MIRACLE NUMBER FOUR

A Song Of The Suburbs

Paul Marriner

Bluescale Publishing

www.bluescalepublishing.co.uk

Bluescale Publishing

ISBN 978-1-9996200-4-2

For the days we smile with
belief and dance with hope

For the days we make memories
to cherish and relive old ones

For the days we find something wonderful to
love and something testing to accept

For the days we are nurtured by
some faith, no matter whose

For the days we laugh until we cry
and cry until we find peace

For the moments

MIRACLE NUMBER FOUR

A Song Of The Suburbs

'God might be out of fashion but
we're not giving up on miracles.'

Chapter 1
Spring 1975
Whispers
'Bridge Over Troubled Water'

In the autumn of 1974 my mother stopped going to work at the bakery. I passed there often, and the ladies in their blue tabards still smiled but stopped speaking. It didn't bother me. It wasn't until the following spring, when out with my sister, that I realised they were offering sympathy. Susan knew. We had been walking to the chemist to collect Mum's prescription – Susan on half-day from the salon and me just home from school – when the smiles and silence at the bakery's open doors stopped her. More accurately, it was the whispering when we'd passed that she noticed. Turning sharply, she spoke slowly and clearly.

'April will bloom again.'

She kept her eyes on them. Usually summer-sky blue, they were dark in the shadow of her lowered head. It was theatrical, menacing even. As we walked away she said, 'Clever, eh?' more to herself than me.

I hesitated. 'I suppose. Because …'

'Because of Mum's maiden name.'

I nodded, pretending to understand.

'You don't get it.'

'Of course I do.'

'What was her surname before marrying Dad?' Susan passed me a can from the canvas shopping bag, warning, 'Do not sing it.'

I dropped back, humming *I'm A Secret Lemonade Drinker* as I followed her to the chemist on the corner, then remembered, 'Oh yeah … it was Bloom.'

The door to the chemist was up a step and took a heavy push to open, as if to dissuade those less committed customers. Susan went first and held the door, just, for me. I stood in a corner, flanked by mysterious cosmetics, aerosols and bottles, sipping from the can and gnawing at a sliver of fingernail. The other customers stopped talking as she went to the pharmacy at the back, a counter raised high, perhaps to claim superiority. I never liked going there for Mum; maybe it was the white coat worn by the man behind the counter, but I was uncomfortable, like the doctor's or headmaster's office. Susan reached up to pass over the prescription, saying she'd collect tomorrow. Turning back, she caught my eye before taking a breath and disturbing the quiet, which even I sensed had become awkward.

'Not talking about something doesn't make it unspeakable.'

No one spoke. I followed her out.

Instead of turning homeward we went to the park, in silence, to the empty roundabout. Susan ushered me on. I was only a couple of months short of fifteen and reluctant – roundabouts were for kids – but she nudged me aboard and started the spin. Every time I came around, her eyes were a little more red. She sang quietly and it took eight or nine rotations before I caught enough of the melody to recognise it, the volume falling and rising as I span away, then back to her. Some evenings Dad played this record continuously on the music centre in the lounge. I stayed away from the room these times; there was no instruction, it just wasn't right to go in.

The roundabout slowed as a young mum approached, toddler in tow, frowning at me. I mouthed an apology as I hopped off but misjudged the speed and bumped heavily into Susan. She caught and held me for a few seconds. We rarely hugged, and I'd rather not, but she was as sad as I thought the song was. Her voice lowered to a whisper as she finished singing: *Bridge Over Troubled Water*. It was a few years until I learnt that sad songs can still offer hope.

We walked on home. I resisted the urge to sing the lemonade advert to try and make her laugh but wanted to be talking. 'Nan and Grandad Bloom were bold.'

'Bold?'

'Naming Mum, April, and her sister, May.'

'They had a sense of humour.'

'Never really thought of it before.' I hadn't.

'Do you think they understood, about blooming again?' she asked.

'Who?'

'The ladies in the bakery.'

I thought for a second. 'Yes. Of course. And is that why the bread Mum used to make is called a bloomer?'

'No. Dork.' Susan laughed. Good.

'Thought not. Shame.'

'Hey, what about the chemist shop? That was smart too, right? The bit about the unspeakable?' she said.

'I don't know. Yes.'

'Their pity makes them feel better than it does us. We don't need it.'

Her sudden anger was troubling. I hadn't taken the silent smiles in the shops for pity, but Susan would not be wrong. Mum's operation was six months ago and the radiotherapy nearly five. Her hair had grown back, and without the sickness and exhaustion of the treatment it had been easy to avoid thinking about the continuing scans; as easy as it had been to avoid the whispered conversations. Susan took a small handkerchief from her cardigan sleeve and pressed it gently under her eyes, not wanting to smudge the dark mascara and blue eye shadow. I was ashamed to have missed the obvious, despite Mum's regular hospital visits. Or had I ignored it? I too should be angry, or scared, or both. 'Mum's still not right, is she?'

'No Mikey. Why else do you think Dad asked Will's mum to write that letter?'

Miracle Number Four

Chapter 2
Summer 1975
Outside Susan's Room
'Seagull'

I heard Mum come up the stairs. I was reading Susan's *New Musical Express* – an article about Billy Connolly would be of interest to Dad, I'd show him tomorrow. From the creak of floorboards I could tell Mum had stopped outside Susan's room, and it was possible to hear Susan's quiet singing. Mum waited for her to stop before knocking and opening the door just wide enough to say, 'That's nice.'

Susan said something that made Mum force a gentle laugh then say, 'Good night,' before knocking on my half-open bedroom door.

'They should play that, shouldn't they?' she asked me.

I looked up and smiled. 'I think they will, Mum.'

Susan had been rehearsing the song all week and had nearly convinced the band to play it.

'What's it called? *Seagull*? It's beautiful and makes sense, though I don't know what it means.' Her face was partly in shadow from the light on the landing, but I could see her eyes moisten. She smiled, just, or perhaps I imagined that.

The next morning, while Mum was at church, I recorded the song from seven inch single to cassette, using Susan's music centre. I borrowed her battered acoustic guitar, nicked fresh batteries from a torch for my cassette player, and shut myself in my bedroom.

Miracle Number Four

Chapter 3
Autumn 1975
April's Miracle
'Unchained Melody'

Despite, or because of, my sister's prophecy in the spring, the lady in the bakery doorway nodded as I passed. Susan's emotion had been no deterrent to them, if anything it evoked more sympathy.

It was half-term, Thursday afternoon, and the clear autumn sky's sun gave less warmth than it promised. The air was still. The smell of fresh bread drifted from the bakery. I lingered, waiting for the whispers.

Years before, in pre-school days, I'd gone there with Mum. I'd waited out back while she worked, fashioning bloomers and French sticks from dough. The bakery was warm and humid, and I'd watched her craft the wheatsheaves for the harvest festival assemblies and church services. She had been an artist with the sheaves, their form growing in the oven as the streaky white dough baked to gold. Often, I'd sat in the corner, leafing through *The Dandy* before I could even read, the sun through the open back door lighting the cartoons. The words in the comic were meaningless but the pictures telling; around me the adult chat and gossip meant nothing, but the sound told its own story. It was a happy place.

Memories I was glad to hold. A kind sadness.

The ladies in the bakery never mentioned Susan's outburst, and it didn't occur to me to still be angry at the whispers. Sometimes there were no whispers at all, and I missed them, though I didn't tell Susan.

I walked on home, bouncing the ball I was carrying, disappointed when it barely came back up. It was punctured.

Home was five minutes. I edged past the car on the drive, spinning the deflating ball slowly, looking for a piercing in the black and white hexagons. There was no obvious damage but I wanted to find it before Dad. The gate was unlocked, and, without looking up, I pushed through to the shaded passage between our house and the neighbour. A faint melody drifted from the open kitchen door. I stopped for a few seconds, wanting to recognise the tune; it might help gauge the mood inside the house. Mum always had the radio or music centre playing. Music was a friend and her enthusiasm for my version of *Seagull* had been all the encouragement I'd needed to keep learning guitar. I listened to the song coming from the house and took a few bars to recognise The Righteous Brothers' *Unchained Melody* – probably the old single from the pile of seven inch records Dad kept on the coffee table, next to the music centre. About a minute and a half through the song there would be a jump as the needle hit a scratch. The black discs, in their tatty covers, were stacked carelessly, unlike the LPs. They were filed meticulously in two small cupboards, either end of the sideboard on which the music centre sat. I listened until the jump then realised Dad's car had been out front. He was home; further reason to judge the mood. Not that there was ever reason to be fearful, but if he was early then why? I gave the ball a last spin, gently drop-kicked it down the alley, and waited at the kitchen door for the music to stop. There was a brief silence followed by Mum's voice, but so quiet I couldn't catch the words. The record played again and Dad said, 'So light on your feet.'

Were they dancing?

I'd last seen them dance to this record during the celebration for Mum's birthday, back in January. She hadn't wanted a fuss. By then the treatment had finished, but she was still having regular scans, the results of which weren't discussed when I was around. Dad had insisted on a party, so they compromised on a gathering at home. We had a small family and weren't close, but relatives seemed genuinely pleased to recognise me. It didn't matter that I hardly knew them, which was comforting somehow. Susan mingled, and if Mum was nervous of her hostess duties, Susan was a capable substitute. Dad took advantage of an audience to stand at the fireplace and tell a few jokes, then called me up. I didn't need to be asked twice and slipped through the crowd of happy friends and relatives. Dad whispered, 'Remember the holiday camp?' and launched straight into a Two Ronnies routine. We'd done a double act in the talent contest which had gone down well. I'd enjoyed the applause, though we'd come second to a six-year-old impersonating Shirley Temple – far more cute than talented. At Mum's party, as Dad finished to polite laughter, he handed over to me. With no time for nerves I told of two ships carrying red and purple paint colliding, and the sailors being marooned. The laughter was real, and I went straight into my favourite six-legged chicken story, trying to remember what Dad had taught me about timing.

Five or six jokes later, he called Mum to join us. She did so reluctantly as he put on a record. Then they danced and afterwards the guests applauded, which I assumed was usual.

Taking confidence from the memory, I went into the kitchen and heard Dad speak softly, '... a miracle. April's miracle.'

I stood at the door to the lounge. Mum and Dad were in the middle of the room, holding each other. His back was to me, her face pressed to his neck. He was not a large man, but Mum was small and his arms enfolded her; though he wasn't big, I never doubted his strength.

'A miracle,' he repeated, 'and everything will be fine.' He spoke unusually quietly and stroked her auburn hair. She was silent, save for an occasional sob, shaking her fragile shoulders. They swayed gently and Dad kissed her forehead. I waited at the door, an intruder wanting to leave but anxious to know what was so miraculous. Mum sensed me and raised her head,

'Mikey … we … I'm …' she started to speak, but words didn't come, her eyes red-rimmed from crying. My chest tightened and stomach churned at the shift from Dad's happiness to Mum's … Mum's what? Fear, confusion, embarrassment? She pulled away from Dad who turned to the door,

'Michael!' He spoke loudly and smiled sincerely, easily and naturally as always. He ran a hand across his thick black Brycleemed hair. 'Where have you been? We just got back. Let's … no. Wait. We should celebrate. April?' He looked to her for approval. She smiled and meant it but perhaps more for him than herself.

'Yes,' she answered softly and then more loudly, 'Yes.'

'Good.' Dad pulled her back to his side and pecked her cheek.

'Frank. You're embarrassing Michael.'

'What? Oh. Ok. Michael, go and get Susan. Tell her we're going out to celebrate.'

I smiled, wanting to show I shared his happiness. 'Ok. But what's the miracle?' And why did Mum look worried?

'We'll tell you over dinner. Let's try the new Berni on the high street. We can tell you and Susan together. Go find her.'

'Will knocked earlier, it's Susan's half-day from the salon, they're probably at the lock-ups,' said Mum.

Dad kissed her full on the lips. I slipped out the door.

Chapter 4
Autumn 1975
Girl On A Tea Chest
'Jeepster'

The lock-ups were little more than half a mile away, where suburb met small industrial estate. I was half-way there, not paying attention, when my name was called from across the road. Vince sat on a low brick wall, bordering a garden at the corner of the street and the cul-de-sac where he lived. His dad owned the garage where my dad worked. We'd hung around together since forever and were in the same school and year. I crossed the road, trotted up to him and pretended to slap his face. 'Made you wince, Vince.'

Vince pretended to hit back. 'On yer bike, Mike,' but without his usual chuckle.

We had been greeting each other this way since primary school and I supposed we would eventually stop, but habits die hard.

I sat on the wall next to him. 'Busy?'

'Number plates. Motorbikes.' He tapped a bookie's pencil on the small notebook in his lap. It lay open at a page, empty save the date and the word *Triumph* written carefully at the top in the style of the motorbike's badge.

'Thought you stopped when you nearly got run over up at the by-pass.'

'I did. But … something to do.'

I exaggerated a look up and down the quiet road. Few cars passed and no motorbikes. 'Why bikes?'

'Fed up with cars. Couldn't write the numbers fast enough.'

'Not many Triumphs yet.' I pointed to the blank page.

We both looked expectantly up and down. I laughed. He didn't. He nodded back to his home at the top of the cul–de–sac. 'They're shouting again.'

'Shouting?' I hesitated. 'Oh. Wanna come with me?'

'Where?'

'The lock-ups. I gotta find Susan.'

'Susan?'

'Yep. Coming?'

'Ok.'

'You know she thinks you're too young, right?' I said, partly to tease but also because I thought he should know.

'I'm nine months older than you.'

'Still nearly a couple of years younger than Susan.'

'I know. And short. She told me. But nothing else to do, while they're,' he indicated back to his house, 'shouting.'

'Ok, but hide the notebook.'

In minutes we were at the entrance to the lock-ups, the garages behind the maisonettes. Access was down a narrow lane, hedged by brambles. Thin tendrils, spiteful with thorns, reached for us. As we neared the garages I heard muffled bass tones, mixed with discordant guitar, trashy drums and cymbals, but it wasn't until the singing began that I recognised the song – an old Marc Bolan track that Susan had been practising round the house for a couple of weeks. The lane's bend straightened to the row of garages. The sky was cloudless and the low sun brightened the faded paintwork on the coloured doors without providing warmth. All were closed save one, the music's source. Outside this garage, sitting on a tea chest, was a girl with golden hair falling straight past her neck and shoulders, almost to her waist. With a second, urgent take, I recognised her. Her hair was bright blonde in the sun and brighter still for flowing down to a black t-shirt and brightest of all for framing black sunglasses. She held a strand of hair to her mouth. I couldn't see her eyes – had never properly looked in her eyes – but it was easy to imagine she was looking at me; an uncomfortably wanted sensation. I smiled in case, conscious as ever of it being lopsided, and slowed to an amble in contrast to a quickening anticipation. She rocked to the music, mouthing the lyrics. I wasn't sure what a jeepster was, but the singer in the lock-up was right when claiming the universe to be 'reclining in her hair'; I didn't know what that meant, but it was surely true of the blonde girl on the tea chest. I'd met her before and seen her fleetingly at one of the band's rehearsals, so knew her, and been increasingly intrigued, but never unexpectedly excited, gently confused, charged.

'Cool glasses,' I said to Vince, who was two yards ahead. 'What?'

'The blonde girl. Cool sunglasses.'

'Sunglasses in October? Cool? You've been watching too much American telly. And what blonde girl?'

'Sitting on the chest.'

'Blonde? Nah, light brown maybe. You're more blonde. She's not at our school. Know her?'

'Sort of. She's blonde.'

'Nah,' Vince repeated, but the word was lost in the music now we were close. The girl who might have been blonde looked up, but the sunglasses were too big and hid not just her eyes but most of her face. I smiled again, just in case, again, and raised a hand in a welcoming wave. She lifted a hand in return and went back to watching the band in the lock-up.

The noise was not yet musical but, with increasing volume as we neared, there was power despite the imbalance and splintering feedback. The 'might be' blonde on the tea chest bobbed in time – perfectly. The bass was now almost lost under crashing drums, wailing guitars and screaming vocals, but all came together on the chorus as I reached the open garage door and the force thumped into my chest. I'd heard Susan's band rehearse before, but this was tangible, within and around me – so much more than sound. Glancing at the girl I was sure she felt the same. How could she not? She now swayed – perhaps to the music, but more, I was sure, to show this moment was shared, though how I couldn't say.

I was fifteen and a third and already worshipped rock, but today the music was new; today rock had purpose, rock was alive, rock was the answer.

Beyond the up-and-over door the interior lay in shadow. In the back a long-haired drummer thrashed at a clutter of drums and cymbals. Beside him, tucked into a corner, the bass player sat on a speaker cabinet, hunched over his instrument. To one side stood a huge figure, guitar resting high on his rounded frame. Two singers looked outwards, posing behind mic stands. One of them, Susan, acknowledged me. The other was lost in head-shaking performance.

The music stuttered to a finish as the various players realised the song's end had been reached. A short silence was shattered by the young man screaming into his microphone, experimenting with yells of differing pitch until a final, 'Goodnight Penscote!'

Susan stepped away from her mic, rolling her eyes at the other singer. The girl on the tea chest stopped chewing her hair to clap with exactly the right level of praise and cool reserve.

'Hi, little brother.' Susan left the garage, taking a crumpled pack of ten cigarettes from the waistband of her jeans.

'Hiya.' I stood to my full height, still two inches short of her, though they were due to the heels she wore.

'Fag, Will?' She turned back to the garage to offer a cigarette to her co-singer.

He shook his head, 'Menthol? They're horrible. Why bother?'

'Yeah, like my dad won't mind if I stink of fags.'

'What's it to him? You're eighteen right?'

'Just. Anyway, I like 'em. Gotta match?' Susan asked. Will pointed towards the girl. Next to her, on the tea chest, lay a pack of Rothmans and matches. She held out the book of matches for me to take and pass on. She still wore the big sunglasses, hiding any expression in her face save a small smile that I returned, forgetting its unevenness.

Will emerged from the garage. Unkempt, lank hair stuck to his forehead, resisting attempts to be shaken free. He took the cigarettes from the tea chest and the sunglasses from the girl. Her eyes were almost too big for the elfin features which suited her petite frame. Though she was pale her clear skin had a faint glow.

'Hi, Petra,' I said as casually as I could. It seemed she took a couple of seconds to let me notice green-hazel eyes before dropping down from the tea chest. She landed lightly on the gravel and brushed a long, disturbed hair from her face. In the garage the remaining band members were quietly jamming another song. Will stood next to Susan, taking her cigarette to light his own before calling,

'What the fuck's that noise?'

'*Highway Star*,' shouted the guitarist, his voice oddly high pitched considering his bulk.

'No, it isn't, Pluto. Not even close.' Will turned back to Susan. 'Is it.' A statement, not a question.

'It's close.' Susan defended the band. She twisted the two studs in her right lobe. 'And anyway, it's a better rock song than *Jeepster*. That's too soft, we shouldn't be playing it.'

'The crowd love a bit of Bolan,' he said, putting on the sunglasses.

'Yeah, all three of 'em.'

'What's a sheepster?' asked Vince. Susan sighed. Petra answered,

'It's jeepster, not sheepster.'

'Oh. What's it mean?'

'Nobody knows,' said Petra.

'Some say it's another name for a vampire,' I offered.

'Some say … but they don't know. Nobody does.' Petra was clear. I was impressed.

'Yep. That's the point,' said Susan, 'and it doesn't really matter. It's too pop and what … four years old? Ancient.' She turned to make sure Will heard that last part.

Vince nodded as if in understanding.

'Just wait 'til the first gig, in a few weeks,' said Will.

'Rehearsing in the works social club when your mates are there isn't a gig,' said Susan.

'You'll see.' He went back into the darkened garage and cursed on tripping over a mic stand that was hard to see wearing sunglasses in the shadows. There was a brief silence until Susan laughed, quickly followed by the rest of us. Will flicked a V-sign.

Susan turned away, squinting into the low sun, wiping a shimmer of sweat from her forehead and drawing lightly on her cigarette. 'You ok, Vince?' She indicated towards his face and a mark on his left temple I hadn't noticed. He touched the slight graze there, then pointed to Susan's cigarette, saying,

'You shouldn't. My old man says it's bad. His heart is knackered.'

'And yet he still smokes.'

'It's how he knows.'

I laughed and was glad when so did Petra.

'It's for my voice,' said Susan. 'You heard of Janis Joplin, right?'

'Of course.' Vince nodded.

She turned to me. 'What's up?' talking loudly over the song which had started again, under Will's direction.

I shouted, 'Dad says come home 'cos we're going out to celebrate.'

She led me to where it was quieter. 'Celebrate what? He didn't finally win the pools did he?'

'I don't know. I thought you might. Something about Mum's miracle.'

'And Dad's home early?'

'Yep.'

'Mum's miracle?'

'Yep.'

'Slowly, what did Dad say?'

'I told you.'

Susan went back into the garage. She spoke to the bass player then took the microphone from its stand, waving goodbyes to the others. Disappointed to be going, I gave a casual half-wave to Petra, who casually half-waved back. She had returned to sitting cross legged on the tea chest, easy and elegant, slipping a bomber jacket around her shoulders and pulling another strand of hair across her mouth. The flares of her jeans draped over clean Dunlop trainers. Susan gave her mic to Vince to carry as we ambled back up the alley, the music fading behind us.

'So, who's Petra and why's she named after a dog?' Vince asked.

'Our mums know each other from St. Gregory's,' I said.

'Oh yeah, I've seen her there,' said Vince. 'And the name?'

'She's older than the dog on *Blue Peter*, so, if anything, the dog was named after her.' I tried not to sound defensive.

'Of course,' said Vince, without obvious sarcasm. 'It is an odd name though.'

'Will's real name is Wilhelm,' Susan said by way of explanation and pronouncing it with a 'V', but Vince's expression remained blank. Susan continued, 'Will's her brother. They sometimes come to ours with their mum. That's how I met him. Their dad's German or something.'

'Which one's Will?' Vince asked.

'The other singer.'

'Oh, him,' Vince acknowledged.

'He's more of a shouter really. Poor Wilhelm. And all that screaming. Thinks he's got the high notes but maybe it's just his voice breaking again. Hopefully, his balls will have dropped all the way by the time we gig.' Susan looked at Vince. He looked away. I laughed. Susan walked a few yards ahead.

'Are Will and Susan … together?' Vince asked me quietly.

'I don't think so. He doesn't come round often. Nor does Petra.'

'You've never mentioned her. And that's when you saw Petra's brown hair, right?'

'Funny boy. It's blonde … today, anyway.'

'Nah. That's blonde,' Vince whispered and pointed at Susan, ahead of us.

'That's dyed. Dreamer,' I whispered back.

We stopped at the corner to Vince's road.

'See ya banjo boy,' Susan said, referring to the shape of the cul-de-sac where he lived.

'Bye, Susan.' Vince handed back the mic. She slipped it into the back pocket of her jeans, mouthpiece protruding.

'You can call me Susie.'

'Can I?'

'No.'

'Oh.'

'Only joking. You can but don't tell anyone else.'

'Right. Bye, Susie. See ya, Mikey.'

'Don't call me Mikey.'

'Too late, mate.'

'Ha. Don't forget your notebook.' I pointed to a small bush just behind the garden wall where we'd sat earlier. He cast a two-finger salute. When out of hearing Susan said, 'You saw that mark on his face?'

'Maybe.' It was an uncomfortable thought.

'His old man's a tosser.'

'But Dad likes him?'

'He has to pretend. Here.' She took the cigarettes from her jeans' waistband. 'Put these somewhere. Dad never suspects you. I'll get them back later. After the celebration. What mood's Dad in?'

'Good.' I slipped the pack into the top of my sock, not visible under flapping jeans.

'And Mum?'

'She's ok. She's up. They were dancing in the back room.'

'Dancing?'

'To that old song they like. The one from the party. When you finished off Mum's drink.'

'*Unchained Melody?*'

'Yep.'

'Dancing?'

'Yes.'

'That's a good sign, right?' Susan asked, unusually seeking reassurance.

'I suppose.'

'And what we celebrating?'

'I told you, Mum's miracle.'

Miracle Number Four

Chapter 5
Autumn 1975
Feeding Chickens
'It's Only Rock And Roll'

Dad worked the Sunday after celebrating 'Mum's miracle', making up hours lost accompanying her to the hospital. He left me in the shed, thinking up excuses not to clean my bike and oil the gears. Fortunately, Susan called me to the house. She was in the kitchen, arranging a boiled egg, soldiers and cup of tea on a tray that was too small.

'Mum's breakfast.' She handed it to me.

'I took it yesterday.' I hadn't avoided one chore just to pick up another.

'Yesterday was Dad's turn.'

'He went to work. I did it.'

'But it was Dad's turn.' Susan was firm, if her logic unconvincing.

'When's it your turn?' I protested.

'C'mon, I made it. You know Mum prefers you taking it.'

'Does she? She won't eat all this and what if she's still asleep?'

'She won't be, though it doesn't make much difference.' Susan gave the smile that was part plea, a little bit apology and a lot 'big-sister knows best', which she usually did.

'Shall I take up the paper?'

Susan looked at the headlines lying on the table. 'No. Dad says all that shitty news is bad for her, though I don't think she cares.'

There was a time I'd knocked before entering, but these days I went straight in; I hated hearing Mum jump at the rap on the door – harsh, no matter how gently I tried. The room was dark. The early November sun barely crept through the gap between closed curtains and didn't reach her, hidden under covers. There was a faint smell of damp towels.

'Mum, breakfast,' I whispered, placing the tray on the bedside table. She murmured something, perhaps a thank you, but didn't move.

'Don't forget your tablets.' I left the door ajar and returned to the kitchen.

'What's on today?' Susan asked.

'Dad wants me to clean my bike and oil the gears. I don't think they need it, but he says they always do.'

'Exciting.' She was sitting at the red Formica-topped kitchen table, eating toast and flicking through a copy of *Cosmopolitan* brought home from the salon.

'Does nymphomaniac mean what I think it does?' I feigned innocence and pointed to a headline in the magazine.

'If you're lucky you'll find out one day. Was Mum up?'

'No.'

Susan turned up the radio. *Feel Like Makin' Love* was playing. 'Bazzer reckons the band should give this a go. Dad likes it, which is odd. What do you think?'

'You're already playing a couple of Bad Company songs.'

'Ha, you've been paying attention. Did Dad say when he's coming home?'

'No.'

'He said he'll take Mum for a drink down the Conservative Club later, but I don't see that happening.' She offered me a slice of toast.

'Now that Mum's supposed to be better, how come she's still in bed?' I licked off the jam before taking a bite.

'Good question. I thought when Dad told us about Mum's miracle it might be a proper moment.'

'Oh yeah, proper.' I nodded.

'I guess you never can tell about them and you can't really know until you've had a few.' Susan had a theory about proper moments; they changed you.

'How many have you had now?' I asked.

'Still only a couple.'

'Only two?' I was pleased as I wasn't sure I'd had any. 'What were they?'

'Well, the first is not for telling ... but you were there for the second.'

'Was I? That's good.'

'No. Not really. Proper moments aren't always good, maybe mostly not.'

'I meant it's good I was there as it means I've had one.' I sounded hopeful.

'No, it doesn't, not necessarily.'

'Why? What was it?'

'The reason I still hate Sundays. When Mum told us about ... you know ... when we first found out. Even though it's ok now, I still fucking hate that moment, didn't see it coming.'

'Oh. Yeah, I suppose.' I didn't remember well the Sunday to which Susan referred, though it was only fourteen months ago. Probably I had been keen to get to the park to play football and, probably, Mum had said I must wait until she came back from church – though I never understood what difference that made. I might have been kicking a ball against the coal bunker or hanging round the shed, watching Dad take something apart. It's likely that when Mum came home she called me in and sat me next to Susan. And Mum would have found a way to tell the news such that it was no big deal and, now I thought of it, immediately after, Dad came in and we played Monopoly. That was unusual for a Sunday afternoon – mostly it was a time for Mum to fiddle with her embroidery while Dad was in the shed, putting back together whatever he'd taken apart in the morning, in working order, naturally. So, now I tried to think of it, I couldn't. Perhaps Susan was right – it wasn't a proper moment for me. I wanted to ask why that might be but could guess the answer. Mum, Dad, Susan, perhaps especially Susan, had hidden much to protect me but I didn't need it anymore.

'Anyway,' she interrupted my thoughts, 'you gotta oil your gears and I have rehearsal. It's cold in the lock-up, so we're rehearsing at Will's house. Coming?'

'Will's house? So Petra will be there.'

'I don't know. Why?'

'Just wondered.'

'Oh, wanna come see? You can oil your gears later.'

'Dad would know if I didn't.'

'Of course.'

'How?'

'Dad magic. It's up to you. I'm going in a few minutes.' She went upstairs, shouting as she reached the top, 'You'll want to change though. Petra might be there and that t-shirt's manky. And there's jam on your nose.'

Wiping a hand across my face – there wasn't any jam – I went down to the shed. I squeezed a few drops of oil from the 3-IN-ONE can onto the bare concrete floor under my bike and ran back to my bedroom. Minutes later I was at the front door, in a clean Led Zeppelin t-shirt and fake leather bomber, waiting for Susan. She talked over her shoulder as she came downstairs.

'… yes Mum, I know. Did you take your tablets?'

Mum tied her dressing gown belt, leant over the banister on the landing and said quietly, 'Of course. It's … what time is it?' She looked small and pale in the grey light of the window on the landing.

'Time for us to go. Did you really take your tablets?' Susan asked again.

'Yes. Where are you going?'

'Band rehearsal, Will's.'

'Is Mikey going?'

I winced at being called Mikey by Mum.

'Yep.'

'Tell Vi I'll see her during the week. You look nice.'

Susan stopped at the bottom of the stairs and turned to look back up, 'Do you think so? This t-shirt's a bit tight over my tits but I think Bazzer likes that.' She made a point of pulling the bottom of the t-shirt down. The Rolling Stones mouth logo she'd drawn on using red felt tip pens was stretched across her chest.

'Susan, please.'

'Go back to bed, Mum. We'll see you later.'

Outside, I asked, 'Do you want Bazzer to?'

'What?'

'Like your tits.'

'Don't talk like that, I'm your big sister. Not sure about Bazzer. Yeah, why not. Here, look after this,' she passed me her microphone, 'and do something with your curls.' She ruffled my blonde hair.

I pushed her hand away. 'I already did.'

'Why this way?' I asked as we passed St. Gregory's church. The nine o'clock Mass had finished and the priest was saying goodbyes to the last few worshippers.

'We're going to Bazzer's first,' Susan said as Father Andrew stepped from the lychgate and called,

'Hello, Michael. How are you?'

I went to church rarely, only when Mum really insisted, which hadn't been for ages. But Father Andrew always spoke as if he knew me, as if I was any other member of his congregation. I usually avoided him, not that I minded being part of the church, as long as I didn't have to go or actually do anything. Before I could answer, he continued,

'Morning, Susan, how's your mother? Haven't seen her in a while. Or you. The choir misses you.'

'Mum's ok thanks,' Susan answered.

'I saw Violet at early Mass. She tells me April is much better. Cured? Prayers have been answered.' Father Andrew spoke slowly but not with hesitation.

'I suppose, but maybe not all, yet,' said Susan.

'Is she not all right?'

'Mostly. But a few more prayers couldn't harm.'

'They never do, Susan,' said Father Andrew, ignoring the sarcasm. Susan walked on, quickening her step. A few yards down the road she muttered, 'Prayers. Bollocks,' as I caught up with her.

'Bollocks?'

She slowed. 'I don't know, Mikey. Maybe. Maybe not. Especially after Mum's miracle, as Dad calls it. Anyway, luckily we'll never know.'

'Luckily?'

'We might not like the answer. C'mon. Bazzer's waiting.'

Bazzer, the band's bass player, was at his front door. In the hall lay a guitar case, next to an amplifier and a speaker cabinet on a trolley made from half a pallet and pram wheels.

'Nice t-shirt,' he said as Susan walked up the garden.

'Thanks. I drew it myself. Probably won't survive a wash.'

'Could you make me one?'

'I expect so.' She pulled the front down, stretching it as she had earlier. Her denim jacket was open and the lips logo clearly visible.

'It's … cool … Hi, Mike.' Bazzer passed the guitar case to her.

'Here.' She passed it on to me.

Bazzer turned back indoors. 'I've got this, it's a heavy bitch.' He rolled the homemade trolley to the door and manoeuvred it clumsily over the threshold, asking Susan, 'Did you bring the mic?'

'Yep. You don't mind me borrowing it?'

'Of course not. A proper singer needs a proper mic, right?'

'Right. I'll get my own soon, tips at the salon are good.'

The quiet roads, lined with mock-Tudor semis, were disturbed by the noise of the trolley rumbling over flagstones. Susan helped Bazzer push it through the alley behind St. Gregory's, skirting the school playing field. We stopped at the exit, leading into an avenue of more thirties semis, where Will lived.

'Fag?' Bazzer took the guitar case from me and found the cigarettes and matches inside, offering them to Susan. 'Need to have one before Will's house, his mum won't let us smoke indoors.'

She took a cigarette and squeezed next to him, sitting on the speaker cabinet. I stood at the alley's exit, as if guarding the way, nibbling at a fingernail. The sky was a blanket of white cloud, but the air was still and I wasn't cold. At the far end of the field, through the diamond-mesh wire fence, I could see a group of boys playing. They would have climbed the fence to get in, careful not to catch skin on the sharp wire at the top but confident on a Sunday the groundsman would be absent. The pitches were cut up from play and the smell of damp earth and grass was spoilt by the cigarettes.

'You smoke with style,' Bazzer said quietly to Susan, and I thought I wasn't meant to hear so didn't laugh.

'Thanks,' she replied, and it sounded sincere.

My thoughts on whether or not I'd smoke when older were interrupted by Will shouting from his gate, some forty yards into the road at the end of the alley. 'About time. C'mon, let's make some noise.'

'I'd rather play some music,' Bazzer said, but Will was out of range.

Will lived in a neat semi in a cloned row of them. He watched as Susan and Bazzer struggled to push the trolley through the narrow gate then went indoors, leaving the front door open. I was there first, as Will's mum came to the door.

'Hi, Mrs. Anders. Ok to come through?' I asked.

'You can call me Vi, you know. Lovely to see you. We've made soda bread. How are you? How's April? Marvellous news, isn't it? How's your dad?'

Before I could answer, she saw the trolley at the gate and called Susan into the house, repeating the welcome and questions, almost verbatim and without waiting for answers.

Susan took the microphone and guitar case from me and followed Will and Bazzer into the front room. As the door opened I could hear a guitar being tuned. Vi touched my arm and guided me to the kitchen. I gave a wistful glance back to the closing front lounge door, catching a glimpse of the equipment packed into the room. I was still teaching myself guitar on Susan's old acoustic and now played it better than she. The front room setting didn't spoil the glamour, and as Susan once told me, 'Rock doesn't have to be born in a basement,' though I suspected the good stuff probably was. I wondered if Petra was in there.

'Ah, don't worry. They'll be twiddlin' and fiddlin' for ages yet. Soda bread? It's just off the hob. I made the buttermilk myself,' Vi said, showing me to a seat at the kitchen table. I was never going to refuse her gentle Irish accent; she was never going to take no for an answer. She was a thin lady, even more than Mum but with an energy that filled far more space.

A movement in the hall caught my eye and I looked up as Petra said, 'I prefer Dad's rye bread.'

She came in from the dark hallway. The kitchen was bright, and I had no doubt her hair was a light enough brown to be considered blonde. 'Hi, Petra.'

She nodded in response.

'You may prefer the rye, but we haven't any,' Vi said to her, and then to me, 'In truth her dad rarely made it and I doubt she remembers the taste anyway. But once or twice a year he sends a loaf from Germany. It's always stale when it gets here.'

'I do remember the taste. Great with Limburger cheese,' said Petra.

'Now I know you're fibbing. That cheese is the foulest smelling of … of something rancid rotting in hell. You hated it. Your father only bought it to rile me. Did I tell you the time we took some in a picnic, parked up but fell asleep and a walker called the police because the smell was so bad she thought we were dead? The copper's face was a picture when we woke up.'

'That's probably not true,' Petra said, but Vi laughed and handed me a plate with a chunk of soda bread and a pat of butter.

The kitchen was warm, and a huge pan sat on the hob, steam rising from the simmering water. Condensation clouded the window over the sink. The back door was open and I could see out to the tidy garden, spoilt by the washline that ran its length, propped in the middle and crowded with billowing sails of drying sheets and towels.

Vi made tea. I filled the silence, 'Smells nice,' nodding at the pan on the hob.

'Dope. Mum's boiling whites,' said Petra. There was an Irish lilt I'd not heard before.

'Oh.' My cheeks reddened. 'Still, smells better now than when they were put in, probably.'

Petra laughed.

'Let's hope so,' said Vi, pouring tea. She let me finish eating before asking, 'And how is your mum? Really.'

'Oh, she's ok, I think. Still sleeps a lot, maybe more than before.' I was guarded. No, not guarded, unsure. I had no need to be wary with Vi. I'd first met her a year or so earlier when she'd become friends with Mum at St. Gregory's.

The muted mess of sound coming from the lounge as instruments were tuned and microphones tested became momentarily clear as Susan came out, quickly closing the door, and asking for a drink of water.

Vi left her seat at the table to find a glass. 'Of course, and is your mum feeling better? Mikey says she's still sleeping a lot. Perhaps it wasn't just the …' she lowered her voice, '… you know.'

'It's ok, we should be able to say it, now it's gone. But no, she isn't properly better, not yet, I don't think, despite what Dad says. Are you coming round this week?'

'Of course. Wednesday. I'll bring a cake.'

'Seeing you cheers her up.'

Vi passed a drink to Susan, rubbing her arm gently as she did so. 'Your father must be relieved.'

'He calls it a miracle,' I said.

Vi looked to Petra and back to me before nodding, 'Perhaps. Who's to say?'

Susan smiled and went back to the lounge, Vi calling after her, 'And tell them no smoking. It smells awful enough after they've been in there.' She turned back to me and Petra. 'Young men and farting. Maybe it would smell better if they did smoke. But best not light a match with all that gas.'

I laughed; Petra looked embarrassed.

Vi picked up a long wooden spatula and stirred the jumble of underwear in the boiling pan before turning off the burner. She used two hands, protected by tea towels, to lift the heavy pot from the hob and pour away the water with a hiss of steam before rinsing the 'whites' under the cold tap. 'Why don't you two go and feed Ingrid and the others. They've not eaten yet today.'

'Ingrid?' I asked.

'Our favourite hen. Come see,' said Petra.

'You have chickens?'

'You don't?' She took a box from a cupboard and led me down the garden, ducking around the washing waving on the line. She moved quickly and lightly. I was sure Vince was wrong about her hair. A breeze blew a tress across her face. She didn't mind.

At the garden's end was a small coop, leaning to one side, in a full enclosure of wire mesh. Behind the mesh, scratching and pecking at mostly bare ground, was a brood of chickens, bobbing and ducking haphazardly. Some saw us approach and came to the wire. Petra made some odd clucking sounds, but I think shaking the box was the main attraction.

'That's Ingrid.' Petra pointed to one of the birds though I wasn't sure which.

'Why Ingrid?'

'Mum's favourite film is *Casablanca*.'

'Oh.' I pretended to understand. 'Do they all have names?'

'Of course, but you won't remember them. Ingrid is the oldest. The red and grey one is prettiest. Niamh.'

'Your mum likes unusual names. Like Petra?' I hesitated before adding, 'Nice name.'

'It's not unusual where my dad's family is from. Germany.'

'Don't the neighbours mind? About the chickens I mean, not your name.' I looked up and down the row of gardens stretching either side, mostly separated by simple waist high diamond-mesh fencing.

'Nah. They don't make much noise. Will's rehearsing is worse. They'll complain in a little while.'

'Who? The chickens?'

'Ha, funny boy. No, the neighbours.' She indicated back to the house from where music could now be heard but the song was not recognisable. 'Wanna feed 'em?' She gave me the box.

'Do they lay eggs?' I threw some ground cereal into the coop.

'Yep, but not every day, and Ingrid only once a week or so. Bless her. Mum says she's past it. We used to have a lot more but there are only so many eggs you can eat. Will hates them.'

'Eggs?'

'No, chickens. Mum's always nagging him to fix the fence to keep the foxes out. Since Dad went it's sort of his job.'

This was the second reference that morning to Petra's dad not being there, and I tried to remember if I should know why. Vi had started visiting Mum a little over a year ago, soon after the diagnosis, often chatting over tea. Petra had occasionally come along, sitting quietly in the corner. Her long hair hadn't seemed quite so blonde in our kitchen.

I watched her kneel at the fence to the coop, close to a couple of chickens, but thoughts were disturbed by the loud crashing of metal on metal. I started but Petra stood calmly, saying, 'There she goes.'

Two gardens away an elderly lady stood outside her back door, smashing a ladle against a tray. The harsh clanging was painful to hear. Between strikes she shouted for the 'bloody racket' to stop – or something like that; the black and brown terrier at her feet barked louder than she could shout.

'She's not a music lover then.'

'Nor's the dog. They hate it when the band play. I suppose it does get a bit loud but it's only for a couple of hours. Silly cow. Mum'll be out in a minute, trying to apologise. Will says Dad wouldn't have. He'd have told her where to go.'

The dog ran up and down the old lady's garden path, barking incessantly with wild excitement or annoyance. I couldn't tell which but thought it was probably protesting as much against the metal clanging as the music, which was now inaudible. 'Do you want me to try?'

'What?'

'Telling her where to go.'

Petra looked at me but didn't answer and, in truth, I was grateful. I had no idea how I might confront the old lady. But if I wasn't brave enough for that, I was brave enough to hold Petra's gaze longer than was comfortable. Her eyes were more green than hazel in this light. Despite the sun, it wasn't warm and the breeze was cold where it touched the sweat on the back of my neck.

'What happened to your jaw?' she eventually asked.

'Eh?'

'Your jaw. I hadn't noticed before, but it's a little ... off.'

'I had an accident, years ago.' My cheeks flushed.

'And?' She smiled.

'Sort of dislocated it.'

'Sort of? Did you get hit?'

'Not exactly.'

'You don't want to tell me. That's ok.'

'No, it's just that …' I took a breath. 'Ok, I stepped on an upturned rake, it sprang up, smacked me in the face and I screamed so hard I dislocated my jaw. It didn't go back quite right.'

She laughed. 'How loud did you scream?'

'I was only six or seven and it hurt, a lot. The worst part was it hurt so much to talk I didn't tell anyone, and Mum thought I was all right until she looked at my face. And now …' I indicated to my mouth, hoping the spot nestling in the side of my nose wasn't obvious, '… it's worse when I smile.'

'It's a funny story.'

'All true.'

The old woman hit her tray again. We looked at her. The terrier was at her feet and barking until whacked across the haunches to shut up. After a brief stare she gave a final smash of ladle against tray and the dog followed her indoors.

'She'll be out again in a little while,' Petra said. 'Dad was useful for some things.'

I hesitated before asking, 'So, how long have your parents been divorced?' Only a few kids at school had divorced parents and they didn't speak about it much, until asked.

'Divorced?' There was a sudden anger. 'You have noticed Mum's Catholic, haven't you? Divorced? As if.'

I couldn't tell if she thought they should or shouldn't be and her anger stopped me asking. I waited. She added,

'Separated. Five years or so. You get used to it. Mum says the only thing she misses now is the … you know …'

'The what?'

Petra hesitated. 'Special cuddles. It's what she calls … you know.'

Perhaps I looked embarrassed as she added, 'My mum tells me everything. I guess she misses him.'

I wanted to stare as her eyes darkened with tears. She shook them away. 'Doesn't matter. Will's ok at fixing the fence. Ingrid's only escaped twice. Besides, who needs two parents, right? Oh shit, sorry. After your mum nearly died from … you know.'

'S'ok, we can say it now. Cancer.'

Mum had still said the word only once, on the Sunday that Susan 'fucking hated'. And now, as I thought of and repeated the word, 'Cancer,' I wondered how it was that 'fucking Sunday', fourteen months ago, wasn't as fresh as yesterday. How was it such a moment for Susan and yet not for me? When Mum had first told us about the breast cancer the word hadn't carried the evil it subsequently developed, to the extent it had not been spoken until today. Such avoidance had helped the word fester a malevolence all its own. Even when Dad mentioned, ten months ago, casually, that the treatment hadn't worked, he'd avoided the word. And when telling us this week about the miracle, that it was gone, still no one said it.

'Were you scared your mum would die?' she asked.

I nodded. 'She had a lump removed and radiotherapy last year but afterwards it got worse, and no one knew what to do. That was a bit scary.' I smiled; perhaps to show how brave I'd been; that had been Mum, Dad and Susan's way.

'A bit scary? No shit, Sherlock,' said Petra, frowning.

'I guess. Anyway, then it shrank, and they don't know why but they've been checking for months and now they say she's ok.'

'And your dad thinks it's a miracle. Do you?'

'I don't know if I believe in them, but happy to if it makes it real.'

'My mum thinks so. Especially because of the letter your dad asked her to write. Speaking of which, do you ever wonder why lady saints aren't called saintesses?'

Before I could answer, the music coming from the house stopped for a few seconds, then started again, louder this time. Petra started towards the kitchen. I followed with an eye on the neighbouring garden. Vi was sitting at the kitchen table, flicking through *Radio Times*, and offered more soda bread which I politely refused even though she said I needed 'building up.' We went through to the front room where the furniture had been pushed to the sides. The band's gear littered the floor space. Will and Susan stood with their backs to the bay window. Petra shouted 'hello' at Susan, but it was lost in the music. We found a gap between the sideboard and drop-leaf dining table, opposite Bazzer who nodded at me. The room did smell but I was close enough to Petra that her soapy, flowery scent was sometimes strong enough. I recognised the song as they reached the final chorus: *Get It On*.

Will stopped singing. The band played the final riff. As the song closed out, Susan spoke into her microphone, '... and meanwhile, I'm still thinking...'

The sudden silence was broken by Will, 'What was that?' It was directed at Susan.

'We said we'd do it like the single. That's what Bolan says, at the end.'

'No it isn't.'

'Yes it is.'

'So what? Just because it's Bolan.'

'Yep, just because. Oh, wait, I get it. You want to say that last part, with your Bolan wig. You do know he's past it?' Susan laughed and gently tugged his dark frizzy hair.

'Piss off. Perms cost a bloody fortune.' Will laughed, but it was forced.

Petra leant towards me and whispered, 'Do you think they've snogged yet?'

'Who?'

'My brother, your sister.'

'I don't know. I don't think she fancies him. What d'you think?'

'Knowing Will, yes. He's more than a year older than her. But then, knowing your sister, maybe not. She doesn't take shit from anyone.'

It was true, and all the more so since a couple of weeks ago when she came home with her hair cut shorter, almost like a blonde Liza Minnelli. We'd seen *Cabaret* at one of the 'film nights' down the Conservative Club – Dad was on the Entertainment Committee – and though the film was X rated he'd sneaked me in too.

Dimitri, the drummer, shook long black hair from his face and counted in the next song: *Rebel Rebel*. Will missed his cue and Bazzer looked up from his bass guitar, rolling his eyes. When they reached the chorus Bazzer stared at Susan and smiled encouragement for her harmonies. She smiled back. I doubted Susan had snogged Will.

It's Only Rock And Roll was next, and I paid close attention. It was one of the songs I was learning on Susan's acoustic.

Four or five tunes later, Dimitri was bored and thrashing the drums, prompting Pluto on guitar to boost the volume of his solos until it was painful. Will shouted for quiet but was ignored. Bazzer, on bass, sighed. Susan muttered something about fresh air and left the room, Petra and I followed. Vi was still at the table but now the kitchen smelt of roasting chicken.

'Vi, you were right about the smell in there. Don't they wash?' Susan asked.

'Not as much as they fart and sweat dear, especially that bigger lad, what do they call him, Pluto? You could stay for lunch but we've only a small bird this week and I've to make three dinners from it. I'm sorry.'

'We should go anyway. Mum's not eating much but might want lunch and Dad's boss asked him to work today.'

'Ah, Lawrence. I know him from church. His confessions take a long time. I expect he's a lot to confess. His wife is lovely but he's an arse, making your father work on a Sunday, when April needs ... well, could do with him being home, I'm sure. Arse.'

Mum saying that would have made me laugh, but from Vi it seemed natural.

'Anyway, you best be going. Look after April, tell her I'll be round Wednesday and maybe we'll go and light a candle. Perhaps she's still feeling a little … lost, just now.'

Susan started to ask a question but was interrupted by Bazzer coming into the kitchen, tapping her on the shoulder, asking, 'Can we work on that song before you go? I've got some ideas.'

'Oh, sorry, I need to go now. But we can give you a hand taking your gear home on the way.'

'Nah, s'ok, I'll hang out here a little longer, if that's ok Mrs E?'

'See you next rehearsal.' Susan waved to him as she led me down the hall to the door.

'And maybe you can do me a t-shirt like yours, but with bigger lips?' he called after her. She turned and nodded as we left the house.

We took the quicker route home.

'Getting on ok with Petra?' Susan asked, when she stopped to light a cigarette.

'I think so. Did you know her dad moved out?'

'Of course.'

'I didn't.'

'You did. At least, you should have.'

'I suppose 'cos everyone knew, no one told me.'

'Sometimes you don't need to be told, just to listen.'

We walked on in near silence save Susan's gentle singing. My ears were ringing from the rehearsal, but I could just make out Susan's quiet voice. 'What's that?'

'The song me and Bazzer are writing. What d'ya think? So far we've only a chorus.'

'And just as blossom's pink and white
So April blooms again
And soon as springtime comes to light
So April blooms again'

'Any good?' she asked.

'Bit slow.'

'Yep, and I don't even know if it's true. I thought so, last week, but …'

Chapter 6
Autumn 1975
Broken Record
'All Along The Watchtower'

The room was mostly dark. Yellow light from the streetlamp seeped through thin curtains at the bay window but was not a disturbance, I was used to similar at home. The camp bed was ok if I didn't fidget, and I might have slept well if not for the dog's bark. It was faint but urgent, loud enough to interrupt sleep, causing meandering, drowsy thoughts. I looked across to Susan and could see the shadowy outline of a body, but her face was turned away. She lay on the camp bed next to mine. The other furniture was pushed to the sides to make room for them – similar to the last time I'd been here, in Vi's front room, but then the chairs and table had made way for amps and drums. The dog barked again, louder, or perhaps I was more awake. And someone was calling, probably upstairs. They called a name, but both the voice and name were unfamiliar. The shout was repeated and now I was fully awake. Vi shouted for Will. The dog barked again. Susan sat up. There were heavy footsteps on the stairs. The barking was constant and Vi said something about a torch.

'Let's see.' I stood by Susan's camp bed and helped her up. Her nylon nightie flashed with static as she pulled her home-made Rolling Stones t-shirt over the top.

'What time is it?' she asked.

'No idea.'

I grabbed a jumper to pull over my pyjamas.

We went into the hallway and felt cold air. The kitchen light was on, and Vi was standing at the open back door, looking out to darkness. The neighbour's terrier was at the far end of the gardens, barking with some mix of anger, fear and excitement.

Susan looked at the clock on the far wall and muttered, 'Nearly half twelve,' as a complaint to no one in particular.

Vi turned. 'Ah, sorry, dears. Kettle's on. Last time that bloody terrier barked like this we lost three chickens to a fox.' She pulled her dressing gown tighter and went back to the kitchen door.

The dog was still barking, and I thought I heard chickens clucking. 'Shall I go and see?'

'It's all right. Will is out there. Can't have guests being bitten by foxes. You stay here.' She patted my arm. 'Susan dear, would you make a pot of tea?'

I looked to the garden, but Will's torch was dim and though I could see the dot of light move, it illuminated nothing. 'I hope Ingrid's ok.'

'She's a smart chicken. She'll be fine,' Petra said, surprising me as she squeezed her slight frame between me and Vi to look out the door. 'Is Will out there?'

'Yes, so the fox will have run and that stupid dog's barking at Will.' Vi tried to sound optimistic but her voice dropped, 'Unless the fox is trapped in the run. Oh ...'

Petra put an arm round her mother. She was taller than Vi and a little taller than me. Her thick towelling dressing gown was too big and the belt wrapped far around her waist. There was a brief lull in the barking during which the chickens could be heard, followed by Will shouting something unintelligible. We stared at the narrow path snaking up the garden, disappearing into the dark. The dog's barking eased and Will emerged from blackness into the meagre light from the kitchen. He held the torch in front of him; it was now all but useless. He was angry, shaking his head, 'Sodding fox.'

Petra and I moved to let him into the kitchen; Vi closed the door behind, asking, 'What happened?'

He sat heavily at the kitchen table, repeating, 'Sodding fox.'

Susan placed a cup of tea in front of him.

'That doesn't help,' said Vi. 'What happened?'

He looked to Petra, 'I'm sorry sis.'

'What?' Petra looked from him to me then back to Will. 'Oh no. Ingrid? Is it Ingrid? Did the fox get Ingrid?'

Will stared into his tea.

Petra began to cry and stepped toward me but before I could react she was past and into Vi's arms.

I looked at Susan and hoped she would know what to say. Vi separated herself from Petra, speaking to Will.

'I told you, didn't I, you lazy git. You needed to fix that fence, you miserable, lazy little bleeder. What would your father say? And now we've lost Ingrid, and others I suppose. You lazy bugger. Go back out there now and tidy up the mess. I won't have your sister seeing them in the morning. Go on, leave that tea, get out.'

I'd never seen Vi angry before, and though she didn't shout, there was a depth to her emotion that must have hurt Will. But he laughed. 'Ingrid is … was … just a chicken. And a fox needs to eat, right?' He looked to me. I looked away.

Petra ran from the kitchen into the back room.

'You're such a dick,' said Susan.

'What? No, it's all right, really. Ingrid's ok. There's been no fox. I don't know what that stupid dog was barking at.' He laughed.

'Then you're an arse as well as a dick,' said Vi, clipping him round the back of the head, but he laughed louder.

Susan caught my eye and indicated I should go and tell Petra.

Earlier that evening, Vi had popped round to ours to drop off an embroidery pattern and some earrings. We were in the lounge, Mum and Dad waiting for Dad's boss, Lawrence, and his wife. They were going out – the plan was for a meal at the new Chinese restaurant in The Broadway, followed by a film at The Odeon. And that, as Vi said to Mum,

'… sounds like a good Saturday night.'

I was watching *The Generation Game*. Susan was up in her room listening to *Straight Shooter*, having bought the cassette on her way home from work that day. I was hoping she'd also be going out so I could nab the cassette for a listen.

'And what film's on?' asked Vi.

Mum looked to Dad, who answered, '*Lisztomania*.'

'Sounds … nice,' Vi said to Mum who shook her head slightly.

'Lawrence says it's a good cast.' Dad stood to look out the front window.

'Daltrey's in it,' I called. 'I want to see it.'

'Too young,' said Dad.

Mum forced a laugh. 'It might not be my cup of tea, but it'll do me good to get out.' She toyed with the pearl earrings borrowed from Vi.

'Of course it will,' Dad said, moving to the sideboard where he sifted through the small pile of single records. 'Though I'd have preferred to go dancing. Like the old days.' He slipped a record from its sleeve and set it on the turntable. 'Especially when you look so beautiful. Doesn't she, Mike?'

I nodded. It was true. Mum wore a simple, knee-length purple dress with a white cardigan draped over her shoulders and a single string of pearls. I wasn't used to seeing her wear make-up. She looked years younger.

'But have you lost more weight?' Vi asked.

That was also true. The dress hung loose but then women were always trying to lose weight, weren't they? So why the hint of criticism in Vi's tone?

Mum said nothing.

'That just makes it easier to take a twirl.' Dad turned up the volume on the music centre. He pulled Mum gently from the chair and took her in dance hold. She stood uncertainly in block heels that were taller than usual.

They both seemed nervous, and the music was certainly not for twirling. The opening bars of *Unchained Melody* were indistinct, and this was not the song as I knew it.

'Remember this?' he asked her as they swayed gently in the small space between the dining table and the fireplace.

She shook her head.

'Of course you do. This is the first song we danced to, back in, what, fifty-five? Hammersmith Palais. Remember?'

She nodded, unconvincingly and with a slight blush. This was the same song they had danced to at her birthday party but an older version.

'Guess where I found it? Last weekend, in Wendrell's record store, while you were trying on that dress. Couldn't leave it there.' Dad eased her into a spin that didn't suit the tempo. They stopped abruptly at the harsh two-tone clang of the doorbell. 'Lawrence and Elsie,' he said, leaving the room.

Mum stood by the fireplace. She caught my eye and held out a hand, looking worried. I went to stand by her.

'... and the drinks are on me. I sold that Audi today,' Lawrence said as he entered the room, Dad just behind. 'Hello, April. Good to see you. You look lovely. It's been too long. And you ...' he hesitated, waiting for the name to come to him, '... Vi.'

'Evening, Lawrence, how's young Vince?' Vi asked.

'He's fine.'

'And Elsie?'

'Waiting in the car. We should get going,' he said, and turned to Mum. She took my hand. Despite her make-up she was pale.

'You can sit up front, next to me.' Lawrence spoke to her. She looked at Dad.

'I ... I just need to say g'night to Susan, she's going out with friends,' she said, and took a step to the door but didn't let go of my hand until we were at the foot of the stairs. I waited there. After a minute Dad came out, with Lawrence behind, and called up. When there was no response to his second call he started up the stairs, but Susan was coming down.

'Mum's not feeling well. Says go on without her.'

'What? What's the matter?' Dad asked then shouted, 'April, come on love, we haven't had a night out for ages.'

Susan stood half-way down the stairs. 'Best not, Dad. Mikey, take Mum a glass of water. She needs to take a tablet.'

I was happy to be away from the awkwardness as Vi now came from the lounge. There was confusion at the foot of the stairs – a confusion that wasn't shared in Susan's firm manner and stance. 'Really Dad, better for Mum to stay home tonight.'

'No, a night out will do her good.'

'Why don't I have a word?' said Lawrence.

'Oh I don't think that's a good idea,' said Vi, stepping between him and the stairs as I came out of the kitchen with a glass of water. Susan ushered me past the men.

I was in Mum's darkened room for less than a minute. She took one of her tablets and gave me a quick hug which I took as a sign she wanted to be alone. By the time I was back downstairs Lawrence had left and the others were in the lounge. Dad was standing over the music centre, watching the single spin gently. Susan was watching Dad. Vi was watching Susan.

They turned to watch me enter and I thought I'd made a mistake, somehow. I tried to think of a joke that might help but, thankfully, couldn't. 'Mum's ok,' I said, for something to say.

'So much for April's miracle,' said Dad.

'Perhaps she's still learning to live normally again.' Vi tried to help.

'That wasn't easy for her at the best of times, I know,' Dad muttered, 'even before the cancer she struggled to … to be herself, to be the mother she wanted. But always I thought she was special, even more so after her third miracle.'

'Third?' asked Vi.

'Three miracles. April and I already had love at first sight and two beautiful kids, then she received the third. I mean, I know I'm not so much into the God thing but why wouldn't he look after his April? I thought it meant she's special.'

'Special?' said Susan. 'So Mum's cancer was special? Special when they hacked away part of her breast and she cried for months afterwards when she looked in the mirror? Or when she was throwing up 'cos of the treatment? Special when it came back, and she sobbed for a week? Yeah, that's really special.' She was struggling to contain anger and looked to me. I had a fleeting memory of the night Dad told me the treatment hadn't worked. Susan had been in the lounge, holding Mum, when he came up to my room? Had he played it down that much? How had they protected me from it?

Dad reached out to Susan. 'But Mum's ok now, and without it coming back we'd never have had the miracle. That shows she's special.' He looked as desperate as he sounded, as desperate as I could imagine.

'It's hard for her,' said Vi.

Dad looked back to the spinning record. 'It's hard for all of us. Circles,' he said quietly, his eyes reddening. I could only just hear him but then jumped as he shouted, 'Fucking circles,' and ripped *Unchained Melody* from the deck. He threw the record to the floor. It didn't break with the first stamp, nor the second, and I winced each time, but it cracked with the third, as did his rage. He sat heavily at the dining table, lit a cigarette and sucked hard before apologising. Susan stood by him and bent over to hug tightly. Her eyes were wet, mascara smeared. My stomach lurched. It hurt to look at Susan or Dad, so I picked up the pieces of the broken record and slipped them back into the paper sleeve, leaving it on the coffee table. I swallowed hard and screwed my eyes shut to prevent myself crying.

Vi spoke to Dad. 'Why don't I take Mike round to mine. Susan's going out isn't she? You and April will have the place to yourselves.'

'It's all right, Vi. A couple of the girls can't make it so we're not going now,' said Susan.

Vi thought for a second before insisting, 'In that case come with me and Mikey. Your mum and dad can have the place to themselves, and you can keep me company.' Her gentle Irish lilt carried a firm instruction. Susan looked to Dad. He dragged on his cigarette.

Vi touched his shoulder as she spoke, 'Leave it ten minutes then go sit with April.'

'And say what?'

'Nothing, for a while. Just sit and hold her. That's worth a lot. She knows you don't understand, but she also knows you care. I'll look after Mike and Susan.'

So Saturday evening was spent in Vi's back room. I sat at one end of the settee, Petra the other, and Susan in the middle, flicking through *Melody Maker*. Vi sat in the armchair. We watched *The Dick Emery Show* but it wasn't funny. I usually watched it with Dad and we'd memorise the better jokes to tell Mum later.

The programme ended and Vi asked Susan to help make tea. Petra picked up the music paper Susan had left open at a review of *Midnight Lightning*.

'You a Hendrix fan?' she asked me, tapping the paper.

'Not so much.'

'Bazzer says he was the dog's bollocks. Reckons Terry's All Stars should play *All Along The Watchtower*.'

'Terry's All Stars?'

'It's what Will wants to call the band.'

'That's a bit American, isn't it?'

'Didn't Susan tell you? Sounds like the chocolates. I guess Will sees himself as Terry which means ...'

'… he thinks it's his band.' Susan interrupted as she brought in a tray with tea and biscuits. 'Which it isn't. Now Terry And The All Stars would be ok. And Terry could be me.'

'What's the difference?' Petra asked.

'And how is Terry a girl's name?' I said.

'As in Teresa?' said Petra.

'Why not? Could be,' said Susan. 'Point is, doesn't have to be Will.

'Perhaps it should be named Bazzer And The All Stars,' said Petra.

'Hmmm, do you think?' said Susan, smiling at Petra.

She blushed slightly as she answered, 'Well he does look a bit like David Essex …'

'… with a broken nose …' interrupted Susan.

'… and bass is the most important instrument in the band,' added Petra.

'Says Bazzer,' Susan said, laughing. 'We'll find out at the debut gig in a few weeks.'

Will and Bazzer came home from The Railway around half-ten. Bazzer teased Petra for the touch of lipstick she wore. She insisted it was just lip balm. I was annoyed at myself – I'd noticed but said nothing.

The camp beds were made up in the front room and Vi went to bed as *Match Of The Day* started. Petra followed at half-time. The rest of us stayed up and Susan laughed at Will and Bazzer's Saturday night football wisdom as Arsenal beat United. When it was over, Bazzer left and I slept until the drama of a possible fox in the garden had woken the household.

I left Susan and Vi in the kitchen, arguing with Will over how much of a dick he was for lying about the fox and Ingrid. The door to the back room was ajar. I bit at a jagged nail then knocked loudly before entering. Light filtered in from the kitchen and hall, and I could see Petra lying face down on the sofa. I made enough noise to be heard. She didn't turn from laying with her face pressed into a cushion. Her long hair, usually straight, was a tangle.

'Ingrid's ok. Susan says Will is a dick. Your mum says he's an arse.'

'I know. I heard.' She sat upright and shook hair from her face. I couldn't see her eyes properly and thought she was no longer crying but not smiling either. 'He is a dick. I fucking hate him. Like I need an older brother anyway. Dick.'

'And arse,' I added.

'Yep. Arse.'

'Fucking …'

'… arse …'

'… hole.'

'Hey that's my brother.' Petra smiled and slapped me round the head with a cushion.

'Shall I offer him out?'

'He's a bit big, don't you think?'

'I'm big enough.'

'Right, nearly as tall as me.'

'Exactly. And I've seen every episode of *Kung Fu*.'

We sat in comfortable silence until Vi came in, checking Petra was all right and suggesting it was time for bed, again.

Susan and I took to our camp beds. She turned and fidgeted. I whispered, 'You ok?'

She turned again. 'Just not tired anymore.'

'Nor me.'

'Was Petra all right?'

'I think so. We decided Will is an arsehole. She's angry with him.'

'He is an arsehole and being angry with family is ok.' She fidgeted some more.

'Susan?'

'Yep?'

'How angry is Dad with Mum? It's just … I mean I never heard him swear like he did earlier, in the house, anyway.'

'He's not angry, he just doesn't know what to do while Mum's getting better.'

'What you said, about Mum's operation, I hadn't thought of it like that.'

'Mum wouldn't want you to. Do not ask her about it.'

'She is ok, isn't she? I mean, obviously she isn't, quite, but Dad goes on about the miracle.'

'He needs to feel he's made a difference. He practically begged Vi to write that letter asking her sister to pray to Saint Teresa in Ireland.'

'I didn't know much about it.'

'It was ages ago. And you did. Anyway, I don't know about miracles, but the cancer's gone. She'll be herself soon.'

'You should have told me.'

'What?'

'More.' I pulled the blanket to my chin.

After a minute Susan rested up on one arm, asking, 'Hey, what about you and Petra?'

'What?'

'You know.'

'What? I think she likes Bazzer.'

'Why wouldn't she? He plays bass in a band and looks a bit like David Essex …'

'… with a broken nose.' I finished.

She laughed, 'Yep, but he's way too old for her. I mean, what is she, sixteen …?'

'… and a bit.'

'Nine, ten months older than you?'

'I guess.'

'So you haven't kissed her yet?' she asked.

'No, 'course not. Haven't asked her out.'

'You will and you'll kiss. I could teach you but that would be weird. The actual kissing is the easy bit, the tricky part is knowing when to make the move. That I can help you with.'

'Yeah, maybe. Susan?'

'Yeah?' She settled under her blankets.

'Do you think I should learn to play bass?'

'Well, you gotta do it for the music, not the girls. But it wouldn't hurt.'

Chapter 7
Autumn 1975
Penscote Bathworks Social Club
'Pretty Woman'

On the last Sunday evening of November, I knocked at Vince's house, hopeful he'd be coming out. He'd missed school Thursday and Friday and hadn't been at work Saturday morning – we washed cars at his dad's garage and the pay was good, considering how little pride we took in our work. Vince opened the door before my second knock, closing it behind him with barely a goodbye to whoever might be home.

'Where've you been?'

Vince didn't answer. It wasn't until we reached the front gate that I saw his sheepskin coat was only half worn. One sleeve draped over his right shoulder. The arm below hung heavily with a plaster cast from elbow to white fingers.

'Whoa, Vince, what the …?'

'Nothing. Fell in the kitchen. Broke my wrist.'

'Really? Which one?'

'Haha.'

With his good hand he pulled his woollen hat down, trying to cover his ears. It was a chilly night. As he tugged down one side so the other rode up. After a comical couple of attempts I did it for him.

'So you've no school for a few days.'

'Not sure. Mum says back on Wednesday, but Dad reckons tomorrow. Dunno how I'm supposed to write.'

'Does it hurt?'

'Not as much as it itches.'

'A knitting needle. That's what you need. When Susan broke her ankle that's how she scratched under the cast.'

'I'll ask her for one later.'

I looked to see if he was joking but couldn't tell in the dark.

Penscote Bathworks was the largest of the factories left here, and its foundry ran twenty-four hours a day. The iron baths were cast and enamelled on site, and the noise and smell was an odd contrast to the polite and regimented terraced houses close by. They were built between the wars, more modern than the industrial terraces of the past, but still covered in soot from the foundry. Now they were the oldest of the town planners' dreams for the new Penscote suburb. It was the foundry that was out of place, together with the railway that terminated there, bringing iron and taking away baths.

Petra's brother, Will, had started work in the offices straight from school. On the far side of the site, where the works met the heathland and municipal golf course between suburbs, was the social club and sports pitches. Will had persuaded the club steward to let the band play a set there this Sunday night, after bingo. The club had its own entrance, a lane that skirted the factory and ended at the gates to the pitches. It was this lane that Vince and I used and, as we passed within twenty yards of the foundry, the heat was welcome. Occasional flashes of vivid orange burst from the hangar-like factory's open doors and were instantly consumed by the black winter night. My short denim jacket was no protection from the cold. I cursed, having to hop-scotch around the rain-filled holes pockmarking the lane, not wanting to spoil my new trainers.

At the social club, the small entrance hall was almost filled by a huge older man behind a table, threatening to break the chair, sucking on a filterless fag. We weren't members but Will had given him a list of guests to admit. He stamped the back of my hand with a small datemark, assuring me it would wash off by Wednesday. He was only marginally more careful stamping the back of Vince's cast before nodding us through with a bored warning not to try buying lager or beer. I joked, '… but vodka's ok?' He didn't laugh.

We went through to the main bar where the band was setting up at the far end, a handwritten poster to one side proclaiming 'Terry And The All Stars' – Susan's design. Pluto, the guitarist, and Dimitri, the drummer, stood off to one side, looking nervous. Petra was standing by Bazzer's amp, watching while he checked and double-checked connections, flicked switches and tweaked knobs. Susan was standing at the bar and from the mono speaker on the wall above her came Orbison's *Pretty Woman*. She sipped from a can of Coke, occasionally spoke to Will, and made notes on the back of a spoiled bingo card. Vince and I threaded a path through the tables, crossed the small dance floor and went to the stage. The regulars at the tables watched us with barely concealed suspicion.

'Hi, Bazzer, Petra,' I said casually, nearly adding that the bar was playing her song. She wore a simple white blouse and dark blue jeans, tight over her slim hips before flaring. There was a single patch sewn over one of the back pockets – a solitary dark red rose. Her hair was long and straighter than ever with an elegance that made the excitement I felt seem childish.

They both nodded.

'All set?'

'Nah,' said Bazzer, 'something's not right.' He didn't look up from fiddling with the cables draped from the guitar to the Vox amp to the cabinet.

'Do you know what you're doing?' I teased.

'Bloody cheek. I am an electrician.'

'Er, apprentice.'

'Bugger off.'

'Anyway, we hope it's a dodgy cable rather than another knackered output transistor,' said Petra.

'Of course,' I agreed.

Vince laughed.

'What are you sniggering at?' she asked him.

'Nothing.' He couldn't tell if she was serious. Neither could I, which I liked.

'Good.' Now she smiled. Unusually, she wore a little eyeshadow, blue. The extra year or two it gave her was appealing. She turned her smile to me and the compliment that I'd just formed became a stutter which became a cough.

'How's your wrist?' she asked Vince. 'I heard you fell on the stairs. Clumsy.'

'Who told you that?'

'My mum spoke to yours after church this morning.'

I started to ask Vince about falling in the kitchen, but he quickly offered, 'Do you guys want to share a Coke? My mum gave me money for tonight. I told her I'd have to pay to get in.' He went to the bar.

Petra stepped down from the stage. 'Is Vince all right? His mum said it's a bad break, but his dad just laughed. My mum thinks he's a prat.'

'Your mum thinks a lot of people are prats,' Bazzer said, hunting through a bag of cables.

'Or arses,' Petra added.

'Which is a good thing,' said Bazzer.

'And she's mostly right,' added Petra.

'And she has a way of saying arse like it must be true,' I added.

Bazzer laughed. 'I know what you mean. Oh, by the way, did Susan tell you I can come over tomorrow for another bass lesson? About six?'

'No, but it's ok and I've been practising.'

'You're learning bass now?' Petra sounded surprised. 'And Bazzer's teaching? At your place?'

'Yep.'

'Oh ... cool.'

'Very,' I said, and meant it.

'He has the knack,' said Bazzer.

My cheeks flushed.

'Tricky without an actual bass guitar,' she teased.

'True, but guess what Dad brought home Friday night?' I tried to sound nonchalant.

The morning after the night a fox didn't attack the chickens, there had been an impromptu rehearsal at Vi's. Petra had gone to church with her mum, reluctantly. Bazzer and Pluto had popped over and although there were no drums they played for an hour or so. Then Susan had worked with Bazzer on their song, despite Will's mocking. I'd watched and listened and, when Bazzer took a cigarette break, joined him in the garden. The chickens at the end of the garden clucked, perhaps expecting food. It was a cloudless mid-November day, but the sun wasn't sufficient to warm us. Bazzer pretended to offer me a cigarette as I sat next to him.

'I'm trying to give up,' I said.

'Haha. Me too, these things are expensive.'

'Better sell some records then.'

'That's the plan. Just gotta write a hit, find a label and keep Will from being a dick. He should let Susan sing lead more.'

'Not many girls fronting rock bands.'

'Susan could. And we need more guitar. Will barely plays, leaving it all to Pluto.'

'Pluto's good right? Has a few of those Blackmore licks?' I asked hesitantly. Susan was my educator in rock and I was learning fast, and loving it, but wary with my opinions when with Bazzer.

'Yeah, but he can't play lead and rhythm. We need another guitar. I'm trying to convince Susan to fill the gap, she's getting better.'

'And what about bass? Always need more, right?'

'Why not, and even when less is more, it's less bass that matters most.' Bazzer drew on his cigarette and blew the smoke away from me.

'Is that one of Susan's?'

'Yep.'

'What does it mean?'

'Fuck knows.'

We laughed.

'Would you teach me?' I asked.

'What?'

'Bass.'

'You're already learning guitar on Susan's acoustic. I hear you're pretty good.'

'But guitar's gravy and bass is the meat.'

'That sounds like your sister again.'

'Nope. Mine. Would you teach me?'

Bazzer took a second to think. 'Maybe. Where? My old man's not keen on too much playing at our place.'

'You could come over to ours.'

'Will Susan be there?'

'I 'spect so.'

'Yeah, why not. You need to stop biting your nails though.'

'Why? Do I need them for bass?'

'No. But they look manky.'

Since then, Bazzer had given me three lessons, Susan had sat in twice and I was trying hard not to bite my nails. After the latest lesson, Dad had asked Bazzer how I was doing and was told I seemed to, 'have the knack'. Two days later, on the Friday, I was in the lounge, bored both with the news I wasn't watching and the maths homework I wasn't doing. Susan was making tea, sardines on toast. As she called me to the table Dad came in carrying a large canvas holdall, similar to an army duffle bag but longer.

'Mum not eating with you? Where is she?' he asked Susan but nodded towards the ceiling, already knowing the answer.

'I haven't disturbed her.'

'No, best not. I'll pop up in a mo. But first ...' he laid the duffle bag next to the table, '... is the kettle on? I need a cuppa.'

'What's that?' I pointed to the old bag.

'What?'

'That.'

'What, that?'

'Yep, that.'

'Nothing.' His dismissive air was exaggerated.

'Well it's a lot of bag for nothing,' said Susan.

'I thought I'd take up a hobby. Something to keep me busy in the winter nights when there's bugger all on telly.'

'And the bag?' I pressed.

'What?'

'That.'

'What? The bag?' He tapped a foot against it.

'Yes, the bag,' said Susan, losing patience.

'Oh, that's the new hobby.'

'What, bag collecting?'

'That's funny, Mike. But no, I'm developing my comedy act for the Conservative Club and thought it might help to drop in the occasional song. So I need to learn guitar and don't want to borrow Susan's.'

'Really?' I dropped my toast to the plate and reached for the bag, but he was quicker.

'Trouble is, I think it's broken already.' He pretended a quizzical look and, finally, pulled out a dark brown electric bass guitar, scratched and scuffed. 'It seems to be missing something. I wanted a six string but it's only got four, so you might as well have it.' He passed it to me, smiling broadly. That it was a three-quarter size bass was momentarily a disappointment, but that didn't matter, and I didn't let it show.

It was mine.

I matched Dad's grin. Susan later remarked it was the only time in fifteen years she'd known me speechless.

On the stage at Penscote Bathworks Social Club, Bazzer replaced the cable from amp to speaker cabinet, turned down the volume and tried a few notes on his guitar, nodding with satisfaction. Someone called out, 'Play something we know.' And a few others laughed.

More people wandered in, and a clutch of younger drinkers crowded the bar. Will had been encouraging people to come down, as had Susan; I recognised some of her friends. This was probably the biggest Sunday night crowd they'd ever had, though I doubted the ten or fifteen older regulars would be that pleased, particularly those that had started dominoes.

Petra and I left Bazzer to tune up, and as we went to the bar I caught a brief smell of her scent – sweet and perhaps marzipan – for a second, until swamped by the burning sulphur of another match being struck. In the morning I expected Susan would smell of the smoke still in her hair and glanced at Petra's – so much hair must take a long while to wash, surely.

'So you've another lesson this week. Will Susan be there?' she asked.

'Sorry?' I hadn't been paying attention. She repeated the question.

'I suppose so,' I replied, speaking loudly to be heard above the growing conversation at the bar.

'Bazzer likes Susan, doesn't he?'

'I guess.' I answered, wondering if it would be odd if I was to smell Petra's hair.

'And your next lesson with Bazzer is tomorrow? I think my mum was gonna pop over to see how your mum's doing. I was gonna come.'

'That's ok.'

'Sure?'

'Yeah, 'course, more than ok,' I said, feeling brave. At the bar Vince was holding two cans of Coke and talking to Susan who was frowning as she asked,

'… knitting needle?'

'For scratching.' He held up the arm with the cast.

'Oh, sure, I get it. Yeah, but your mum'll have one.'

'Nah, I asked.'

'As you like. I'll find one and Mike can bring it over.'

'Ta.' Vince handed one of the Coke cans to me and I offered it to Petra for the first sip.

More people came in, brandishing the date stamp on their hand. The band had worked hard to gather a crowd. When Dad entered I nudged Susan and we went over, Vince and Petra following.

'Where's Mum?' I asked.

Dad removed his heavy coat and scarf and hesitated before answering. 'It's a bit cold for her. But she's sure the show will go well, and I've got to take pictures.' He held up his camera.

'Mum said she'd come. It's our first proper gig,' Susan said.

'I know, Princess, but she's … well it's cold and there's all these people and … you know.'

'Yeah, I know,' Susan said, with no bitterness. 'We've a gig booked at the college in a couple of weeks. Maybe then.'

'The college? I don't know, Princess, maybe.'

'But …' I started. Susan shook her head, almost imperceptibly.

'I know, Mikey. I know.' Dad put an arm around me and hugged tight and I was glad Susan had stopped me. 'So, when are you going on?' he asked.

'A few minutes.'

'Nervous?' Dad asked.

'Not much, well maybe a little, but that's a good thing, right?' Susan smiled. 'Anyway, it's really just another rehearsal but with a few more people, mostly pals.'

She was nearly convincing, but I was nervous for her.

Conversation at the bar grew louder. Will tapped Susan's shoulder, nodded acknowledgement at Dad, and led her to the stage. The Club Steward announced the winning ticket for the meat raffle while the band finished fussing with instruments and mics and lined up to start. The regulars at their tables stayed seated and some groaned as the main lights dimmed and the stage lights brightened. The crowd the band had brought down, perhaps thirty or forty people, shuffled away from the bar and closer to the stage. The spotlights and metallic strip-curtain backdrop offered flashes of glamour, but the club's dour brown decor was a challenge. The crowd quietened as Will gave a look to his bandmates, mouthed a count and Pluto's guitar filled the bar with the opening riff from *Rebel Rebel*. It was much louder than rehearsals and Petra took half a step back; I took half a step forward. Will's permed hair bobbed up and down, and he occasionally stroked his guitar. Susan stepped in time to the riff, driven by the beat, rocking the mic stand on its heavy metal base. Dimitri battered his drums and Pluto played faster. I looked to Dad and matched his smile. Penscote Bathworks Social Club was rockin'. Even the regulars tapped toes – mostly.

The set, just eleven songs, passed quickly. I concentrated on Bazzer, who didn't move much, and though he didn't try to excite the crowd it seemed he wasn't just playing an instrument – he gave it life.

Susan took lead vocals on a couple of songs and was no longer just big sister. She sang and moved with emotion and knowing beyond her years.

Yes, they made a few mistakes. Sometimes Pluto's solos were too loud or not loud enough. And yes, Will wasn't nearly as funny as he thought between songs, despite the partisan crowd's laughter. Occasional feedback caused wincing pain but that was ok, this was music, live. The band had passion; the band lived the music; the small, packed dance floor bounced with energy. Though I'd heard these songs many times in rehearsals, tonight they were fresh.

Dad was impressed, transfixed and, thankfully, didn't hear the spiteful shout between songs from the back to, 'Get Andy Pandy off the bleedin' stage.' Susan was wearing striped dungarees which I'd told her, subtly – perhaps too subtly – wasn't a great look.

They finished with *Under My Wheels* and didn't play an encore.

Vince reminded me, 'Alice Cooper's real name …'

'… is Vince. You tell me every time.' I laughed to show I didn't mind.

'Because it's true every time,' he said. Which made me laugh more.

The cheers faded, the main lights came back on, and there was a rush back to the bar that had the regulars moaning again. Terry And The All Stars spent a couple of minutes congratulating each other then began packing away. Susan came down from the stage where Dad was waiting. They hugged.

'Mum would be so proud.'

Susan forced a smile. 'Next time, eh?'

'Next time, Princess.' Dad swallowed hard. 'I better get back. And I'm so proud of you. You were amazing. I took lots of pictures.'

He squeezed her again, said, 'Don't be late,' and was gone.

I bumped against Susan. 'Where did you learn to do that? You were the dog's bollocks.'

'Thanks little brother.' Her blue eyes were both darker and sparkling for holding tears.

'You ok?'

'Yeah, just wanted Mum to see.'

'She'll come next time. After all, what's the point of a miracle if nothing's different?'

'Yeah, next time.' She took a deep breath to catch her tears. 'C'mon, help pack this lot away. No such thing as a free show.'

'Well at least now we know what we'll be doing when we leave school,' said Petra, following me up on stage.

'What's that?'

'Roadies.'

'Nah, we'll be up there with 'em.'

'You maybe. And yours is like that?' Petra pointed to Bazzer's guitar.

'Nearly. Mine's smaller, a junior bass.'

Petra laughed, 'What, like a tiny guitar for a tiny player?'

'Sort of.' I laughed.

'Well that's your band name then,' said Petra. 'JB. Junior Bass.'

Bazzer laughed but coming from Petra, I thought JB sounded all right.

Chapter 8
Winter 1975/76
Penscote College Of Art
'Seven Seas Of Rhye'

On Friday 12th December, Terry And The All Stars played the Art College Christmas concert.

Dimitri, retaking CSEs and studying drama, had persuaded the college to give a full forty-five minutes to Terry And The All Stars – not difficult because the jazz club had folded, the poetry society was struggling, and this year's orchestra was short three violins, an oboe and a flute. It helped that Dimitri was particularly friendly with Miss Portel, the new drama teacher tasked with organising the concert.

I went there after school to help set up the gear. A faded red Ford Escort van was parked close to the hall's back door. A young man in dirty jeans, burgundy Fred Perry polo shirt and a short denim jacket was leaning against the driver's door, trying to light a cigarette in the wind. As Susan and I approached he patted the van's roof. 'Like it?' His voice was deep, and though he was short, that didn't detract from his physical presence – he was broad and heavy, but not overweight.

He didn't smile but I thought him pleased with himself.

'This is Steve, my brother.' Bazzer made introductions.

'Nice van,' said Susan, then she looked at Bazzer. 'For us?'

'Terry And The All Stars.'

'You've not passed your test yet. Has he?' she asked.

'I don't know, but he can drive.'

Steve was first to the back of the van, pulling out amps, speakers and stands, passing lighter items to me and Susan.

I watched the band set up the gear, paying close attention, then joined them in the wings to watch the opening acts.

After the Shakespeare comedy excerpt, at which no one laughed except Miss Portel and, a split second later, Dimitri, Petra joined me. She had come along to cheer on Will, she said, though of course I hoped I might also have been a reason. Steve stood with us, saying little, even in response to my excited praise as the band opened with *Seven Seas Of Rhye* – but they made a right hash of it. The intro was sloppy, they came in too fast, Will couldn't hit the top notes and the harmonies were poor. I caught Petra's eye. She winced, and shouted above the music, 'I told him he's no Freddie, but ...' she shrugged.

It took a couple of songs for them to relax, and I thought that being on this proper stage with harsh lighting wasn't helping. Nor did an audience of sceptical students. But gradually the band upped the energy and volume, and by the time they played *Time's Out*, one of Bazzer's own, they'd clawed it back. Thanks to Bazzer's lessons I was watching him with new understanding but, time and again, my eye was drawn to Susan. Though Will led on most songs, she was more and more the centre of attention. Her short mop of blonde hair was somehow rebellious and her cheesecloth skirt, cotton vest and crochet waistcoat were a homage to Joplin – a big step up from the Andy Pandy dungarees. Many of the youths in the crowd were captivated and I could see why – she was both obvious and mysterious, a young woman, curves accentuated by movement, but still youthful, no older than them, attainable, yet out of reach. And she may have been playing to an art college, but she sang every note as if packing out The Marquee or Wembley's Empire Pool.

Mum would have been proud.

They finished with *School's Out*, which I thought cheesy as term was nearly finished, but what the hell. Stage side, Petra and I joined the shouts for more. As the calls subsided Petra asked, 'Jealous?'

'Of ...?'

'Susan, maybe?'

'Not jealous but it would be cool to be alongside. Wouldn't it?'

'Not for me. But for you? Yeah, I can see it. Is that why you're not getting your hair cut?'

'Do I look a bit like Frampton?' I asked hopefully.

'A bit, though as your jaw is … skew-whiff, more like Leo Sayer. But let your hair grow, and Frampton? Maybe.'

I tried to hide a crooked grin as the house lights went up and the magic of the gig was lost in the returning hall. The wooden boards on the walls listing winners of various awards down the years were suddenly old, irrelevant.

'Looks like we've lost our job as roadies,' said Petra, motioning to Steve. He was already disconnecting the PA and coiling cables.

'And he drives a van.'

'That little red thing? My mum saw it earlier when they brought it round to pick up the PA. She reckons he's nicked it from the Post Office.'

We each picked up a guitar case and some cables to follow Steve outside. The others were standing around watching him load the gear, explaining, '… it only fits one way, for fuck's sake.'

'Oh, by the way,' Petra whispered to me, 'if Steve offers you a cigarette, my mum says to say no.'

'But Susan smokes.'

'Not Steve's type of smoke.'

'Oh, right,' I said, sort of understanding.

On the following Monday, Dimitri was hanging round the common room, bumming fags, when an older student approached. Apparently he'd seen the concert, wanted the band to play his twenty-first party and was happy to pay the going rate.

Terry And The All Stars had eight weeks to learn enough songs to fill two sets and decide what the going rate should be.

Miracle Number Four

Chapter 9
Winter 1975/76
Saint Teresa's Tears
'Young Americans'

The run up to Christmas was a busy time. Now in the last year at secondary school I had more homework, and was expected to do chores around the house. In truth, washing up occasionally and vacuuming upstairs once a week was no hardship, but it interrupted bass practise, or sharing new jokes with Dad or, highlight of the week, hanging around Petra's when Terry And The All Stars rehearsed.

The second highlight of the week was Monday's bass lesson. I'd rush to finish homework before tea – or simply not do it – to be ready when Bazzer came round, on his way home from work. Susan would sometimes sit in and listen, which I didn't mind as Bazzer offered more praise. Now that I had my own guitar, I was a quick learner. Sometimes, after the lesson, and if Dad was working late, Bazzer and Susan would use the front room to work on their own songs – I was ushered out and the door closed behind me. When I teased her about rarely hearing music she claimed they were writing lyrics. Mum was usually in the conservatory. Since Dad's miracle claims, she had been spending a lot of time there, embroidery hoop in her lap, needle held carefully, though rarely actively engaged. When I asked what she was making she'd say,

'… still deciding and, meantime, watching the flowers,' then indicate to the garden. But in winter, in the dark, that was no longer believable.

I didn't know, but in early December Dad had taken Bazzer to one side and asked how I was getting on with the bass. Bazzer told him I was doing well, better than well, but, '… without an amp and cabinet couldn't go far.' The conversation had quickly led to finding secondhand equipment so I could make real progress. Bazzer knew a guy who was shifting some gear and would make sure it was in good working order. Dad was easily persuaded, had worked sufficient overtime to afford it, and I guess Bazzer was happy to be able to impress Susan's father.

Result? I was happy as the proverbial pig in shit with my Christmas presents. Come New Year's Eve, the neighbours less so. Dad brokered a deal – I wouldn't play with the volume above two in the evening and not at all on Saturday afternoons – the neighbour insisted on quiet while watching the horse racing. This caveat was also invoked on New Year's Day; *Grandstand* was showing the Cheltenham meet. As a result, Thursday afternoon, 1st January, I was bored. Dad was at work and Mum was in the conservatory, occasionally adding stitches to the muslin cloth stretched across a small embroidery hoop – she had finally decided it would be an apple tree with white or pink blossom. Susan, with New Year's Day off from the salon, was napping on the couch, recovering from the previous night.

'Where you going?' she asked as I forced on trainers with laces tied.

'Bazzer's. There's a loose connection or something on one of the pick-ups.' I indicated to the duffle bag at my side, holding my precious bass. 'Gonna ask him to have a look.'

'You and that guitar.' She raised herself slowly to sitting. 'And?'

'Nothing. It suits you. Give me a minute, I'll come with. Fresh air might shift this head and Mum wants Vi's cake tin returned. They were back yesterday. We'll stop on the way.'

'I can give Petra that present.' I was happy for the chance. I hadn't seen her for a couple of weeks. She and Vi had spent Christmas in Ireland with family.

'Mum!' Susan shouted through to the conservatory then winced, 'Bugger, that hurts,' and held her head. 'Ask if she wants to come.'

Mum appeared not to have heard Susan's shout or me come in. 'Mum?' I called gently. She didn't stir. Her eyes were closed, and she was still. The embroidery hoop was on the floor. I picked it up and laid it in her lap. She didn't move. I went back to the lounge.

The sky was grey without threatening rain but the January cold was enough to make us hurry. We walked to Bazzer's via Petra's and she seemed pleased to see me. It had only been two weeks and I knew her smile well, but saw it anew. After we exchanged gifts – I gave her David Bowie's album *Young Americans* on cassette and she gave me a guitar strap; the perfect present – I suggested she come along with us.

'As long as you're back in time for us to go to New Year's Day Mass,' said Vi.

At Bazzer's front door there were muffled shouts, and he could just be made out through the semi-opaque glass. As the door opened we heard the dull thud of music from inside. A dishevelled Bazzer nodded along, out of time. His heavy eyes brightened as Susan said, 'Afternoon, band bruv, you look rough.'

'Heavy night.'

'Looks like it got heavier after I left.'

He nodded. 'And less fun.'

'Happy New Year, Bazzer,' I said.

Bazzer winced, I was talking loud. He managed a brief smile, asking, 'JB, Petra, you guys ok?'

'Practising hard. Thanks for helping my dad sort out the amp and speaker.'

'Oh yeah, sure, no problem. All working?'

'Great.'

'And the neighbours said thanks too,' added Susan.

'I do need some help though,' I took my guitar from the duffle bag. 'I think one of the pick-ups is knackered.'

Bazzer reached to take it from me but stalled at the angry shout from the front room.

'Oi! Barry! Shut the door! It's cold.'

Another voice, this time female, shouted, 'Yeah! I'm freezing my tits off.'

'Yeah, yeah,' Bazzer called over his shoulder then more quietly said to Susan, 'My brother.'

'What? With tits?' Susan asked as the owner of the female voice came from the front room. I thought she was probably in her early twenties. She wore faded jeans and a tight t-shirt with a hand drawn Rolling Stones logo. She was as tall as Bazzer and probably broader, strong but not athletic. The t-shirt was similar to Susan's homemade effort but not as well drawn. As she came down the hall I smelled burning, tinged with a sickly sweetness. 'Hi, Sofia. Happy New Year.' Susan greeted her.

'Happy New Year, Susie. Hi, Petra. Barry, your brother says to come in or go away, but whatever, shut the door.'

Sofia went back inside.

'She came home with Steve, last night,' Bazzer said to Susan.

'I expect she did.' Susan half-smiled.

Bazzer reached for the guitar. 'I'm not sure I'm up for looking at it right now, JB. Can you leave it with me?'

'Sure. Still ok for a lesson Monday though?'

'Of course, but I'll get it back to you before then. Can't miss practise.' He looked to Susan. 'You staying?'

'Yeah, for a while.' Susan stepped through the door and turned. 'Tell Mum I'll be back to make tea.'

As the front door closed Petra said, 'I always thought it was Bazzer for Bassman, not Barry.'

'Any idea who the girl was?' I asked.

'Sofia. She works down The Railway. I go to school with her sister, Kay.'

'I see why she complained about freezing her ...' I stopped myself, just.

'Really?' Petra gave a slight shake of her head then frowned. 'I made that t-shirt for Bazzer.'

'Looks good.'

'Not as good as the one your sister made.'

'Even so, I wouldn't mind ... you know ... a t-shirt like that,' I hinted.

'Better ask Sofia,' she said, deadpan, and I couldn't tell if she joked.

We walked back without talking much and I tried not to fill the silence with rambling nonsense or second-rate jokes. It wasn't far, but by the time we were back at Petra's the afternoon winter darkness was falling quickly and cold was settling on us. At the gate she touched my arm and, for a second, I thought she was going to kiss me. She didn't, of course, but said, 'I forgot. Mum said to tell your dad we went back to see Saint Teresa and said another prayer. Like he asked. But Mum also said that doesn't mean he shouldn't also say one, or more.'

'Saint Teresa?'

'Well, to be more accurate, a statue of her, in Ireland. The real Teresa died a few hundred years ago, in Spain I think.'

'Haha. The statue that Dad reckons made for Mum's cure?'

'Is there another?'

I laughed at Petra's response, but it wasn't that funny. This was about Mum. Dad must have asked Vi to pray again. 'So you went to the statue?'

'Yep, Mum and me and some of her ... sisters, I think, or more cousins, went down to the caves by the bay. They live in Glaskild, near the sea. The caves are really cool, when it's not raining. In the biggest one there's this statue of Saint Teresa. They say if you pray to her and she cries it comes true.'

'And did she cry?'

'Which time?' she asked.

'Either.' I tried to be patient, though the answer was suddenly important.

'I don't know. Maybe. It was dark. Creepy. My mum says when she was a girl they used to sneak into the caves at night and that's where she kissed her first boyfriend, Niall. She was eighteen. Came to England a year or two later and lost her virginity to my dad, on the back of a bus when they hid upstairs and got locked in the depot. That time she prayed to Saint Teresa not to be pregnant.'

'You and your mum share everything, don't you?' I didn't care about the back of the bus; I cared about statues crying, or not.

'Don't you?'

'Not the small stuff so much.'

She looked thoughtful. '... which must make the big stuff seem bigger than it is. It's never just another part of the story.'

I took a second to work through that. 'I guess so.'

'That's not a good thing. Is it?'

'Not always.' I agreed

'Anyway, don't say anything to Father Andrew about it.'

'What? Your mum on the back of a bus?'

'No, idiot. Saint Teresa. Mum doesn't think he believes in all miracles.' She left me at the gate, turning at the door to call, 'Thanks for the present.'

I held up the guitar strap, 'Likewise, see you next rehearsal?'

'Maybe.'

'Did you try that guitar strap yet?' Susan asked as I helped her make tea. She had come home from Bazzer's an hour or so after me. Mum was in the conservatory; Dad was in the shed.

'It's ace. And I guess it was Petra's idea.'

'Yep, she's cool.'

'Yep. But I was wondering ... should I have kissed her or something?'

'Or something?' Susan laughed.

'I mean not like a proper kiss, but maybe a peck on the cheek, to say thanks. It's such a cool present.'

'Nah, probably not. That'd be like a brother, sister thing. When you finally do kiss you don't want that. Don't worry, like I said, when it's time I'll help you. Trust me.'

'Do you think she really liked the cassette?'

'Did she look properly pleased?'

'I think so.'

'The best thing would be for her not to have liked it but to have pretended sufficiently well to convince you she did.'

'Oh, I see.'

'Do you?'

'Sort of.'

'So, was Petra pretending?'

'I don't think so. Though I now hope she was. It's hard to tell with her.' My words drifted away.

'What's the matter?'

'Did you know Dad asked Vi to say more prayers for Mum?'

'When?'

I told Susan what Petra had said about Saint Teresa's cave and asked if I should tell Dad.

'Doesn't sound like she said much.' Susan frowned. 'I mean, did the statue cry or not?'

'She didn't know.'

'That's not much to tell Dad.'

'Do you ever wonder what if Vi had never written that letter?'

'No. But miracle or not, Mum deserved it as much as anyone, letter or no letter. Here.' She passed me a sandwich plate. 'I'll bring a cup of tea through in a minute.'

I went to the conservatory where Mum was sitting on an old armchair, embroidery still in her lap, and put the plate on the table next to her.

'Cold in here Mum.'

'Not so bad.' She patted the blanket on her lap and round her legs.

Standing at the French doors, I felt the draught on my face through the ill-fitting frames. I looked to the garden but the blackness reflected the conservatory lights back at me.

'Mum.' I didn't turn.

'Yes, Mikey?'

'Petra said she and Vi visited that statue, in Ireland, like Dad asked.' I was hesitant and tried to take the worry from my voice.

'Did she? She's a lovely girl. Steady. You should spend more time with her.'

I paused, not knowing what to make of that and instead asked, 'Did they need to go to Saint Teresa again?'

'Not really. The cancer's gone.'

'But did Dad ask her ... to pray?'

'I expect so, but I just need to ... buck up, as they say.'

Susan came in with a cup, steam evaporating into the chilly air. She saw the look on my face as I turned from the garden. 'All ok?'

'Yes, dear,' said Mum.

'Mike?' Susan asked.

'I told Mum that Vi went to the statue.'

'She needn't have,' said Mum.

'But Dad asked her,' I said.

'You know your father.' She spoke quietly. 'And you can't blame him. It's not been easy for him, or you. So why wouldn't he?'

I began a question but Susan shook her head, almost imperceptibly.

'Besides,' said Mum, shifting in her chair to sit more upright, 'you know what your father says about these miracles.' She looked to Susan. 'There are ...'

'... three types, Mum.' Susan finished the sentence.

'And we need them all. Don't we?' she said.

I stood away from the doors, back into the centre of the conservatory. It started to rain but only lightly and the drumming on the plastic roof was not distracting.

'And they are …?' Susan encouraged Mum, taking her hand.

'Love at first sight, children and God's work.' Mum looked serious. 'But I think there's a fourth.'

'Miracle?' I looked at her.

She stared past me. 'Peace.'

Miracle Number Four

Chapter 10
Winter 1975/76
The Golden Suite
'Saturday Night's Alright For Fighting'

'Seventh February, nineteen seventy six. The Golden Suite, Penscote Town Hall. The day the All Stars broke through. We gotta play the song.' Will's frustration was clear.

'I don't care. I don't want to play it,' said Bazzer.

'The guy with the birthday wants it for his parents. And he's paying.'

'I don't care.'

'But we've rehearsed it. You said you'd play it.'

'I've changed my mind.' Bazzer lit a cigarette without offering one to Will.

'Susan. Tell him,' Will said, as she came into the cramped space being used as a dressing room and to store guitar cases. I sat in the corner pretending to read the *New Musical Express*.

'Tell him what?' Susan asked.

'We need to play *The Last Waltz* at the end of the gig.'

'I'm not playing it,' Bazzer said.

'Why not?' Susan asked.

'It's shit.'

'We've rehearsed it,' she reminded.

'That's what I said.' Will lit a cigarette from his own pack.

'Because you'll sing anything,' said Bazzer. 'You know he's been rehearsing *Delilah* with Pluto on an acoustic 'cos he thinks his new next-door neighbour likes it and he fancies her. He'll sing anything to be liked.'

Pluto looked up from the guitar he was tuning and nodded.

Susan laughed. 'The woman just moved in? She must be thirty if she's a day. And what about the husband? He'll beat the crap out of you.'

'It's a good song, like *The Last Waltz*,' Will tried.

'No it isn't and I'm not playing it.' Bazzer was adamant.

'We're being paid for it. And I've given up *Seven Seas Of Rhye* to Susan.'

'That's true,' said Susan, taking Bazzer's arm and leading him outside.

'Which, by the way, doesn't work without a piano,' Will called to their backs, sounding hurt.

Pluto strummed his guitar and Will sang *Delilah*.

I tried not to laugh and wandered into The Golden Suite, where they would be playing that night. Dimitri was fiddling with the set-up of the drums while Steve complained, '… of course it's right,' as he rerouted cables. The guitar amps flanked the silver sparkle drum kit and the wall behind was curtained with a heavy dark blue velvet. On the front skin of the kick drum Susan had drawn the band's name. Above it, Dimitri had written *Ludwig* in black felt tip pen.

'Hi, Dimitri,' I called to him.

'Hiya, JB. They still arguing back there?'

'Yep. Hey, Steve?' I tapped him on the shoulder.

'Yeah?' He looked up from the mic stand he was trying to stop from flopping to the floor.

'How do you know the person at the door's a drummer?' 'Dunno.'

I made sure Dimitri was paying attention before completing the joke. 'Because the knocking gets faster.'

Steve looked at me but didn't react. Dimitri pretended to be insulted and cursed something in Greek before throwing a drumstick.

Though there was an hour to go before the party would start, I was already excited. It was easy to imagine fronting my own band, even playing my own music, one day. But there would be no envy at watching my sister. My time would come. I stood at a mic, feeling the pulse of air behind me from Dimitri's kick drum as it was tuned, and looked out to the empty room. It was large enough for a couple of hundred people. There was a temporary stage, only a foot high but enough to make a difference. A couple of spotlights could be directed at the band. The bar at the far end was being readied and the room decorated for a party. Pairs of balloons were tied underneath wall lamps, some of them already deflating, and on each of the tables edging the dance floor was a flower decoration, sprinkled with glitter. Above the bar was a banner proclaiming 'happy birthday', and off to one side was a buffet with a two-tier cake centrepiece. Next to the stage was Susan's new, bigger, brighter band poster. This was Terry And The All Stars' biggest gig and who could say what might come from it? As for *The Last Waltz*, Will had a point, but so did Bazzer. Steve moved me aside as he checked cable runs again.

I went outside to find Susan. The Golden Suite was on the first floor, and at the end of the corridor the fire escape door was ajar. It led to a stairway, and I stood on the balcony. It was a dry, sunny day, warmer outside than in. Hearing murmurs from below I looked down through the iron grate and took a second to unravel the scene, the tangled bodies. Bazzer was sitting on almost the bottom step and Susan was astride him. Their faces were melded. They were both fully clothed, but Bazzer's hand was slipped up the front of Susan's t-shirt and she rocked against him. They radiated a primal energy. The passion within and from them both was a revelation and carried an urgency I'd never seen before. There was no romance and no subtlety. I felt guilty and watched for only a few seconds, but the image of intense, honest lust stayed with me.

It was not a stretch to imagine such an encounter leading to a proper moment, as Susan might say. That it was my sister wasn't a shock, it was somehow reassuring. If it happened to her, it could, would, happen to me, one day. And why not soon. I went back inside to ask Will if Petra was coming tonight.

The hall was packed, the bar busy and the food scoffed. Terry And The All Stars went on as the buffet queue dwindled. The room lights dimmed. The band carefully picked their way through the gear and cables to take their places on stage in the dark. I stood off to one side, next to Steve, finishing a fishpaste sandwich despite feeling nervous for Susan.

Will raised a hand to catch the barman's attention and two spotlights burst into white. Seconds later the band crashed into *Under My Wheels*. They'd rehearsed this opening until fingers bled, and, from the opening bars, played with attack and confidence, both in themselves and each other. Susan was more centre stage, closer to leading the band with a seductive mix of easy charm and stirring energy. The guests had come to drink and dance; the music was a force, an invitation to submit. It took just a song and a half for the first few women to be dancing and the third song, *You Really Got Me*, for the first of the younger men to be dragged up. By the fifth song, *Rebel Rebel*, the floor was more than half full. Will and Susan were charismatic on stage, the music moving through them, enticing more dancers to the floor, managing the show with spontaneity and confidence. Even Pluto was animated, filling nearly half the stage – such lightness of movement from the big guy was oddly mesmerising. Dimitri's face was hidden behind the long black hair sweeping to and fro with his beat. Bazzer swayed gently, but timely, eyes often closed, his bass driving the feeling that brought life to the dance. They finished the first set with Bazzer's song, and it fitted perfectly. During the break, the Birthday Boy bought the band a drink. Steve moaned at having to buy his own but brought back a shandy for me. It was going well; shame Petra wasn't there.

The second set had the crowd jumping and edging ever closer to the stage. A couple of drunks yelled for requests, and another shouted at Susan to, '… get yer kit off!' and thought it was funny.

'You should be so lucky,' said Susan, laughing but not easily. She wore denim flares, plain white linen shirt and a light, flower patterned scarf tied close to her neck. The outfit was understated, directing focus to her voice – strong, real. But the drunk was beyond such discernment; the drunk was a prick.

'See me afterwards, you'll be the lucky one,' he shouted back, with no humour.

I was standing next to Steve and felt him tense.

Bazzer counted in the last song, *Born To Run*. The drunk sang along. At the chorus he put a foot on the stage. His red, leering features were shiny with sweat as he lurched into the spotlight. He reached for the mic, but Susan took a step back without missing a beat, leaving him to clutch at air, his friends laughing at him. Steve edged closer, placing a hand on my chest as if to make sure I stayed. The drunk tripped back off the stage and fell heavily to the dance floor, raising more laughter. He struggled to his feet then tottered off to the bar. Steve relaxed back alongside me but was now focused on watching the crowd close to the stage. The song ended and Will milked the applause until the crowd genuinely cheered for an encore. Susan whispered something to Bazzer then called for the band to finish with *The Last Waltz*. The Birthday Boy ushered his parents to the floor, nodding thanks to the band. Though the older couple's dance was not a waltz it was a gentle sway of love, warmth and celebration and couples of all ages appeared from the darkness to join them. Will added another chorus to the song, and the band followed him seamlessly to the set's end.

The barman shouted last orders and turned up the lights, but it was another half hour before the more persistent drinkers left. Will, Bazzer, Dimitri and Pluto hung around, trying to get a final pint for free, while Steve and I packed away the PA – me under supervision. An older guy asked Steve for the band's contact details, hinting he'd like to book them for a do at the local Armed Forces Club. Steve pointed him towards Will.

I went with Bazzer to the makeshift dressing room to gather the guitar cases. As I opened the door I heard Susan. She'd gone there to change out of her stage jeans.

'Just fuck off. What's wrong with you? You're pissed and a dick … just … no.' Her voice cracked as she shouted.

Bazzer pushed past me. Susan was backed up against a table and the obnoxious guy from the crowd was pressing himself against her. Her ripped blouse was on the floor and one bra strap hung loose over her shoulder. The man grunted and Susan tried to push him away, but he had full grip of her upper arms, turning white under his spiteful squeeze. She was still wearing jeans though the top button was undone, and the fly half unzipped.

'Piss off!' Susan shouted but the man didn't react until he heard Bazzer's garbled shout of fury. He turned and let go of Susan, shame in his face.

I don't think I was angry, the scene didn't seem real, and I was slow to react, but Bazzer took a step and swung at the drunk. He ducked and though the fist barely connected with the top of his head he stumbled. Bazzer was on him, hitting wildly. The man was heavier and taller and pushed him off, throwing blind punches as he struggled to his feet, shouting vague obscenities, forcing Bazzer backwards. A surge of fear flared in my chest, and some instinct to protect pushed me to jump forward and shove the man away. A fist caught me a glancing blow on the cheek, and I think I cried out, more in shock than pain. The room was a sudden blitz. Susan screamed. She jumped on the man's back, locking arms around his neck but he shrugged her off. I grabbed at his swinging arms. Bazzer renewed his attack. Susan kicked out at his shins, stamped at his knees. The cacophony brought the others. Steve stopped in the doorway. In less than a second he understood. He dragged me aside, I landed awkwardly against a table, banging a rib, and he exploded into the bigger man, a furious onslaught of fists, elbows and boots – both instinctive and practised. The man went down, cowering from the attack, crying for help, unable to defend himself. It was a blisteringly violent assault with astonishing intensity, and it took Bazzer to push Steve off the man, shouting at him to stop before he, '…killed the fucker.' Susan joined him, attempting to calm Steve and restrain his flailing arms while the man lay on the floor, curled, bleeding, whimpering.

'I'm ok, Steve, I'm ok, it's all right, it's sorted, you've sorted it, thank you, thank you …' Susan said in an increasingly quiet voice as Steve calmed and let himself be pulled away. His chest heaved as his breathing slowed.

'Ouch,' said Dimitri, standing just inside the door. Pluto peered over his shoulder. The drunk struggled to get to his feet and all but crawled from the room, blood dripping from nose, mouth and a cut above his eye. Steve shrugged off Bazzer, looking for me. The anger in his eyes dissipated in an instant.

'JB? Sorry, so sorry, mate, you ok? JB? I'm sorry.'

My heart was racing. I winced as I stood up straight. 'S'ok Steve. I'm ok. You did good, I'm glad.' I looked to Susan. Bazzer was draping his jacket around her shoulders, and zipping up her jeans, hiding her from us, asking if she was ok. She didn't answer, but nodded as she trembled, though from shock, anger or fear I couldn't tell. I went to stand close to her, not knowing what to do. My ribs hurt and my hands were shaking, as much as Susan's as she raised hers to my cheek, asking,

'Ok?'

I nodded, pretended a smile, tried a joke. 'Rock and roll eh? *Saturday Night's Alright For Fighting*. Besides, he barely touched me. Lucky Steve got to him before I did.'

'Oh, Mikey.' She hugged me and let her tears flow.

Bazzer rested a hand on Susan's shoulder and motioned to us to leave.

We went back to the party room. The decorations were still up but few lights were on and the detritus from the party was sad.

'Hey, JB, really sorry.' Steve apologised again.

'Really, no problem. I'm glad you came in.'

Steve half-smiled.

Dimitri said to Pluto, 'I've never seen Steve look pleased before. This shit brings out a happy side.'

'Yeah, a real Sunny Steve,' said Pluto sarcastically, but moving quickly out of the way to let Steve pass as he picked up the PA amplifier.

'Better get the van loaded,' said Sunny Steve.

Chapter 11
Winter 1975/76
Mass
'Downtown'

The white and pink blossom on the embroidery's apple tree was starting to bloom, 'Like you, Mum,' I said when I found her in the conservatory. I pointed to the hoop in her lap. I couldn't tell if she heard the reference.

She looked up and smiled briefly.

'It's a bit early isn't it? For a Sunday? Have you had breakfast?' I asked.

'I'm not hungry.'

'You never are Mum, but …'

She was fully dressed in a green, light woollen frock, with a heavier cardigan over her shoulders. Her face was made up and her hair formed into a neat bun. She was wearing her Sunday best shoes. 'I don't want to be late.'

'What for?'

'Mass.'

It was the Sunday morning after the party gig. Dad was still in bed. Susan was still in bed. I'd woken hungry with thoughts of the previous night both exciting and unsettling. There was a small red mark on my cheek but no pain, and my ribs were ok if I didn't stretch or twist. I'd gone downstairs and made tea and toast before hearing the cough from the conservatory.

'It's …' I checked the clock on the mantelpiece in the lounge, 'nearly eight. What time is Mass?'

'Nine. It's a ten-minute walk.'

'You haven't been for ages.'

'I know, Mikey. But I want to. I'm better now and should go and say proper thanks. It's just … it's … I know it's the right thing, but I don't understand if I'm the right person to be thankful. I should be more grateful, but I've been so tired and feel a little sick. Is it cold out?'

'S'ok Mum,' I answered vaguely, concerned that she was asking me if she should go and I had no reason to say no, except it didn't feel right she should be out on her own.

'I miss the church. And the sewing club and the bakery. Do you remember when I used to take you there?'

I nodded and knelt, placing the embroidery hoop carefully on the floor, holding her hands. They were cold, clammy, and smelt of Nivea. 'Yes Mum. Of course.'

'I don't know if I want to go back to work. I feel I should and would like to, but I don't see how I can, not yet. I'm not good enough.'

'Well enough?'

'No. Good enough.'

There was such conviction in her voice that it was not enough to just deny it, but what else did I have? 'Don't be silly, Mum. Of course you are.' I let go her hands and put my arms fully around her in an awkward cuddle, saying, 'It'll be all right.'

She had said this to me countless times and I'd always believed her, and it had been all right. But today it was hard to believe myself.

'I need to start again. Mass today would be a new beginning, wouldn't it? Sorry, Mike. So sorry.' And now her voice carried a deep despair. With a sudden clarity that was frightening, I was drowning with her, and it was too much to bear. I pulled away and was then ashamed.

'It's ok,' she said and brushed the tear from my cheek. 'Will you come to Mass with me?' she asked with desperation.

'Of course.'

'And can we go on a picnic, when it's warmer? It's been a long time.'

'Of course. In a few weeks.'

'We can call in at the bakery on the way, for a fresh loaf.'

'Of course.'

The cold in the conservatory settled heavily. It was not the cold after a crisp snowfall or of a clear winter's day. It was a suffocating, grey cold. I still held Mum's hands but when I looked at her she was staring into the garden. Her suggestion of a picnic was a fantasy; except it was also a memory: Late afternoon, height of summer, school holidays. Dad leaving work early, driving to the nature reserve, walking the tight, overgrown alley towards the canal and the fields beyond, running ahead and being called back when out of sight, Dad catching up as we neared the canal, always worried about the water, keeping all safe, across the small bridge and into the fields, a secluded corner under tree shade, a hamper of cold drinks, warm bread from the bakery, doorstep sandwiches. Slow time, time slow. Hide and seek in the bushes. Mum pretending not to know where, finding and holding me. Holding me. Dad calling for us. Mum giggling and shushing, then releasing me to burst into the open and throw myself into Dad's arms, Mum just behind, Dad catching her too; never doubted, invincible. Long shadows under the trees. Mum sitting on the grass, singing *Downtown*. Susan joining in, already catching the harmonies. A memory. Or a fantasy? No, a memory. It had been real, it still was. I swallowed a sob. My chest was heavy. It was hard to breathe.

'I'll ... I'll see if Dad and Susan want to come. You stay here.'

Dad held Mum's hand on the short walk to St. Gregory's, Susan and me a yard behind. He left us at the lychgate, lighting a cigarette and saying he'd be there when we finished. Inside the cold church, Vi and Petra were surprised to see us and budged up on their pew to make room. I took the hymn book from the rack in front and flicked through to the numbers listed on the board by the pulpit. I didn't recognise them. It had been a long time. As the service progressed I occasionally tried to whisper a question to Petra, but she was either more committed a Catholic than I realised or similarly bewildered; she kept telling me to hush.

I occasionally glanced at Mum but her head was down, even when standing to sing. She took communion, encouraged by Vi to join the queue in the aisle, and, when it was her turn, I thought Father Andrew's smile genuine.

As the service worked through the rituals I watched Father Andrew ever more closely. He spoke both English and Latin and was the centre of attention, glamourised in garish robes, master of the content of the service, managing the time, directing the players and controlling the congregation. No, not congregation – audience. A performance I could admire without being entertained, educated or involved.

Mass finished. Mum said, hesitantly, she should say hello to Father Andrew and Vi and Petra went with her. Susan and I went to the back of the church. Without the distraction of the service it was cold and poorly lit. The elaborate, confusing stained-glass window behind the altar might be glorious with the colour of sunlight, but on a grey winter morning was dull and muddled.

'You sang well,' I told Susan as we sat near the font, hoping to take some warmth from the old cast iron radiators. I should have dressed more sensibly. Susan rewound her long woollen scarf round her neck. The congregation were filing to the door quickly; it was warmer outside.

'It's been a long time, but I remembered most of the hymns, though my voice is really rough from last night. And I'm knackered. I'm glad I came though. Mum seems better for it too.' She reached to her ear, a habit, but there was only one earring there. 'Shit.'

'What's up?'

'I forgot. Lost one last night.'

'Last night?'

'Drunken prick.' She touched her ear again.

'Is it sore?'

'No.' She answered quickly and looked away.

I didn't like the silence. 'What are they doing?' I indicated towards the altar where Mum, Vi and Petra loitered, waiting their turn for a word with the priest.

'I don't know. I think Mum just wants to say hello to Father Andrew, it's been a while. I suppose Vi is there to … I dunno, be there. As for Petra, where Vi goes, so goes Petra.'

'What do you mean?'

'I don't know. I just mean they are close, closer than me … we … and Mum, I guess. Good for them.' There was no malice or envy in Susan's voice.

I hunched a little closer to the radiator. It made no difference. 'Do you like Petra?' I asked.

'Does it matter?'

'I suppose.'

'For what it's worth I think she's pretty and a smart kid, but maybe sometimes too cool.' Susan fiddled with her scarf.

'What d'ya mean?'

'Like when she made a t-shirt for Bazzer, but he gave it to Sofia. It didn't seem to bother her much.'

'Maybe she's just good at pretending.'

'Maybe. Or what about that thing with Saint Teresa. The statue that might have cried.'

'Oh yeah. And …?'

'I don't know, Mikey. I mean, if I'd been in a cave, with a statue that started crying, and thought that might really be a … a miracle, then wouldn't that be a moment to remember, as a proper moment? They don't come along often, but when they do maybe they can be so cool it's not right to be too cool about them.'

'I don't get it.'

'I'm just saying that a crying statue might be a moment, that's all.'

'What? So maybe it didn't cry?'

'I don't know. But it just seems kinda important, to know if it did or not. The thing about moments …

afterwards, something needs to be different, or you need to be different, otherwise, is it a moment?'

'You think if the statue didn't cry Mum's not going to get better.'

'I'm not saying that and maybe Mum doesn't need another miracle, just more or less pills. She came out today, didn't she?'

'But if the statue didn't cry then what's the point of Mum coming here?' I thought about how badly the morning had started in the conservatory. 'Maybe not everyone has moments like you?' I challenged.

'I don't see why not.' She nodded thoughtfully. 'And you should be thinking about your own moments. You know, sometimes you have to go looking for them ...' Susan indicated towards Petra. 'You still haven't asked her out, have you?'

'She probably thinks I'm a kid.'

'You are, but so's she. Now's your chance. She's coming over, probably bored waiting. Whatever she says doesn't mean the future can't change or that your imagination stops.'

'What?'

'I'll see if Mum's ok.' She left me and smiled at Petra as they crossed.

'They're still waiting for Father Andrew,' said Petra as she took the chair vacated by Susan, checking the radiator. She pulled the sheepskin collar of her denim jacket tighter, asking, 'Is your mum all right? Seems ... nervous.'

'She doesn't get out much.'

'That's really not funny.'

'You're right. Sorry. I think it's 'cos she hasn't been here for a while. She's worried what Father Andrew will say.'

'He'll be all right and if not, my mum will put him straight. And now Susan's there too. I hear she and Bazzer are going out together now.'

'Far as I know … talking of going out, want to go to the cinema?' The question was more rushed than I wanted but it was too late now.

'What's on?'

'Dunno. Does it matter?'

'Probably.'

'I don't think so.'

Petra thought for a second. 'Oh, you mean, like, go to the cinema … together, sort of?'

'Yep, rather than me and you.'

'Ok, but you do know I'm a lot older than you, don't you?'

'Nine months.'

'And a bit and I don't think we should sit in the back row. Not first time.'

'Ok. But that means maybe second time? You know The Drifters song, *Kissin' In The Back Row,* right?' My bravado was thin, but charming, I hoped.

'I was thinking more of their other one, *Like Sister And Brother.*'

'Sharp. And funny. And you do know the rest of the words, don't you?'

'Maybe.' Petra laughed.

'That's nice though.'

'What is?'

'When you forget someone might be watching and …'

'And …'

'Just laugh.'

'You should be on the screen.'

'It's true though.'

'And?'

'I'm glad.' I forced my most serious expression, the one I hoped most resembled Redford in *The Great Gatsby.* Wasn't his jaw just a little uneven?

'Just how old do you think you are?'

Miracle Number Four

Chapter 12
Winter 1975/76
The Sewing Machine
'Like Sister And Brother'

There was little shelter at the bus stop opposite the tube station, and my Harrington was too light for the cold wind. I pulled the zip to the top, stiffened the collar as best I could and jammed my hands into the pockets. I could see through the entrance to the tube to the clock above the ticket office. I was eight minutes early, as if I was ever going to be late. A small but steady flow of football fans filtered into the station. Their red and white scarves marked them as supporting Brentford – one of the nearest clubs easily reached by underground and bus. They heard the train rumble over the bridge above them and broke into a run, not bothering with tickets. I checked the station clock again, then jumped at the sound of my name, shouted by Vince, leaving the newsagent.

'Hey! Mike, where's yer bike?' He crossed at the zebra and stood close as if waiting for my, 'Vince/wince,' response, but I just nodded.

'Where you going?' he asked.

'Cinema, with Petra.'

'Oh. You didn't say earlier. New jacket?' He tugged gently at the collar of my Harrington. 'Nice. What you gonna see?'

'*One Flew Over The Cuckoo's Nest.*'

'Really? You know the new Pink Panther film is still showing?'

'Petra's choice.'

'Ok. I'll give it a go.'

'It's sort of a date.'

'Just sort of? Then I'll sort of come.'

'It is a date.'

'Then I'll definitely come.'

'Haha. Nah, just me and Petra,' I said, looking over his shoulder as she crossed the street towards us. She wore a green and white horizontally striped top with a blue collar under her denim jacket. Her jeans were heavily flared and long enough to hide her shoes. She moved lightly, as if not wanting to leave a mark, but with a confident swing in her narrow hips. I hoped my nervous excitement didn't show.

Vince followed my line of sight. 'S'ok, I've got stuff to do. Hi, Petra. See ya later,' he said as she joined us. He walked away but five yards on turned, saying, 'It's not as funny as Pink Panther though.'

I waved Vince away and turned to Petra, thinking of Susan's advice. 'Hi, you look ...' I'd forgotten exactly what Susan had said and out came, '... old?' as a faltering question.

'Old?'

'Er, no, not old, though you do.'

Petra looked at me, bemused, and I was grateful for the bus arriving. I followed her up the tightly curved steps to the top deck. We sat a few rows from the back, and I briefly caught her almond scent – but all too briefly as the man in front lit a cigarette. Still, her perfume was enough to enhance my nerves in a way I didn't understand and was new. We chatted briefly about the Terry And The All Stars gig the previous night and agreed it was going really well until they played *Obladi Oblada*. Then we gently, sort of, admitted to each other that it hadn't been going that well before then either – but hey, what to expect from a forces social club? And, as Petra said, 'Susan seemed nervous, not talking much to the crowd between songs and letting Will take centre-stage. And what was with wearing a heavy wool cardigan?'

I nodded, uncomfortable with criticising Susan, and we sat in awkward silence which I wanted to fill but remembered Susan's wisdom.

The previous night, after tea, I'd helped Susan wash up. Dad was in the front room, listening to old records, and Mum was in the conservatory, embroidering.

'You don't have to help every night,' Susan said, passing me a soapy plate.

'Haha,' I pretended to laugh, recognising the sarcasm. 'It's my third time this week.'

'Second.'

'Maybe,' I carefully swirled the tea towel around the plate, 'but we don't want to be late for tonight's gig. Do we?'

'Oh, so you're coming then?' Susan asked in mock surprise. I smiled then we lapsed into silence until Susan asked, 'You've rubbed the rose off that plate. What's the matter?'

'Nothing.'

'Good.'

'Just wondered ...'

'Yes?'

'You know I'm going to the pictures with Petra tomorrow?'

'You may have mentioned it. *One Flew Over The Cuckoo's Nest*. Romantic.'

'I was just thinking, you might, you know, have some ideas on what to do.'

'What to do? Easy. Don't be a dork and make sure to enjoy the film, that way if it doesn't go well at least you'll not have wasted money.'

'Haha. Funny, but ...'

She passed another plate. 'Ok, take control but don't be pushy and ask, don't tell. Listen more than talk, which I know you'll find hard, and pay small, sincere compliments. Don't make a joke out of everything and be sure to pay for the tickets. Don't try to put your arm around her in the cinema, you're too short for it to be comfortable for both of you, and do not, under any circumstances, try the disgusting hole in the bottom of the popcorn bag trick.'

'What's the popcorn bag thing?'

'Doesn't matter, just don't do it. And do not say Petra looks nice or pretty.'

'Why not?'

'It's naff. You can do better.'

'Can I?'

'Of course. When you see her say that you like her dress or jacket or shoes or hair and say, casually, it makes her look sophisticated, mature and you're fortunate to be at her side. Don't say it too seriously but make sure she knows you mean it. Oh, and if she's wearing a David Cassidy fan scarf just come straight home.'

Susan had given me a lot to consider. As the bus pulled up outside Ealing ABC cinema I suddenly said, 'You look older. Not old.'

'What?' Petra asked.

'As in … grown up. And I'm lucky.'

She looked at me, perplexed, then nudged we should be getting off.

At the cinema I gently insisted on buying tickets and popcorn; the car wash job paid ok.

The bus ride home was spent discussing the film – it wasn't as humourous as I'd hoped, and Petra explained why it wasn't meant to be. I didn't mention that I'd not always given the film full attention. Susan's advice about not trying to put my arm around Petra had conflicted with an instinct to find a way to be closer. In the end I settled on the excitement of leaning towards her in the dark as being enough, occasionally brushing shoulders, elbows or fingers, when both reaching for popcorn together – not that I even liked popcorn. I also didn't ask Petra if she knew of the 'hole in the popcorn bag' trick – in case she did.

Though spring was coming, the evening sky darkened early and hinted at drizzle. We hopped from the bus back at the station entrance. While I considered asking Petra if I could walk her home, taking more of Susan's advice, Petra

said, 'Coming round for tea?' and was on her way. I
followed.

The band's van was parked outside Petra's house,
windscreen fogged, driver's window lowered an inch with
occasional whisps of smoke slipping through the gap. I
waved at Sunny Steve and went to the car. Petra made for
the house as the rain started.

Steve wound down the window.

'Hi, Sunny. Wotchya doin'?'

'Waiting JB. It's what I do a lot of.' He said it as if
expecting me to appreciate some underlying philosophical
point.

'Yeah … er, what for?'

'Bazzer wants me to stay out here while he and Will get
a few things straight. We might need the van to carry back
some gear. Been here fuckin' ages. Ten minutes and I'm
either goin' home or goin' in.' He indicated up the garden
path. 'Is Vi in?'

'Dunno. Been to the pictures with Petra.'

'Oh. What d'ya see?'

'One Flew Over The Cuckoo's Nest.'

'I heard that's shit.'

I thought for a second before answering, 'Not when it's
a date.'

'Dirty little sod. Back row was it?' Sunny Steve pulled on
the cigarette.

I just smiled. Cold rain dribbled inside my jacket collar.
'I'm going in. You?'

'Nah. But tell my brother I'm getting pissed off and cold
out here and I'll be in to sort it out soon if they can't.'

'Ok,' I said, as if I understood.

Vi was out and I went through the front door left open
by Petra. Will was in the kitchen, shouting at Bazzer.

Since playing the town hall party three weeks previously, the arguments had increased in both frequency and intensity, and it all came down to *The Last Waltz*.

A week after that gig, the band had gathered in The Railway on a Sunday lunchtime. Sofia was behind the bar, Susan told her I'd drink only Coke.

Sunny Steve sat apart, smoking heavily and drinking Bell's, occasionally visiting the bar for hushed conversations with Sofia or the landlord.

'No more waltzes,' had been Bazzer's opening argument, 'for the good of the band's future.'

'Really? And is shagging the singer for the good of the band?' Will sarcastically mimicked Bazzer.

'You're such a dick, Will.' Susan said, calmly. 'We're not shagging. Point is we played *The Last Waltz* at that party and some of us think that should be the very last waltz we ever play.'

'So, you don't like paying gigs?'

'We don't want to play to mums and dads.'

'Then I suppose I'll keep hold of this.' Will took a thin roll of fivers from his inside pocket. 'Thirty quid. Picked it up this morning. They liked us. Might want us back next year. Thirty quid between five of us.'

Bazzer looked over to his brother, a couple of tables away. 'Six.'

'Bollocks.' Will was dismissive.

'What about all the loading and petrol and use of the van?' said Bazzer. 'Tax and insurance too.'

Sunny Steve looked up from his scotch. He wasn't smiling.

'Taxed and insured?' Will sneered.

'No van, no gig. So Steve gets a share.' Bazzer was firm.

'Seems fair,' added Dimitri.

'Yeah, just 'cos you need someone to carry all your junk,' said Will.

Dimitri looked up from his cigarette and said, 'Drums,' which was all the explanation needed.

'It's fair, Will,' Susan said.

Will thought for few seconds. 'Tell you what. Fair shares for Steve and in return we play parties if they pay well.'

Dimitri and Pluto nodded.

Bazzer said, 'No.'

Susan looked to me, 'As our biggest fan, what d'ya reckon?'

But before I could think of how to tactfully suggest I doubted Led Zeppelin ever played a birthday party, Susan continued, 'Ok, at least until we have enough of our own songs and have bought some decent gear. Then we do our own thing. Speaking of which, some of that money,' she pointed to the roll of fivers on the table, 'should go in a band pot. Our PA's shit.'

'Sorted,' said Will, 'So keep Friday twenty seventh free. We're playing the Armed Forces Club. Fifty quid but they've asked for *The Twist, Obladi Oblada* and *The Last Waltz*. We've three weeks.'

'And so it begins,' said Susan.

On the way home from the pub I'd asked Susan, 'So you and Bazzer aren't shagging?'

'Not yet.'

'And when you do, will that be a moment?'

'I bloody hope so.'

Now, in Vi's kitchen as Petra and I returned from the cinema, Will was adamant. 'They loved it. The older crowd knew it and got up to dance.'

'And you want to be known for playing *The Twist*? Besides, that's the same crowd that shouted for *The Hokey Cokey*.' Bazzer couldn't keep anger from his voice.

'Which would have made for a good encore.'

Petra and I watched from the kitchen door, the two young men oblivious to our presence.

'Never mind the song, you've gone round the bloody twist. We're never playing it again. End of argument.' Bazzer turned to leave but Will grabbed his arm,

'What, because shaggable Susan doesn't like it? Gonna get your psycho brother in here to beat me up?'

There was a second's silence in which I thought Bazzer was going to hit out, but Petra said something quietly. I didn't catch it, but Bazzer and Will realised they were being watched.

'Your brother's mad. I'm not playing those poxy songs again,' Bazzer told Petra after taking a breath.

'Except for cash, eh?' Will smirked and turned to me. 'JB, even you have to admit no one was dancing until we played *The Twist.*'

'Which just means it's the wrong audience, not the right song,' I said, feeling brave.

'Bollocks. That sounds like something your sister would say.'

I smiled, taking it as a compliment. Bazzer asked, 'JB, ring and see if Susan's around. Maybe she can make him see sense.'

The phone was on the small table by the front door.

Susan picked up after five or six rings and used her telephone voice for the greeting before recognising me.

'Hi, sis. What you doin'?'

There was a pause before she replied. 'Mum's not well again. I'm … I'm sitting with her. I don't know what else to do. Where are you?' There was a catch in Susan's voice that I didn't recognise, a hint of fear.

'Round Petra's. Bazzer and Will are having a row. Can you come round?'

'Is Vi there?'

'No. Why?'

'Doesn't matter. Tell Bazzer I can't come now. They'll have to sort it out themselves. I gotta go. If you see Vi can you ask her to come round here?'

'Will do.' I replaced the receiver and went back to the kitchen. 'Susan can't come round. Mum's not well. I better go home.'

'Me too. Steve's waiting. We'll finish this at next rehearsal.' Bazzer left the kitchen. I followed.

Petra came to the front door with us and for an instant I thought she was going to peck me on the cheek. Instead, we stood awkwardly until I said, 'Thanks for coming to the pictures. Bowie's got a film out soon. Shall we make that the next one?'

'Next one?' She smiled and started humming *Like Sister And Brother.* I laughed, genuinely, and hoped she really did know all the lyrics.

The rain was lashing so I asked Bazzer for a lift in the back of the van and was home in minutes, going in through the side alley and kitchen. The house was dark and quiet; no radio played and the television was off. Mum and Susan sat in the conservatory. It was cold and the dim lamp offered little encouragement. Mum stared into the darkness of the garden, perhaps to the small dirty window of the shed and the light of the naked bulb within. The blanket was over her legs and the small embroidery hoop lay on her lap, muslin cloth stretched tight.

'Hi, Mum.'

She jumped as I jolted her back from the night outside. Her eyes were red. 'Oh, Mikey. Where have you been?'

'Pictures, with Petra.'

'Sorry. I forgot. Again.' She looked away. 'Was it good?'

'Yeah.' I turned to Susan. 'Wotchya doin'?'

She stood. 'Cup of tea, Mum?'

'No thanks.'

'Sure? I'm having one.' She left the conservatory, indicating I should follow.

I waited for Susan to put on the kettle before asking, 'What's the matter with Mum?'

'The usual.'

'Yeah, but she seems more upset.'

'I made a mistake, Mikey. I'm such an idiot.' Her blue eyes were dark with rising tears.

'What do you mean?' To see her troubled was frightening. She didn't answer. Her hand went to her ear, fiddling with the solitary earring. I asked again. She lowered her voice,

'Mum was sitting in the conservatory, fussing with that embroidery, and we started talking about last night's gig and how it went and she was really interested, you know, not ... dreamy like some days and we talked about the band and me and Bazzer, she really likes him, and ... and it was really cool. But I wanted ... needed ... to tell someone ... you know ... it's been ... nagging ... and worrying and I thought she'd understand about it.'

'It?'

'That stupid thing with the drunk guy.'

'Drunk guy?'

'A few weeks ago. The town hall gig. How dumb I was to let the prick into the room.'

'Oh, that prick.'

'I keep thinking how stupid I was, how fucking thick to let him in ... I dunno ... I suppose I just thought he wanted to say how good we were, 'cos we were ... then he grabbed me and ...'

'Hurt you?'

'Not really, nothing really happened, I was lucky I suppose, but how stupid. Me. I never thought I could be that ... but ... I keep thinking about it. If you and Bazzer hadn't come in ...' her voice tailed away. She was crying and I was scared. I took half a step as if to hug her because I didn't know what else to do and, in truth, was a little relieved when she turned away.

'And then, I thought, for a second, it would help, to mention it to Mum. We were just chatting, about stuff, and it was so easy, for a change, and just ... normal ... but that thing, it's been bugging me and then I stupidly told her. No details and I made sure to say I was all right and I didn't tell her about Sunny Steve or that you saw, but I just wanted her to know that I'd fucked up … and she …'

'What?'

'… just started crying and rocking and saying she was so sorry she hadn't been there, to stop him. Then she started saying it wasn't my fault and she knew, really, what it was like and how it must have felt and how terrifying it could be and how long the fear could last. And she was crying and … and worst thing is, it was like she really did understand, and then I had no way of helping her. Oh Mike, it was just fucking awful.'

I began to speak but had no idea what to say.

'Then Dad came in and wanted to know why Mum was crying, but she just kept saying it'll be all right and rocking. Then he cuddled her and eventually she stopped sobbing. Then he started crying and went down the shed. God, Mike, it's shit.'

We watched the steam from the kettle disperse under the kitchen cabinets and I had two false starts at saying something, anything, until: 'It wasn't … isn't … your fault. None of it. You or Mum or Dad.'

Susan took a tissue from a sleeve to wipe her nose and forced a smile. 'Thank you. Take Dad a cup of tea but don't tell him you know anything … about anything.'

Part of me was glad to be away from Susan and Mum. Part was anxious to understand more and didn't want to have to pretend to Dad everything was all right. But the largest part just wished I knew how to make Mum better, how to make all of it … better. As Susan said, it really was shit.

I called loudly on pushing the door and went into the shed. It was colder in there than out, despite the one bar electric fire under the workbench. It smelt of metal and oil, and on the bench was a disassembled sewing machine, the parts carefully laid out, the smaller pieces safe in various glass jars. There was a bulb hanging from the ceiling and an articulated desk lamp on the bench, crouched threateningly over, and harshly illuminating, a small electric motor. Dad was hunched on a stool.

'Hi, Mikey.'

'Tea. And Biscuits.'

'Not those lemon puff things I hope. Can't work these fiddly pieces with sticky fingers.' He smiled.

'Nah, proper digestives.'

'Smashing. How was the film?'

'Good.'

He took the tea and biscuits. 'What was it?'

'*One Flew Over The Cuckoo's Nest.*'

'Not heard of that.'

'Me neither.'

'But you ... haha, very funny. I'll do the jokes. While you're here, have a look at this motor, just at the top, there's a hole down the centre, can you see a small grommet stuck? I can't find the bugger and think it dropped down there. I didn't bring reading glasses.'

'I can't see anything.'

'Sure? A small grommet?'

I looked again. I didn't know what a grommet was but felt sure if it was there I'd see it. 'No. Sorry.'

'I need to find it Mike. I can't fix this otherwise and I promised your mother.'

'You will Dad. You always do.'

'Do you think? I don't know anymore.' He looked at me and raised a tired, unconvincing half-smile. 'Maybe sometimes things are just broken beyond fixing.' He turned the motor over in his hands, searching for a clue, again. 'Is Mum still in the conservatory?'

I nodded.

'Did you know the doc said Mum's depressed.'

'Yes, Dad.'

'I haven't told anyone. I don't know what it means. I thought I did but ...'

He put the motor down and cupped the mug of tea. 'Me and your mum used to love the cinema,' he said without looking at me. 'The first film we saw was *Mandy*, back in fifty-five. Such a sad film. Mum cried and I wanted to, but didn't. I wish I had. You know Mikey, first chance you get to cry when you're with Petra? Do it. Forget all that 'be a man' rubbish. The earlier she sees you cry the better and easier for later, when you really need to. The longer you leave it, the harder it is.' He looked out through the shed window, out into the darkness and up to the house, 'Thanks for the tea, say I'll be up in a minute.'

Miracle Number Four

Chapter 13
Winter 1975/76
The Guitar Lesson
'Can't Get Enough'

The Monday after the Armed Forces Club gig, Susan was dishing up steak and kidney pie, Dad warning her not to slice off a finger as she opened the tin, then calling me down from my bedroom. The television was on, we didn't talk much over dinner, but Dad said, 'Lawrence caught me at work today. One of the mechanics, ex-army guy, told him you guys were good the other night. He said your band was shit-hot, which is a good thing, right?'

Susan laughed.

'Lawrence asked why I hadn't got you a gig down the Conservative Club. I'm Secretary for the Entertainment Committee this year.'

'Dad, c'mon, Terry And The All Stars at the club?'

'You played the Armed Forces Club.'

'Yeah, and to be honest, it wasn't great.'

'If I can convince them, you'll get paid. And you'll be doing me a favour. I was supposed to arrange something for March but haven't got round to it.'

'No way if it's a stag night,' said Susan. 'I'm not going on after comedians and strippers.'

'No more strippers. That was a bad idea. The members' wives were not happy. But I might get a couple of comedians in. The members like a laugh, it'll give me the chance to do a turn, and they can bring the wives. I needn't do the blue routine.'

'We're a rock band, Dad, not cabaret.'

'I know, but we pay well, and I did promise the committee I'd arrange something.'

'You know what we play, right? It's not exactly *Come Dancing.*'

'Perhaps not, but there is a new member who works for EMI.'

'EMI? He'll be there?'

'I expect so.'

'What do you think, Mike?' Susan asked.

'Don't do it. I mean, it's hardly The Marquee, is it?'

'How much is a new PA these days?' Dad asked.

'Almost as much as our fee for playing Conservative Clubs,' said Susan.

'No fucking way.'

I closed the door to Vi's front room, shutting out Bazzer's vehement refusal. 'Sounds like they need to chat about it,' I said to Petra, joining her in the back room. It was the Thursday after Dad's request, and they were rehearsing and arguing while Vi popped round to see Mum. Usually, Petra and I would hang out with the band but tonight I'd suggested we watch *Top Of The Pops* and *The Liver Birds*.

'I think Susan may have just mentioned that the Conservative Club have asked for a couple of songs for the next gig. I think *Green Grass Of Home* was mentioned and …' I was interrupted by a shout, clearly audible through the wall,

'… *Tie A Fucking Yellow Ribbon* …that's taking the piss.'

'Oh. Yeah, that was another one.'

'Yellow Ribbon? Susan agreed to that? There's no way Bazzer will play it,' said Petra.

There were raised voices from the front room.

'Sounds like Will doesn't mind,' I said, 'and Susan is just thinking about the money. Three or four decent paying gigs then they can sort out a better PA, some songs of their own and play some proper venues.'

'… *Unchained Melody*! …' they heard through the wall. 'You have noticed we don't have a piano, let alone a fucking string section. And we've only two weeks.' Bazzer sounded genuinely amazed at the idea.

'I forgot about that one,' I said. 'It's Mum and Dad's favourite. They danced to it on their first date, at Hammersmith Palais. It's special for them.'

'It'll need to be, to get Bazzer to play it.'

We sat on the settee with an empty place between us. The news was just finishing. The arguing next door grew louder the more muddled it became. More voices joined in.

'Oh, I brought this.' Without standing, I tugged awkwardly from a back pocket to pull out a cassette. 'I recorded Monday's John Peel show. Thought you might like it.' I was surprised at my nervousness.

'All of it?' she seemed genuinely surprised but then the programme had been from eleven to midnight.

'You mentioned it was a bit late and I was still up so …'

Petra took the cassette with a sincere, 'Thanks,' and we sat in silence until Petra asked, 'You ok?'

'Yeah, 'course.'

'Sure? You're not saying much, not like you, and the news isn't that interesting.'

'I guess not … it's … I was thinking. If the band play the Conservative Club gig shall we … do you want, to go?'

'I 'spect they'll need a hand with gear, as always.'

'No, I mean, shall we go, a bit like the cinema.'

'Eh?'

'I'll pay for the tickets.'

'Pay?'

'It includes scampi in a basket.'

'Oh, I see … like a proper date? More proper than the cinema?' Petra sounded sceptical.

'Not that that's not proper, but yeah, I guess … more proper.'

'What is scampi?'

'Nobody knows. But you'll love it.'

'Do I need to learn how to slow dance?'

The arguing quietened as the music started in the next room.

'Only if they play *Unchained Melody*.'

We sat in silence again until I asked, 'So shall I? Get tickets?'

'Yeah, why not,' she said, shifting across the settee to sit closer to me, her leg resting against mine. She smelt clean and sweet, not of perfume. I wanted to turn to kiss her but didn't move and hoped my face wasn't as red as it felt. I should have turned off the main light before sitting.

As *Top Of The Pops* started, Susan came from the front room. Petra took her leg slightly away from mine. The movement was imperceptible, the change in pressure immense. Susan sat heavily in the arm-chair muttering, '…Joplin never sang about yellow bloody ribbons.'

I laughed until she told me to shut up.

'So, set list settled then?' Dad asked as he came in from the shed. It was the day after the abandoned rehearsal.

I was at the kitchen table, finishing, sort of, some maths homework. 'I don't know. I don't even know if they're gonna play the gig.'

'Tell Susan the main reason is so I can take your mother to see the band, oh and for us to dance. It might be the only way I can get her out.'

'Er, that song you like is the one causing most rucks. Bazzer really doesn't want to do it.'

'I need to know by tomorrow. Is he still here?'

I indicated to the front room. 'He's showing Susan some stuff on acoustic.'

'Really? I'm not hearing any guitar. Go and ask if they want tea and don't bother to knock.'

I went straight in. Bazzer was sitting in the armchair, Susan was sitting on the floor, leaning back between his legs, holding her acoustic guitar. Bazzer was reaching over her shoulder, demonstrating chords. He sat back quickly as the door opened. I smelt the Charlie perfume that was Susan's favourite and worn only when going out, or staying in, with Bazzer.

'Hi, guys. Bit dark in here. Shall I turn on the big light?'

'Piss off,' said Susan.

'And Bazzer, never thought I'd see the day.' I shook my head.

'Hail the prodigy, JB. You ok?'

'I was until, well I mean, c'mon Bazzer. Who'd have thought it? You, of all people.'

'What?'

'Playing a six string. Susan, what have you done to him?'

'Ha bloody ha. He's a very good guitarist and an excellent teacher.'

'Hmmm, maybe, but you need to make more noise with that guitar. Dad's not convinced.'

'Dad knows,' said Susan.

'Knows what?' Bazzer asked.

'He just … knows.'

'Yep. He knows,' I said, enjoying Bazzer's discomfort and taking the guitar from Susan to strum a few chords – the opening bars to *Can't Get Enough*.

'Look who's talking about six-strings,' said Bazzer. 'Nearly as good as your bass playing.'

I shrugged, trying to appear modest but not feeling it.

'Don't tell him. He's hard to live with as it is.' Susan took back the guitar. 'What's up?'

'Dad says do you want a cup of tea?'

'What do you think?'

'That's a no then. Oh, he also wants to know if you're gonna do the gig.'

'Tell him we haven't decided.'

'He really wants you to play that song for him and Mum. He thinks it'll convince her to have a night out. And she hasn't seen the band yet.'

'*Unchained Melody*?' Bazzer asked.

'Yep, he really wants you to,' I stressed.

Susan, still leaning back against Bazzer, angled and lifted herself enough to peck him on the cheek.

'I don't like it, you don't like it …' Bazzer protested.

'I know but they do. For Mum?' she asked.

'We've got to change the key for you.'

'I know, but ...' she kissed him again.

I left them, turning on the main light and leaving the door open behind me.

'Very mature,' Susan called after me.

Dad smiled, appreciating the joke. 'They're too busy for tea I suppose?'

'Way too busy. But it looks like they'll play the gig.'

'Join me to watch telly? Your mum's gone to bed.'

As we went into the back room I heard chords. They might have been the opening bars of *Unchained Melody*.

Chapter 14
Winter 1975/76
The Conservative Club
'Tumbling Dice'

Terry And The All Stars played the Conservative Club on Saturday 20th March 1976. The hall's tables had been pushed back to clear a dance floor. There was the rise and fall of conversation and a steady stream of people to and from the bar in the next room. The repro art deco wall lamps provided little illumination. Lights hung under the ceiling's browning polystyrene tiles, focused on the front of the stage, where I helped Steve run cables. I squinted through these spotlights but could barely make out the people at the back of the hall.

Dad had asked Vi to keep Mum company – he was busy organising the evening and performing his own routine – and they had a table at the front. Petra and I sat with them. Mum and Vi drank vodka and Coke and I asked Susan to buy me a pint of lager and a half for Petra, her choice. I still had the car wash job and gave Susan the money.

It wasn't one of the Entertainment Committee's finest nights.

Dad's stand-up routine went well. He had practised in front of me and the mirror and was genuinely funny. He had stage presence and was likeable and finished with the joke about the man obtaining expensive gifts for his wife (Punchline: 'But darling, I'm not made of bricks.'). Terry And The All Stars followed, at just after nine, and by twenty past the audience was unimpressed. The Conservative Club was more *La Bamba* than *Highway Star*.

Dad's grin was fading despite pride at Susan's performance. Much of the audience drifted away to the bar area and half-way through the first set few were left. The Entertainment Committee Chairman called Dad to one side 'for a chat'.

Confidence drained from the band. They messed up the intro to *Tumbling Dice* and had to start again. Instead of looking to the audience their heads were dropping, even Will and Susan's. Behind them, Dimitri and Bazzer exchanged 'told you so' looks. Only Pluto seemed his usual self but, as Sunny Steve later told me, that was probably due to the weed he'd been smoking out back. I learnt later that Sunny Steve sold it to him.

In the interval a disappointed Susan came to sit with us, and Mum and Vi were loyally enthusiastic. It was the first time Mum had seen or heard her perform in public and she hugged her, genuinely impressed. Dad was in the kitchen, encouraging the chef to get the scampi in a basket out more quickly. Bazzer stood next to Susan. He said little but occasionally rubbed her shoulder, or moved an invisible stray hair from her face, or bent down to gently rest a hand on her leg; a simple gesture to let her know he was there.

Dad came into the hall from the kitchen as the first of the scampi baskets was brought out and motioned to Susan it was time to get back on stage. As the others came back in, Will was arguing against playing the second set.

'And let down my dad? You can piss off but I'm going on,' was Susan's immediate response.

Until that point Will might have had some support from Bazzer; not now.

They started the second set with *Seven Seas Of Rhye*. It lacked energy and the audience weren't engaged – maybe they'd played it too often, or maybe it was still missing the piano, or maybe the scampi really was that good. I still didn't know what scampi was. The third song finished, and the last chord faded into the hall to an almost complete lack of response which was, I supposed, better then polite and insincere applause. I said so to Petra, but she didn't agree. Looking at Mum, I could see her watching Susan intently, smiling falsely. Trying not to be obvious, she took a small plastic tub from her handbag, tipped out some tablets and swallowed them with vodka and Coke. Vi said something and Mum looked guilty until Vi smiled gently and nodded understandingly. Vince's dad, Lawrence, stood just inside the door, watching.

On stage, the band were shrinking; the playing was uncertain, their movements stiff. There were no shadows under the blazing spotlights, nowhere for the band to shelter. Between songs the audience's murmurs of discontent grew louder. This was a new type of shame for me; the embarrassment of others: Mum; Dad; Susan; the band. It was an embarrassment that was neither mine to feel nor fix but still I felt sick.

I started rehearsing excuses to make them all feel better but knew I could offer no real comfort. Then I saw Mum dab at a tear and in that second, as her façade crumbled, true vulnerability was exposed – a vulnerability that was both a cause and consequence of her depression; a vulnerability to her loved one's tribulations – every hurt, slight, embarrassment and disappointment that Susan and I suffered, so did she, ten-fold, a hundred-fold; a vulnerability to loving that was as much a curse as a joy. Though I would not have been able to articulate what I saw, the anguish it brought was clear.

I was close to crying for her. 'I'll be back in a minute,' I told Petra.

'Where you going?'

'To find Dad. I don't think Mum's well.'

'Ok, but don't be long, I think the band are about to wrap it up.'

While I'd been distracted, Will had announced they would play only two more songs. They were ditching most of the second set and going straight to *Obladi Oblada*. This had not been agreed with the band.

'You're joking, right?' Susan whispered across the stage. The audience didn't hear. They didn't need to, to know something was wrong.

Will smirked and began strumming the simple, repetitive chords. They'd come up with an arrangement that, in

Bazzer's view, 'Just about makes it playable and recognisable. Just about.'

Some of the audience sang along with the chorus and two couples danced. The song stumbled to a finish and the audience applauded.

'And this is our last tonight. Thanks for being ... an audience,' said Will over the staccato plucking of his guitar, beginning *Delilah*. I hoped this was some kind of pre-arranged joke of which Petra and I were unaware, but it wasn't. Dimitri look confused, Pluto bemused. Susan and Bazzer looked close to murder. Will looked like he didn't give a fuck.

Will conducted the audience through two extra choruses of *Delilah* and tried a third, but Bazzer stopped playing, Dimitri followed and the failed chorus dribbled away. A few people clapped. Bazzer confronted Will while they were still on stage, but I could see some truth in Will's sarcasm,

'... yeah, 'cos they really wanted *Suffragette City,* and I'm sure they're gonna invite us back next week to play it. We'll probably have to learn *Paranoid* for them too.'

Susan seethed.

The remaining small audience didn't know what to do. Lawrence watched from the side. Sunny Steve went to get the cases from the van.

Dad lit another cigarette and approached the stage. 'I'm sorry Susan. My fault.'

'Was the guy from EMI here?'

'No.'

'Thank God for that.'

'To be honest, he works in accounts, doesn't have anything to do with the recording side anyway. I really am sorry though, about tonight.'

'No, Dad, my fault. I knew we shouldn't have played.'

'Remind me,' said Will, 'was it the wrong songs to the right audience or the wrong audience for the right songs or the wrong songs and the wrong audience or ...? I knew

116

Delilah and *Obladi* would go down well. No one listens …
hey, Frank, we still get paid right?'

'Not until you play *Unchained Melody*. It's in the contract.'
Dad laughed unconvincingly and went back to Mum. I
looked at Susan and went on stage, taking Will's guitar from
its stand. It was still plugged in. Before I could slip the strap
over my shoulder it was snatched by Will, shaking his head,
and then from Will by Bazzer who was not to be denied.
Bazzer started *Unchained Melody*. Susan took a mic that was
still plugged into the PA and sang the first verse – they'd
changed the key for her, and it was a simple arrangement.
The depth of feeling in Susan's voice carried the song. It
was still dark in the hall as Dad took Mum's hand. She
looked nervously at the now empty dancefloor and Dad
whispered something. They swayed with the rhythm then
stood still as Dad held her tight, hoping to settle her tears.

Susan finished singing. Bazzer handed the guitar back to
Will, 'B is flat. No wonder you sounded shit.'

Will sneered.

The few people at the back of the hall finished their
drinks and drifted away.

On the dance floor, Dad still held Mum. A sob caught
in her throat.

Susan called to me, 'Get some water from the bar.'

'I'll come with, I could do with a last drink,' said Vi.

Lawrence was standing in the doorway. 'That went well,'
he said as we passed, though it wasn't clear which part of
the evening he meant.

Vi didn't stop walking as she said, 'Feck off yer spiteful
bastard.'

Dad had taken Mum and Vi home. The hall was empty, the
stage lights off and the wall lights barely made shadows. The
bar staff collected glasses and it smelt of spilt beer. Sunny
Steve had finished loading the van and was sitting on stage

with the band, all smoking apart from me and Petra. There was as much confusion as disappointment.

'We got paid, yes?' Bazzer asked.

Susan nodded.

'Then I say add it to the band pot, split it six ways and Will can piss off, taking his shitty PA and drooping mic stand with him.' Bazzer spoke as if the break-up was of no consequence.

I looked from Bazzer to Susan to Will and finally to Petra.

Will stood. 'Suits me. Fucking *Highway Star* at a Conservative Club? Bunch of dicks.' He indicated to Petra she should follow. She stood, saying to me, 'Nearly had that dance, eh?'

'Nearly. Next time?'

'Maybe. Shame, as I'd been practicing.'

'Really?' I asked.

Petra just smiled and joined Will at the door where he called over his shoulder, 'I'll be round for the money,' waved a hand with exaggerated nonchalance and left.

'Well that went easier than I thought,' said Bazzer.

Pluto stood, waddled across the stage and carefully down the steps at the side. 'I'm going.'

'Ok, see you at next rehearsal.'

'No, I mean with Will. I'm off. I need proper paying gigs and Will's got more chance of them I reckon.'

'But …'

'No bad feelings. See you around. Give my share to Steve and I'll get it off him later in the week.'

The earlier confusion and disappointment mushroomed into bewilderment and demoralisation.

Susan dragged on her cigarette. 'Did not see that coming. And then there were three. Unless …' she looked to Dimitri.

'Nah, I'm with you guys. No drummer ever pulled after playing *Tie A Yellow Ribbon*.'

Sunny Steve took the van while Bazzer walked Susan home – it was only ten minutes but he insisted and I followed a couple of yards behind. I went in and left them outside the front door.

'Mum and Dad have gone to bed.' I handed her a cup of tea when she came in. 'So, what next for Terry And The All Stars?'

'Nothing next. They are done. Whatever happens will be new. I never liked that name.'

'Feels like a big thing though.'

'Nah. It was always coming. Did you see how calm Bazzer was? He knew. It'll lead to new opportunities. Speaking of which, you missed one tonight ...' She sipped on her tea, looking over the mug.

'What?'

'How come a guy who is desperate to get up on stage to tell jokes or spank a guitar doesn't have the balls to ask a girl to dance?'

'What d'you mean?'

'I saw. When we played Mum and Dad's song and they danced, I saw you looking at Petra, wondering whether she'd say yes to a dance or not.'

'She'd have said yes.'

'Hmmm, then why not ask?'

'It was for Mum and Dad. Special.'

'Could have been special for you too. Just depends.'

'On what?'

'If you get a hard-on or not.' She laughed at her own joke.

'Haha. Funny.'

'I know. But you know what to do if that does happen right?'

I hesitated. 'Stupid question. I'm not talking about it with you.'

'Who better? Only a girl can tell you the right thing and I'm the only one you can trust. So do you know?'

'Of course.'

'Liar.'

'You're obviously desperate to tell me.'

'Not if you don't want to know. If you're not worried about making a fool of yourself … if you don't care, then …' Susan sipped from the tea.

'I know what to do.'

'No you don't. No boy does on the first dance. You've just two choices. Leave a gap and hope it goes away or pull the girl closer and hope it gets bigger. Either way she'll know.'

'That's not funny.'

'It's true. So why didn't you ask Petra to dance tonight.'

'I told you. It was Mum and Dad's. Was Mum ok afterwards? I didn't really see.'

'Don't know. It was a really big deal for her to come out. And she went shopping during the week and came to the salon for her hair. So maybe she's getting better.'

'Maybe the miracle is beginning to work again.'

'Maybe.'

There was a cynicism in Susan's voice that I didn't want to dwell on. 'Anyway, I can think of better songs for my first slow dance with Petra. Though after tonight I don't suppose there'll be one.'

'Why not?'

'No Will, no Pluto, no All Stars, no Petra.'

'Rubbish. Will splitting was just a matter of time. It has nothing to do with you and Petra. You'll take her to the cinema again, take her out and you'll dance.'

'Not if her mum's there, watching, like tonight. That wouldn't have helped,' I said defensively.

'What, you mean with the hard-on?'

'Haha, still not funny. Speaking of Vi. Did you hear her tell Lawrence to fuck off?'

'You're joking.'

'Straight up.'

'Why?'

'Dunno. She just walked past him and told him to fuck off. She meant it too.'

'Vi?'

'Yep.'

'You'll have to ask Petra. Ring her in the morning. I'm going to bed.'

'Ok. Susan?'

'Yep?'

'Sorry about Terry And The All Stars.'

'People, time and music moves on. So will we.'

Miracle Number Four

Chapter 15
Spring 1976
A Moment Or Two
'Shining Star'

Guitarist/Vocalist wanted. M or F. West London. Rock originals and covers. Looking to write and gig soon. Must have own equipment and transport. Influences Joplin to Zeppelin, Wonder to Winwood to Who, Nyro to Bad Co. Under 23. No drugs. No alkies. Must be free to start now.

It had taken a couple of days following the band break up to fashion the advert. When Susan finally showed it, I asked, 'Alkies?'

'Alcoholics.'

'Is that spelt right?'

'It'll do.'

'And West London? Not really.'

'As close as matters and Penscote just doesn't sound right ... for a rock band.'

'Nyro to Bad Co.? Not many will know her. If it wasn't for you and Bazzer, I wouldn't.'

'That's good. Narrows the field.'

'What about Bowie or Deep Purple or the Stones, Yardbirds, Floyd, Faces or ...?'

'... we only have fifty words and those bands are included in there.'

'Are they?'

'Sort of.'

'Ok. Where's it going?'

'Local papers.'

'Not *NME* or *Melody Maker*?'

'Not yet.'

In the two weeks since placing the advert they'd auditioned seven guitarists/vocalists M or F. I was there for a few, sitting quietly on the tea chest in the corner of the lockup. It was odd without Petra. Susan thought it best, what with the Will situation and all, and Sunny Steve knew a guy that could lend a PA until they had enough cash to buy their own.

They narrowed the auditionees to two and callbacks were arranged for the first Saturday in April, in the room above The Railway. It was cold and damp but free, thanks to Sunny Steve sweet talking the landlord's wife.

Meantime, Bazzer was regularly at our place to give me bass, and Susan guitar lessons. By April I knew three quarters of the songs on the old Terry And The All Stars' set list and had all but given up biting my nails.

The day after the callback auditions, over tea, I asked Susan, 'Can a proper moment last longer than a … moment?' It was just the two of us; egg, chips and beans. Mum was in the conservatory, not eating with us, again. Dad was not yet home from work – Sunday paid double time.

'Not really. It's either a moment or it's not,' said Susan.

'You sure?'

'Yep, take that Sunday, when Mum told us, you know. It took her, what, ten minutes to get to it, but there was a single point when I knew what she meant, really understood. That was the moment. And it's not always the same time as when it actually happened, it's more to do with when it hits you. Why?'

'Just wondered.'

'Why? Had a moment?'

'Maybe … sort of.'

The first 'sort of' moment, the previous day, had been upstairs in The Railway. The curtains were closed but the afternoon sun slipped through gaps. I opened the door and the newly disturbed air swirled dust in the stripes of light. There was a small disused bar at one end, and the tables and chairs had been stacked against the dark wood panelled walls. The air was stale enough to taste. Susan followed me in, taking a small aerosol from her bag and giving three or four squirts of perfume, which made no difference.

'I hope I don't need to pee, God knows what the loo will be like. Open some windows, Mike.'

The rest of the instruments and gear was brought in and I helped set up. Then they sent me to the shops for cans and crisps.

The first callback blew it almost immediately. They'd agreed beforehand the songs to play but whatever Bazzer and Susan had seen in him at the first audition was gone. His timing was off, his solos were tame, his voice was thin. After just three songs they knew; he knew; I, sitting quietly on the dusty bar, knew, and was careful not to catch the guy's eye. The audition finished awkwardly and was barely discussed while we waited for the next.

The second callback started with more promise. His lead work was good though the rhythm work on *All Day And All Of The Night* was laboured. They tried *Brown Sugar* but there were too many wrong chords. They stopped and started it four times, each time Bazzer explaining where the guy had gone wrong and trying to help, but frustrations were growing. Dimitri suggested a fag break, but Bazzer wanted to get it done, so they tried *My Generation*. The guy had a good voice, accurate pitch and power to spare, and it was going ok until the second key change. The guy missed it. Bazzer stopped playing, forced a smile and called to Dimitri to count it off again. This time was even better, until the second key change. Missed again.

'Sorry, I . . .' the auditionee started to apologise but Susan said not to worry. They'd try again but did he know the key changes? He said he thought so but when Bazzer offered to show him, he was happy to pass over the guitar. Bazzer started to explain but a few bars in called to me,

'JB. Grab the bass. Can't do this without.'

'What?' I hadn't been paying attention.

'The bass. You know this one. I need it so I can show the guitar part.'

I looked to Susan. She laughed and nodded. 'You do know it.'

'Not that well. And not on your full size.'

'Bollocks. You've been learning it for months. Get your arse over here.' Bazzer was adamant.

I slipped from the bar top, matching Susan's broad smile.

'I'll count you in,' said Dimitri, 'don't be nervous.'

'Oh, he isn't,' laughed Susan.

It was true, the most nervous person in the room was the auditionee, looking on. I wasn't perfect, the excitement meant I snatched more than a few notes and missed others, but I nailed the bass break and even offered some harmonies. The band hit the key changes spot on and try hard as I might, the joy in my smile outshone any desire to appear cool.

The second 'maybe' moment was a few hours later that same day, when I'd taken Petra to a disco. I'd been given tickets by Vince's new mate Oskar. Oskar had started at school in January.

When it came to school, I was indifferent. It just ... was. I was academically and athletically average, but the teachers knew me by the cheek which I kept just the right side of respectful, more by luck than judgement. It helped that I finally learnt when to stop talking in class. It also helped they remembered and liked Susan. I was told I could do well in exams if ... big if ... I put as much effort into school as the guitar. But that acknowledgement was tempered with a second – it was never going to happen. In the meantime, I was popular enough with some of the kids but not too many, and wasn't a threat to any. Even the music teacher quite liked me – the only pupil he did – for taking an interest in at least some of the classical musical pieces he tried to impress the class with. I never understood why he persevered with us – a testament to either sheer stubbornness or passion for the music; I'll give him the latter.

When Oskar started, three things marked him out: much taller than his classmates; a haircut that hadn't come from the barber's opposite the station; he was Polish. To begin with, it made little difference to me; Oskar was in the same class as Vince. But as the evenings stretched a little longer each week, Vince moaned at me for either having a lesson with Bazzer or being too busy practising to spend time down the park. We still washed cars on Saturdays and his dad was a generous boss, surprisingly, but gradually we hung out less. The moaning subsided as Vince got to know the new kid – Oskar. Vince was soon spending more time with him than me, but occasionally all three of us gathered in the small cafe by the tube station. Sofia, now Sunny Steve's regular girlfriend, was behind the counter. She worked both there and The Railway and didn't mind us making a pot of tea last half an hour and a Kit-Kat go three ways – not easy with four-fingers. One afternoon, after school, Oskar was talking, in good English, about the upcoming disco at the Polish Community Centre. I was already thinking about how to ask Petra to go with me. The tickets should have cost fifty pence each but Oskar had a few to give away and, as a friend of Vince, did I want a couple?

With tickets in hand I'd gone home via Petra's. Vi ushered me in. I hadn't seen her since Will had left the band a couple of weeks before.

Petra was out back, feeding the chickens.

'How's Ingrid?' I called. Petra was at the coop, throwing in grain.

'Hungry. Wotchya doin'?'

I held the tickets in front of me.

'You ok?' she asked. 'You look worried.'

I'd rehearsed this situation on the way over but hadn't reckoned with such nerves. 'Nah, 'course not. You ok?'

'Yep.'

'Wotchya doin'?'

'I just asked you that.' She laughed. It was the unpractised laugh that charmed. She wore a t-shirt with a hand drawn version of the cover for *The Dark Side Of The Moon*.

'Nice t-shirt.'

'Thanks, my friend Kay did this one. She's good.'

'You should wear it next Saturday. Here.' I showed her the tickets.

Petra took the tickets. 'A disco? Not really your scene is it?'

'Music is music.'

'You don't really believe that.'

'No, but to be honest, it's not easy to dance to…,' I pointed to Petra's t-shirt, '… Floyd.'

'We're gonna dance?' she teased.

'To the slow ones,' my bravado returned, 'and tickets are free. Oskar gave them to me.'

'Oskar?'

'Vince's new mate.'

'Oh yeah. I've seen them hanging around.'

'I'll pick you up at seven.'

'What, on your bike?'

I laughed. 'So that's a yes then. See you Saturday.'

I left before she could refuse.

The journey to the Polish Community Centre took longer than expected. I talked all the way. Petra asked me to slow down but I was lost in the joy of taking part in the day's earlier audition and the anticipation of this proper date. By the fourth time of describing the events in the room above The Railway, Petra gently reminded me we were here for the disco and led me from the bus by hand; it was warm and soft, of course, but the surprise was exciting, almost a shock. She held my hand tightly and the flush of tension thrilled. The contact was a promise.

'Took *my* hand ...' I explained, twice, to Vince at the kitchen hatch selling soft drinks to the hall. Petra was with Oskar at the table they'd claimed. 'Get it? I didn't take hers, she took mine.'

Vince assured me he 'got it'.

'Smells good too.'

'Her hand?' Vince was dubious.

'All of her.'

'Don't tell me, tell her.'

Which was good advice. We threaded our way across the busy dance floor, shouting, 'Excuse Me,' and 'Sorry,' to be heard above the music as we bumped our way back to the table. Vince sat down next to Oskar. The DJ played *Shining Star* and Petra took to the dance floor. Her shuffle turned to a sway then a disco side-step, bang on the beat. She burst from shadow to colour and back in the flashing lights and was both in her own world and, it seemed, enticing me to join her. I was never going to refuse, despite shortcomings; I had little dancing skill and wished I'd asked Susan. We danced for a handful of tracks without touching or talking, the music was too loud, then sat to take a drink. Vince shouted that he and Oskar were going outside for a cigarette, Oskar didn't want any of the organisers to know he smoked.

'They're really pally, aren't they?' said Petra, shouting to be heard.

'Are they?' I wasn't paying attention.

'And I didn't know Vince smoked.'

'Does he? I've never seen him.'

'Doesn't he?'

'Don't know.' I was more concerned with second-guessing Petra's reaction were I to take her hand, or say how much I liked her perfume, or that I liked watching her dance, or that the green cotton dress, tight to her figure, was a good match to her eyes.

It was the first time I'd spent a whole evening in a disco – usually I was too bored to stay at the youth club efforts. But here, the repeated action of getting a can from the kitchen hatch, sitting to watch the dancers, especially Petra, and occasionally being coaxed on to the floor, was no hardship. Around ten o'clock the DJ announced there were just three songs left as he placed the needle on a single. I recognised *I'm Not In Love*. For the first time that evening I initiated a dance. My heart was banging as I stood and nodded toward the quickly filling floor, ignoring Vince and Oskar's smirks. Petra joined me. Taking a glance round the room I copied others, wrapping my arms around her shoulders and pulling her close. I had grown just a little taller than her over the last couple of months and she melded into me, placing her arms around me and resting her head on my chest. We rocked and turned slowly on the spot. The lighting was subdued and our place on the dancefloor personal and discrete. Her perfume was urgent and sweet and her softness unexpected. Two or three minutes into the song I had to ease myself a little away from her, but she pulled me back, more tightly than before. She lifted her face and kissed me gently and briefly on the lips, smiling as she laid her head back on my chest. I would be forever grateful to 10cc. As the song ended we kissed again, this time with a little more pressure, but still only briefly, and I led her back to the table. My desire was to also dance the next slow song, but my instinct was to close on the amazing high point of that first dance. It was easier to celebrate as special when also unique.

I saw her home. We held hands on the bus, even up and down the stairs which was awkward, and all the way to her door which she opened before turning and kissing me. It was still a gentle kiss and we hugged only briefly. But though the kiss was on my lips for just a few seconds the pressure lasted far longer.

'Oh, and say thanks to Susan. Her smooch advice made sense.' Petra laughed and shut the door. I was nearly home before remembering what Susan had said. Reliving that slow dance was easy with Petra's perfume still on me.

'So did you? Have a moment? When?' Susan asked, slapping hard at the bottom of the ketchup, aimed at her chips.

'Not sure, maybe two. Yesterday. One was …'

Susan interrupted, 'Whoa, no need to tell me. I mean you can, when, if, you're sure they were moments. But best wait a few days, in case you change your mind. Nothing worse than declaring a moment then finding out you were wrong. You'll know for sure in a few days, or weeks. Pass the vinegar.'

I handed her the Sarsons.

'And, on the subject of yesterday. What're you doing tonight?' she asked.

'Why?'

'Why do you answer a question with a question?'

'Why not?'

'Funny. Me, Bazzer and Dimitri are working on some new stuff tonight. Wanna play?'

'Me?'

'You're doing it again. Yep, you. It's only until we find the new guitarist but after yesterday, turns out you'll have to play bass and Bazzer will take lead. We've run out of people to audition and ads in *NME* are too expensive. Oh, and JB, save up for a proper bass.' Susan's suggestion was so casual that it took me a few seconds to grasp the significance. I just managed to stop any exclamation and forced a calmness, saying,

Miracle Number Four

'Well, if you think you and Bazzer can cover the guitar parts then I guess I'm available.'

Chapter 16
Spring 1976
The Broken Dove
'That's The Way Of The World'

The days immediately after the disco were both thrilling and disappointing. On the downside, Petra had to go with her mother to visit some cousins on the coast for a couple of days. On the plus side, the new band, the band I was now in, our band, my band, had a new name – Rocknow Station – and though it was no one's favourite, it was no one's last choice. Dad thought it was good, naturally, while Mum thought it confusing without knowing why, but then said she liked that.

At the first Rocknow Station rehearsal, in the manky room above The Railway, they plugged in Bazzer's bass and gave me a mic. It turned out the years of singing in my bedroom had helped a little. Bazzer was easily good enough to take on lead guitar and he convinced Susan she was easily good enough to sing lead as well as play rhythm. I was a little embarrassed at their genuine reactions to flattering each other. Dimitri pretended to stick fingers down his throat and gag but promised to try some backing vocals. In short, the band was complete, and we believed in ourselves. Will and Pluto were history. Sunny Steve was happy – one less person in the band meant better shareouts. We had a new name and a new energy. Within days Sunny Steve had arranged for a gig at Zamara'z, a club in nearby Twickenham. The manager owed him a favour; Sunny Steve didn't elaborate. We had until 19th June, ten and a half weeks.

I was leaving the station, returning home, when the movement from the figure at the café's window caught my eye. Vince waved me in. There were no other customers and the air was still, despite the door being open. Sofia was on the till. We exchanged nods.

I sat with Vince at the table by the window. 'Not seen you around much.'

'Yeah, sorry, you've been a bit busy. Petra, I suppose.' He apologised sarcastically.

'She's been away a few days, back today though.'

'Oh, so band stuff then.'

That was true and I'd just come from Patrick's Pianos, our nearest instrument shop, checking the price of new guitars. I'd come away disillusioned. At the rate we got paid for washing cars it would take years.

'What about you? Up to much?' I asked.

'Revising.' He didn't look up from his cup.

I waited for the overhead rumbling of a train to pass before asking, 'Already?' with more than a hint of disbelief. We were due exams this summer, but they were a month away.

'My old man's insisting.' He pulled a pack of Players from a pocket and lit a cigarette. 'And he's decided I'm going into the business, apprentice mechanic.'

'Is that a bad thing? My dad started that way. Didn't yours? It's an all-right job.'

'Is it? Not if you care sweet Fanny Adams about cars.'

'Er, what about collecting number plates?'

'That was last year. And it's no reason to be a grease monkey.'

'Ok. So you told him no?'

'Funny. When did anyone?'

'Did you try?'

'He got angry, of course, but at least he doesn't try to slap me about, now I'm as tall as him.' Vince looked away. Though we'd always suspected – make that, known – his dad hit him, this was the first time in all these years it had been said. What sort of friend had I been that it had taken this long?

The silence was difficult, so I asked, 'What do you want to do?'

'Dunno. Oskar's going to college for A levels. I probably won't even pass CSEs.' He stared at his tea.

I hunted for something positive. 'If Dimitri can re-take CSEs at college so can you. I'll probably be there.'

'Dimitri's a Greek drummer,' he said, as if it explained everything.

I nodded, having no answer to that, then tried, 'Wanna come to my gaff for tea? Susan's probably making something. If not, I'll do sardines on toast.'

'No thanks. I might pop round to Oskar's.'

'Susan'll be home soon. You haven't seen her for ages.'

'So?'

'You used to hang around with us.'

'Things change.'

'And people adapt.'

'Deep. One of Susan's?'

'My own.'

We sat quietly for a minute until a couple of boys we recognised from school came in. They joked with Sofia and ordered Cokes.

'Your class,' I said to Vince.

'Yep, and a couple of dicks,' he said, loud enough to be heard.

'What are the chances of that? Both named Richard eh?' I tried to break the sudden tension.

'Funny,' said Vince but he wasn't smiling and glanced over often to the two other boys. Their sniggers grew to laughter, their smiles to sneers.

Twenty minutes later, in Vi's kitchen, I tried to replay how it had gone wrong so quickly. I sat at the table, leaning back, face to the ceiling as Vi cleaned the split over my left eye. It stung. A lot. The bruise beneath throbbed. I breathed shallow to manage the pain of my right ribs. My left ankle ached.

Vince stood to one side. His face was bruised and there was a plaster stuck horizontally across his nose. His bottom lip was swollen, and he held a cold, soaked tea towel around his right wrist.

As Vi turned back to the sink for more clean water I looked to my hands, again. Though bruised on a couple of knuckles they were mostly unmarked. I flexed my fingers. All was ok. My newly unbitten nails were intact. My wrists were not injured. Some comfort.

'You could do with a stitch or maybe two,' said Vi. 'I'd better call your dad. Will he be home yet?' She looked to the clock, it was shortly past five.

'No,' I said, 'but it's stopped bleeding.'

It hadn't and she made me look up to the ceiling again.

From the café, Vince and I had gone to Vi's because it was close, the volume of blood on my shirt and Vince's face had looked serious and I didn't want to upset my mum.

We heard the front door close and Petra calling out, 'Mum,' and then, 'What the ... fu ... hell?' as she saw us. I tried to look at her, but the blood seeped into my eye, causing me to blink, causing more blood to flow.

'Put the kettle on, Petra. Tea with lots of sugar,' suggested Vi, now padding a handkerchief hard against my wound.

'Well?' Petra asked.

'I still don't know,' said Vi, pressing ever more firmly.

I started to speak but stopped. It hurt my ribs to take a breath to talk and, besides, I didn't know for sure. Except it had happened quickly, very quickly.

'We were in the café. A couple of dicks from school wanted a fight. They got one,' said Vince.

'Why?' asked Petra.

'They don't like me.' Vince looked down.

'Luckily, they love me,' I said, filling Vince's silence.

Vi took my left hand and placed it over the handkerchief.

Vince fingered the plaster on his nose. 'Anyway, we gave as good as we got.'

I doubted that.

After the fight, Sofia had helped us but suggested we leave before her boss returned. On the way to Vi's, Vince had asked me not to tell his dad what the other boys had been saying.

I had no reason to disagree and, besides, I was in pain, shaking, and my heart beat so hard and fast it hurt the bruised ribs. Oh, and my ankle hurt. How had that happened?

'... bum boy and superstar together. No surprise ...' one of the boys had said, sure to be heard.

'Pass the Vaseline,' said the other.

It hadn't been obvious to me, stupidly I suppose, that they were talking about us until Vince tensed and repeated, 'Brainless dicks.'

Before I'd finished asking what they meant, one of the boys had thrown a can. Vince told him to, 'Fuck off.' A chair was pushed at me, cracking into my knees. The first boy kicked at Vince who fell over as he went to stand and the other threw a punch at me, then an elbow, another punch and a kick and a knee and a punch and a ... who knew what ... as I scrabbled to my feet. Heart pounding, pumped with sudden adrenalin, I didn't feel pain and swung blindly, breath held, eyes screwed shut, barely connecting with the boy.

Sofia was there in seconds, screaming and shouting, flailing at the attackers with the rounders bat from under the counter. She cracked the boy attacking me on the shoulder and he cried out in pain but was laughing as he stumbled out to the street. I looked over to Vince who was underneath his attacker. Vince's arms and hands covered his face and head, and he wasn't catching many punches. Sofia grabbed the boy by the hair and dragged him to the door.

He laughed with his partner, and they jogged away. It was all done in less than half a minute. I had no anger, no fear; I just shook with adrenalin that was no longer needed and a sudden headache from pumping, coursing blood, not from wounds. My thoughts were jumbled. It might not have been real if not for Vince's moans and the blood dripping down my brow and into my eye.

Vi waited until some colour came back to our faces before letting Vince walk home and ringing my dad. She had wanted to go with us to A&E but Dad said no need and Petra said a small scar might look, '... dashing,'; emphasising the 'small'.

By the time we got to hospital the bleeding had stopped but I was shaking again. Dad came up with a story for Mum about me falling and banging my head on a table in the café. When we got home Susan took our dinners from the oven, but I had no appetite. The three stitches had hurt, my head hurt and, more than anything, my pride hurt. I thought about the fight and how I'd failed; how I'd been scared and hit out indiscriminately, not landing one true punch; how I'd wanted to cry on the walk to Vi's and was embarrassed as we passed the bakery and newsagent; how I'd not pressed Vince on the reason for the boys' aggression; how I'd been stupid enough not to see it coming.

'You look terrible,' said Susan, taking my barely touched plate away. 'When you want to, tell me all about it. But later. First, change shirts, throw that one in the bin, in a bag, and go and see if Mum's awake. She was worried but went to bed early. Then we'll go to rehearsal.'

I gently washed my face, found a mostly clean t-shirt and waited outside Mum's bedroom for a few seconds. When I heard movement I entered. She was sitting up in bed, an unopened *People's Friend* magazine on her lap. My three stitches were spidery black threads, pinching together the angry red gash splitting my left eyebrow. My cheek and eye socket were swollen and the bruise beginning to darken. I winced when bending over to hug her.

'Oh, Mikey,' she put a hand to her mouth, 'that looks so sore, so sore.'

'It's ok, Mum. Not as bad as it looks.'

'Really? Dad said you tripped in the café and smacked your face on a table?' It was a question.

'Something like that. It happened so fast, I'm not sure. But it's ok. Worst thing was the stitches.'

'Vince's mum rang me while you were at the hospital. Dad didn't mention you were with Vince.'

'Didn't he?'

She rested a hand gently on my cheek while she looked at me, then took my hand. 'No shame in losing a fight, Mikey, as long as it's for a good cause.'

'No fight, Mum.' I pretended, though it was some comfort to think that the cause was a good one, even if I wasn't entirely sure what it was.

'I'm glad you're spending so much time with Petra, but you won't forget about Vince, will you?'

I thought it an odd thing to say and changed the subject, 'Did you go out today?'

'I did a bit in the garden. It's looking nice, isn't it?'

'Very. And did you eat?'

'A little.'

'Good. And taking the new pills?'

'Of course.' She smiled uneasily.

I smiled sympathetically. I wanted to ask if they were making any difference but thought I knew the answer.

Susan and I carried our guitars through the public bar of The Railway on our way to the upstairs room, ignoring the unimaginative quips from the regulars. Sofia, working shifts in the pub in the evenings, waved us to the bar.

'You ok, JB?' She asked with genuine concern. Now that she was Sunny Steve's girlfriend she called me 'JB'.

'Yeah and thanks for … earlier.'

'No problem, and so you know, I told Steve who those kids are. They won't be doing that again, Steve's on it … them.'

I smiled thanks. I hadn't thought they would but …?

Up in the room Bazzer offered, 'Ouch,' on seeing me.

'No worries. You should see the other guy.'

'That's the third time he's tried that joke,' said Susan, 'It's still not funny.'

The rehearsal was subdued, despite Bazzer reminding us it was less than ten weeks to the debut gig; my first ever. Knowing the new songs to the point of instinct wasn't optional. But my guitar was heavier than usual, the bruising to my ribs telling, and Sofia's comments weighed on me, especially when Sunny Steve came in, wanting to test some new equipment with the cobbled together PA. We took a break while Steve unravelled cables and, rather than engage in conversation with the others, I went to him. Steve welcomed the help, saying, 'Thanks, JB, but don't bend down, that eye looks bad and from what Sofia said you might be concussed. I know a bit about that.' He didn't laugh.

'Talking of which, Sofia mentioned … you … know the kids?' I asked.

'She knows their names. Don't worry. I'll find them. This is Rocknow Station. We stand together. It's them that'll fall. And Vince is one of ours too. I don't care what his … fancies might be.' Steve didn't look up from his work and his voice was sincere.

'Fancies? I hadn't really … you know … thought about it …' and I hadn't, until that day, 'but, I was gonna say, about the two … dicks, best not, you know, do anything. I … we … Rocknow … don't want you in trouble. We need you and they are just a couple of dicks.' I tried to laugh but it made my bruised cheek smart.

'You sure? I know you're a good kid and all, but sometimes you need to draw a line.'

'No, really, s'ok, best … you know, let sleeping dogs lie and all …'

'Sleeping dogs?' Steve repeated.

'Sleeping dogs?' Dimitri asked as he wandered over.

'Yep,' I said, 'New band from down south. Shit-hot, apparently.' I changed the subject.

'Yeah, really? Like that last one you suggested. A Stitch In Time? I'm not as thick as I look.'

'That would be difficult,' I agreed, patting him on the back. 'Oh, by the way, do you know why drummers have loads of kids?'

'What?'

'They're rubbish at the rhythm method.'

Dimitri thought for a second then said, deadpan, 'What if they're not Catholics?'

I laughed and my cheek hurt again.

It was close to closing time when rehearsal finished and the pub was all but empty. I was on the way out, worrying that Dad would tell me off for being out late mid-week, when Sofia called me over again. 'Steve tells me you don't need him to sort out those tossers. You sure?'

I nodded.

'You're a good kid, JB, but sometimes you have to meet stuff head on. Nip it in the bud. We just don't want you to be picked on.'

'I know, but really, they're just … dicks. If anything else happens I'll talk to Sunny Steve. Promise.'

'Ok, but maybe I'll slip some senna in their tea.' Sofia reached across the bar and pecked me on the good cheek.

I couldn't deny the thought of Sunny Steve beating the shit out of them appealed, nearly as much as Sofia giving them the trots. But though it suited me for others to think I was forgiving, the truth was that if Steve did intervene I'd just feel guilty and a coward for not dealing with it myself; not to mention what Petra might think. Or Vince? And what about his 'fancies' as Steve had called them? I didn't really know what Steve meant, except, of course, I did. Now that I thought about it, Vince never talked about girls, except he did – my sister. What did that mean? And what I really didn't know was what it meant to me and him. And I didn't understand why I needed to get beaten up before I even asked myself the question.

I slept badly. Lying on the right hurt my ribs; lying on the left hurt my face, lying on my back, bizarrely, hurt my ankle.

Petra talked her way out of church on Easter Sunday and came round to our place instead. Dad was out; a monthly visit to the market for meat for our chest freezer. Mum was in the conservatory, no surprises, and I was in the front room, sifting through Dad's old vinyl for anything Bazzer might consider interesting. It was a dry, sunny April day.

'That'll scar. Quite heroic looking,' Petra said as I opened the front door. The stitches above my eye were feeling tighter every day, which I supposed was a good thing. She kissed me on the lips, looking thoughtful for a second before, 'Hmmm, interesting, you don't kiss lopsided.'

I laughed but before I could respond she asked, 'What do you think to this?' passing me a record as I led her into the house.

'Earth Wind And Fire?'

'*That's The Way Of The World*. Kay reckons this is the album of the year, already.'

'Kay?'

'Sofia's sister, at my school, remember?'

I put the record on the turntable, and we sat on the settee, shoulders and thighs carefully brushing. I didn't pay much attention to the music and when I spoke it was unplanned and a surprise, to both of us.

'That smell … you … smell really nice. What is it?'

'Blasé. I borrowed it from Kay. Like it?'

'Very much. Smells just the way you should.' I wanted to be both sincere and sophisticated. I had no way of knowing if I'd succeeded. Since the disco date, I had imagined scenarios in which we kissed ever more 'properly'. What that meant wasn't entirely clear, but I'd spent nearly as much time on that as bass practise. Thankfully, the old settee was a two-seater, sagging in the middle, and we were both gradually slipping towards each other.

'I meant the album. Kay knows a thing or two.' She indicated to the record player.

'Oh, yeah. Bass player's pretty good.'

Petra laughed lightly. We listened in silence while the first side played. She took my hand and I didn't let go until needing to turn over the record. The air was warm and still and the curtains half-closed. Though nervous I was also confident. We had been building slowly to this point of hesitant passion. She slipped her hair behind her ear and turned to me as I sat back down. It was such a definite act that I even relaxed, a little. We settled closer and I put an arm around her, tilting my face to hers. Her perfume was stronger, the pressure of her thigh was firmer and her breathing as shallow as mine. Our lips touched. She raised her hand to the back of my head, pulling me closer.

The crash of breaking glass snatched us apart.

There was a short confusion; neither was sure the other had heard it.

There was a sob from the kitchen. Mum.

We sat rigid, still against each other.

More sobbing.

I withdrew my arm.

Mum was leaning over the kitchen sink, taking her weight on thin arms, weeping between intense, painful sighs that wracked her small frame. Pieces of a small glass dove lay on the floor at her feet, surrounded by grains of different coloured sands. The body was intact, but the head detached.

Sunshine flooded the kitchen through the window and Mum was a hunched silhouette. She turned as I called but all she said was,

'Sorry.'

'Mum?' I repeated, taking her under the arms and gently easing her away from the sink. She caught her breath as she stood on a shard of glass, drawing blood. I apologised and settled her in a chair, asking Petra, standing in the doorway, to call Susan from her bedroom.

Mum was now crying silently but repeating her, 'I'm sorry,' mantra, seemingly oblivious to Susan cleaning her foot and placing a plaster over the small cut. Petra and I watched, me expecting Susan to find out what had caused the upset, but Susan had her own mantra,

'It'll be all right, Mum, it'll be all right ...'

I carefully gathered up the glass and tried to salvage the coloured sand. It seemed important not to discard anything, so I left it in a dustpan at the side of the sink.

Mum stopped crying after a few minutes and stood cautiously, saying she'd lie down for a while and not to tell Dad. Susan helped her from the kitchen, stifling her own tears.

Back in the lounge, Petra and I sat back on the sofa, not touching.

'You ok?' she asked.

'Better than Mum.' I pretended to laugh.

'Why do you do that?'

'What?'

'You know.'

'Dunno. I forget sometimes she's still not well.'

'Forget?'

It was probably more truthful to say avoid, not forget. I pretended to smile, 'I'm not even sure what's wrong. I don't think anyone is. She saw a different doc and he said it might be schizophrenia, not depression, but wasn't sure. I don't know what schizophrenia is. Something about hallucinations and voices? You'd think one of them might be a happy one.'

'Still joking?'

'Sorry. I ... you know.' I looked away.

She rubbed my arm. 'She's taking pills though?'

'New ones. She's down the doctor's a lot and we're down the chemist as much, so I suppose she's taking them.' I went to the record deck, restarted the second side of the album and sat back next to Petra, again, still not touching. 'It's been a shit week for her.'

'And you,' she indicated to my bruised face, 'And Ingrid. She died yesterday and one of my aunts in Ireland is really poorly.'

'Ingrid the chicken?'

'Is there another Ingrid?'

'Oh, I'm sorry, that is shit. You didn't say.'

'She was old, for a chicken. My aunt is a bigger worry. I need to bury her later.'

'Your aunt?'

'It's not funny.'

'Sorry. Will your aunt get better?'

'Don't know. Lots of prayers are being said for her.'

We listened to the music for a couple of tracks then I asked, 'When you were in Ireland and Vi prayed to the statue ... for Mum ...'

'...yeah?'

'... did Saint Teresa really ... you know ... cry?'

'It was dark. My mum thinks so.'

'And you?'

'Does it matter?'

'I don't think I've ever really believed it, but if I ... we ... don't ... then who will? And otherwise, why should we believe Mum doesn't need to be so unhappy?'

'Does that make sense?'

'I don't know.'

We buried Ingrid that afternoon, in the abandoned vegetable patch behind the chicken coop. Vi was back from church and said a few words. Will turned up and suggested the best way to remember Ingrid would be roasted. No one laughed though I did think it funny. Petra cried a little, trying to hide behind the long hair she pulled across her mouth and I was able to offer some comfort, I thought, but felt bad I'd been unable to provide the same for Mum earlier.

Chapter 17
Spring 1976
Under The Yew Tree
'She Moves To Still'

The first Saturday of May was traditionally reserved for St. Gregory's spring fete. Vi had been baking and manned the cake stall for the first hour. Petra was to meet her there and called in at The Railway on the way, to collect me. I was with Bazzer and Dimitri in the upstairs room, grabbing a couple of hours practise, having already spent the morning cleaning cars. Susan wasn't with us, being needed in the salon on Saturdays, but there was plenty for the rest of us to rehearse. We had the room until two-thirty, by which time the landlord would be trying to catch a nap between lunchtime and evening sessions.

Petra came in as we started *She Moves To Still,* a song written by Susan and Bazzer, but which I was trying to sing. The song was a mid-tempo bluesy number which I really didn't think I had the voice for but, as Petra told me on the way to the fete, Winwoods don't come along often. It was supposed to make me feel better. It didn't. Taking Petra's willing hand did. She wore a red, cotton pinafore dress with a bright white t-shirt beneath. Her long hair, nearly blonde, really, and slender figure lent an appearance both athletic and feminine. Her face was make-up free but there was an air of sophistication in the choice, a confidence that she was pretty enough not to need more colour, her green eyes were sufficient, both telling all, and yet concealing enough. I was not only desiring, I was proud. We walked past the station and parade of shops, so familiar to me, but with some renewed sense of belonging.

The fete was bustling by the time we arrived. The grounds of the vicarage were only just big enough for the clutter of tents and marquees. Cotton bunting fluttered and a hand-painted sign of welcome was strung over the side gate to the garden. There was a constant flow of people in and out, five pence entry fee, hand stamp as proof of payment, and a noisy chatter, forcing Petra to raise her voice as we wandered the stalls.

'By the way, Will's after a bass player. Wants to know if you'll join his new band. Will And The All Stars.'

We stopped at the tombola tent, Petra hunting through her purse for five pence.

'You're joking right?' I passed her a coin.

'No.'

'Taking the piss?'

'No. He reckons if you're good enough for Bazzer then you can probably play a bit and says he'll get you paying gigs.'

'He already has a bass player. Besides, Will And The All Stars? Seriously? That's rubbish.'

'I know, I told him. But you know what he's like. And he wants to ditch the bass player he has but can't do that until he finds another one. Oh, and talking of paid work, do you think Susan could get me a Saturday job at the salon, washing hair or something?'

'I'll ask. That's how she got into hairdressing.'

'I'm not getting into hairdressing. I don't have the patience for all those blue rinses, but I need a Saturday job.'

'You could wash cars with me and Vince. I'll ask his dad.'

'No way would I work for him. Hey, I've won jewellery.' The lady behind the table handed over a leather bracelet, thin strips glued at each end into a clasp. She assured Petra it was new. It was too big for Petra's petite wrist, close to slipping over her hand.

'Pretty?' She showed it to me.

'I guess.'

'So what shall I tell Will?'

'Say I'm all about the music, not the money. Besides, imagine what Susan would say.'

'Do.'

'Do?'

'Not say. Susan would cut your balls off. Nice to be asked though, eh? Maybe you could play in both bands.'

'I've enough trouble learning the songs for Rocknow Station. Not sure I'm up to it.'

'JB? Nervous?' she teased.

'Maybe, a bit, 'specially if I've got to sing.'

'Don't worry, I heard Bazzer tell your sister he reckons you'll do the business. You know Bazzer, if he didn't think you'd be ok then ...' she drew a pretend knife across her throat. 'It's all about the band.'

We moved on to the cake stall. The woman behind the table pointed to the other side of the garden. Vi was there, talking to another stallholder. 'Didn't know your dad was coming,' said Petra.

'Vince's dad's garage are running the secondhand book tent and Dad's been roped in. He wasn't happy. Says he's enough to do on a weekend. He doesn't go to church and hasn't read a book since he left school, unless you count Haynes manuals.'

We strolled across the lawn. A tall man glided alongside, his all-black attire incongruous amongst the spring dresses and shorts.

'Hello, Petra, Michael. How are you both? Lovely to see you here.'

'Father Andrew, hi,' said Petra.

'That's a fine scar you have there, Michael.' The stitches had been taken out the previous day, but the wound still looked fresh.

'You should see the other guy.'

'We've a boxing club if you've the knack for it.'

'He definitely doesn't and daren't hurt his hands,' said Petra as we reached Dad's book stall.

'Hello, Violet. The word on the WI stall is that your cakes are a triumph,' said Father Andrew, entering the small marquee. 'And who's this looking after the stall for Lawrence?'

'Frank, April's husband.' Vi made the introductions.

'Of course. We've met, haven't we?'

'On and off, over the years,' said Dad.

'Thanks for helping Lawrence run the stall. Where is he?'

'You know his dodgy ticker? He had a turn last night,' said Dad.

'But Frank's sold a lot of books, probably more than Lawrence would. He's the gift of the gab,' said Vi.

'Selling? This is giving them away.' Dad laughed.

'Every little helps. How is April? We haven't seen her in church for a while,' said Father Andrew.

'She's … resting, still. And, to tell the truth, up and down.'

'Is there anything I or the church can do?'

'Well perhaps a top up on the miracle, just to move things along a little quicker,' Dad joked.

'Miracle?' asked Father Andrew.

'Saint Teresa's tears and all?' Dad looked to Vi.

'Glaskild,' said Vi, quietly. 'We said prayers last year.'

'Just before April started getting better. And the cancer has gone. Not many can say that,' Dad added, looking to me for confirmation.

'Ah, Glaskild's Saint Teresa. Down by the sea,' said Father Andrew. 'I've heard of it.'

Vi nodded.

'It's encouraging to think it may have helped,' said Father Andrew, 'if not quite a miracle.'

'Well I'm no Catholic, but …' Dad let his words tail off.

Father Andrew's smile was fixed. I watched him, trying to guess his thoughts. After a pause that was close to uncomfortable, Father Andrew said, 'I suppose it's a kind of miracle.'

Dad seemed relieved, 'And as I always say, there's three types. Love at first sight, children and God's work.' It was both a mischief and a challenge.

The smile on Father Andrew's mouth was a sneer for a second before he caught it, 'Three you say?' And I thought he was about to tell Dad he was wrong.

'Don't forget Mum's fourth,' I said. 'Peace.' And it was more a challenge than a mischief.

Father Andrew started to speak, stopped, sighed and said, 'Ah, then your mother's a wise lady. Anyway, it's been a pleasure to meet you again, Frank. Vi, might I have word?' He ushered her away.

Dad watched them leave.

Petra looked through the boxes. I waited patiently, pretending to be interested in the books and laughed when she asked, dead-pan, 'What do you think came first, the alphabet or the dictionary? After all, the letters might have been known but not in that order.'

Which was a fair point.

We wandered the other stalls until we found the secondhand records and cassettes. The spring sun was warm, and I was happy to take the shade of the small marquee, sifting through vinyl. Petra stood just outside, claiming her pale Irish and German complexion needed all the help it could get, despite me disagreeing. I found a cheap copy of *L.A. Woman* which I thought Bazzer would appreciate and turned to ask Petra her opinion. She was lit by bright sunshine and framed by the marquee entrance, a strand of hair pulled across her mouth, thoughtful, as so often. Behind her was the happy fete – busy, haphazard, noisy. The contrast with her poise and easy smile made me pause. Though her small features were fine and sharp, they were open and warm. Before I could ask her opinion on the album, I saw two youths stop outside the tent; the two that had attacked me and Vince. Something must have played in my face as Petra asked, 'You all right?' then followed my look and guessed, 'Them?'

I nodded. My chest tightened and my legs wavered. They recognised me. A mix of fear and anger brought a rushed confusion, but I might have waited a second or two before acting if one of the youths hadn't laughed so loudly. I dropped the record onto the table. With no thought and sudden rage I brushed past the hand raised by Petra.

'Superstar,' the larger of the two boys said, 'what are the chances? S'ok, no problem.'

I stopped just short, my face inches from his as I looked up, but I had no plan or instinct or force to make them feel my anger and frustration. They understood and smirked.

'Really,' said the other, 'it's ok. Sofia told us you know that Steve.'

'So fucking what?' I wanted an argument.

'We heard of him. Tell Sofia we said sorry.'

They began to walk away.

'Piss off,' I said.

They laughed. One turned. 'Girlfriend's a looker though, hope your boyfriend isn't jealous.'

'Fuck off.'

They went. They didn't care. Nothing I could do or say was a threat to them. If not for Sunny Steve, they'd care even less. I fumed at my helplessness.

'Bollocks to 'em,' Petra said.

'I could have let Sunny Steve sort them. I should've.'

'That wouldn't make you feel better.'

'It might. Wankers.'

'And why call you superstar?'

'Taking the piss. I suppose they know I play guitar. Word gets round school.'

'And boyfriend?'

'Something to do with Vince, I suppose.'

She thought for a second, 'Does he prefer boys? It wouldn't be a surprise. Not that it's a bad thing.'

'Not sure what you mean.' I didn't want to talk about it.

'And he's been hanging round that Oskar a lot lately.'

'Me and Vince used to hang around a lot.'

'You guys hang around together. Vince tends to hang round Oskar. It's different.'

'So is Oskar ... girly?'

'Not really.'

'That doesn't make sense then.'

'Not to you maybe. Don't worry. More importantly, you heard them say your girlfriend's a looker?' Petra laughed.

'They did, you are,' I said, but not lightly. My anger was still tight.

'What? Girlfriend or looker?' Petra glanced around. The fete was busy enough that we were inconspicuous.

'Both.'

She pecked me quickly on the cheek but then, a little more slowly, on the lips. My rage at the youths was flushed into a thrill, a desire. I grabbed her hand and we slipped between the stalls and tents, past the vicarage and towards the church. A path wound through the graveyard, under the trees. Out of sight of the fete, I stopped under a yew, its shadow deepened by that of the church. It was cool here, but my forehead was damp with sweat. My breathlessness was not from running.

'Here?' she asked as she eased away a little.

'It's a place of love and worship.'

She laughed. 'Worship?'

'You do have a cool laugh.'

'You just like having someone appreciate your jokes.'

I was still holding her hand. I hesitated, but these were nerves of excitement, and tugged her closer. She pulled her hand free and, before I could think I'd made a mistake, scanned the cemetery, taking a step to be against me. We kissed. Not as before, not gently, not teasing, not hinting, but with abandon and no consideration, no plan; with honest lust and sweet desire. She was petite, light, but heavy against me; her mouth on mine, my tongue with hers, our breathing quick; her small breasts to my chest, her hair in my hands. She smelt both of perfume and herself. I didn't feel my own arousal until Petra pressed her hips to me. There was a pause, the slightest of pauses, then she pulled herself in harder. I nuzzled her neck, heard the moan that barely escaped, unsure if it was mine or hers. We kissed again and again until I pulled away, not sure what to do next and not wanting to spoil anything.

We held each other.

I hoped to God this would turn out to be a moment and Susan would be right. Maybe they did change you, or make you do or feel something different. Holding Petra, my senses racing, it was easy to believe at least one of those would be true.

The moment was broken when Petra stood away and winced, in pain.

'You ok?'

'Yep, 'course.' But she winced again.

'What's the matter?'

She whispered, 'My monthly. Cramps. Sorry.' Her pale cheeks flushed. She looked away, pressing a hand to her stomach. 'Sorry.'

I took a couple of seconds to make sense of the words then smiled with what I hoped would appear sympathy. 'Sorry? What for? Hey, I've an older sister. I know about this stuff.' I spoke quickly, also embarrassed.

She looked at me.

'Well, ok, I don't *know*. But you don't need to say sorry. I'm sorry. Did I hold too tight or … or something? Should we go to the chemists? They might have some tablets. Or we could check with Susan, at the salon. She might have something. I don't mind. We …'

'Shut up.' She rested her arms around my neck and her head on my shoulder. I leant back against the tree. The graves around us were mostly untended and the long grass and meadow flowers vibrant. With birds and insects, the cemetery teemed with random life among the regimented stones. The shadow of the church was welcoming, not threatening, and the quiet was comforting, not dark.

We stayed that way under the tree until Petra took the tombola stall leather bracelet from her wrist, broke the clasp free and separated the strips of leather. She gave three to me, keeping three for herself. We each tied our new bracelets round our wrists.

Chapter 18
Summer 1976
The Mole
'Tomorrow Belongs To Me'

This was the summer I turned sixteen and pretentiously claimed it to be, '... the summer I grew up.'

Susan saw it as the summer we all, '... grew older, not the same thing at all.'

I was in exam hell and my lack of revision should have been a worry. Susan was trying to enjoy her hairdressing training at the salon. Bazzer was finishing his electrician apprenticeship and using his skills to patch up the band's flaky PA. Dimitri was still in college, doing as little as he could get away with – which, being a handsome Greek drummer with charm to match his locks and beard, was quite a lot.

We were rehearsing often and, thanks to Bazzer, with discipline. And if that wasn't enough, Bazzer was round our house at least twice a week. Partly he came to continue my bass lessons and to impart his views on the history of rock music and which bands I should listen to. But mostly it was to see Susan. She told Dad, frequently, that Bazzer deserved payment for giving me lessons. He responded that allowing Bazzer close to his daughter was reward enough, and laughed gently at Bazzer's embarrassment. Mum, when she was there, laughed on cue, but I didn't think it light or natural. Most of the time she was in her bedroom or the conservatory, slowly adding to the embroidery, not hiding or avoiding, but unsure and anxious. Sometimes I asked her why, as gently as I could, but she couldn't say, and I couldn't understand. That she was unhappy was a confusing heaviness for her, both mental and physical, but it was the occasional fleeting glimpse of despair in her face that was

155

frightening and meant I didn't ask often, despite feeling ashamed.

Thankfully, Dad rarely asked how school was going. I'd convinced myself that if the debut gig went well qualifications were unnecessary. And even if I wanted to revise, there was no time if I wanted to see Petra more – which I did, whenever she wasn't revising. Her O Levels were still to come, and she was smart enough that they mattered, far more than my lesser CSEs. But she came to some rehearsals, and we occasionally hung out at the youth club with Vince and Oskar, caught a few bands at local pubs like The Red Lion, standing inconspicuously in a corner to check out the opposition, and made time for the cinema, sitting closer to the back row each time. I'd grown noticeably in the last few months, an inch, maybe two, taller and a little broader but still slim; skinny, Susan claimed. Petra hadn't grown taller, and though her figure had filled out a little, she was still lithe and her features fine. She occasionally let Susan trim her hair, but not to take any length, just to even the ends which were now down to her waist. After cutting, in our front room with a bathtowel on the floor to catch hair, Susan would take time to brush it through. I wondered if it would be weird to ask to do that – and decided it would, for now.

It was Petra who encouraged me to grow my hair longer. The suggestion was made a couple of days after we'd seen a re-released *Tommy*. We were at my home, listening to an album Bazzer had lent – Cream's *Wheels Of Fire* – and though we agreed we didn't 'get it', played it all the way through in deference to Bazzer's wisdom. That it was a double album, and we were nearly through the fourth side, was a testament to our faith in Bazzer. Towards the end Petra commented that, regardless of the music, a band like that needed a recognisable front man, a Daltrey, a Plant, a Frampton – all of whom had blondish, long, shaggy hair. I laughed childishly when she said 'shaggy' and shut up quickly when she frowned.

Later that evening I caught sight of my reflection and yes, my hair was more blonde than brown and yes, needed a cut – but not for a while.

When I casually mentioned to Susan that Petra had casually mentioned longer hair, she agreed, with the proviso that I, '… understand something's different if she's telling you what to look like.'

I didn't get what she meant. More importantly it was an indication that at least one other person, Petra, saw my future as I dreamt my own.

When not practising, rehearsing or revising, Petra and I hung round the park. The warmer and lighter evenings were slow and easy and we fell into a routine of meeting up by the roundabout after tea, wandering to the off-licence for a can of Coke, holding hands, then back to the park to sit on the bench by the swings, not letting hands go. Sometimes we talked a lot, often we didn't. Occasionally, Vince and Oskar joined us. I'd bring my tiny AM radio to listen to Radio Caroline. Always, I would walk her home. If the light was fading we'd kiss on the porch, each time with increasing abandon. Then I'd go home and practise when I should have been revising.

One Saturday evening in May, Bazzer brought in fish and chips for all, paid for by Dad. It was a treat he insisted on, an old fashioned family Saturday night to celebrate the end of my CSE exams, as he told Vi when she came round. I doubted there was much to celebrate. Susan and Bazzer transferred the food to hot plates from the oven, while Dad put on an old Shadows album, calling to Bazzer he should listen to some, '… proper guitar.'

Susan nudged him and he pushed his hair away from his face to murmur an agreement that Dad couldn't hear. I took in salt, vinegar, ketchup and cutlery. Vi made a pot of tea.

Petra buttered bread. For a couple of minutes the downstairs was a procession of dedicated preparation until there were seven of us squeezed around the dining table. There were comments on how good the fish was, Vi thanking Dad for buying, Bazzer insisting he'd contribute, Susan telling him not to be silly, and me slipping in a joke about the saddest fish being a battered sole, which Petra explained to Vi. Mum ate sparingly, avoiding eye contact.

'I s'pose you two are going down The Railway later?' Dad asked Susan and Bazzer, piling chips into a butty.

'It's Sofia's birthday. They'll do a lock-in I expect.'

'Can we come?' I asked, meaning me and Petra.

'We're not rehearsing tonight,' Susan said, and Dad was quick to add,

'No. Too young. And we're having a family night in. *New Faces* is on.'

I groaned.

'I've been asked to do a turn at the summer ball and need some ideas. *New Faces* usually has a comedian or two. Besides, Mum likes it. And Vi,' Dad explained.

'We're just here for the fish and chips,' teased Vi, sprinkling salt and smiling.

'But you can stay a while.'

'For a while,' agreed Vi, 'and I ...' she looked at Petra, 'we, also wanted to let you know we might need to go back to Ireland for a little while. My sister's taken a turn for the worse.'

Mum looked to Dad. I looked to Petra.

'I'm sorry, Vi. For how long?' Mum asked.

'Not sure. A few weeks perhaps. Nothing's arranged yet.'

'What about the salon job?' I asked. Susan had helped get Petra a Saturday job at the salon.

'I don't know. What do you think?' Petra looked to Susan.

'I think Eileen will have the hump. I told her what a good worker you'd be.'

'Sorry.'

'Never mind, we'll cross that bridge when it comes.'

'Would you tell her for me?' Petra asked cautiously.

'I could, but if you'd like to get back in there when you return, you'd be better talking to her yourself. Explain about your aunt,' said Susan.

Petra looked down.

'I'll come with,' I offered.

The table went quiet.

Susan laughed quietly. 'Leave it with me.'

'But still, you don't want to lose the job. Do you have to go?' I tried to make it a casual question.

'Ah, I'm sorry Mikey, but my sister's proper poorly and we should see her,' Vi answered for Petra.

'Yes, you should go,' said Mum, not looking up from her barely touched food.

'You'll be all right,' said Vi, 'and we won't leave until Petra's finished her O Levels.'

'Two or three weeks then?' I asked but no one answered. The table went quiet again. Again, Susan broke the silence.

'JB, this'll cheer you up. Tell him, Bazzer.'

I was embarrassed it was so obvious I needed cheering but shouldn't have been. These people knew me, and I should be grateful for that.

Bazzer glanced round the table. I was amused that Bazzer's stage confidence was not so easily transferred.

'Go on,' prompted Susan.

'It's no big deal. I ... we ... think that you need your own bass. Full size, I mean. Can't keep playing mine and your junior one's too ... junior.'

Susan interrupted. 'So, we got you a proper bass. A Fender something or other. Secondhand, bit knocked about, but Bazzer has fixed it up and it's yours. You can pay us back out of gig earnings, a few quid at a time.'

'It's in the van, outside. Decent hard case too,' Bazzer finished.

'Full size, Fender?' I was disbelieving. 'That's ... I'll pay you back. I already have money saved from the car wash job. What colour? How many pick-ups? You're not taking the mickey? Really?'

Susan smiled at Bazzer. He looked both embarrassed and proud.

Mum put down her knife to reach over and squeeze first my hand, and then Susan's.

'Does that mean you won't be JB anymore?' Petra asked.

'Nah,' said Susan, 'he'll always be JB.'

Dad offered to pay for the guitar, but Mum said quietly, 'No, as a musician he needs to pay for it, from his earnings. A proper musician. It's who you are, as well as what you do.'

I was speechless. She understood.

Susan told Bazzer to bring the guitar in from the van. I spent the rest of supper interrogating Bazzer about the pick-ups, tone controls, headstock, and repeating that the sunburst fade finish was exactly what I'd wanted. Dad teased that it was missing two strings, of course.

Everyone pitched in to clear the table, Dad keen to settle down before *New Faces* started. Susan and Bazzer went to her room to work on some lyrics, Dad shouting after them to, '… leave the door open.'

'I'm eighteen and three-quarters,' she called from the bottom of the stairs.

'Exactly,' he shouted back as he ushered everyone through to the back room.

Mum said something to him, quietly, almost a whisper, which I didn't hear but he said, 'Oh come on love, just for a little while.'

'Are you all right, April?' Vi asked.

'I thought I might have an early night. It's tiring.'

'What is?' Vi reached over to take her hand.

'All of it. And I don't mind, really, but I just hoped it would be better, by now.'

'It will, April, it will.' Dad moved to sit next to Mum, and put an arm around her.

'Yes, I think it will, but for now I just wish I didn't think about it so much.'

I wanted to ask what was so tiring, but with Dad and Vi nodding it seemed like something I should already know. I was pleased when Dad suggested Petra and I wash up.

'We're going to listen to records in the front room,' I called, as Petra and I left the kitchen.

'Door open,' Dad called back.

I turned on the dim standard lamp and closed the door, taking my new guitar from its case and placing it carefully on the armchair for examination, again. Petra took an album from the bag she had brought and set it on the turntable, sitting next to me on the sofa as the first track from *Tomorrow Belongs To Me* began.

'Alex Harvey Band?' I asked.

'Sensational. So they say.'

'Haha. Funny.' I fiddled with the leather bracelet and moved it from my right wrist to the left.

'So it doesn't catch on the new guitar?' Petra guessed, holding up her arm to show she was wearing her matching bracelet. 'It's cool of Susan and Bazzer to buy it for you together. They'll be engaged soon I expect.'

'Maybe.' I agreed then took a breath before asking, 'When will you know when you're going to Ireland?'

'I don't know. Soon.'

'My mum's gonna miss yours.'

'She'll be ok. Won't she?'

'I suppose. Is Will going with you?'

'No. He's just started a new job at the bathworks. He can't get time off. And someone needs to feed the chickens.'

'You could stay here with Will then.'

'My aunt's very poorly. Mum wants me to go.'

'Do you?'

'I should.'

'But you could stay here with Will.'

'Maybe. Have you started biting your nails again?'

'No. Are you still sucking your hair when no one's looking?' I took my hand from my mouth to fiddle with the bracelet. 'Anyway, how ill is your aunt?'

'Very.' She hesitated before adding, 'Cancer.'

I reached over to brush an imaginary piece of fluff from the guitar's headstock and gave the E string a satisfying twang. 'Does your aunt live near that statue, for Saint Teresa?'

'Yep.'

'And they prayed for her?' I rested back alongside her.

'Of course.'

'Did Saint Teresa cry?'

'I don't know. C'mon, I'll be going home soon.' She leant towards me.

We kissed with relaxed passion. Since the day of the fete and cemetery we were more obvious with each other and it had been easy to slip into instant fervour. It was no longer necessary to hesitate or plan. It was ok if the setting wasn't perfect or the timing a little awkward. There was confidence that this was a shared desire, comfort that neither understood what we were doing, and excitement at where it might ... must ... lead. Forgetting, not ignoring, the next room, we pressed together on the settee, kissing quickly then slowly, lightly, then deep. Petra cradled the back of my head and I stroked her back, daring to ease my hand to her hip, then her thigh. She kissed me harder. She smelt both sweet and musky and felt both firm and yielding. With no thought, as my impulse quickened, so my chest tightened, and I raised a hand to cup her breast. Though delicate, petite, it was heavy in my touch. Petra's response was an urgent tension.

The sound of the door handle turning jolted us apart. We sat awkwardly, my arm still around Petra's shoulder.

'Ha, nearly,' Susan laughed as she entered.

'We're just listening to ...,' I waved vaguely at the record deck.

'Of course. It's warm in here, you two look quite flushed. Me and Bazzer are going down The Railway. Just thought we'd say g'bye.'

Behind her in the doorway Bazzer waved apologetically.

As she turned to go, Dad shouted from the back room, 'Hey, you lot, come and settle this. There's a band on and I reckon they're miming but Vi thinks not. You guys are the musicians. You should know.'

Susan went to see. Reluctantly Petra and I joined them, and Dad asked us to put on the kettle. My sigh was in exasperation; The Sensational Alex Harvey Band still played in the front room.

Susan and Bazzer went to the pub. Petra and I waited for the kettle to boil and were persuaded into a game of Newmarket. Dad provided everyone's twenty-five pence stake.

It was not half an hour later that the phone rang and the concern in Dad's voice stopped the game. The call ended with him promising to, '... be there in five minutes,' and calling from the hall, 'there's been some trouble at The Railway, we should pop round.'

'Susan?' Mum didn't hide her panic.

'No. That was her on the payphone at the pub. She's fine. It's Vince. Susan says we should take him home.'

Dad went upstairs for a jacket. Petra followed me out and sat on the telephone seat as I put on trainers.

'Don't forget Kay's albums.' I nodded towards the front room.

'I'll leave 'em here. Have a proper listen. You can bring them back during the week. My mum's working lates and Will is usually at rehearsals on Thursday nights.' She finished with a whisper as Dad came down the stairs.

We walked to The Railway to find Vince sitting on the car park's low brick wall, Susan standing over him. She answered Dad's question.

'He tried to buy a drink but Sofia's not behind the bar tonight. The new girl told him to go away, but less polite. He got arsey and before me or Bazzer could step in, there was a row and then the landlord threatened to lump him and Vince knocked over a glass, by accident, and someone started shouting then Sunny Steve brought him out here.'

'Is he drunk?' Dad asked.

'Don't know. He's talking rubbish and slurring but doesn't smell of beer. He seems happy enough.'

'Let's take him home.'

'Home?' I tapped Dad's arm. 'You know what his dad's like. Should we wait a bit?'

Susan agreed.

Dad thought for a few seconds. 'Ok. For a little while. You stay with him, I'm popping in for a pint.'

'You going back in?' I asked Susan.

'In a minute. I'll have a fag out here first. Best Dad doesn't see.'

'He knows.'

'Of course.'

Vince stood and began walking to the shops.

'Where you going?' I called after him.

'Launderette, drink machine, I want a can.' Vince shouted over his shoulder.

'This is not how I want to spend Saturday night. Bazzer in the pub with my dad while I watch someone's grey knickers in a tumble drier. Is that a skid mark? It's revolting.' Susan turned from the rumbling machine.

'Sorry,' Vince mumbled.

'It's ok. They're not your knickers,' I tried to joke. Vince laughed and sipped from a can of Vimto. The door to the street was open and the evening was warm, exaggerating the damp of the launderette. The sun had set below the parade of shops, but the neon lights barely spilt through the plate glass to the pavement, leaving the launderette both contained and exposed, stage-like. Vince and I sat on the bench in the window.

'You don't need to stay,' I said to Susan. 'Tell Dad we're here and I'll wait for him.'

'I'll give it ten and another fag.'

I looked to the red plastic clock above the washing instructions on the wall. It was just gone nine.

'Skid mark. Haha. I just got that.' Vince laughed, almost a giggle.

'What have you been drinking, Vince?'

'Nothing. Fancied a lager top though. Sofia wouldn't serve me.'

'That wasn't Sofia. You should have asked someone to get it for you.'

'You?' Vince looked to Susan.

'No, I think you've had enough, whether you've been drinking or not.'

'And that's why I wish I had a big sister. You're pretty tonight.' Vince turned to me. 'Not you. Susie. But, you know,' he paused, alternately smiling and frowning, 'I've never really fancied your sister, just wanted one like her. Can I have a fag?' He switched back to Susan.

'Since when do you smoke?' She passed him the pack and a box of matches.

'Since … since my old man wants me to be a mechanic.' He laughed, then was serious. 'Do you know who I do fancy?'

'No,' said Susan, 'and your secret is safe with us.' She humoured him and turned back to the machines.

'Yep. Secret.'

'He is drunk, or something,' said Susan.

'Susie's a good big sister.'

Susan indicated I should join her at the driers. Not bothering to whisper, the machines were loud, she said, 'I didn't tell Dad, but I think Sunny Steve gave Vince a joint earlier. Oh my God! Those sheets … is that blood?' Susan's face was a contortion of disgust.

I stood beside her, watching through the porthole as the sheets rose and toppled. We were both repulsed and hypnotised by the tumbling linen. To the melody of *Saturday Night At The Movies* I sang, 'Boring night at the launderette, who knows whose knickers we'll see…'

Vince sniggered.

'Hilarious.' Susan was sarcastic.

'If it helps, I'd rather be home, with Petra. Before she goes back to Ireland.'

'It doesn't help. Anyway, she'll be back.'

'Yeah but … a few weeks … that's …'

'… an age. I get it,' Susan looked at me, 'and will feel even longer. But hey, the Zamara'z gig is soon. Concentrate on rehearsals and practise. And you heard what Mum called you earlier.'

'A proper musician? She really gets it, right?'

'Right. Don't let her down. And you need to get used to your new guitar.'

'I'll pay you back.'

'Good.'

'You and Bazzer went halves?'

'Something like that.'

'Petra thinks you and Bazzer will be engaged soon.'

'Does she? I'm way too young,' Susan laughed quietly.

'That would be a moment, right?'

'You'd hope so.'

'I suppose you and Bazzer have had a few more?' I asked. The washing bundled to a halt as the drier finished.

'Maybe.' Susan was cautious.

'What if Petra meets someone in Ireland? Before me and her have any … moments.'

'She might not be going. Anyway, I hope you weren't just about to have a moment when I came into the front room tonight.'

'No. 'course not.'

'Good. They're not just about sex.'

'I know.'

'But speaking of sex, have you two?'

'Mind your own business.' I looked over my shoulder to Vince, looking vacantly out of the window.

'Fair enough,' said Susan, 'and I know she's already sixteen but you're not yet.'

'Next month,' I said defensively.

'And she's Catholic.'

'So are we, sort of.'

'Barely and not proper, not like Mum and Vi and maybe Petra. They don't believe in contraception. Though it doesn't seem to stop Collette at the salon, but that's not the point.'

'What is?'

'Sex with Petra isn't necessarily gonna be special first time and you better not get her pregnant. Never mind Dad, I'll kill you.'

'We're not stupid.'

'Really? And it needs to be Petra's idea or not at all. And even then, it better be more special for her than you. That way there'll be more special times to come.'

'What?'

'If I have to explain, then maybe you just … shouldn't, yet. But, in case …' she rummaged in her small denim handbag and found two condoms. 'Do not let Dad find them and if he does, do not tell him where you got them.'

Embarrassed, I slipped the two small foil packets into my back pocket. I wasn't sure I wanted them. While the fantasy appealed, the reality might be daunting, but then I couldn't say no to the fulfilment at which they hinted and which I so desired. I wanted to understand better Susan's advice but she had moved on, telling me to keep an eye on Vince. She was going back to the pub. 'See ya, Vince.'

Vince watched her leave then called me over.

'Susie isn't my secret.'

'Just as well, 'cos it wouldn't be a good one.'

'Oskar.'

'What?'

'Oskar's the secret.'

'You have been smoking something. What are you on about?'

'Nothing. Doesn't matter. I'm a fucking idiot.'

'What about Oskar?'

'Petra hasn't said anything?'

'Not really, at least, not much.'

Vince started to speak, stopped then whispered, 'Shit,' and ran outside. He threw up on the pavement as Dad arrived and waited for Vince to stop heaving.

'You better stay with us tonight. I'll ring your father.'

I struggled to sleep, alternating between reliving, and enhancing, that evening's brief intimacy with Petra, and worrying that she might be going away. I woke early and went downstairs. Crumpled sheets and pillows were discarded on the sofa, the candy striped cotton incongruous against the browns and oranges of the wallpaper and furniture. An unused plastic bowl was on the floor.

'Vince left half hour ago,' Dad said from the kitchen, 'by the time I came down he'd gone.' He cradled a cup of tea. The radio was on low volume. 'Did you find out what he was drinking?'

'No.'

'His dad wasn't happy when I rang him.'

'That's not what you said last night.'

'No point in Vince worrying.'

I watched Dad sip. He looked tired but, when he caught me looking, smiled and asked, 'What's on today then?'

'Practise. Need to try the new guitar.'

'Your bike needs a clean and the front brakes look skew-whiff.'

'I hardly ride it.'

'Summer's nearly here. You will. I'll give you a hand checking, then I need to set up Mum's new sewing machine. You can help with that. She'll be needing it soon.'

My lack of enthusiasm matched his lack of conviction.

I cycled to Petra's on Thursday evening, canvas shopping bag swinging from the handlebars, containing Kay's albums. There was a drizzle and my Harrington was a darker shade of green when I arrived, my hair flat to my head. Petra laughed at my flares tucked into my socks. She took my jacket and passed me a tea towel to dry my hair.

'How're the chickens? Do the others miss Ingrid?' I asked.

'Not as much as me and Mum.'

'Is Will looking after the fence?'

'Just about. He spends most of his time practising with his new band.'

'Like tonight?'

'No, something happened. He's watching telly.'

'Oh.'

'S'ok, we can go upstairs. Bring Kay's albums.'

I followed her. This was my first time in her room. It was tidy and plain and smelt of soap. A mono record player and cassette player topped a chest of drawers and the bedside table held three tidy stacks: books; singles; cassettes. The light cotton yellow blind was down, filtering the low summer sun into the room. There was just one poster on the wall, over the bed: Peter Frampton.

'You know he doesn't play bass, right?'

'Haha. Here.' Petra threw me a black t-shirt with The Who logo hand-drawn. 'It's the third attempt.'

'Mine? That's so cool. Thanks.'

'It's not as good as Kay could do.'

'It is.' I held it up.

'It isn't. Try it on. I did one for me too.'

She turned her back and began removing her blouse. I hesitated. Without turning she said, 'Best wait outside.'

'This fits well,' I said, from the landing.

'Show me.'

169

We looked at ourselves in the mirror and laughed in unison. 'Let's not wear them at the same time though.'

'Best not,' said Petra, clicking play on her cassette player. 'Guess who this is,' she challenged, sitting on the bed.

I sat beside her but half raised myself to tug from a back pocket the odd change, door key and one of the sealed foil packets that dug into my flesh. As it dropped to the bed I realised the mistake and placed a hand over it, trying to pretend it wasn't there. Petra took a couple of seconds to make sense of what she'd seen. 'What's that?'

'Er ...' I fumbled for words, any words. 'Shit, I forgot.'

'Forgot? Forgot you had a johnny in your pocket? Saturday was good but ...'

'Sorry.'

'You remembered I'm Catholic, right?'

'Of course.'

'And ...?'

'I didn't mean we should try it.'

'Try ... it?'

'Not it, as in ... it. I mean I just thought, like Susan did, you know, just in case, not that we should, or shouldn't.'

'Susan? She thinks you, we ... need one. What have you told her?'

'Nothing. She said we shouldn't. But, just in case ...'

'You bought one anyway? I hope it wasn't from the chemist in the parade. They know my mum.'

'Susan gave it to me.'

'Susan?'

'Yeah, but that doesn't mean she thinks we should. And you are Catholic and all that.'

'Oh, so if I wasn't Catholic, you think I would?'

'I'm sorry. I didn't mean to bring them. I'd forgotten they were there.'

'You've more than one?'

I pulled out the second packet from the same pocket. 'I didn't want to leave them in my bedroom.'

'Of course not,' she answered with heavy sarcasm, 'but you think we might ... you know?'

'I suppose. One day?'

'Only suppose? You don't want to?'

'No. Yes. Of course, but not now.'

'Now, as in today? But tomorrow's ok?'

'Yes. No. Not tomorrow, especially, but one day, it would be ... nice, wouldn't it?'

'Nice?'

'No. Not nice.'

'It wouldn't be nice?'

'I don't know. I'm sorry. I shouldn't have brought them.'

She half-laughed, finding a small, zipped compartment for them in her purse. 'I'm not that much of a Catholic. I'll look after them and, maybe, one day, I'll remind you, but it'll be a while yet. I need to talk to Mum first.'

'Wow, you really do share everything. Steely Dan.' I said, referring to the cassette and keen to change the subject.

'Kay made a copy for me.' She stored her handbag in the bedside table.

'Bazzer says it's pretty good.'

'Never mind Bazzer. What do you think?'

I listened for half a minute. 'S'ok but needs ...'

'... more bass, I know,' she interrupted, laughed, then leant over to kiss me.

'Oi JB! Leave my sister alone and turn that shit off,' said Will, standing on the landing, looking into Petra's room. I hadn't heard him come up the stairs. 'No one dances to that. Come to tell me you want to join my band? I hear you can sing a bit too. I might have a job for you, and we've got three paid gigs lined up already.'

'No thanks, I don't know any Bay City Roller songs.'

'Very funny. But seriously, turn that off.' Will indicated to the cassette.

Petra turned the volume up. Will went to his room, calling, 'Matching t-shirts is naff,' before slamming the door.

'He's probably come up for a joint. He knows Mum won't be home for a couple of hours. Dad would never have let him. He gets them from Sunny Steve.' Petra explained.

'He's not the only one.'

'You don't ...'

'No. Dad would kill me.'

'Susan?'

'Not sure. Fags yes, but weed? Don't know. Haven't smelt it but anyway she's over eighteen. Can do what she likes.'

'Who then?'

I hesitated, unsure if I was breaking a confidence but wanting to share with Petra. 'Vince. At least we think so. You know he was chucked out of The Railway on Saturday? He was acting weird, and Susan thinks Sunny Steve gave him a joint.'

'Acting weird?'

'A bit strange. He also said he had a secret, but ... you know what you said about Vince hanging round Oskar.'

'What? Like the other day, in the park. You weren't there, probably at rehearsal, again. Oskar said something about going back to Poland for the summer and Vince got the hump. A bit arsey, then looked all upset. Like he needs Oskar around.'

'Yeah, that's the secret.'

Petra was thoughtful. 'Not a surprise. Poor Vince. Don't you think?'

'I don't know. I'm not sure what it means.'

'Really?'

'I mean, I know what it means, but not what it really ... means. I suppose I've not thought about it much.'

'Maybe you're just too busy being you.' She said with a hint of criticism. 'Point is, if he told you, he wants you to know. Probably needs someone to know. We should go down the park, see if he's there.'

'Or we could stay here and listen to Steely Dan.'

'No, we should see if he's ok. But not in matching clothes,' she said, standing and removing her t-shirt. I tried not to be seen watching but she said, 'What? No difference to a bikini top.'

I pretended indifference, not commenting that I hadn't actually seen her in a bikini, and wondering why she hadn't let me in the room when she first changed into the t-shirt.

'A girl at school,' she continued, 'had a belly-button piercing last week. Just looks silly if you ask me.'

I nodded, distracted. There was a small mole to the left of her chest, just next to the start of the gentle swell at the top of her breast. I looked away, just.

Miracle Number Four

Chapter 19
Summer 1976
The Party
'Tears Of A Clown'

'Twenty years ago today. Eleventh June, Nineteen Fifty Six. It was a Monday.'

'Twenty years,' Mum agreed with Dad.

They sat opposite each other at the small dining table in the kitchen. I stood by the toaster, waiting for it to pop.

'Twenty years today, Mike. Your mother wore a cream …'

'Ivory,' she interrupted.

'… dress. Delicate embroidery, by Mum, long sleeves, long veil. Like a net curtain.'

'It's called voile.'

'Of course. Beautiful, Mum and the dress. It's in the loft. I bet it still fits. Twenty years. And do you know the first song we ever danced to, Mike?'

'*Unchained Melody*, Dad.'

'Jimmy Young's original. Hammersmith Palais. Special song, special nights, special lady. Dance?' Dad went round to her side, holding out a hand.

'Later. Lots to do for tonight.' Mum took the hand and stood but neatly swerved to one side and out to the hall.

I laughed and buttered hot toast.

It was a Friday, and Dad had taken the day from work. Mum had taken a lot of pills.

Lawrence had complained about Dad being off work but, for once, Dad insisted. It was a special day, and we were hosting a party. There was much to organise. Mum had been reluctant until Dad sifted through the old photographs, showing those of their special day, including inside the church. They had persuaded the priest that although Dad wasn't Catholic any children would be raised as such. That they had, loosely, was a source of some pride to Mum. That

175

they hadn't, quite, was a guilt I think she struggled with, especially as neither Susan nor I went to the Catholic school, like Petra.

I went with Dad to the off-licence where he negotiated a sale or return deal for beer, lager and soft drinks – he had spirits at home, having stocked up over the last few months.

Susan took the afternoon from the salon to make sandwiches. Vi and Petra made cakes. I stayed out the way by tuning and retuning both my bass and Susan's new acoustic; I inherited the old one – to which I fitted new strings. Mum flitted through the house, adding decorations, straightening cards, rearranging furniture. It was a hot, heavy day and she slowed as the afternoon wore on. By five, she had been persuaded to nap for half an hour. Vi and Petra went home to change. Dad readied the music centre and set up some flashing lights that Bazzer had built, using a set of old traffic lights Sunny Steve had 'found'.

Bazzer was the first guest. He checked to make sure Dad had set the lights up properly then went upstairs to see if Susan was ready.

By eight, more guests had arrived, including Dad's workmates, keen to start on the free bar set up in the conservatory. Vi and Petra were also among the first to arrive and my compliment that Petra's floral print cotton dress was 'a summer treat, just like you,' had been part Susan's and part my idea. Her smile and kiss, while Vi was watching, made the forethought worthwhile. We wore our matching bracelets, with no prior agreement.

By nine, some of Mum's old sewing group friends had arrived, then Lawrence, with his wife, Elsie, and Vince and Oskar in tow. Dimitri followed and when I told him where Bazzer was, went straight upstairs and into Susan's room without knocking. From the bottom step I heard Susan shout an insult and the thud of something heavy against the door. Dimitri retreated, laughing. As he passed me on the way down he said, 'I wouldn't let someone do that to my sister if they're not engaged.' He winked and went to find a beer.

Dad moved between rooms, switching records, serving drinks, telling jokes, offering cigarettes. Mum stood in a corner of the conservatory, sipping sherry and thanking guests for coming. She looked regal in a lilac cotton, sleeveless dress, though the neckline was high. She never wore low cut dresses even though no scars from her operation would be visible.

Petra and I squeezed on the telephone chair in the hall, watching the comings and goings, guessing the next song as quickly as we could from the opening bars, and shaking our heads at some of Dad's choices – *Yellow Submarine?!* We each had a can of Carling, though I didn't much like the taste.

Susan and Bazzer finally came downstairs as Sunny Steve came in with Sofia and her younger sister, Kay. Susan took Sunny Steve to one side and though I couldn't hear, Susan's manner was firm and Steve both shook his head and nodded obediently.

I said, 'Hello,' to Kay and tried not to be conspicuous as I listened to her and Petra gossiping. Their chatter was effortless and bonding, the content irrelevant, the sharing was all.

More guests arrived.

The house was crammed, the music centre blasted, Bazzer's traffic lights flashed furiously, and Dad worried if there was enough beer. Lawrence held court in the front room. Vince and Oskar sat in the kitchen. Dimitri appeared to be chatting up one of Mum's sewing club friends, disregarding, or perhaps relishing, the age gap.

I finished my Carling, enjoying relaxed senses and mild dizziness. The last time I'd felt this had been Christmas, when Susan sneaked me a couple of after dinner sherries. Dad had known. I smiled at Petra and indicated we should go to the conservatory for another drink. We edged through the crowd, Kay following, casually picked up a can each from the makeshift bar and went out to the garden. The sun had dropped below the roofs, and we sat on the small lawn. The noise and light from the house placed the party as if on a giant screen. The conservatory was an organised clutter of drinkers, smokers and chatters, ebbing and flowing to and from the lounge. Mum stood in a corner, quietly smiling, occasionally answering a question. The kitchen was less crowded, and we could see Vince and Oskar.

'What do you think of Oskar? Fancy him?' Petra asked Kay.

'He's all right. Looks good. Dresses well. Talks a bit odd though.' Kay was overly matter-of-fact.

'He's Polish. Do you want me to set you up?' I asked.

'And upset Vince?' said Petra.

'Why?' Kay asked.

'Vince is all right,' I said.

Petra laughed. 'I'm not saying he isn't. I like him. I'm just saying he might not like Kay being with Oskar.'

'Oh, Vince is the one you told me about?' Kay remembered.

'Yep. And he's a lovely guy. But he pays a lot of attention to Oskar.'

'What about Oskar then?'

'I don't know. Let's find out.' Petra left Kay and me in semi-darkness on the lawn and went up to the house, tapping on the kitchen window. She motioned to the two boys they should join her. They came out through the back door, ignoring two figures arguing in the alley.

I watched the three of them walk over, silhouetted against the house lights. Petra introduced the boys to Kay and there was no awkwardness as they swapped potential common acquaintances and moaned about the exam timetable.

For me, the chatter and music drifted into the background. The air was warm but the grass cooling. A gentle carelessness lightened my thoughts.

'What are you smiling at?' Petra disturbed me.

I lifted my can. 'The Carling is cold, the night is hot, I'm with friends and my girlfriend is the prettiest one here.'

'You're half-cut already,' she teased.

'Which doesn't mean it isn't all true.'

The evening turned quickly.

Kay and Oskar had clicked and, even I had to admit, they looked suited. Oskar was tall and athletic and hadn't broken out in spots. Kay was both taller and more full than Petra, upright and strong and her dress cut low at the front. She looked older than her sixteen and a half years. Both she and Oskar had knowingly fashionable haircuts. Why wouldn't Oskar take an interest? I would, if not for Petra.

'You're staring.' Petra whispered.

'What?'

'At Kay. Staring.'

'No I'm not.'

Petra used me to push herself to standing, but not in a gentle way. 'You are. And so is Vince. In a different way.'

That was true. Though they sat mostly in shadow I could see Vince, not quite sulking, smoking furtively, casting glances at Kay and Oskar.

I watched Petra go to the conservatory. Mum was still there, still in the corner, still sipping sherry. She lit a cigarette, I rarely saw her smoke, but extinguished it after only a couple of drags. Her smile was fixed, and she avoided eye contact with the guests. She lit another cigarette. I had an impulse to go to her. Half-way to the house I crossed Petra, returning with a can. She looked away but I stopped her.

'I wasn't staring at Kay.'

'You were. Vince still is.' She nodded to the three shadows sitting on the lawn.

'I know we've sort of joked about it, but you really think Vince fancies Oskar?' I asked, looking to deflect the conversation away from me.

'I don't care. It's his business. I'm more interested in you gawping at Kay. And Vince is your friend. No matter who he fancies. You should be more interested in how he's feeling than how Kay looks.'

'What? Hang on. You brought Kay and introduced her to Oskar.'

'And your point is?'

'Have you been drinking? Oh wait, yes.' I pointed to the fresh can in her hand.

She brushed past me, returning to the shadows on the lawn.

Before I could decide whether to go with Petra or to Mum, I was called.

'Hey, JB!' It was a whispered shout from the end of the alley leading to the back door. Sunny Steve was beckoning. I went over.

'Sofia's ill.' Steve directed me down the side of the house. Sofia was sitting on the step to the kitchen, head in hands, vomit at her feet. 'Needs to throw up.'

'Bit late for that, Sunny.'

Sofia looked up. Though the alley was dark there was sufficient light through the kitchen door glass that I could see her mascara had run, streaking her cheeks. 'JB?'

'Hi, Sofia. You ok?'

'Not really.' She started crying. The streaks blackened further.

'Steve can take you to the bathroom.'

'No!' Sofia's reaction was immediate. 'Get him away.'

Sunny Steve looked apologetic, offering, 'Too much to drink and maybe a little ...' he imitated smoking. 'You take her.'

'I think you should.'

'No,' Sofia was adamant. She pulled a compact from her small handbag and could see enough of herself in the poor light to cry harder. 'Bathroom,' she said, using the kitchen door to pull herself to standing.

I looked at Sunny Steve who didn't move and found myself half-following, half-guiding Sofia through the crowded house, apologising randomly and vaguely, as I directed her up the stairs. The looks of disgust or bemusement or occasional sympathy from the party guests were embarrassing. The bathroom was to the left of the landing at the top of the stairs, but the door was shut and didn't yield to my push. Sofia stumbled and fell to her knees, her crying turning to moans of self-pity. I helped her to my room and sat her on the bed. The half-closed door left her in shadow.

'Wait here a minute. Please don't throw up. I'll get a bowl.' I turned to leave but she caught my wrist.

'JB. You're a good kid. You know, a good kid. Steve's a prick.' She pulled me down to sit beside her. 'A good kid. I've always liked you. Crooked smile is cute,' she stroked my cheek, then my eyebrow, 'scar is … cool.'

I smelt the alcohol on her breath and the sickly-sweet odour of whatever she had been smoking in her hair. But beyond that was an aroma of perfume that was somehow not worn but innate, essential. She was bigger and heavier than me and easily pulled me into her, softer than Petra and both desirable and desiring in a more primal way. She liked my uneven face. I was close to losing my thoughts to instinct when I heard,

'Mum? Mum?'

Close to panic I pushed myself away from Sofia, took a breath and went out to the landing.

'Petra? You all right?'

She was surprised to see me, nearly as shocked as I was to see her.

'Your mum asked me to find mine. I think she needs some help? Or something. Have you … Jesus.'

Petra's face showed the horror of seeing Sofia walk out of my bedroom behind me, fiddling with the front of her button up dress.

'What's the matter with you? Are you obsessed with tits or something? Kay's, now Sofia's! Mine aren't big enough?' Petra was more upset than angry.

'No, of course not. I mean, yes, they are, but I'm not obsessed. I wasn't ... we weren't.'

'Then why is she hanging out her dress?'

'What?' I looked to see Sofia still struggling with buttons. I hadn't noticed before but now, two cans of Carling down, my attention was caught. To say she was 'hanging out' was an exaggeration but perhaps not much. I had a fleeting memory of Petra's mole.

'Oh my God. See. Obsessed. But don't worry. Dick. Go back to Sofia. I'm looking for my mum, not you. Your mum needs her.'

One of Dad's Conservative Club friends was standing on the top stair, laughing at the scene. 'Don't mind me. Just waiting for the loo.'

'Fuck off,' said Sofia.

The man laughed harder. Petra shoved past him on the way downstairs. A woman came from the bathroom and Sofia pushed past me to get there, ignoring the man's protest.

I went back to my room and sat on the bed. The noise from the party downstairs was irritating. The constant stream of guests to the bathroom was irritating. That Sofia had been so stupid was irritating. That I had been even more stupid was, well, even more stupid. That Petra had misunderstood was frustrating. Or had she? Would it have been a misunderstanding even two minutes later? Fucking idiot. Stupid. The music from the party was louder. Someone, please tell me not Dad, had put on *Three Steps To Heaven* and turned up the volume. This was not the party I had imagined.

I needed a distraction. Closing the door and nearly shutting out the music downstairs, I picked up Susan's old acoustic, strumming the opening to *Seagull* – I might need to play it at the Zamara'z gig in a few weeks and needed to be better, much better. But tonight it was not in my fingers. After less than a minute I set the guitar down and stood at the window, looking out to the garden. Light from the house gave an orange tint to the otherwise dark outlines of Petra and my friends. Mum was now outside with Vi. I wondered what Petra had said to them and watched as she walked back to the house with Oskar and Kay.

I waited, I don't know how long, before wandering downstairs. It must have been late as most guests had drifted away. Dad was sifting through the seven-inch singles in the dark front room. Vi was in the kitchen, washing glasses and passing them to Susan who dried. I heard the opening to *Unchained Melody,* followed by Dad calling me to go and bring Mum. I found her still in the conservatory and wondered if the glass in her hand was the original sherry. She followed me back to the front room where my happily drunk father held her close to dance. I stood in a corner, watching. Susan came in, dragging Bazzer who looked uncomfortable until she pulled him to her and kissed him as they turned slowly to the music. Mum watched them over Dad's shoulder and smiled. The traffic lights still flashed and the bouncing red, orange and greens were a confusing splatter of sudden light, suddenly gone, suddenly back. A couple I didn't know leant heavily against each other and swayed clumsily. The Righteous Brothers sang. The room smelt of incense; I've no idea why. In the far corner a woman sat on a man's lap, their faces joined, his hands roaming and pressing. I thought I knew the woman, then recognised Dimitri's long hair. She was much older than him but there was confidence in Dimitri's lust. Then I thought about how little older Sofia was than me and left the room. From the dark hall I could see the kitchen. Vi was at the sink, still washing glasses. She didn't see the man come in through the back door. His movements were sharp, hard and somehow absurd as he unhesitatingly grabbed her. She called out in disturbed surprise as he pressed into her from behind, hands reaching round to her front, his face buried into the side of her neck, mumbling. She called out again, this time scared and pushed herself away from the sink, trying to turn. But he held her tight, and she half screamed something I couldn't understand as she rocked backwards against the table. He crashed into it hard, the shock causing him to let her go and she was able to spin round. There was fear and anger in her face, and she slapped him twice before backing away. The scene was theatrical, unreal, farcical, and I looked to the front room, expecting someone, perhaps Dad, to run out, but time and movement was frozen. Nothing happened until Vi scrabbled to grab something, anything, and cutlery came to hand. The man stood away from the table and was gone, returning through the back door. As he went I saw his face – Lawrence; Dad's boss, Vince's dad. Vi was left standing at the sink, breathing hard, studying the spoon in her hand. She didn't look down the hall but closed the back door and went to the sink, steadying herself on the worktop.

'Where have you been?' Vince was still under the apple tree and offered me a cigarette which I declined, then his can, which I took.

I sipped. 'That's horrible warm.' I handed it back, wanting to mention seeing his Dad with Vi in the kitchen, but to what end? And I was almost doubting it had happened. Why would it have? How would it have? Might Vince have seen it through the kitchen window? 'Is your mum still here?' I asked instead.

'Nah, she got bored with Dad's drinking and left ages ago. He doesn't care what the doc says about his heart. She's fed up telling him.'

'Is your Dad about?'

'I think he just left. Through the alley. You missed Sofia chasing Sunny Steve with a stiletto.'

'Is this how parties are supposed to go? Dimitri got off with a woman who taught us in junior school.'

'My mum and dad's are much worse, or better, depending on your view, I suppose. Oh, and Oskar walked Kay and Petra home earlier. Sounds like you've been a prat.'

Someone put on *Tears Of A Clown* and turned up the volume.

I took the can for another sip. 'I know. Not so much as I nearly was, but yeah. Petra says I'm obsessed with tits.'

'We heard. You're nearly sixteen. Of course you are.'

'You?'

'Not as much as I sometimes wish.'

I looked at him. The light from the conservatory barely reached us and his eyes were in shadow, but also dark.

'Do you? Wish that?' I asked.

'Sometimes. It would make things simpler.'

'I don't really understand.'

'Nor do I.'

'Did you mind Oskar taking Kay and Petra home?'

Vince dragged on his cigarette before whispering, 'Yes.'

'After what you said the other night, does it mean you and Oskar … you know?'

'No. But …'

'You, er, like him?'

'A bit.'

I took the cigarette from him, inhaled awkwardly, coughed violently then said, 'Is it ok if I don't get it?'

'It's ok for you, but what if I don't.'

It was true that I didn't 'get it'. Of course I knew what was meant by 'queer' or 'poof' and at school we used the terms as casual insults, but we didn't appreciate, or even try to, what it really meant to those that were, not that we knew any, as far as we knew. Did they? I don't know. Vince didn't, for sure, I don't think, and we had no idea that our casual ignorance and disdain could be truly hurtful. I had no idea how lonely and confused Vince might have been. Except even I could now see he probably was.

I forced a laugh. 'Petra was right. Doesn't matter who you fancy. Though, I must admit to being a bit surprised it's not me.'

He took back the cigarette. 'You? Too skinny and too funny. Besides, they say people we fancy let us down and I don't want that to be you.'

I was glad of the night's shadows making it difficult to be sure if Vince was crying or not.

Chapter 20
Summer 1976
The Compilation Tape
'Show Me The Way'

I was not the only one late for work at the garage on Saturday. Many of the mechanics had been at the party. Some overslept and came in late, one didn't bother at all, risking Lawrence's wrath. Dad managed to be on time, just, but then he had the keys and felt obliged. They needn't have worried. Lawrence was late, not arriving until gone nine-thirty and shutting himself away in the office out back. With the blinds lowered and door to the workshop closed it was almost a sanctuary. It had a second door leading to the alley out back so he could come and go as he pleased. It was his habit to enter through the workshop to make sure it was known he was in, but leave via the back door, unseen.

By half-ten I had washed, lazily, a Ford Cortina, and popped to the bakery for a sausage roll and pasty run, taking orders from the mechanics and keeping the change. Dad was at the reception desk, telling me to crack on with the next car – the keys were on the board in Lawrence's office. I hesitated. I had avoided thinking about Lawrence and Vi in the kitchen the previous night; more concerned with making things right with Petra. What if Lawrence had seen me in the hallway? But Dad was insistent and taking the chance I hadn't been seen was preferable to explaining why I didn't want to go to the office. Besides, the dreamlike, make that nightmare, nature of what had happened in the kitchen remained a confusion.

I knocked on the office, first softly, then harder, and was relieved there was no answer. Perhaps Lawrence had left by the back. I knocked again before turning the handle and easing the door open. The office was in semi-darkness. The blinds to the workshop were shut but the fire door out back to the alley was ajar, letting in a sliver of sunlight. Lawrence

187

wasn't at his desk. The key-board was on the wall behind the empty chair. I took a step in but pulled up sharply at the deep throated moan from behind the door, from behind me. It was so quiet that I might have imagined it, were it not repeated. I jumped forward, further into the office, suddenly frightened, turning involuntarily to see. No one stood there. Lawrence was lying on the floor, crumpled awkwardly against the filing cabinet, one hand to his face, blood glistening on the hard tiles, another moan on his lips.

I ran from the office, shouting for Dad.

By the time the ambulance arrived Lawrence had been propped up against the filing cabinet. He had sipped water between moans but offered no explanation, not even when Elsie turned up and he was loaded in the ambulance.

'It's the best place for him.' Dad pressed her arm to assure her, and stepped back to join the small crowd in front of the garage. She squeezed alongside the stretcher in the back.

Vince and I watched the ambulance leave. I told him, 'My dad'll take you to hospital later but I'm off to rehearsal in a minute. You should come along.'

'No lights or sirens. That's good, right?'

'Gotta be.'

'He fell?'

'I suppose. And bashed his head.'

'Is Petra going to your rehearsal?'

'No. We haven't spoken.'

'Well, it was only last night.'

'Spoken to Oskar?' I asked.

'No way, and what we talked about, that's a secret, right?' There was a hint of panic in his voice.

'Of course.'

'Come on, Frank, join us. Father Andrew will forgive your heathen ways. It's what we do. Forgiveness.' Vi was waiting outside St. Gregory's. Dad had walked there with Mum and me.

'No thanks, Vi. Not after my last conversation with Father Andrew. Besides, Susan is at home with Bazzer, and I don't trust the dirty little sod. I'll pop back and keep them on their toes.'

'Frank,' Mum chided gently.

'Well he is,' said Dad, 'They all are at that age. What is he? Twenty-one? You lot go and enjoy, I suppose.'

'We won't be here long, Frank,' Vi said without smiling. 'Just feel like it, eh?'

'And there I was thinking you might have a bit more faith these days,' said Vi, looking at Mum. 'Anyway, I'll pop round afterwards if that's all right. I've a favour to ask.'

'Is Petra coming?' I asked.

'She stayed home today. Perhaps she's still a bit under the weather following Friday's party.' Vi looked at me a second or two longer than necessary.

'She did have a can or two,' Dad laughed.

'That'll be it,' Vi agreed.

I followed her and Mum into church.

At Friday's party, Vi had asked Mum to come to Sunday Mass. They would be celebrating The Ascension. Mum had agreed, hoping Susan would also attend but by the time Sunday arrived, Susan had convinced me it was better I should go, after all, '… Petra will be there and Bazzer will be here. We've another song to work on.'

So, Sunday morning, here I was, but here Petra wasn't. Perhaps that was for the best. The service and proceedings continued around me, and I stood and sat on Mum's cues, enjoying the choir and recognising a couple of the hymns this time. The sermon made references to The Ascension. It meant nothing to me but its significance was obviously deep; the congregation deeply attentive. My thoughts wandered, but were drawn back sharply by Father Andrew's end notices, when he asked the congregation to include in their prayers a fellow member, 'Lawrence Stills, in hospital after suffering a heart attack.'

'Enjoy the service?' Susan asked. She was in the kitchen when we returned from mass. Bazzer wasn't there.

'I'm glad I went,' said Mum, 'I wasn't sure when I woke but I'm glad I did and feel better now. I'd forgotten how important The Ascension is. Christ rose to heaven while the apostles watched.'

'And they didn't think it a bit … odd?' I asked.

'Ha, always looking for the joke.' She patted my hand.

'You did well to go,' Vi agreed. 'And you Mike? Enjoy it?' she asked.

'The organ and choir were good.'

Dad came in from the garden, keen to share news but Vi stopped him to explain they'd already heard.

'Elsie rang while you were out,' he answered Vi's question. 'Apparently Lawrence was doing ok until the early hours when he had a heart attack. She said he's comfortable. But they always say that.'

'How's Elsie?' Vi asked.

'Shocked. Scared. Crying. I said I'd take her up the hospital later. Perhaps with his heart problem it was to be expected.' He put on the kettle.

'Anyway,' said Vi, 'I've some news of my own.' She was serious.

'Let's sit in the conservatory,' said Mum, leading Susan through.

I stood in the hall, picking at a partly bitten nail. On the walk home from church I'd avoided being left alone with Vi but was now caught off guard. As the kitchen emptied she ushered me to the front room. Dad stayed in the kitchen, waiting for the tea to brew.

She forced a smile. 'I hope poor Vince is all right. Perhaps you should pop round to see him. After all,

Lawrence is his father, even if he's an arse. Like you on Friday night, I hear.'

I held a breath. Had she seen me on Friday, when Lawrence attacked her?

'With that older girl, Sofia is it?' she explained.

I breathed out. 'What? No. I didn't do anything. Sofia was gonna throw up. Steve asked me to help. I … nothing happened.'

'Ah, well I hope not, but it's not me you've to convince, is it? Sometimes you need the things you don't do to be seen. And Petra has a stubborn streak twice her size.'

'Really, I …' I wanted to say more, to convince Vi I hadn't touched Sofia, but she was gone.

Dad opened the French doors to the garden. 'I'm so sorry Vi. Really, so sorry. You must go. We understand. She's family.'

Vi had just told us she was going back to Ireland to look after her poorly sister. Very poorly. Mum said nothing and the slight colour she had found during the morning's walk home from church was gone.

'When?' I asked.

'Probably Tuesday. We have to.' Vi made a show of checking her watch. 'I need to make a few phone calls so better get back. But I have a favour to ask. Will you look after the chickens while we're gone?'

'Well you royally fucked up at the party.' Susan laughed. We were walking to rehearsal on Sunday afternoon and well out of earshot of Mum, oddly seeing us off at the front door.

'What?'

'I rang Sofia this morning. You got lucky. She'd have eaten you alive. She says sorry. Oh, and you needn't worry about Sunny Steve. Apparently he understands.'

'I never thought he wouldn't.' I tried to sound confident. Getting on Steve's wrong side was to be avoided. 'Will you tell Petra before she goes away? Or should I pop round to see her now?'

'No time.' Susan was firm. 'We've got the use of The Railway this afternoon and we need it. Only a fortnight to go.'

'We rehearsed yesterday.'

'Which is how we know we need to rehearse today.'

'Shame she wasn't at church this morning.'

'I suppose Friday night is why she wasn't. Anyway, nothing wrong with a little jealousy, as long as it's completely unfounded. Especially as she's going away for a while.' Susan stopped out of sight of home and rested her acoustic against her hip to light a cigarette. 'And Vi didn't mention going away until you came home?'

'I guess she didn't want to worry Mum.'

'I suppose. How was church?'

'Ok. Mum seemed to enjoy and afterwards she said it was important to have been, that The Ascension really mattered, that it was an escape.'

'For who?'

'Don't know. I don't really get it.'

'Nor me. But what do I know about religion? Sweet FA. Music is ours, eh?' She tried to joke. 'Speaking of which, if we're going to play *April Blooms Again* at Zamara'z we really need to sort those harmonies.'

I nodded, then, 'Susan?'

'Yep?'

'You will tell Petra nothing happened?'

'Of course.'

'But don't tell Mum or Dad anything.'

'Mum might be able to help.'

'Do you think?'

Susan hesitated. 'No, I guess not.'

Petra and I sat on the swings, feet on floor, barely swaying to and fro but in time with each other. The sun was low, perhaps only ten minutes from slipping behind the row of houses backing onto the park. The trees made an avenue of the main path from the gate to the play area and cast long shadows. There were a few older boys still playing football and one or two dogs being walked, but no younger kids on the slide or roundabout, having long gone home. I was tired. It had been a long day. First school, then being nagged about a poor last-ever school report, then bass practise, never a chore, but I couldn't concentrate on the coming gig and gave up. Instead, I'd found a blank C90 cassette and made a tape for Petra. Now I was waiting for the right time to give it to her. She passed me a can of Coke. I sipped before asking, 'You do believe what Susan told you, about the party? About Sofia?'

She took the strand of hair she'd been chewing from her mouth. 'Honestly? I'm not sure. Though as Sunny Steve hasn't kicked shit out of you …'

'I'm sorry.' I tried to sound sincere without grovelling.

'Suppose it's ok. As Susan said, Sofia's got nice tits.'

'I do the jokes. And anyway, they're really not as nice as … you know.' I half-nodded towards her.

'I'll take that as a compliment,' Petra blushed a little, 'but it doesn't mean forgiveness, yet.'

There was nothing to forgive but I was learning and knew better than protesting too much. 'And you're still going to Ireland with your mum, right?' I returned the can.

'Tomorrow. Have to.'

'What about exams?'

'All finished, last one today. You really don't pay attention do you?'

'Your aunt's that ill?'

'I guess.'

'And you don't know how long for?'

'No. And Will is already half-way there.'

'Already?' I kicked at the groove of compacted earth under the swing.

'He had to.'

'What about his job, at the bathworks?'

'I don't know. Maybe they'll keep it for him.' Her turn to kick at the dirt.

'So why can't he look after your aunt?'

'Will? He … it doesn't matter, and anyway, it's not about looking after her, there's loads of aunts and cousins for that. Mum just wants to be there. She has to go. Really. Just has to.'

'My mum kind of needs yours, still.'

'She went to church. Isn't she nearly better?'

'Some days, not others. And what about your Saturday job, in the salon?'

'Susan will tell them for me.'

'I suppose. But you'll miss the Zamara'z gig. There's a party afterwards.'

'I'm sorry. About the gig, not the party. I didn't enjoy the last one.'

I wanted to ask if Petra knew about Lawrence and Vi but guessed she would. I hadn't spoken to anyone about it, not even Susan, and as the days passed, the memory faded. I was beginning to doubt it had happened but, in all honesty, was grateful for the doubt.

She continued, 'Oh, but a party doesn't mean you should … you know … go with Sofia.'

'Go?'

'You know … go.'

'Oh, no way, Steve really would kill me.'

'Really? That's the reason?' Petra stopped her swing. Her green eyes were close to black in the fading light.

'No, I didn't mean it like that … I mean … here.' I took the cassette tape from my Harrington's pocket. 'Ireland's a long way.'

'JB, you're embarrassed.'

'No,' I lied. 'Vince helped. I had to borrow a couple of singles from him. You were right about him and Oskar, which I still don't get.'

'You're neanderthal. Poor Vince. Oskar walked Kay home on Friday.'

'Yep, poor Vince. And he's got his dad's heart attack to think about.'

'Don't feel sorry for that prick.' Her anger was sudden.

I took a few seconds to think about the right question but before I could ask it, her smile was back. She read through the track listing. 'This is your best handwriting.'

It was. And much better than the two attempts in the bin at home.

'Side two, track one is my favourite,' I lied, though it was true to say it was the most important song there.

'What, because it has a good bass line?' Petra teased, then read from the listing, '*Show Me The Way*.'

'No.'

The darkening sky was streaked with orange, magenta and yellow as the scattering light filtered through the clouds. The sun was gone.

'And this is for your birthday.' She passed me a neatly wrapped package. 'To be opened on the day.' She stood and moved as if to peck me on the cheek but stopped. 'I need to go, finish packing. Remember, stay away from Sofia at parties.' She forced a laugh.

I had no other argument to convince her that going to Ireland was a bad idea. She knew them all and was still going.

I walked her home, not quite holding hands, and on the porch waited for her to make the first move to kiss. She did but it lacked urgency and passion. We hugged lightly for a while. I tried to think of something witty to say, but all I had was, 'Sorry.'

Mum, Dad and Susan were watching a sitcom on television, or at least, staring at the corner where the television stood. There was no laughter.

'Hi, you ok?' Susan asked, ushering me back into the kitchen and whispering, 'Vi popped round to say goodbye. She could be gone some time. Mum's upset.'

'And Petra's going with her.'

'Where Vi goes …'

'… Petra goes,' I finished.

'I'm sorry, Mike. I bet it feels shit. But she can't stay here by herself.'

I didn't see why not, or maybe stay at ours, but no one was going to believe me.

'Especially as Will has gone already,' Susan added.

'I heard.'

She lowered her voice. 'And you know why?'

'To look after the aunt. Sort of.'

'Maybe. But Bazzer thinks it's something to do with Vince's dad being in hospital.'

'Why?'

'Something Will said to Pluto, who's still friends with Dimitri who told Bazzer. Jesus, band gossip, it's worse than the salon.'

'Will and Lawrence?' I repeated for my own benefit.

'Maybe. Maybe that's why he's already left. But silver linings and all that. Will's new band were meant to be playing their debut down at The Cross Keys next month. Bazzer rang them. The gig's ours now. Our second.'

'And the second Petra will miss.'

Chapter 21
Summer 1976
Zamara'z
'Rock And Roll'

It was dry and sunny on Saturday, 19th June. Rocknow Station gathered at Steve and Bazzer's just after lunch, going over the set list, debating whether we were playing too many originals. Susan complained I was noisy and chatty. She trimmed everyone's hair, except mine; I refused. Steve went out into the garden every half hour to look up and complain about the weather should it rain while loading into Zamara'z later – it never looked like rain. Dimitri sat in the corner, flicking through an old copy of *Men Only* that Bazzer swore was either his dad's or brother's when Susan asked. Then she snatched it from Dimitri when I got bored and looked over his shoulder. Vince came round to ask if we needed help with the gear, knowing it was the only way he would get into Zamara'z. Steve reluctantly agreed, just in case it rained and the load needed to be done, 'Sharpish.' Vince and Steve sat in the kitchen and discussed the load order while smoking a joint. It seemed a natural progression for Vince and I didn't question it.

Bazzer and Steve's dad wasn't there. He never was and no one asked.

Steve and Vince loaded the van just after three. Susan and Bazzer made beans on toast for all and called us to the kitchen.

'Hey Dimitri, what do Ginger Baker and black coffee have in common?' I asked as we sat.

'I don't know, JB, but I've a feeling I'm about to.'

'They both suck without Cream.'

No one laughed. I hadn't told it well. 'I'm saving the best for later, at Zamara'z.'

Susan was the last to sit at the now crowded kitchen table. 'Mikey, you can talk to the audience a little between songs but no jokes. There's a change to the set. Here.' She handed us each a sheet of paper with a handwritten list.

The others took a minute to read, all except Bazzer, the only one not surprised.

'You've missed out *April Blooms Again*,' I said, 'we have the harmonies sussed.'

Susan started to speak but Bazzer caught her eye and was quicker, 'It's just not right for Zamara'z. And, JB, really, no jokes tonight.'

Leaning close to me, Susan spoke quietly, 'Been thinking about Thursday, a lot. I know it sounds stupid, but I don't want to tempt fate or something, not that I believe in that shit. Touch wood,' she tried to joke, tapping the body of the guitar leaning against the wall beside us.

I didn't laugh.

The previous Thursday, I'd fed the chickens as usual, after complaining, as usual, and was close to convincing Dad that it would be better to build our own coop and keep them at home. I'd made a sandwich for me and Mum and we'd sat in the kitchen, listening to the lunchtime radio show. She hadn't said much, I'd done nearly all the talking, but that was usual.

About two, I heard Susan call out to say she was home. It was half-day at the salon. I shouted down from my room then went back to the letter I was trying to write to Petra. She'd been gone two days. I could hear Susan moving about downstairs, probably making a cup of tea, as was her routine, then I heard her on the stairs.

'Ok?' She poked her head round my door.

'You should knock.'

'Why? In case you're knocking one out?' She laughed and motioned to the Sun page 3 calendar on my wall.

'Haha,' I laughed sarcastically. 'I'm writing to Petra.'

'Good. Where's Mum?'

'Downstairs? Garden?'

'No. And not in her bedroom.'

'Sure?'

Susan ignored the question, checked her own room then the bathroom, then double-checked Mum's.

'Nope.'

'Must be in the garden,' I said.

'How do you not know? You've been here all day.'

'I've been practising up here since lunch. Only two days to Zamara'z.'

Susan gave me her disappointed teacher look and went back downstairs, shouting for Mum. I followed.

'Was she all right this morning?' Susan asked over her shoulder.

'Seemed ok at lunch.'

'Let's try the shops.' There was worry, or perhaps fear, in Susan's voice.

I followed her out. We checked the parade, especially the bakery and the chemist. No sign of Mum, and Susan's fear became mine. On to the doctor's; no sign, nor at the library. I could feel my own rising panic feeding on Susan's. We jogged to St. Gregory's. There were a couple of people in the cemetery. A woman walked from the west entrance. She carried a bundle of wilting flowers and left the door open behind her.

'You check inside, I'll check the graveyard.'

I went into the church, waiting just inside the door for my eyes to accustom. I was more hopeful of finding Mum here – expecting, even, and walked the nave almost on tiptoe, the stone floor being noisy. In the front row sat a petite woman and I held my breath trying to calm my excitement so as not to make her jump. Though my eyes had adjusted it was still dark. I quickened my pace and drew alongside, smiling. The woman sensed my presence and turned. It wasn't Mum. My frozen grin was an embarrassment and I hurried back down the aisle, stopping at the door to look again over the pews in case I'd missed her. I hadn't. The short-lived joy knotted in my chest. Father Andrew emerged from behind the altar and I left the church.

'No?' Susan asked.

I shook my head.

'We need to tell Dad.'

'He'll be angry at me.'

'So?' She was frightened and my thoughts were a runaway train of possibilities, racing as fast as my heart, sparked by my own fear.

Into the park on the way to the garage. Now running. Me in front. I was stopped by Susan shouting, 'Is that Mum?'

A hundred yards or so away, sitting on the grass under the shade of a tree, was a woman in blue slacks and a yellow blouse. Was it?

Mum looked up when we were maybe thirty yards away. She was lounging on an old car blanket and was startled, taking a few seconds to recognise us before putting down the plastic cup from which she drank. She had brought a flask, of tea, probably, and a pack of Cadburys Mini Rolls, one of which was half-eaten.

'What are you doing?' Susan asked sharply.

Mum looked confused. We looked at each other and joined her on the blanket. I had a sudden anger, first at Mum and then with myself. Stupid. I should have known to check here first. This was our park; only good things had ever happened here. She was always going to be here; always safe.

'We've been looking for you everywhere,' Susan said through tears, now of relief.

'What's wrong. Oh Susie, don't cry.'

'I'm sorry, Mum. Why are you here?'

'I just wanted a picnic. But I didn't have anything in, so …' She indicated to the flask and Mini Rolls. 'But I wasn't going to walk far. So I came here. It's peaceful.'

It was. The noise of children playing added to the serenity of my park. It didn't need silence to provide calm.

'It feels ok to be tired here. Safe. It's good you're here.' She lay back on the blanket, looking at the sky before closing her eyes. I had no more idea than Susan what to say. With eyes shut Mum said, 'I'm sorry I feel so tired, all the time. No, not tired, weary.'

'Don't be sorry,' said Susan.

Without looking, Mum held out her hand for Susan to hold.

'Is that why you're in bed so much?' Susan asked, taking the hand.

'Not really. It's no safer than anywhere else, but sometimes I don't know how to get up, or why, except there are lots of reasons. Too many. And I really do want to be my old self, but what if that's not who I should be?' A bead of a tear formed in the corner of her eye. 'It doesn't matter though, or change anything,' she whispered.

'What doesn't, Mum?' I asked.

She sat up and gently took my hand away from my mouth to stop my nail-biting. 'How much I love you. That never changes. I just wish it was the only hurt. It would be worth it.'

'I love you, Mum.' Of course, but now it brought a pain I hadn't known. 'What can I do?'

She had no answer.

We'd taken Mum home and hadn't told Dad.

Now, in Bazzer's kitchen, as the others tucked into the pre-gig meal, Bazzer repeated, 'Remember, JB, no jokes between songs.'

Back stage at Zamara'z, two toilets had been knocked together and partially converted, serving as a dressing room, though it still smelt like, 'a binman's khazi,' as Dimitri put it. We changed into the stage costumes on which we'd agreed, though they were much the same as our usual clothes. No one was following Kiss's lead. I wore my cleanest jeans with a new t-shirt, a US Army jeep over a single star. I don't know why. Only Susan looked much different – she wore jeans and a gypsy style blouse with a bold flower print. There was a drawstring, the ends tied close at her neck rather than showing her shoulders. Her short mop of blonde hair was spiky. Her eye make-up was theatrically dark, after advice from Sofia, who had swapped her shift at the pub to be here and was laying out sausage rolls for later.

Vince waited at the dressing room door for the signal from Steve, standing stage-side, that it was time to go on. I was first out, on the way asking Vince, 'Do I look enough like Frampton?' and trying to mask a lopsided grin.

'Close enough.' Vince laughed and walked with me from the trashy dressing room, squeezing past empty beer barrels and crates of used bottles, to the stage. It was a small club with a small bar and a small stage, just a couple of feet above the dance floor. It smelt of last night's fags and beer. Apart from the lights behind the bar and those pointed at the stage it was ill-lit, and only the restless murmur of the crowd was an indication of how many might be waiting in the dark. I cut short thoughts that this was my debut. That didn't prevent clammy hands. Wiping them on my jeans made little difference and I wished I'd let Susan trim the fringe sticking to my forehead. I kept telling myself Winwood was as young as me when he first gigged, so was Page, Jackson, Frampton, Kossoff, Marriott, Wonder. It was no comfort – they were musical geniuses. I was a skinny suburban kid with a secondhand bass and a few jokes up my sleeve that I wasn't allowed to use.

The rest of Rocknow Station gathered next to me stage-side. We smiled at each other, and I realised they were just as nervous. Susan said to me, but loud enough for all to hear, 'It's ok to be tense, scared even. It's not ok to freeze.'

She nodded to Bazzer who was but a step short from leading us out when a big voice called from behind,

'Oi! This is not the fucking Partridge Family. Who's the kid?' The big voice was a contrast to the stature. A short man with neat hair and fine features stood behind them. He wore a pin striped suit and striped tie with Windsor knot, incongruous to the surroundings.

I froze.

'Hi, Algie.' Sunny Steve stepped between him and me.

'Algie?' Dimitri sniggered. Algie span round, pointing with two fingers, a cigarette jammed between them.

'Don't, son, just don't.' He turned his accusation to Susan. 'And she's centre stage? This isn't what you sold me, Steve.'

'Who's she? The cat's mother? Who the fuck are you?' said Susan.

'I'm the man paying your wages tonight, sweetheart.' Algie smiled. 'So you better be as good as Steve says. We don't get many girls fronting bands here, and those that do, need to have some front.'

'There's nothing wrong with my front.'

'Good. But you might want to undo that.' He raised a hand to the tied-up drawstring at her neckline. She brushed it aside. He turned back to me. 'And you'll be the wonderkid I've heard about. I hope you're as special as made out. That pissy lot out there are more Jimi Hendrix than Jimmy Osmond. Go slay the buggers, pretty boy.'

No turning back.

I followed the others on stage. Somewhere between the curtain and microphone my nerves bloomed to excitement. I was lightheaded and my heart beat sharply. There was fear of failing but, intoxicatingly, there was bright anticipation, hope of success and desire for recognition. The doubts that had been growing since the night Petra said goodbye were still there, but the need to play, the compulsion to perform was stronger.

The crowd gave an ironic cheer then sarcastic applause as we readied ourselves with final tunings. Susan adjusted the height of the stand in front of her and started to introduce the band, but stopped, glanced sideways to me, smiled and said, 'Fuck it, let's play,' into the mic. She signalled to Dimitri behind her back. He beat his sticks together for the count. The opening bars for *Under My Wheels* burst from the speaker stack, exploding into and across Zamara'z. I punched all my being into those first notes and was lifted with sound, a visceral force. The band, our band, my band, was alive and whole. I was barely able to control the energy, feeling the flow both within and from me.

We ripped through the beginning of the set.

We were tight, the music was heavy, our touch was light. Susan and I shared vocals but she was centre stage, urging or settling the crowd to suit the song, animated or still, driving and directing. And between songs the cheering crowd was its own music, both giving back, and asking for more. As Dimitri pounded the introduction to *Rock And Roll,* I looked out to the audience. Squinting past the spotlights, I saw the crowd had edged forward. A few were dancing but most were just there to listen, to feel, to be a part of us. The faces were indistinct in the dark and it wasn't until the song finished that I saw Dad, almost pinned against a wall, cigarette in one hand, pint in the other. I watched him until he caught my eye and his smile shone with pride.

The set closed with a ragged version of *Highway Star,* and we played *Stay With Me* for an encore – sung by Susan to her limit, voice cracking at the end of the set, lyrics unchanged. I doubted Zamara'z had seen or heard better. The final chord was lost in cheers, whistles and applause. Bazzer gave a shallow bow and Dimitri came from behind his kit, waving at a couple of girls close to the stage. I stood at the mic, bass guitar hanging, uneven smile fixed in place, still surfing on adrenalin. It didn't matter that I had no notion of what was expected of me, of what to do next. With no arrogance or pride I simply soaked in the thrill of knowing, of loving, something that could be experienced no other way. I looked at Susan. She looked exhausted and serious until I caught her eye. She nodded and grinned.

We stayed on stage for a couple of minutes, congratulating and thanking each other, apologising for unnoticed mistakes – I made a lot – and wishing we could do it again. Some people came on stage, mostly to be close to Susan; Bazzer made sure to stand next to her. Dad waited for the crowd to thin before climbing up to hug me and Susan. I was last to leave the stage.

The converted toilet smelt no better after the performance, though sweat, tobacco and weed was adding to the mix. The neon strip light was dimmed by the piece of net curtain that someone had draped under it, using drawing pins on the ceiling. There was no hot water and the sausage rolls were cold but we didn't care, soaked in gig afterglow. Susan sat on Bazzer's lap, sharing a bottle of pale ale between feverish kisses. Dimitri sat on the moth-eaten sofa, trying to persuade the two girls he had brought back to join him. They were more interested in Sunny Steve who was rolling joints with the offer that, 'Only the first is free.' Kay came out of the toilet cubicle, tucking in her blouse. I took two bottles of pale ale from the make-shift bar, opened them and passed one to her. 'Hi, didn't see you out front.'

'Sofia sneaked me in through the back. Reckons the manager, Algie, wouldn't let me in as I'm not eighteen. Don't I look it?'

'Dressed like that, yes.'

Kay grinned openly, very different to Petra's thoughtful smile. She had dressed similar to her sister for the night – a short black skirt with large RAF roundels and a plain white satin blouse with wing collars. The top three buttons were undone. 'Petra's right. You do have an uneven smile, a little bit.'

'I know. How was the set?' I asked.

'Good. You guys need some funk though.'

I thought Petra might have said something similar if she'd been here and said so.

'Probably. Hey, JB, I'm really sorry she went away. You ok? Have you guys been writing?'

'A little.' In the eleven days since she'd left I'd received two letters and replied to the first. Truth was, I hadn't yet replied to the second – there were only so many ways to say I'd been spending my day feeding chickens or practising for the gig. I had not the balls to write what I really wanted. 'But she'll be back soon,' I told Kay.

'I'm not so sure. I got another letter this morning. Her aunt is proper poorly.'

I wanted to ask more, but without showing I hadn't heard that from Petra. I nodded, vaguely.

'Is Vince around?' she asked.

'Helping to pack up, I think. I'm surprised Steve lets him.'

'He likes being around the band. You know his dad's out of hospital? Vince has started at the garage. He hates it.'

I nodded. We had stopped going to school, exams had finished, the wide world beckoned, and Vince's dad was already involving him in the garage.

'He won't last there,' she whispered as Vince came in, cursing. He raised a hand to show a red gash on his finger. 'Dimitri, you need to sort out that poxy wing nut on the tom holder. Nearly sliced off a finger.'

'That's why I let you pack away the kit.' Dimitri laughed.

I gave Vince my bottle and opened another, though I didn't like the taste.

'Hang on, I've a plaster somewhere.' Kay went to her bag.

'I didn't know you two were friends now?' I said quietly to Vince.

'We're not, really. But she and Oskar ... at least, she thought, Oskar and her might, but then he went back to Warsaw or somewhere. He didn't tell her until the day he left. No different from me, really. So, she turned up at my house with a couple of albums in a plastic bag, pretending she thought I might like them but mainly as an excuse to ask about Oskar.'

'And?'

'She's cool. And my mum was happy. Keeps going on about it. Dad too.'

I hesitated. 'You … we, haven't really spoken much about, you know, stuff. Like, you and Oskar?' My uncertainty left it a question. 'Did you … talk to him before he left?'

'Sure.'

'About, you know.'

'Of course not, idiot.'

I hesitated again, longer. 'Do you miss him?'

'Do you miss Petra?'

'Is it the same?' I asked, and immediately regretted it.

'Isn't it?'

'I'm sorry. I don't know. You don't talk about it.'

'You mean as much as you talk about Petra? No one does.'

Before I could answer, Kay returned to wrap a plaster round the bleeding finger. It was too small to properly cover the wound.

Sofia came into the crowded room with a bottle of Vodka. 'Your mate Algie did me a deal on the price.' She held it as a trophy to show Steve.

'You can be sure Algie's still made money on it. Tight bastard.'

'Algie's all right,' said Vince. 'When he saw I was bleeding all over the stage he gave me a hankie.'

'Sunny doesn't trust anyone,' said Sofia, ushering the two girls waiting for joints out the door. One of them protested, but only briefly as Sofia stood to her full height.

Vince, Kay and I stood just inside the door. I watched the room. As the gig adrenalin waned I floated between sadness and gentle euphoria. I occasionally sipped from the pale ale and frequently asked Kay and Vince if it really had gone well, despite knowing Vince was always going to say yes.

'And what about our own songs? Go down ok?' I asked this time.

'It was a good mix.'

'And Susan was great, wasn't she?'

'Always. Algie says you may be the prodigy but it's Susan the punters will pay to see.' Vince went to drink from his bottle, but a hand reached over his shoulder to take it.

'You three could cost my licence.' It was Algie. He took our bottles. 'But who knew the little feller had such a big voice? Well done son. JB is it?'

Algie's paternal smile disappeared as he turned to Sunny Steve. 'Where was the second encore?'

'You're not paying enough for two.' Steve's voice was light, but his eyes didn't smile. 'Here.' He passed Algie a couple of freshly rolled joints.

Algie slipped them into a top pocket. 'I'm gonna ask round the kids, see what they thought. See if they want you back.'

Susan pushed herself away from Bazzer. 'They will. Enough front for you?'

'Never enough, darling. You guys were good but don't kid yourselves, you ain't Zeppelin.'

'Yet,' said Dimitri.

Algie laughed. 'We'll see.' He turned to go but Sunny Steve took a step to block his exit, holding out a hand.

'Cash.'

'Come and see me at the end of the evening. It'll come out the takings.' Algie tried to casually brush Steve's hand aside but it didn't move.

I held my breath, watching Steve, whose calm presence carried its own threat, his jeans and t-shirt contrasting with Algie's formal suit. I'd never met anyone wearing cufflinks before. Algie forced a smile and pulled a wad of notes from an inside pocket, holding on to some pride by insisting, 'But next time it's two sets and an encore.'

'So there will be a next time,' Susan called after him.

'Don't be here long.' Algie gestured to the joints laid on the table. 'We often get the Bill wandering round after closing time.' He went out but his small head popped back.

'Look after that, it's a nasty cut.' He indicated to the plaster on Vince's hand, growing a small line of claret. 'And don't touch anything.'

'Worried about blood stains?'

'No, infection. This place is bloody filthy. Actually c'mon, I've got a first aid kit in the office, let's put a proper dressing on it before you get tetanus.' He walked away and Vince followed.

I collected a couple of cans of Coke, taking one back to Kay.

'You and Vince getting on ok?' I asked.

'What d'you mean?'

'Nothing. Just wondered.'

'Because of that thing with Oskar?' Kay guessed easily.

'I suppose. I don't really get it.'

'Nor me, but that's ok. Me and Vince have a laugh. That's all. His mum likes me. So does his dad but he's such a creep. Vince doesn't say much about Oskar or talk about that stuff. Not like you talk about Petra.'

'Who told you that?'

'Vince. Who else?'

'I need a jimmy.' I gave her my can to hold and went to the toilet cubicle.

When I came out Steve and Sofia were at the fire escape door, cuddling and sharing a joint. Kay was sitting on the sofa next to Dimitri. Her skirt had ridden up when she sat down. I purposely looked away. Sofia called over her shoulder, 'That's my little sister, don't be a perv,' and threw a joint at him. 'Kay, if you must, then kiss, but no tongues and do not let him touch you. Dimitri, don't you get enough?'

'Only porn stars die wishing they'd had less sex.' Dimitri spoke seriously.

Kay rolled her eyes; Dimitri laughed and took his hand from her thigh.

I heard Bazzer offer Susan a drink and her refusal as I went over to my guitar case. I knelt down to open it and check I'd stored my precious instrument properly. Of course I had, and lying on top was the original set list. I took it out. Susan left Bazzer to cross the room and gently pull me to standing. 'I'm sorry Petra wasn't here. It was a great gig. Your first. You were amazing and it might turn out to be a moment.'

I didn't say, but it was hard to believe that, without Petra there. Instead, I passed her the paper, saying, 'Not knowing where Mum was on Thursday was my fault, not hers. We should have played *April Blooms Again* tonight.'

Chapter 22
Summer 1976
Still
'Sound Of Silence'

The Tuesday after the Zamara'z gig was my sixteenth birthday, at last. Susan and Dad went in to work later so we could have breakfast together. They both gave me cash towards a new amp. Over tea and toast Mum said she wanted to go to confession. Dad joked she could have, 'Nothing to confess.'

'I've enough,' she said, 'and need to apologise to Father Andrew for not being there. And how else to get ready for a fresh start, leaving stuff behind. I feel I'm close.'

'You don't owe anyone an apology.' Dad looked at me for support. I nodded.

'Maybe,' Mum continued, 'but I promised Vi I'd light a candle for her sister and say a prayer for Lawrence.'

'Mike'll walk with you,' Dad said as he left for work.

After breakfast I went to my bedroom to open the present Petra had left. It was a black t-shirt with a hand-drawn 'Rocknow Station' logo – the lettering cleverly fashioned into the image of a thundering locomotive. The post had included an envelope with an Irish postmark, and I opened it with expectation, but the card's message was a simple *Many Happy Returns* and was as disappointing as the t-shirt was welcomed.

Mum went to confession mid-morning. It had been months, maybe years, since her last one and I thought she'd be nervous. She wasn't. On the way, she spoke of how long she had known Father Andrew, remembering her first confession with him and how he had put her at ease. She talked of the days she had helped with the church flowers, before the cancer, and how Father Andrew had visited her in hospital and how the prayers had helped. She was quietly excited about this confession but, like Dad, I didn't understand why, or what she could have to confess.

I waited on a bench in the cemetery from where I could see the yew tree under which I'd kissed Petra. How long would Mum be? I'd never been to confession. Anytime Mum had tried to press me, Dad had helped me avoid it. What would I confess? I thought of what had nearly happened with Sofia. But it was only nearly. I was happy to assume there was no need to confess temptation, only action, otherwise confession boxes would be forever full and the priests would never get anything else done – whatever it was they did. I fiddled with the leather bracelet. Did kissing Petra in the graveyard count? The church was imposing, almost domineering, towering over the tree. But of all the feelings that memory held and provoked, guilt was not one, and there was no way I'd let it be. Still, it was odd. Though I barely qualified as Catholic, this was 'my' church. I couldn't explain or understand why, but it was easy to believe how much it meant to Mum and the desire to believe in her miracle was as important as the need for it to be true.

She seemed relaxed when she came out, if not especially happy; a normal post-confession state, for all I knew. Not that it mattered. That she was gently smiling was enough. She wore dark blue slacks and a cream light jersey wool twinset. She was elegant and classy. Anytime – the few times – she smiled, she was pretty and young again. We just hadn't found a way to help her smile more.

Thursday morning brought more clear skies. The summer was promising to be good. I spent the time practising a little but, mostly, staring at my guitar. It was easier to relive the Zamara'z gig than start getting ready for the next one. It was hard to forget Petra had gone away; been taken away.

I went down to the garden and sat next to Mum on the bench. She was embroidering, slowly and carefully. Her simple light blue blouse and cotton skirt with a flower print were bright and young, in contrast to her weary sigh. 'Ok, Mikey?' she asked.

'Yep,' I lied. 'You?'

'It's a beautiful day,' she said without looking up.

'How's the apple tree?' I indicated to the threaded image.

'Nearly done.'

'It's taken a long time.'

'It's been a long year, I know. But nearly done.'

We sat quietly until I asked, 'Did Vi say when she's coming back?'

'No. It was a rush. I know you miss Petra.' She brushed a finger across the bracelet on my wrist.

'I suppose.'

'Vi told me Petra will miss you. Never mind what happened at the party.'

It was the first time I realised Mum had been told what an idiot I'd been. Which made me a bigger idiot. Of course she would have known.

'But it's ok. It came to nothing and I'm sure Petra will be all right with you. And you know in your heart if there's anything to forgive. I didn't always think that. I used to think it must have been my fault and I needed to be forgiven, but since talking to Father Andrew I don't believe that anymore.'

'I don't understand, Mum.'

'Anyway, it's ok to miss Petra. I miss Vi. But after a while it'll be fine. They needed to go.' She turned to me. Her eyes were dark and wet and, despite the sun her cheeks were pale. 'It's been a long year,' she repeated, 'but it will be fine, it really will.' She put down the embroidery and raised an arm. I shuffled along the bench to hug her more closely.

'Mum?'

'Yes?'

'You ok?'

'Very tired. But I don't mind it anymore. And you'll be ok. I've spent my life scared of missing the future, even though it frightens me, but now it's ok. Would you promise me something, Mikey?'

'Of course.'

'Don't try to be liked by everyone. They don't all deserve to like you. Be and play what you feel, not what others want you to.'

After lunch I went to the park, my park, but without Petra's company it was empty. Joining a kick-about didn't help and I wandered home past the station parade.

In the kitchen I poured a glass of cream soda and took it to the lounge. Radio 2 was playing. Out of habit I waited a couple of seconds to recognise the song *Sound of Silence* – Susan loved this song, but I didn't see how we could fit it into our set. I went through to the conservatory. Mum sat in her chair, eyes closed. It was warm under the plastic corrugated roofing and the gentle wind that came through the open door was welcome.

The breeze fluttered the net curtains. It had tipped to the floor an ornament from the windowsill – the small glass dove filled with tiers of coloured sands from the Isle Of Wight that Dad had repaired. It was only a year or two ago we were there, and Mum had insisted on a dove, not a swan. On August bank holidays we'd go down to a friend's caravan near Freshwater. We usually drove down on the Thursday, Dad borrowing a bigger car from the garage forecourt, and stay over the weekend. I didn't miss going, but was glad to have the memories: chasing blow-up beach balls into the sea; Coke and crisps in the club house in the evenings while Dad entered the talent contest; playing rummy or sevens in the caravan when it rained; a bag of crab legs on the sea front; listening to Mum and Dad daydream of a future living near the sea with visiting grandchildren. Nothing unusual or exotic; everything obvious and shared. A family just like the others and, similarly, just as unique.

I replaced the dove, thankful it had not broken again.

The now completed embroidery of the apple tree in blossom lay in Mum's lap. Her eyes were still closed, and her head bowed. Still.

With the door open there was some bird chatter and insect hum. The high sun cast short, dark shadows. Occasionally a child's shout could be heard, floating from the park, carrying laughter, promising joy. There was a small patch of lavender underneath the apple tree at the bottom of the garden and the beginnings of fruit hidden within the branches and leaves. The garden's borders were crowded with the yellows, blues and reds from flowers and shrubs. The lawn was browning from the sun and the earth smelt both old and fresh. The afternoon sky was open summer blue, streaked with aircraft trails. Just outside the conservatory was a long-abandoned hutch. I turned from the garden, thinking to ask Mum if we should get another rabbit, but it was just a notion of the instant.

Mum was still and quiet; eyes closed.

A chaffinch darted from a hedge to the apple tree.

'Mum?'

Still, Mum was quiet.

'Mum?'

Still.

My breath was stayed in sudden fear. I watched for a few seconds. Realisation burst into shock and the shock was the moment.

Mum was still, for the moment and forever.

Miracle Number Four

Chapter 23
Summer 1976
The Process
'That's The Way Of The World'

Vince and I sat on the bench near the swings. It was early evening. The summer was relentlessly hot and dry. Heat seeped from the tarmac around the playground. Tree shadows were long but didn't reach us, and I squinted at the low sun. A dog sniffed with disappointment at the dust in the tray at the foot of the granite water fountain. A few boys played football, two smaller children played on the slide and another on the swings.

It was nearly two weeks since Mum had passed away in the conservatory – the only person using the term 'died' was Father Andrew. The funeral would be on Thursday, 8th July, the day after next.

I'd just come from home where Father Andrew had been speaking to us about the service.

Susan had made tea and we'd sat in the front room being awkwardly polite until Father Andrew took control.

I wasn't paying attention and had to be asked again, 'Mikey? What would you like to put in?' Father Andrew touched my arm.

'Put in where?'

'The coffin. For April.'

I must have looked blank as he repeated the question and Dad said, 'She'll be keeping her wedding ring and there'll be a picture of us all on the pillow.'

'Pillow?' It hadn't occurred to me there would be a pillow in the coffin. Father Andrew had suggested Mum be laid out at home for a couple of days but Dad refused, thankfully. Neither Susan nor I had gone to see Mum at the funeral directors though I think Dad had, but never asked him about it.

'Father Andrew has suggested we write letters for her,' said Susan.

'Will you?' I asked.

'I don't know. You don't have to,' she said.

'But it might help with the process,' added Father Andrew.

'But it's up to you,' Susan told me.

'Of course,' said Father Andrew. 'There's time for you to think about it. Let's talk about the process on the day.'

'Process,' Susan repeated.

'It helps to be familiar with the process.'

'Process?' This time it was a question.

'Yes Susan. If it's a smooth process …'

The cup exploded as it hit the mantelpiece. It was thrown with violence, knocking over a picture. The breaking glass and frame were an echo of the shattering china. The room was suddenly quiet, but only for an instant.

'It's not a fucking process!' Susan screamed. 'If you say it one more time …' Her tears were of rage. Dad tried to hold her, but she pushed free, '… go on, say it, just one more time, I fucking dare you.' Susan stood over the table.

I hoped Father Andrew would say it, Susan had a right to vent and rage.

'I'm sorry Susan,' said Father Andrew, 'and I know it's been a hard few years, for you all, but especially for April. At least now she is at peace.'

Susan tried to speak but her anger was so raw that she had not the words. There was a tight silence. I asked,

'How do you know?'

It wasn't a challenge or dispute but a simple, sincere question. It wasn't that I thought Father Andrew was necessarily wrong or lying. But if Mum's miracle, just eight months ago, could be worth so little, then why should we believe him? Father Andrew smiled benevolently. Susan broke from the room.

I paid no attention to the rest of the process.

'Susie told Father Andrew to fuck off?' Vince was impressed.

'Yep.'

'I wish I had a sister like that.'

'Bollocks to him. He knows bugger all. He doesn't know how she died, never mind why. No one does.'

'Your mum didn't die of cancer?'

'No, they don't know the cause. So much for fucking miracles. And you know Petra and Vi aren't coming back for the funeral? We waited to see if they would. But they can't and Father Andrew says we need to 'move forward'. As if that means anything. Anyway, they're not coming back. I guess people don't.' I didn't hide the bitter tone, then tried to glance at Vince without catching his eye, 'Will's not coming back either.'

Vince hesitated before asking, 'Will? Why would he?'

I hesitated, then, 'We had the police round last week.'

'About your mum?'

'No. Why would you think that? About Will. They wanted to know if I'd seen him on the morning I found your dad in his office.'

'And?'

'I didn't.'

'Oh. Did they say why they wanted to know?'

'No.'

Vince made a vague noise but, before I could ask if he had an idea why, he pointed towards the main path running from the gate. 'Kay. I told her we'd be here. I can give her back this.' He showed me a plastic bag. Inside was an album: *That's The Way Of The World*. 'Heard it?' he asked.

I remembered listening to it with Petra but shrugged.

'Vince, JB,' Kay greeted us. I hadn't seen her since the Zamara'z gig, two and a bit weeks ago.

'Here, not really my thing.' Vince passed her the album.

'Philistine.' She turned to me. 'JB, so sorry about your mum.'

I nodded what I supposed would be taken as thanks. It was a nod I'd perfected over the last couple of weeks. I'd found that most people didn't know what to say next and either left me so they could talk to Dad, or expected me to help them. How should I know? They were the adults for fuck's sake. I preferred it when they moved away and left me in the corner.

'Really sorry, JB.' Kay repeated, smiling, not with pity or mirth but with something like ... I dunno, hope? Whatever, I thought she meant it.

'Thanks, Kay, really.'

'How's it been?'

'Shit. And now my old man is nagging me about getting a job. Says it'll be good for me.'

'You can take my place at the garage if you like,' Vince said with no humour.

Kay sat next to me, opened a bottle of Coke and offered it round. Vince lit a cigarette. Kay declined his offer. He didn't bother offering to me. We sat without talking, and though I didn't particularly want to be there, I didn't want to go home. Bazzer and Susan would be in the lounge, looking at the television with Dad. No one was watching it these days, just staring at the pictures, Susan occasionally insisting on making a pot of tea, Bazzer keen to help her in the kitchen, Dad staring.

'Oh shit.'

'What?' We followed Vince's nod. The two lads Vince and I had fought in the station café were in the park. They were still fifty yards or more away when they recognised us.

The bigger of the boys stopped a couple of yards short, talking at me. 'Who's this?' he indicated to Kay. 'Does your girlfriend know you've got someone else on the go? Not to mention Gloria here.' He indicated to Vince.

The other boy sniggered.

'That's as funny as your fat ugly mother farting in a lift, prick,' I said with no humour.

The boy thought for a second. 'That would be funny. And don't be so touchy. Talking of mums, we heard yours died. Sorry, honest. Were you there?' The apology was far less sincere than the morbid curiosity.

'Who told you?'

'My sister works in the bakers. And honest, we're sorry.'

'Piss off.' My heart beat faster and I felt a little faint.

'No need for that. Just wondered if you ...'

'Fuck off.'

'Easy. We heard you were there. What did she look like when ...'

The question wasn't finished. Lost in desperate anger, I grabbed the Coke from Kay and jumped forward, swinging the bottle at the boy's face. He threw himself back, taking but a glancing blow on the forehead.

The bottle slipped from my grasp to bounce yards away, spinning and fizzing its contents across the play area. Before the boy could recover his stance, I was at him, flailing arms, shouting abuse, kicking wildly, raging indiscriminately.

Kay screamed.

It was done in just seconds, but seconds for which I had no memory. I stood over my tormentor, gasping for breath, cheeks wet with tears, blood on my knuckles from clumsy punches sliding off his face and onto tarmac. The boy at my feet was hunched into a ball, covering his face, pleading. The other boy was terrified into frozen silence.

Vince took my arm.

'Home?' asked Kay.

I looked at her for a few seconds before nodding, 'Yes please, I've got a letter to write.'

Susan removed both studs from her right ear lobe and turned away from her dressing table mirror. I was sitting on the bed, not watching her, not wanting to disturb her and not wanting her to talk to me – what was there to say? A sketch of Janis Joplin looked down at me, somehow challenging, but I didn't want to be in my own room and wasn't ready to go downstairs. I wore a new black blazer style jacket, old grey school trousers, white shirt, one of Dad's black ties and black shoes. Ordinarily I wouldn't wear shoes upstairs, but these had not yet been worn outdoors, the price was still on the sole. My top button was done up, something I'd never bothered with for school, but the temptation to tug the tie loose was easy to resist. It simply wouldn't be the right thing. Some things, on this day, were easy to accept as 'the done thing'. Susan finished adding some eye shadow and mascara then took from her wardrobe the new dark blue dress. It was elegant, matching her new shoes. She slipped the dress over her head, pulling it down carefully so as not to put in creases. She turned back to the mirror, reached for a stick of lipstick and hesitated before replacing it, unused. I may have sighed or murmured, I'm not sure, but something made Susan sit next to me, saying, 'It's only half-nine. We've plenty of time.'

There was a knock on the open bedroom door and a woman with dyed reddish hair and tired eyes in a pale face came in. She tried to take up even less space than her petite frame needed.

'Hi, Aunt May. You ok?' Susan asked. Our aunt had come round early, there was much to do, though little of importance.

'Your dad thought you might like to wear these?' She handed Susan a velvet covered jewellery box – Mum's pearls. 'They were your nan's. She always said they're natural, not cultured. I don't know about that, but they are lovely, and your dad thought ... you know ... you could wear them, if you want to.'

'Why don't you wear them, Aunt May?'

'They were your mum's.'

'And your mum's before that.'

'I think your dad would really like it if you wore them today.'

Aunt May looked to me for support.

I took the box from her and passed it to Susan. She opened the lid. The sheen of the pearls was a shifting, oily kaleidoscope nestling in dark green velvet. Aunt May briefly rested a hand on my shoulder then left the room saying she'd put the kettle on, there was time for a cuppa. Just lately there had always been time for a cuppa.

'I've been wondering … thinking, really …,' I said.

'About?' Susan asked, trying to settle down her mop of blonde hair.

'Lots of things …'

'Me too.'

'Moments.'

'Moments?'

'I'm thinking there might be one today, or a few of them, or even one long one. What do you think?'

'I think you're right.'

'But I'm thinking maybe there are two types.'

'Two?'

'As you say, those you don't see coming, don't realise until afterwards, maybe when they've made you think, or do something different.'

Susan nodded, 'And?'

'Maybe there's another type. Maybe you see them coming or realise while they're happening. And maybe these are just as important, maybe more, and what you do and say at these times is going to be remembered and you want to look back at these ones and see and hear the person you wanted to be and that's not always the person you really were … at the time.'

'Woah, slow down. Who do you want to be today?'

'I don't know, but I'm scared about what's going to happen and if I'll cry too much, or not enough, or at the wrong time, or not at all. I still can't really imagine Mum won't be home later and I'm shit scared that I might suddenly understand in the middle of the service, and it'll feel worse than now, even. Is that possible? And I won't know what to do. And whatever, none of it makes any difference and I really want Mum and Dad and you to remember that I did it right. I want Mum to know.'

Susan took my hand, careful not to hurt the bruised knuckles. 'Don't think about it. We know how much you love her. Whatever you do is right. As for what anyone else thinks? Who gives a fuck. Today it's just the four of us, even if we're saying goodbye, and the time is ours, and it will be precious, just like all the other times we've had with Mum. Today will be precious.'

She took the pearls from the box and handed them to me. I draped and fastened them round her neck. Taking tissues from the box by her makeup, we dried our eyes.

Downstairs, Aunt May poured tea. The back room was full of flowers. They had been turning up for the last hour. One of the largest was from the bakery, in the shape of a harvest festival sheaf. I didn't read the card. Dad was in the conservatory, staring at Mum's chair. On the table next to it was the finished embroidery of the apple tree in blossom. Dad looked to us and held up a piece of paper with some handwritten notes. 'The music for the ceremony. I've asked for *Unchained Melody* when they bring Mum into church. They didn't have it, so I gave them a cassette.' His eyes were red, his shoulders hunched.

Susan and I went to him. We held each other and cried again.

Nothing had prepared me for the walk from the church to the grave. Father Andrew lied. Knowing the *process* hadn't helped. There had been nothing to warn me that a shining sun would not prevent shivering. No one had told me it would take a cold, desolate age for everyone to gather round the open grave or that I would be so watched. It was easy for the few relatives to put an arm round me, squeeze and walk on; easy for them, at least, it seemed. At the graveside, Dad and Aunt May were on one side of me, Susan and Bazzer the other. Petra wasn't there. Her latest letter had arrived a couple of days earlier; she was sorry, again, that she wouldn't be back. I fiddled with the leather bracelet. The church had not appeared busy with mourners, but here, around the grave, it was a crowd. I avoided looking around, aware of the mix of black and navy coats and hats; so many highly polished shoes trampling grass already browned from the drought. Father Andrew controlled proceedings and they were better for being less personal than the eulogy from the earlier Mass.

I kept my head bowed. I barely saw the coffin being lowered and didn't look up until the clumsy movement to the right was a distraction. Father Andrew had picked up some earth and was a step away from dropping it on the coffin, in the shadow of its own grave. Dad gripped the dirt filled hand, stopping the throw. The instant tension between the men rippled through the crowd. Dad whispered something, unintelligible but fierce. I understood; Dad was not yet ready to say goodbye. Nor was I. Father Andrew let the earth slip through his fingers.

It was not until most had left the graveside that I noticed the splash of colour. Out on the main path stood Dimitri, Sunny Steve and Sofia. The shadow of the yew tree was close to hiding them, but Sofia's bright yellow neck scarf caught my eye. I looked over. Dimitri half raised a hand in acknowledgement. Sunny Steve gave a solitary nod. Sofia placed a hand over her heart. I cried again.

Back home I watched Susan hand out tea and sandwiches while Dad sat in the corner – seemingly numb but surely swamped with despair. I realised I had been wrong about the funeral. It wasn't a moment. It never came close. I knew only one moment – the instant I'd understood Mum was still, forever, the instant I'd known she'd gone. That was the moment. Up until that point nothing could be counted as one; since then, it was hard to believe anything else could.

If there had been little normality in the time leading up to the funeral, there was even less in the days after. Aunt May had stayed for a while and, though her presence wasn't welcomed because of what it represented, she made a difference. She cared, she watched, she brought us together when needed and separated us when necessary. She was an echo of Mum and I was glad when she left. Dad and Susan stayed from work, needlessly filling the house, hopelessly trying not to think. The week after Mum's funeral, I helped Dad build a chicken coop where the vegetable patch had been and we brought the birds from Vi's to ours. Visiting to feed them every day had quickly become a chore, and Vi had written to say she was going to rent out the house as she didn't expect to be home for a few months. At some other time it would have been funny to see us trying to catch and keep the birds in the car for the short drive to ours.

Having to feed them at the bottom of our garden quickly became no less a chore.

School was finished and the strength of Dad's suggestions that I go and find a job increased as the days passed. He arranged for me to work more in the garage – washing cars, tidying up. Vince was also there, shadowing the mechanics.

On the first day I was ready for a surfeit of sympathy, though all my pre-prepared answers were nowhere close to explaining my despairing confusion. I had no words to tell people how I felt because I had no understanding – not just of what I felt, but what had happened, was still happening, or, most frightening, wouldn't, couldn't, happen again; ever again. That Mum wasn't there was always, well, there. Sometimes it was distant recognition, as if she might be up in her bedroom, and sometimes it was shocking and in my gut, as I understood she wasn't anywhere anymore. But worse were the fleeting glimpses of what it meant for her never to be there with me again. She was gone; the future I'd never thought about but relied on, was gone. I was not alone, I had Dad and Susan, except I could not be more alone. Without a mother, how was I supposed to be a son? But I came to sense that deep fear's blackness swell and learned to pretend and ignore.

No one at the garage asked how I was.

The next day, rather than go back there I went into Patrick's Pianos, the instrument shop, practically begged for a job, and started work the following Saturday. Selling guitars was easy, drumsticks easier; pianos not so much. I think the manager took me on because he was trying to sell more guitars to younger customers – which meant he was happy for me to turn up in jeans and let my hair grow, though later, when reviewing the piano sales figures, he complained that I was putting off the more mature customers. But I was soon at home there. When there were no customers he'd knock out some old boogie woogie or rag time tune and I'd strum along happily. He was ok. He loved music.

Dad was pleased I was working, even if selling guitars wasn't really, in his words, 'A working man's job.' That, of course, assumed I wanted to be a working man.

I wrote to tell Petra and her prompt reply was full of encouragement, not to mention a hint that she and Vi might be back. Petra wanted to go to college and hoped to work with animals.

At home I saw Dad and Susan's pain but was quick to deflect them. This brought guilt; guilt that I had no way to help them; guilt I tried to assuage by not asking them for help, a cycle of guilt and despair.

And all the time the apple tree embroidery lay there.

Why hadn't I come home earlier that day?

Why did they not blame me? Perhaps they did.

Miracle Number Four

Chapter 24
Summer 1976
Minor Chords
'Miracle Number Four'

I knocked once and entered Susan's room without waiting. 'If you're going to practise those minor chords at least tune the bloody thing first.'

She sat on her bed.

I took the guitar from her, 'Worse than nails on a blackboard,' and gently plucked the strings, listening as I tweaked the machine head screws.

'Thought you were never coming.' Susan fanned herself with an old copy of *Streetlife* magazine. Though the window was open there was no breeze. She settled back against a pillow. 'What you doing tonight?'

'Not a lot.'

'Got a letter to write to Petra? I see another came from Ireland today. Have you been replying?'

I nodded. Petra had sent five letters – everyday news and sarcastic complaints about her boring village – and I'd replied three times. All our letters had ended with, 'missing you,' or something similar, and I wondered why they didn't start with that.

'Good. Then this one can wait a couple of days. Tonight we've got the room above The Railway, to rehearse. Turns out Algie has a mate who used to be in the record business and wants to hear us.'

'At Zamara'z?'

'No. That's the bad news. It's a pub miles away. Some place called,' she stopped fanning to check the notes scribbled on the back of the magazine, 'Oakjack Ford. New Forest. We've got three weeks.'

I played a few chords.

'*Seagull*? We'll include it if you want,' said Susan.

229

My strumming faltered to silence. 'I'm not sure I want to, yet.'

'Play *Seagull*?'

'No, gig. It's been less than two weeks since …'

'The funeral, I know. I said the same to Bazzer.'

'And?'

'He asked what Mum would have said.'

'That was a cheap trick.'

'That's what I said. But he's right. And I asked Dad. He said what else are we going to do?'

'Apart from Bazzer, I haven't seen the band since …' I handed back the guitar.

'The funeral, I know,' said Susan.

I followed Susan into The Railway, more than ever feeling an intruder. But nothing was different. Four weeks on from Mum's death and nothing was different here. On seeing our guitar cases some regulars called for a song, as usual, while others settled on taking the piss because of my age, as always. Sofia ran from behind the bar to hug us, me especially close. I let myself be pulled into her, ignoring the drinkers' catcalls and obscene comments. When she let go she said, 'Sorry, JB,' and dabbed away her tears.

The manky room upstairs was no cleaner and the smell was worse. Steve had set up most of the gear and Dimitri was tuning his drums, stopping as Susan kissed Bazzer hello.

'Hey, JB,' called Dimitri, 'how many bass players does it take to change a light bulb?'

'I give in.'

'Only one, but the guitarist has to show him first.' Dimitri laughed and gave a short flourish on the snare and a cymbal.

I smiled broadly to show I appreciated Dimitri's 'welcome home'. Bazzer passed me a piece of paper, saying, 'Some ideas for the set list. One band, two sets, twenty-four songs, five of them originals, one encore.'

'That's more than at Zamara'z.'

'Then we better get playing,' Susan called over as she picked up a guitar.

For the next few weeks we relied on Bazzer. He held us together; quietly and firmly, he held us. Rehearsals went ahead, the PA was upgraded with money borrowed from Dad – his idea and he insisted; Mum had had a small insurance policy with the Pru – arguments were smoothed, the set list was agreed. Bazzer nudged and coaxed us into being Rocknow Station. When Dad said he really didn't mind, honest, that Susan and I were spending a lot of time rehearsing and very little at home, it was Bazzer who took us all out to Sunday lunch at The White Oak. He gave in politely when Dad insisted on paying half the bill, an arrangement that satisfied both their egos. I offered to pay my share but was happy to be refused – selling guitars at Patrick's didn't pay well.

The band was coming together but it was still a doleful time.

Susan tried, but could no longer fit seamlessly into the salon's arcane hierarchy and social world, despite that having been her forté at school.

Dad tried to sort through Mum's wardrobe but simply couldn't, nor could he give away the new sewing machine, back in its box.

We tried to live with Mum's guidance but without her presence. We tried to cherish memories but how, when still resentful? We pretended to understand, but true comprehension was too painful.

Dad spent days looking through old photographs, not enjoying, but anxious to choose the right ones. Three, black and white, were framed and hung in the lounge: Mum and Dad emerging from church on their wedding day; Mum in her white confirmation dress; Mum, Susan and I having a picnic. A fourth frame hung alongside, displaying Mum's apple tree embroidery. I don't remember Dad looking at the pictures after they were hung, and he put the albums in the loft.

Aunt May stayed with us occasionally. I slept on a camp bed downstairs while she had my room. She wanted to go to St. Gregory's for Sunday Mass; she went alone. We let her down.

At the garage, Vince found himself caught between his father, who was the boss, and the workshop floor. He tried, and largely succeeded, in convincing his father that a mechanic's apprenticeship was not for him, but Lawrence's stubbornness wouldn't allow him to let Vince leave. Lawrence was not fully recovered from the heart attack and despite spending less time at the garage was determined that Vince should earn his legacy. Kay and Vince became close friends and he confided in me that he really liked her. What Vince meant by 'liked' wasn't clear.

The chickens laid fewer eggs, perhaps missing Petra and Vi.

Dimitri found and subsequently lost a job at C&A because he refused to get his hair trimmed, though he did keep his beard neat. I didn't bother trying to grow a beard. The blonde fuzz on my top lip needed a blade just a couple of times a week.

Sunny Steve and Sofia nearly broke up during a period of frequent bickering that coincided with him smoking too much weed. She put him straight.

The sun weighed heavily on the country. What was warming became oppressive. The temperature rose and the rain had long stopped. Heaths, woods and forests burnt.

We played the Oakjack Ford gig and went down a storm.

Chapter 25
Summer 1976
The Rocknow Obsession
'Raindrops Keep Falling On My Head'

I liked Saturdays at Patrick's Pianos. The mornings were busy, mostly with kids – like I was a veteran, ha – then we had a mid-day lull until the afternoon when it picked up again; local musicians finding they needed new strings or sticks or cables or whatever for that night's gig. I liked chatting with those guys, they were mostly gently cynical and self-deprecating. A few were bitter about lack of success but I didn't mind; I didn't see my future like that. My future would be more like the occasional big names that dropped in – Pete Townshend once, Kenney Jones a couple of times and, bizarrely, Keith Richards asking if we had the guitar tabs for Brown Sugar. We didn't, and though I knew the song well, I didn't offer to show him. I regretted that, as I wrote in a letter to Petra that same night. But the guys I liked chatting to most were the roadies. It didn't matter if they were with a known band or pub beginners, their cynicism and contempt was relentless and often hilarious. I lapped up the stories.

The Saturday after the Oakjack Ford gig, Bazzer came in and loitered round the guitar racks until the shop manager was busy demonstrating a piano. Then he came to me at the till, and I discreetly slid over a pack of his preferred strings which he pocketed. He bought a couple of plectrums for the sake of appearances.

'By the way,' he told me, 'Rehearsal down The Railway tomorrow afternoon.'

'Why?'

'Tell you at the band meeting, your place, eight tonight,' he said and was gone.

I was watching television with Dad when the doorbell rang and Susan came down to let in Bazzer and Dimitri. I joined them in the kitchen. Bazzer spoke first.

'Algie from Zamara'z rang this morning. The ex-producer landlord at that pub we played, told him we had potential but aren't ready for the big time.'

'Dick,' said Susan, 'but he said potential right?'

'And wants us back, according to Algie. I told him it's too far and he agreed but then said he'd been let down by a band for next Saturday and did we want the slot at Zamara'z? Two sets this time.'

There was, naturally, full and immediate agreement.

'But' Bazzer waited for us to calm, 'he says he's only paying the same as last time and only wants a couple of originals.'

'Why?'

'Because we're still not ready for the big time.'

'Zamara'z, big time? Wanker,' said Dimitri.

I laughed. No one else did.

Susan looked thoughtful and hunted through a kitchen drawer for a small pad and a couple of pencils. 'Think about that last gig at Oakjack Ford and Zamara'z before then.' This was serious Susan, whom I'd seen a lot of these past few weeks.

'What?'

'No questions.'

Dimitri started to speak but she put a finger to her lips and whispered, 'Think about the gigs.' A minute later she passed us each a slip of paper and a pencil. 'Ok, now write down the three things that are most important to you, above all others. The things you think about most. Care about most. Want most. And I don't mean crap like a Ferrari.'

Yep, this was serious Susan.

She collected the papers, adding her own as she laid them in a neat row on the kitchen table. In a variety of scrawls, excepting Susan's precision, the slips showed:

Susan: Family, Bazzer, Rocknow Station
Bazzer: Susan, Rocknow Station, Bruce
Dimitri: Rocknow Station, Girls
Me: Dad, Susan, Rocknow Station, Rocknow Station

'Bazzer, you've written Bruce. Really?'

'Why not?' Bruce was the dog he and Steve had adopted a few weeks earlier.

'Dimitri, you've only put two,' Susan pointed out.

He took the paper back, adding, 'and their sisters'.

Susan took it back, saying, 'Well at least it doesn't say their mothers,' then pointed to mine, 'and you've put Rocknow Station twice.'

'I know.'

Susan laughed, at last. 'Point is, we've all put Rocknow Station. But what does that mean? 'Cos it has to mean more than playing covers. Any band can learn them, so we could have written 'A Band'. We didn't, we all wrote Rocknow Station. And that only means something if we play our music, our way, else we might as well play along to records in our bedrooms.'

There was positive murmuring.

'So, you've written it down.' She tapped the table. 'Rocknow Station has to be something that happens, not just something to pass the time. We should stop the covers gigs, write our own material and make Rocknow Station what it can be.'

'And what can it be?' Dimitri asked.

'Rocknow Station. No other band can be that. So, let's play Zamara'z, fill the sets with as many of our own as we can and show Algie what a prick he is.'

Bazzer stood and hugged her. I wondered if he'd known about the speech. I smiled at Dimitri who smiled back; he believed Susan as much as I did, though he asked, 'Is it too late to add mothers to my list?'

As they left to go to The Railway, I drew Susan to one side, 'That was risky.'

'Nah, I never doubted.' She turned at the front door. 'Look after Dad tonight. He had a bad day today. I'll be back soon after eleven.'

Through August, the heatwave was a dense blanket, laying heavy, wilting bodies and spirits. The novelty of sunshine was abandoned and queuing for water at a standpipe was an unsettling reality. Tempers were frayed and neighbours turned on each other.

Inside Zamara'z on Saturday 21st, the air was stifling. The crowd was slow to enter, preferring to hang around outside as long as possible. We were due on at eight and, despite Sofia's best attempts, the atmosphere in the toilet/dressing room was strained. I was nervous in a new way. Before, I'd been worried about making mistakes or looking stupid in front of a crowd. Tonight, I was anxious about Rocknow Station. What if it turned out we were all wrong? What if we couldn't make Rocknow Station everything it could be? What if even that obvious aspiration was beyond us? Worst of all, what if I was the one who held it back? I was more unsettled before a gig than I'd ever been, though, to be fair, it was only my third.

Standing stage-side, I could see there weren't many people in the club, and as it passed eight o'clock, Algie told us to wait another few minutes, there was a still a queue outside. We waited as told. It was humid and smelt of stale alcohol and tobacco beyond just last night's; the odours were deep in the club's fabric. My new black and white check Ben Sherman, Kay's choice, stuck to my back. The crowd was still coming in slowly, clogging the bar at the back of the hall, shouting drink orders, calling for the band to start. Algie told us to wait a bit longer. Then someone dropped a glass. A youth with now wet jeans pushed another aside, tripping a young woman who reached out to stop herself by grabbing someone's shirt; a button was ripped, a hand was raised, an angry insult was shouted, another man was shoved, and a woman slapped him round the head. The crowd filtering through found themselves being pushed from behind into the growing quarrel. Voices were raised further, insults turned to threats, a slap became a punch. The scuffle turned to a disjointed dogfight. Algie motioned to us to stay and jumped from the stage, calling for the door bouncers to come in. Sunny Steve took up station on the floor in front of the stage, daring anyone to come near the gear.

Instinctively I took a step back, into Susan who pushed me out, 'Bollocks to Algie.'

I understood and we plugged in as Susan called to Dimitri to, '… count it in hard,' and we knew what she meant.

After the gig, Algie brought a bottle of Johnnie Walker to the toilet/dressing room though I wasn't allowed as much as a taste. He was pleased with us but still didn't offer to pay 'the going rate'. We didn't care. Rocknow Station had blown the fight off the dance floor. Yes, it was disappointing that we'd pulled *April Blooms Again* from the set, again, but that was ok, after tonight I was sure there were gigs to come. We had another level inside us.

In my spare time at Patrick's, and when the boss was out, I tried songwriting. I worked on Susan's *April Blooms Again*, making it a heavy blues rock number with close harmonies. She liked it. Then I tried a song of my own. I had an idea for a simple, soulful tune built around a melancholy refrain, strummed on an acoustic guitar. I didn't know where it would go but had a title; *Miracle Number Four*. The problem was that much as I liked the evolving melody, the sentiment was hard to think about; it was hard to think of Mum; it was hard to remind myself this was a song she would never hear.

Rain fell at the end of August, a few days before Petra's birthday. I'd sent a card and a light silver chain with the letter 'P'; the one with a silver heart hadn't felt quite right. The more I missed her, the more mundane became our letters, which I didn't understand.

I was at the shop, demonstrating a copy of a Fender guitar when we heard, rather than saw, the first splashes on the plate glass front. I went outside with the customer, hoping to build some tenuous rapport that might lead to a sale. I tried a joke, 'Maybe it'll rain money, it's such a *change* in the weather,' and though he laughed politely he didn't come back in with me to buy the guitar. I was left standing in the rain. The parade was busy and the shoppers smiled as they darted between shops to avoid the heavy drops. I grinned too. Though this was not *my* parade, I liked it here. In some ways it was better than mine – Mum had not worked at the bakery or bought groceries or used the chemist; I had not walked with Petra to the newsagent, or station café, or waited at the bus stop. I stood for a minute, a melody playing in my mind, perhaps a new song? But I shook it away, I still hadn't finished *Miracle Number Four*.

From inside the shop I heard the manager playing *'Raindrops Keep Falling On My Head,'* on the Bechstein delivered that morning, and went back inside. It was my turn to make tea.

We threw ourselves into Rocknow Station, hustling for gigs, writing our own material, playing local pubs and clubs, trying to build a following, writing more, writing better, gradually dropping the covers, trusting ourselves, improving the band gear, learning as musicians. And we were pretty good. Bazzer cajoled and praised, Susan challenged, Dimitri practised hard, in every sense, and was a powerhouse on drums. We played Zamara'z regularly and Algie dropped hints about us needing, 'A dedicated manager.'

Rocknow Station became our obsession.

I occasionally worried that it stopped me missing Petra. I wanted to write more often, or to be truthful, I wanted her to, but I thought she'd be back soon, and we could pick up from somewhere before that party. Besides, I knew the secret of her mole and thought of it often.

That Rocknow Station stopped me thinking about Mum was often a blessing but sometimes a worry – especially when refining *Miracle Number Four*. I couldn't work on it without fear; I needed fear for it to be right.

At home, Susan had much to worry about. She worried Dad was spending too much time in the front room with his records while she was keeping the house going between gigs and rehearsals. I knew I should have been doing more but there was always a good reason – though of course not good enough. Dad was still working at the garage but not getting much else done. He stopped nagging about oiling my bike and the garden was increasingly untidy.

We went to the graveyard on the 25th of September, a Saturday. Dad called it a quarterly anniversary. That didn't feel right to me. I'd always thought of anniversaries as events to be celebrated. Three months and a day since Mum died did not qualify. Susan had passed her test and took me in the old orange Mini Dad found for her. He would soon finish work at the garage for the day and we waited in silence on the bench under the yew tree, my thoughts drifting from Mum to Petra and back. From here I could see Mum's plain granite stone, lying pillow-like at the head of the grave. It had been there just a couple of weeks and was still fresh. Could a slab of rock be fresh? I shrugged at the thought.

'You ok?' Susan reacted to the movement. I shrugged again. I couldn't read the headstone from here but had no need:

April Oppen
1933 – 1976
As blossom's pink and white
So April blooms again

As springtime comes to light
So April blooms again

It had taken us weeks following the funeral to agree the epitaph. Dad had wanted a simple *'Wife and mother, loving and loved. A melody unchained. Rest in Peace'*. I liked the 'melody unchained' part but was uneasy about the 'RIP'. If the miracle hadn't made a difference, I still didn't get how anyone could know that. But I didn't protest, being scared someone might prove me right. So Dad's simple message was gaining gradual acceptance until he heard Susan practicing *April Blooms Again* in the bathroom and, sung as Susan did, was as convincing and hopeful an epitaph as any of us could wish for. Mind you, on her day, Susan could sing the gas bill and make you cry.

We had finally put the song in our set, and I had learned to sing it with false sentiment – letting go would have been crippling. Here, at the grave, I played with the leather bracelet on my left wrist. After having nearly lost it at a gig, I now wore it only on special occasions, and it occurred to me that perhaps wearing it today meant Dad was right in some way about the anniversary.

'Your family is missed in church.' Father Andrew made me jump. He had crept up on us in his graveyard. He sounded genuine, but then he usually did. 'How are you? How's your father?'

Susan motioned to the lychgate. Dad was walking through.

After polite conversation there was a lull which Susan took as the chance to go over to Mum's grave. She had a bunch of bright yellow, tightly packed roses not yet in full bloom.

'I'll leave you in peace,' said Father Andrew.

There was that word again.

We stood in silence over Mum's grave. Susan muttered, 'Sorry,' as she placed the flowers at the headstone.

I wanted someone to say something about Mum we all knew. I looked at Dad. He said nothing, but his face, so often blank of late, held a question. And I knew what was to come.

'I've just never really got it, Mikey.'

Here it was.

'They said it wasn't the cancer. So what was it?' Dad's face was wet from crying.

'They said they didn't know,' said Susan.

'What, so she just went to sleep and didn't wake up. That's not right. She wouldn't do that to us.'

'I don't know, Dad.' I stepped back a yard. I'd waited for this conversation. I didn't want it, but he did. He needed it.

'Tell me, again. You spoke to her in the morning, she was in the garden, embroidering. She said she was tired. You went to the park. When you came back the embroidery was done, and she was gone.'

That was it. I wished there was more. There wasn't. Except, sometimes, when I forgot and found myself thinking about it, no, not thinking, not remembering, but reliving it, there was more. She wasn't tired – a least not in the way I told Dad and Susan. But I had no way of explaining properly. Yes, I could tell them that Mum was weary, exhausted. But that wasn't what she meant. I think she meant she was done, finished, accepting of not being here anymore and I wish maybe she'd said that. I might not have gone to the park. But I did. I apologised to Dad again. He thought I was apologising for not being able to explain why Mum died.

'And the embroidery was finished when you got back.?' he asked, again.

'Yes, Dad.'

He looked at me but didn't ask the questions he wanted – why were you at the park? Why didn't you go home earlier? And then his guilt at putting that on me slumped his shoulders and hunched his back and he hugged me until it was hard to breathe.

Susan cried silently.

Algie was giving us more gigs, and we were at Zamara'z that night so were going on to Bazzer's from the graveyard. Though we were reluctant to leave Dad sitting under the yew tree, he was insistent. We insisted he come to the gig later and he insisted he would. I didn't believe him. Susan didn't try hard to convince him and seemed drained.

'Susan?' I said quietly as we passed through the lychgate.

'Yep.'

'Had any moments lately?'

'Not for a while. You?'

'Still just the one.'

'The one?'

'Finding Mum.'

On the drive to Bazzer's the only thing she said was, 'I can't sing it tonight,' and I knew which song she meant.

Chapter 26
Autumn 1976
Rules
'Movin' On'

Thanks mainly to Algie's contacts, by mid-November I'd already played nearly twenty gigs. I was never happier than on stage.

We played Zamara'z three or four times a month. I liked the feeling of being known there, which was comforting, but it never detracted from the thrill of performing, which was never comfortable. Algie was now encouraging us to play more originals – not that we needed to be asked twice – and he was spending a little more on promotion. Susan and Kay designed posters. Sofia handed out leaflets to customers at the café and pub. I did likewise at Patrick's and kept a few complementary tickets on the shop counter, making sure to keep our poster visible on the 'gigs' notice board. Though Vince had just turned seventeen he was working two or three evenings a week at Zamara'z. Sometimes behind the bar, sometimes on the door – not as a bouncer – and sometimes just clearing up. It didn't pay much, but he enjoyed it more than the mechanic apprenticeship he was still trying to escape. I didn't spend much time with Vince these days and I suppose that since *that* party things were a little different, even though I don't believe either of us wanted them to be.

When we played Zamara'z, Sofia would do what she could to make the toilet/changing room smell less and look cleaner. Vol au vents were served and there was Blue Nun as well as vodka, beers and Coke. Kay helped Sofia while Vince helped Steve on stage. Kay sort of took charge of band costumes, though apart from Susan, that meant little more to the rest of us than a different t-shirt and jeans. Sometimes, they were even clean. Susan, Sofia and, to a lesser extent, Kay, would only let me drink one bottle of pale ale which was ok, as I didn't like the taste of the other stuff. No one let me anywhere near Steve's joints – which was also fine with me. I had the feeling that without their watching I might have tried and was scared I'd like it, though I was still not smoking cigarettes. Susan gave up smoking, for her voice. Thinking back to those early days at the lock-up, there was some irony there.

After a gig on the last Saturday in October, Dimitri had, as usual, brought some girls back to the converted toilet now known as 'Chez Sofia's'. They were different every time but always attractive and vital, smart and cool – though as time went on I learnt that my judgement was affected by after-gig excitement which took an hour or two to dissipate. In the meantime, everything was funnier, smarter, sexier. Not that I knew much about 'sexier', except, of course, I knew enough to see it definitely applied to the girl with the halter neck crochet top sitting next to Dimitri. I was standing in a corner with Vince and Kay, as usual. Algie was talking to Steve. Both looked serious and Algie kept tight hold of the thin roll of cash in his hand. I was blowing on a too hot sausage roll – Sofia had brought in a new-fangled microwave oven – when the girl with the crochet top left Dimitri on the sofa. In the poor light it was hard to tell how old she was, but certainly older than me. Everyone was. She was also taller than me. I'd put on another couple of inches that year and was now as tall as Dad and taller than Susan, but not as tall as this girl. Her hair was darker than Susan's but almost the same style – a style I'd rarely seen on others.

'Thanks,' I mumbled as the girl in the crochet top said she enjoyed the gig. My long hair, uncut for months, was in my eyes and plastered to my sweating forehead. I wanted to brush it aside but thought that might be uncool.

'I'm Lynn. Or Coco. If you prefer.'

'Mike or ...'

'... JB. Which I prefer,' she interrupted, standing close, almost edging Vince and Kay aside. Her face was a couple of inches from mine and her breath smelt of tomato juice from her Bloody Mary. I didn't mind. Since Petra had left, I'd nearly kissed only four other girls and each time either Susan or Sofia had quickly put a stop to anything going further. This time it was Kay's turn to interrupt with a pointed,

'So, JB. Heard from Petra lately?' She smiled, adding for Coco's benefit, 'Petra's his girlfriend.'

I don't think Coco was bothered but it was enough to make me draw back. She turned away as Sofia called her name, waving a joint, asking, 'Yes?'

Coco looked to me. 'Fancy sharing?'

I hesitated. Kay gave me a stern look. 'No, I'm ok,' I said, and watched Coco sashay away.

Half an hour later I was on stage, restringing Susan's guitar. All our gear had been packed away and the stage was left with a couple of house monitors and mic stands at the front. Scuffed white and yellow tape marked the floor, stage marks from some long forgotten performance.

'Bit sad, isn't it? An empty stage,' Kay said, joining me.

'Nah, exciting. Waiting for the next band, and because it's empty, the possibilities are endless. Who might be next? Stones, Bad Company, Zeppelin, Purple?'

'You would think that.' She laughed. 'What are you doing?'

I showed her. 'Restringing. I tried doing it back there,' I nodded stage-side, 'but it was too noisy.' The real reason was that unusually, after a gig, I was tired, and to tell the truth, a little resentful that I had to hang around. I had no way of getting home without a lift.

'Dimitri brought back four girls, and one of them brought a couple of guys, Sofia's not happy and Steve's doing a lot of business out the fire door.'

'Susan's gonna have to put a stop to that.'

Kay stood behind a mic stand. 'If she doesn't, Algie will. Did you know that's not his real name? Vince told me it's John.'

'No way. If anyone's an Algie, Algie is.'

'He wanted to be more memorable.' She looked out to the empty dance floor.

'Give us a song then,' a last and lonely drinker shouted from the bar.

I laughed. 'We could do with another singer. I've heard you. You can hold a note. Join us?' I asked Kay.

'No thanks. You guys don't play enough funk for me. Besides, I don't fancy being stared at.'

I could see what she meant. She was a few months short of seventeen and in the last few months had blossomed. Her figure was full, and she had lost any puppy fat she might have had. Like her sister, she held herself tall. Her hair, though not nearly as long as Petra's, was thick and wavy, unruly but never untidy. She didn't take herself seriously but knew her worth. I found myself staring at her.

She moved away from the mic.

'Being looked at sort of comes with the gig,' I said.

'No shit, Sherlock. I'd settle for my designs being admired.'

Kay was starting a fashion course at Chiswick Polytechnic and always moaning we looked boring on stage. She didn't. Tonight she wore a simple black denim waistcoat with no t-shirt or blouse and a black cotton skirt with a bold pattern of gold and silver balloons. It was easy to imagine the effect had the spotlights been on.

'You should let me come up with the band style.'

'Ok.'

'You don't mean that. You don't trust me.'

'You like Earth, Wind and Fire. I've seen their stage costumes.'

'You could carry it.'

'Not as well as you.' I hoped I didn't look guilty, having noticed Kay's waistcoat gaping as she sat next to me on the stage. A dark blue bra nearly matched her waistcoat colour. We fell silent as I replaced another string. Eventually Kay said, 'Heard from Petra lately?'

'I got a letter last week. You?' I concentrated on the guitar.

'Yep. She's got a job, on a farm.'

'I heard. She wants to be a vet's nurse. What's Will doing?'

'Don't know. She never mentions him. You know her aunt died last week?'

I didn't and said, 'Finally,' before I realised how awful that sounded.

'Perhaps she'll be back soon.'

'I hope so.' I did. I no longer knew if we were still 'going out' and our letters no longer gave clues. 'Did she ever mention the night of the party?' I asked hesitantly.

'What? When she caught you in bed with my sister?' She laughed.

'It wasn't like that. Ask Sofia.'

'I did. She can't remember what happened.'

'Nothing is what happened.'

'Ok, I believe you.'

The silence was a little awkward until she said, 'It's hard, isn't it, when everyone else is a couple.'

I must have looked confused. She continued, 'Susan and Bazzer, Steve and my sister, Dimitri and … whoever.'

'You and Vince?'

'Not like that.'

'You guys could be,' I told her. 'You laugh a lot, like a couple, which just leaves me. The only rock star in town who's a virgin.'

'The virgin bit I believe. Rock star? Not so much.'

'Funny.'

'Thanks. Sorry for chasing Coco away, earlier.'

'S'ok. I have a feeling she was only after me for my body. Who wants that? Besides, I am still with Petra, right?'

'Of course, and don't feel sorry for yourself. I'm still a virgin too.'

'Should we have some sort of pact?'

'Is that the line you tried on my sister?'

'Nothing happened.'

Kay smiled, 'Don't worry, that scar's quite dashing. Your turn will come,' she left the stage but turned to add, 'besides, you're a rock star.'

As I finished restringing the guitar, Vince came through a door at the back of the bar. I asked where he'd been.

'Algie's office. Just talking.' I wondered why he'd added that. He sat beside me on stage, taking Kay's place.

'Talking?'

'Talking.'

'Ok. Philosophy? History? Politics?' I tried to tease lightly.

'Ha bloody ha. I know you think it's odd but that's 'cos it's easy for you. You have a plan.'

I thought for a few seconds before replying, 'More of a dream, to be honest.'

'It'll work out. Algie says there are rules.'

'Rules?'

'For the suburb. For Penscote. He says it's like there's a set of rules and ten thousand paths, and when you fit, it's easy, you find a way.'

'I don't know what that means. We don't fit the rules.'

'Most do.'

'Really. Rocknow Station?' I asked sceptically. 'We go where the music takes us. This is rock and roll.'

'Is it? Look where we are. It's not like we're starting a revolution.'

'Sounds a load of bollocks to me.'

'Easy to say when the rules give you a path. Kid picks up guitar, joins band, meets sweetheart, gets his chance, local hero makes good.'

Nothing was said for a minute until he mumbled, 'Algie's offered me a full-time job here. I'm leaving the garage.'

'Your dad will go apeshit.'

'That's why I'm moving out. Sod my old man.'

I took a couple of seconds to let this sink in then asked, 'Where you gonna live?'

'Sunny Steve and Bazzer said I can stay with them 'til their old man comes back. It'll be a while. He got eighteen months this time.'

'What? He's in prison?'

Vince just looked at me.

'I didn't know.'

'Really?' he said.

'Never mind. But you moving out, one of Algie's rules?'

'They're not his and he says the rules might not give me a path. Maybe I'll need to write new ones.'

'Rules or paths.'

'Both'

'I don't get it.'

'It makes sense when Algie tells it.'

I strummed the guitar, nodding with satisfaction at the tuning, and played the opening to '*Movin' On*'.

Vince nearly smiled.

Miracle Number Four

Chapter 27
Autumn 1976
Richard, The Red Cow
'Under My Wheels

Earlier in the summer, The Ramones had played The Roundhouse. Though Punk Rock had been attracting attention in the music press, The Ramones gig was a catalyst and punk bands were crashing onto the scene weekly, making national headlines. Algie told us not to worry. We didn't. He told us to do our thing. We did. As we wrote and performed more original material, so our sound developed; not always in the direction we planned, and we were described in one local paper as Bad Company meeting Steely Dan. We'd take that, and were confident and buoyed by the small following we were building.

Bands like The Sex Pistols, The Damned and The Clash were filling London pubs and we'd checked out their gigs. I'd been blown away by the energy and jealous of the audience reaction and passion, but realistic enough to see they were not Rocknow Station's competition. I believed we were being held back by lack of keyboards and we'd even auditioned a couple, but they were either Rick Wakeman or Gilbert O'Sullivan. We wanted something in between.

There was room for punk alongside rock, disco, heavy metal, prog, funk, soul, reggae, pop, RnB and, of course, us. But it would be a lie to say we didn't have a slight crisis of confidence when Algie announced he'd got us a gig at The Red Cow, Hammersmith, in November. He wasn't our official manager, but we were happy to piggy-back on his contacts. It would be our biggest gig so far, not for audience size but prestige. A lot of well-known bands had already played there this year, and though we had a Wednesday night, not the most popular, it still mattered. We had a support slot and that was ok, we still had two sets, albeit short ones. There were enough people there to fill the room without packing it and smoke hung heavy, closing in the dark walls. We opened with *Under My Wheels*, as usual, but then played mostly originals, and the audience, although not particularly enthusiastic, were appreciative, especially of Susan. She had developed a stage persona and knew when to show an edge, when to up a gear and how to work a tired crowd. But above all, she really could sing, play guitar and, as Dimitri said, look 'rock' sexy, not 'page three' sexy, when she wanted to, and though she was my sister I knew what he meant.

At the interval, I hung around on stage while the others went to join Algie at the bar – I still looked my age thanks to facial hair that stubbornly refused to grow. It turned out shaving every day when not needed didn't make a beard grow faster, it just made your face sore. As far as I could tell, Algie was pleased with how the gig was going and that was important tonight – though we didn't need him to tell us.

From the stage I watched the crowd, especially the tall young woman edging her way through the drinkers, careful not to spill from the glasses she carried, or to nudge another. Most of the crowd was scruffy, if not outright punk, but she wore tight jeans with little flare, basketball shoes, a black bomber with plain red t-shirt underneath and a black flat cap. I couldn't see her eyes, but she had sharp cheekbones and full red lips. Kay would likely have appreciated her style. I watched her work through the crowd until she reached two young guys, about my age I guessed. Was that why she went to the bar? More chance of being served? One of the guys was tall and broad, the other slightly built with jet black hair and glasses, and as he turned to take the drink from the girl I saw he had an Asian appearance.

It took me a second to remember the name and place: Richard, Oakjack Ford, August – our first gig after Mum died.

I'd met him when he'd been sitting outside that pub called Devil's Peat. He was dark haired, tanned and cool. I remember the girl he was with watched him – it was not the girl here tonight.

That night I'd been high from playing and the joy of an audience, and was still performing when I'd met him during the interval. I'd chatted too much and too quickly, probably boasting and almost certainly talking bollocks, pretending to be more than I was, wearing sunglasses outside when the sun was gone. And after the show, I think I showed off by involving Sunny Steve's presence to settle an argument that was nothing to do with me. I may also have been exaggerating when I told the girl with Richard that she should audition to sing with us, but it was true when I agreed with Richard that we needed a keyboard player.

It turned out both he and the girl he was with that night had lost parents.

'My dad's dead.' Richard had said. No fuss, no self-pity, no explanation. It just was. He didn't carry it, let alone show it, but it was with him. His father's death was a reason, but never an excuse. It was as if never forgotten but such a part of him that it didn't need to be remembered. I envied Richard.

I'd joked of writing a song about three kids with dead mums and dads. I was at the stage where I'd moved on from avoiding talking about Mum to making jokes then regretting them.

It had been a long drive home from Oakjack Ford in a knackered Transit. As usual we'd started the journey talking fast and loud and over each other but sometime around one in the morning, somewhere near Guildford, we'd quietened.

Looking out the window but talking to me, Susan had said, 'You shouldn't do that.'

'What?'

'It's ok on stage. Makes sense. But when it's over it's over.'

'What?'

'And I get that you're still up and it's ok to still be JB with us, but no need to take it to others.'

'What are you on about?'

'The showing off. Not needed.'

'When?'

She shifted to face me. 'With those kids during the interval and at the end? Showing off on stage, part of the show, is ok. But not when it's for your own benefit. You don't need to impress anyone. And you shouldn't have involved Steve. He's not for hire.'

'I don't get it.'

'Think about it. Remember what Mum used to say. Don't try to be liked by everyone.'

Here, a few months later in The Red Cow, I went over to him. 'Richard,' I said when I was close, but still having to shout over pub conversation.

He nodded, 'JB. I was gonna come over and say hi.'

'How do we sound tonight?' I know I should have asked something more polite, perhaps how he was, for example.

'Not bad, better than last time, but still need a keyboard.' He smiled.

'Ha, I know, I keep saying. You still playing?'

'More than ever.'

'Good.' I turned to the guy and girl he was with. 'Hi. I'm JB.'

'We know,' said the girl, 'Richard told us.' She smiled, but I wasn't sure it was real. I was going to ask about her musical tastes, sure that I'd be able to turn the conversation to Rocknow Station but recalled Susan's criticism on the way back from Oakjack Ford. Instead, I asked Richard if this was a local gig for him and how Blue Jean Jenny was – the name of the girl he had been with that night came to me – and what he'd been doing since Oakjack Ford.

'Cleaning cars, mostly. My stepdad works at a car showroom. You full time with the band?'

'Not quite. Still have to work. I sell guitars in Patrick's Pianos, near Hounlsow West tube.'

'No way. My mum used to work there.'

'Patrick's?'

'Yep, trying to sell pianos. She's a great player but rubbish at selling.'

'I've only sold two keyboards in four months. Guitars? No problem, but piano? No clue. I was …'

'… JB, we're back on. And we need to tighten up this set. Algie says someone from Chrysalis is down tonight.' Dimitri tapped me on the shoulder but smiled at the tall girl – Kay was once embarrassed to tell me it was a smile that made you feel like the only girl in the room – the sort of cliché a girl doesn't mind. The girl smiled back, a more open smile than for me. The guy she was with frowned.

'Gotta go,' I said. 'Hey, why don't you come down to Patrick's. They gave me a job so you'll get one easy, especially if they know your mum.'

Richard said he'd see.

I tried to find him afterwards for a drink, but he'd left.

We stayed to watch the headline band and, though they went down ok, I honestly thought we were tighter and just, well, better. Algie said the guy from Chrysalis thought so too, though he did think we could do with a touch of keys, oh, and Rocknow Station was a shit name.

Miracle Number Four

Chapter 28
Winter 1976/77
The Double Act
'You've Got A Friend'

I was late, again. Four weeks until Christmas and customers were steadily increasing. I was late. I couldn't blame the buses. I couldn't blame a gig the night before, such an excuse was never acceptable. I was simply late, again. I went into the shop through the front door and was knocked back by the surge of music flowing from the Bechstein. A swirl of notes and chords, simultaneously random and irresistibly coherent filled the shop. I had not heard the piano sound this way before; not so much louder but full, dense and yet also lighter and ethereal.

The shop manager was standing next to the piano. Next to him was a young woman with dark red hair – lighter roots, shaggy, collar length. And next to her was a slim young man with thick dark hair, neatly cut and parted. The three of them blocked my view of the piano stool. They heard the doorbell and the music stopped. As they turned I saw the pianist – a tiny woman, feet barely touching the pedals from the stool on which she sat. She smiled at me, a bright smile touched with shyness, and looked to the young man. He nodded at me and, with a second take, I recognised Richard. He was slender and paler than when we'd last met at The Red Cow – the time I'd suggested he try for a job here at Patrick's. It had to be his mother at the piano. I later learned she was Vietnamese.

Back in November I'd mentioned bumping into Richard to the boss, who'd told me Richard's mother 'Couldn't sell a life-buoy to a drowning man,' but was touched by, 'The hand of Apollo,' when it came to playing piano. My blank expression had forced him to explain that Apollo was the Greek god of music and Richard's mother was a pianist of, 'Extraordinary, gifted, sophisticated, sensitive, powerful, creative, technical …' I'd stopped him there. I'd got the gist. And here she was. I was no classical aficionado, but I could feel she was special.

She played for a couple of minutes until a customer came in – a regular, after guitar strings, again. I served him, jokingly asking how he managed to break so many, but may have offended him. As he left, Richard introduced me to his mother and the young woman. Her smile was warm and a little uneven; of course I noticed. She was confident but not arrogant.

Richard's mother was tiny, with a tentative smile, holding a genuine modesty, as if embarrassed that she should gain so much joy from her playing and excited that others might too. The boss told me Richard was going to be helping in the piano and keyboard section – part time to begin with – and I was honestly pleased; some company my age in the shop was welcome, the boss was often out, leaving me alone.

The next day, Richard was in before me, wearing a pair of smart Farah trousers, a plain Ben Sherman and a black Harrington. His shoes were clean and his thick dark hair sharply parted. His tortoise shell spectacles sat squarely on his face, not tilted like an afterthought. I was scruffy; though the first thing he said after hello was, 'Cool t-shirt.' It boldly proclaimed 'Genesis' across the chest. I wasn't much of a fan, but it was the only clean one that had come to hand. It turned out Richard was an ok player but, more importantly, had a quiet confidence with customers that I envied. In his first fortnight he sold two Yahama keyboards; more than his mother ever did.

It took Richard far less time than me to recognise we could piss about the shop all day if we wanted, pretending to work, but if we didn't sell then one of us would probably be gone. And I could see it being me – his shoes were clean every day and his hair combed. My Adidas Sambas were close to ruin, and I still wasn't letting Susan trim my hair.

On his fourth day, while I was playing *You've Got A Friend* to demonstrate a guitar, Richard left the piano section to wander past, commenting casually to the customer, 'He's good but, to be honest, that guitar makes him sound better.' I instinctively handed it over to the customer as Richard walked away. Richard returned a couple of minutes later to nod appreciatively at the customer's playing. The guitar was sold. I earned a small commission and shared it with Richard.

It was the start of a double act. It would be a lie to say sales went through the roof, but they ticked gradually higher, and we sometimes invited customers back just to play with us and have a cup of coffee. The manager hated the idea of people hanging round not buying but loved the look of a busy shop.

If demonstrating a guitar, I'd play something Richard knew – *Angie* was popular – and he would subtly enhance it, adding touches of piano or keyboard. Then he'd make the, 'It's all down to the guitar, you try it,' suggestion. Once the customer had played a little, Richard again joined in subtly. He wasn't the pianist his mum was, but was good at listening, following and adding just the right touch at just the right time. It would often sound good; often the sale was nailed.

I'd do the same for him when it came to keyboards.

It didn't always work. We learnt that experienced musicians didn't fall for it, and it put off beginners. But we got good at recognising when to try.

Having two of us there also meant I could be late occasionally, usually if the previous night's gig had been a trek. And it worked both ways; Richard often rang in sick, usually with headaches, and I could cover for him.

In the third week, I learnt to cover Richard in other circumstances. I was sitting in the storeroom grabbing a nap, the boss was out, when Richard put his head round the door.

'I need some help. Customer has some questions on the Rhodes.' He motioned towards the front of the shop. Through the door I could see a man sitting at an electric piano. 'He wants to know what the hammer tips are made of.'

'It's got hammers inside?' I half-joked. Richard only half-laughed. 'If the answer's not in there I'm probably not gonna be much good, but ...' I took from Richard the catalogue he'd brought, leafed through and quickly found the specification. 'It says neoprene rubber. Whatever that is.'

I passed the catalogue back to him, but he didn't take it. 'Just in case something else needs to be looked up will you take the sale?'

It was an odd request but as I'd spent the morning snoozing I couldn't refuse. I didn't close the deal and as I went back to the guitar, section Richard joined me.

'Sorry.'

'Why?' I asked.

'For not making the sale.'

'That's down to me. Don't worry.'

'I'm sorry I couldn't use the catalogue.'

'S'ok.'

'Really sorry.' Richard looked worried.

'Really, don't be.'

He half-turned away then back, 'I ... it's ... because ...' his words falling away.

'What's up?'

'Sometimes, some days worse than others, I don't see words properly, when they're written down. I see the letters but not the words.'

'Don't see them?'

'I'm dyslexic.'

'What's that?'

He looked worried, scared even, though of the dyslexia or me knowing, I couldn't tell. 'Letters get jumbled. I can't read them.'

'Like the letters move about?'

'No, but they just don't make words.'

'But you can read music when you play piano?'

'Not well. It's mostly by ear and rote.'

'It's just as well we don't bother with sheet music then.' I picked up an acoustic and started strumming, motioning to Richard he should sit at the Rhodes Fender. We jammed around a twelve-bar blues riff for a couple of minutes, Richard following my lead closely. 'That dicklexis is no problem then.'

'Dyslexia.'

'Who the fuck thought it a good idea to name a problem with reading letters dixelisa?'

Richard looked at me but didn't smile.

'You should come along to a rehearsal, jam with us. I keep saying we need some keyboards.'

'I've seen you guys live. I'm not good enough.'

'For a jam on a Sunday afternoon? Of course you are. You'll soon be up to speed. Just gotta play more, with others. And bring Anika. I want to meet her.' I did. Richard had spoken of his Czech girlfriend; not a lot and never boasting, but always with pride though sometimes also a little sadness which I didn't understand.

'Maybe.'

In Richard's second week, a cocky girl breezed into the shop – full punk, crusty piercings, cheap looking tattoo and a tub's worth of hair gel plastered into pink spikes bursting from her skull. She wore a raccoon mask of black make-up but her smile was cute. I liked her even more when she said she'd seen me play, though she spoilt it by adding our music was, 'Shit.' The word sounded odd for being uttered in such a well-spoken manner.

I was standing behind the counter. I laughed and called to Richard, 'Well, my mum did warn me we can't please everyone,' then asked her, 'What can we do for you?'

'Drumsticks.'

We didn't carry a huge stock, but I let her try a few pairs. She found some that suited her small hands and as I turned to get a paper bag she grabbed the sticks, said, 'Ta-ra,' and ran out.

Stunned into inaction, Richard and I watched, then laughed. By the time we got to the door she was long gone.

'Do you know her?' Richard asked.

'Nope.'

'She knew you, or at least the band. And that's something you don't see every day.'

'What? A punk thief?'

'No, a girl drummer. What do we tell the boss?'

We decided not to mention it.

She came back a fortnight later, the boss was out again. She was only a little embarrassed. 'Sorry. I needed the sticks for rehearsal that night but was skint.'

'And you've come back to pay?' Richard asked hopefully. I was with another customer but listening.

'No. I've come for more. That last pair were crap. They broke.'

'But you were thinking of paying this time?'

'I suppose.'

And that time she did. Afterwards Richard felt guilty for not refusing to serve her or somehow making her pay for the stolen pair. But as I told him, 'She had a cute smile.' We named her Safety Pin Sally.

In the week before Christmas I was glad for Wednesday half-day closing. It was far too busy for my liking but the manager trusted us to lock up. Or, rather, trusted Richard. So we did, a half hour early. We pulled the blinds down, set up the Fender Rhodes and I plugged in my bass. We jammed for a while then I talked him through the piano part I had in mind for my song: *Miracle Number Four*. It took but a couple of run-throughs for Richard to improve on it. We stopped for a cup of tea from the flask Anika had made for him – me piss-taking as you can imagine.

'So, why's it called *Miracle Number Four*?' Richard asked as I spooned in more sugar. I pretended to concentrate on stirring but he asked again.

'Something my mum said. It made sense at the time,' I mumbled.

'And?'

I passed him the spoon. 'And I thought it was a good name for a song.'

Richard removed his spectacles and cleaned them with a handkerchief before asking, 'And?'

'And it's taking me bloody months to get right, so maybe it's just a shit song title.' I understated my frustration at the song not taking shape easily.

'What happened to miracles one, two and three?'

I took an acoustic guitar from the wall and strummed a couple of bars before singing,

'One is in the eyes of two
Two is bringing life anew
Heaven sent is number three
And four is where you pray to be'

I stopped and asked, 'Get it?'

'Not really.'

'It's what my dad says. Miracle one is love at first sight, two is children and three is God's work.'

'Deep. The song makes it sound a bit complicated, why not keep it simple, like the simple soul you are?' he teased, 'And what's number four?'

'The one my mum wanted.' I hung the guitar in the rack, speaking with my back to him. I wasn't sure he heard. I wasn't sure I wanted him to. He sipped carefully from his cup then said,

'You talk nonstop about everything but your mum. What did she want?'

'Probably to have lived a bit longer.' My false bravado was embarrassing for both of us, so I picked up my bass, said, 'Let's try it again,' and counted off the intro to *Miracle Number Four*. Richard froze. He looked at me and smiled. I smiled back and counted off again. He missed it. He looked down at the keyboard. His smile faded.

'Richard?'

'It's gone.' His hands dropped into his lap. Behind his glasses, his eyes moistened.

'What do you mean?'

'It's just gone. I don't know what I played.'

'You've forgotten?'

'No, it's as if it never happened.'

I started to ask more but there was fear in his face as he said to help him through to the stock room. 'Could you ring Anika please? Number's in jacket,' he said before closing the door.

I handled the phone conversation awkwardly, not having spoken to her before, but she was soon there, parking her Citroen round the back.

'I am for Richard,' she said. The accent was endearing but the wording odd.

I left them alone for a few minutes, hanging around where they could see me, in case I could help, or something.

'JB.' Richard called me over. 'You can lock up ok?'

'Of course.'

'Let's go.' Anika touched his shoulder.

'Is there anything I can do?' I wanted to ask what the hell the matter was.

Richard looked at Anika and nodded. 'I'm not as well as I could be.'

'I think I worked that out.'

'Sometimes I don't know what just happened.'

'That's ok.'

'And sometimes I have headaches and … stuff.'

'Stuff?'

'I don't see properly.'

'Or at all,' Anika added.

'I don't get it. Is it like the dyslexia?' I said.

'No,' he said with head bowed.

'We go now?' Anika asked.

Richard nodded.

'See you tomorrow?' I asked.

Anika shook her head. 'And not for a few weeks.'

'What?' I thought I'd misheard.

'You haven't told him?' Anika asked Richard, who shrugged an apology,

'I've got some … stuff to sort out.'

Christmas was as bad as I could have imagined. Without Mum it was meaningless. With no Petra it was lonely, and if I felt that, what would Dad be feeling about Mum? I didn't have the balls to imagine. We exchanged unimaginative gifts and Bazzer came round for dinner though he was unusually tense until the third glass of sherry.

Algie turned out to be a great booking agent and kept us busier than we wanted through the festive period but, though the gigs went ok, we weren't what you'd call a party band. Fortunately, we didn't have a gig on New Year's Eve. Unfortunately, Susan and I stayed in with Dad, who insisted we listen to Big Ben at twelve then went to bed. Shortly afterwards the band turned up, mostly drunk and over emotional, especially Bazzer. Susan was curt with him, and he didn't seem to understand. They didn't stay long, just checking in on us. When they left I missed Mum and Petra even more.

Miracle Number Four

Chapter 29
Winter 1976/77
Red Ice Rising
'April Blooms Again'

The *NME* journalist poured a glass of Jack Daniel's and offered it to me.

'No thanks,' I graciously declined. 'I'm in the studio later.'

'Dedicated to the music?' He took it for himself.

I shrugged modestly.

'So, JB,' he took a notebook and pen from his tatty jacket, 'the new band name. Where's it from?'

I laughed gently. 'Good question, Charles. And I know some fans think it's linked to our passion for speaking up for the man in the street, giving them a voice, but that's just a part of it.'

'Really, JB? Tell our readers more.'

'Well, we'd just played The Marquee ...'

'Wardour Street?'

'Is there another?'

'Hahaha.'

'Anyway, we'd played a couple of encores and the crowd were calling for a third, when Dimitri, just off-stage, said something about how hot we were, and he didn't mean the temperature, then Susie said, yeah, but cool too, then Bazzer said something like, and we are on the way up. So I said ...'

'Yes?'

'That makes us Red Ice Rising.'

'Ha, I get it.'

'The band liked it too. The suits from EMI weren't sure but hey, we don't need their permission, and the rest, as they say, is history.'

And in my imagination Red Ice Rising was on the front page of *NME* – a grainy black and grey photo, the heads of a packed crowd, arms raised to the sweltering, rocking band on a tight stage, Susan picked out by a spotlight, the rest of us partly in shadow, blurred in movement, the newspaper damp with sweat, beat pounding off the page.

'JB, pay attention.' Algie brought me back to the here and now – outside The Half Moon, Putney. 'I'm paying for the guy's beer, all night, so you lot need to be tight.'

As if we needed reminding; as if we were ever anything but.

To be fair to Algie he'd done his part in badgering a journalist from *NME* to come down. I wondered if I should be nervous, but wasn't. The Half Moon, Putney was a great venue to debut the new name: Red Ice Rising. Out of nowhere, Dimitri had suggested it a week into the new year, and we all liked it; not to mention we didn't have anything better. When we asked Dimitri, he wouldn't tell us where the name came from.

At first we were pissed off with Algie for arranging a support slot but it was The Half Moon, so no way would we turn it down. More daunting was that it would be the first gig under the new band name. Kay had designed a logo and drawn it on the front of Dimitri's kick drum, and we had badgered everyone we knew to come down. Though entry was free, Sofia came up with the idea of printing tickets with 'complementary' stamped across them and giving them away, making people think they were being invited personally. It worked well, though she and Sunny Steve got thrown out of four pubs and a couple of clubs when the managers caught them. Susan and Kay refined the logo and drew it on some t-shirts; Sofia persuaded a few friends to wear them on the night. The logo was also used on the posters they stuck up in the station café and some of the shop windows, including the bakery.

It was a good night. These days we played only two covers, opening sets with *Under My Wheels* and playing *Stay With Me* for the encore. Everything in between was an original and *April Blooms Again* was a highlight of the set. Susan's voice nearly cracked in the first chorus but that brought the story alive and such a sweet melody with a heavy blues background meant it was a song to feel, not hear. As the last note faded, Susan's face slipped into a gentle smile which Bazzer took a second to share. Then we exploded into the rest of the set.

Gigging regularly had given us confidence and we knew the songs and each other well. If one of us took a track somewhere else we could follow and jam, then bring it back seamlessly. I know it's boastful, but if you wanted to hear a shit-hot, tight and loud, honest blues/rock band with more than a hint of the west coast – California, not Weston-Super-Mare – great female lead and some decent harmonies in a smoking, packed venue, then you came to watch Red Ice Rising. And Susan had a special skill – she could lose herself in the gig but still hold a distance from the audience. Some part of her was immersed in her own performance while another gauged the crowd, their mood, their reaction, and she could manage them whilst directing us – always subtle but always in control, though you wouldn't know it from the floor. I was different. I was saturated with the sound and atmosphere, aware of the crowd reaction but as part of it, not trying to guide it. I suppose I should have been trying to see if I could work out who the journalist was, but when the first song started that no longer seemed important.

The Half Moon crowd loved Red Ice Rising. Even when the shit hit the fan. Perhaps more so.

Kay wore a denim jumpsuit with a US flag patch and probably didn't mean to leave the top three buttons undone, but she did. Half-way through *Dreams That Kill*, Dimitri stopped playing to grab a cowbell, clamber from behind his kit, shove a path through the crowd and smash it on the head of the dick that had been bothering Kay since the opening song. It was the first time I realised there was something serious between them and it would have been sweet if not for the bloke's two mates who wanted to take it outside. Fortunately, Steve was there and his calm but ever-present threat of extreme violence worked. Somehow it was understood that he was prepared to take things further than anyone else; he just was; he simply could. Dimitri said he'd handle it, but Steve wasn't going to take the chance, telling him, 'You might not have the best hands for a drummer, but they're the only ones you've got.'

Most of the crowd cheered Dimitri as he returned to his kit. Kay was pleasantly and attractively embarrassed. I caught sight of Algie. He wasn't smiling.

After the gig we packed up sharpish.

The following week's *NME* had a write up; only 250 words, but still, in the *NME*, so it mattered, though Bazzer complained it focused on the fight rather than the music. To be honest, I was more interested in the part that read 'the women in the crowd were drawn to the young Frampton lookalike, and probably not for his inventive bass parts.' The stick I took from Dimitri was worth it. I resisted sending the clip in a letter to Petra.

Chapter 30
Winter 1976/77
Judas
'Behind Blue Eyes'

Richard came back to the shop on the 24th of January. It was a shock. Not because I hadn't expected it, but because he was somehow ... less. He was still much better dressed than either me or the boss and wore a woollen flat cap at a stylish angle, but his shirt flapped and his belt was a notch tighter, causing his trousers to crumple round the waist. He was paler too and his eyes darker and wet, but without shine. Most shocking was the removal of his cap. His head had been shaved and was growing back but there were patches of smooth baldness, as if hair had never been there. My face must have showed something – though he left off his jacket, he replaced the cap. On welcoming him, it seemed the boss knew far more than I did about his reasons for being away, which I resented. I'd thought Richard and I had formed a good partnership in the short time he'd been there. I'd asked the boss what was going on but he'd side-stepped my questions.

I'd had a gig the previous night, second in a row, somewhere up the A1, and though we were used to sleeping in the Transit on the way home, the next mornings were still a challenge. As I took coffee first to the boss and then Richard, he said to me, 'You look a bit rough,' with a hesitant smile.

He wasn't wrong. I'd barely washed, and the t-shirt might not have been clean. I'd liberally sprayed the Denim For Men I'd received from Kay for Christmas but perhaps it was wearing off.

'Thanks. Whereas you look really well, like you've been on holiday. Spain was it? or Greece? You should have been more careful out in the sun though. And maybe not over-indulged in the tavernas. Have you put on weight?'

I immediately regretted it. I'd tried to be funny but instead sounded bitter and, to make it worse, Richard apologised,

'I know, I'm sorry. I should have told you I was going to be away.'

'Away?' It hardly seemed to explain how frail he looked and sounded. I waited. He was about to say more when a customer came in and he was quick to serve them. I went out back to tidy the stock room, whether it needed it or not.

'Shit. Safety Pin Sally stole more sticks,' Richard called to me. I'd only been out back a couple of minutes and he was behind the counter. By the time I went through to the shop he was out the door after her.

Safety Pin Sally had again waited for the manager to leave before coming in. I suppose because she'd paid last time Richard was less suspicious, but she hadn't even pretended to try the sticks, just grabbed two pairs and ran. Richard went after her.

I waited in the shop; no idea which way they'd gone. Richard was back, alone and with no sticks, in less than a couple of minutes. He was even more pale and had lost his cap. Though not breathing heavily he looked drained, exhausted and kept touching his missing hair. Without talking he went through to the back and hunted clumsily through his jacket pockets until finding a pair of sunglasses and a small plastic tub. He asked, 'Water?' while struggling to pop off the top. I came back with a glass and took the tub from him; he'd hadn't been able to get the container top off.

'How many tablets?'

'Six.'

'Six? I read the handwritten dosage instruction on the label. Six was not the number.

'Six. Please.'

I shook them into his hand. He gulped them in two swallows and went into the stock room, turning off the light. There were no windows and he sat on the floor, now wearing the sunglasses.

'Should I call Anika again?'

'No. Please, close the door.'

Richard came out from the stock room about an hour later, apologising.

'What for?' I asked.

'Being stupid. Running after Safety Pin Sally.' Behind the counter we had a rack of baseball caps advertising *Fender*. I don't think we sold any. Richard took a black one with white logo and slipped it on, trying to make it look natural.

'Cool shades, by the way,' I said, 'Cap, not so much. Way too American. What's going on? Are you sure we shouldn't call Anika?'

He looked confused and muttered, 'Sure we shouldn't?' as if working out what it meant. 'Yes. Don't call.'

'Ok, should you go home?'

'Not on the bus.' He removed the sunglasses. He was still pale but with dark shadows under dark eyes which had receded into their sockets.

'Sooner one of us passes our driving test the better.' I tried to keep it light. Richard was a couple of months from turning seventeen. I still had five months to go.

'It won't be me,' he said, cryptically.

I served a couple of customers, including an older guy who claimed to have accompanied Frank Sinatra in a Las Vegas night club but then I heard him on one of our Yamaha keyboards so maybe I got that wrong. When he'd left I made coffee and waited.

Richard was sitting at a Rhodes piano, playing snippets of songs I didn't recognise, and which were slow and sad. Eventually he spoke. 'You know *Blinded By The Light*?'

'Of course. Manfred Mann or Springsteen version?'

'Manfred. One day, with the band, can we play it?'

'We can try. Keyboard part will be down to you.'

He slowly played the song's intro on the piano then dunked a bourbon biscuit into his tea, lifting it just as it collapsed. 'Shit.'

I waited.

He pushed the mug away. 'What's the most important thing we have in common?'

'We both fancy your girlfriend?'

'Haha. No, serious.'

'I am. Why? Don't you? 'cos if not ...'

'You've got a girlfriend. Remember?'

'I guess. Though she hasn't written for a couple of weeks.'

'You have written to her though?'

'Sort of.' My last letter had included the news that we'd given all the chickens away to the petting farm. In her reply she said she understood but the part about, 'Still missing Ingrid,' made me feel guilty, even though Ingrid had died long ago.

'Well, you talk about Petra a lot.'

'I just rabbit. Full stop. Doesn't mean anything.'

'Doesn't it? I know she's tiny, but strong. Big green eyes in delicate face, smart, funny, hair down to her, your words, lovely arse, and cool until she's caught out laughing, which is even more cool. And that's what you say after she's been gone what, seven months is it?'

I was embarrassed into looking away.

'See? I know all about her.'

We both laughed, even though it wasn't true; he didn't know about her mole.

'Anyway,' Richard said, 'that's not what I'm talking about. What's the most important thing?'

'Music.'

'Even more. But we've never spoken about it.'

'More important than girls or music?'

'Seriously.'

'I don't know.'

Richard took a few seconds, weighing whether to speak or not. 'Dead parents.'

I put my cup down slowly.

'You don't talk about your mum. I don't talk about my dad.' He picked up his mug, sipped, grimaced at the mushy biscuit, and put it down again.

'What's to say?' It sounded harsher than I intended, especially when I added, 'Besides, there's something else you haven't talked about. Like the state you're in and needing tablets today?'

'Sorry. They're just painkillers.'

'What for?'

'Pain.'

'Haha.' I spoke sarcastically.

'Sorry. Stuff like today, with Safety Pin Sally. It was stupid to run after her. I should have known. Sudden movements, heart pumping faster, adrenalin surge, makes it ... worse.'

'It?'

Richard looked at me from under the cap. 'Tumour. Brain. The docs don't call it that, they talk about my issue or problem or challenge. Fucking cowards.'

I had no words.

'I don't mean that,' he said, 'I'm the same. It's why I call it Judas instead. It's why I was away, radiotherapy.' He gestured to his head. 'They say the hair will grow again.'

I held my breath. I had a memory of Mum and a conversation which included the words tumour and cancer. Putting either of those in a sentence next to the word brain could not be a good thing. I was suddenly scared and then ashamed. I had no right to fear. Oddly, I wanted to ask him if, when they'd told him, it had been a moment. And if it hadn't, surely it was a harbinger of moments to come?

He looked at me, waiting.

I spoke slowly, 'Ok ... so, just to be clear, do you want me to call it your tumour or Judas?'

Richard forced a laugh. 'Judas, I suppose.'

'The whole traitor thing? I get it.'

'Partly, but also, without Judas where would Jesus have been?'

'That I don't get.'

'It just feels like Jesus needed a Judas, so, traitor or not, maybe I need mine, maybe there's something more to come.'

I didn't understand, but Richard's calmness meant I didn't feel the need to ask.

'You should come along on Sunday, to rehearsal. We can try *Blinded By the Light* if you want.'

I knocked on Susan's door and waited to be invited. She called me in but I hesitated. Sometime in the past few months I'd stopped asking her stuff and she'd stopped telling; not a conscious choice, just a change, brought on most by her not being around too much. When we weren't gigging or rehearsing we were talking about the band or she was out – she and Bazzer saw each other almost every day.

'New picture?' I nodded towards a poster of a misty mountain range; ethereal and calming but vacant.

'Covers that damp patch.' Her room was tidy but in need of decoration. So was mine. We'd done little to the house over the last few months and when I say 'we', I suppose I mean Dad.

'Guess what?' I challenged.

'Ok, what?'

'I told you about the new guy in the shop. Turns out he has a brain tumour. I invited him along to Sunday rehearsal, he wants to jam, keyboards.'

'Tumour? Rehearsal? I'm not sure how those two things are related but yeah, why not.'

'Should I ask Bazzer?'

'Why? It's not up to him,' she said with no humour. 'You haven't realised yet, but you're the band's heart now, since you're singing lead half the time. It's cool.'

'Nah, it'll always be you.'

She smiled, but not easily. 'Anyway, what's up?'

'Nothing.'

'Really?' She sat up. 'Hey, how're those changes to *Miracle Number Four* coming?'

'Well, if you mixed *Behind Blue Eyes* with *Sara Smile* and *Seagull* you'd get ...'

'... a mess?'

'Yep. Don't see it being ready anytime soon. I don't know if it's supposed to be a celebration or a protest.'

'That's deep, for you. So c'mon, what's up?'

'Nothing. Just wondered what you thought about tomorrow?'

'Mum's birthday?' She looked at me. 'You don't want to go to the cemetery.' We might not talk as often but there was still no hiding. 'Dad and I are taking time off work.'

Next morning I rang the shop and Richard covered for me.

'At least it's not raining,' I said as the first drops fell. Dad didn't laugh. We were parked close to the cemetery. Susan was behind us in her Mini, ready to go on to work afterwards.

The rain was no worse after a minute so Susan flashed headlights and left her car, pulling her mac tight around her and wrestling with a collapsible umbrella that lived up to its name. Dad and I followed her to Mum's grave where I laid flowers. The grave was well tended, and I realised that Dad was still coming here regularly without me and Susan knowing – or perhaps she did, and I hadn't picked up on it.

It was but a minute before Susan gave up trying to stop her tears and cried unashamedly. I was glad as it gave me permission too. Dad cuddled us both and sighed. I thought there might be some words of wisdom coming. Instead he said, 'I miss the vegetable patch, Mum liked fresh cabbage but without her what's the point?'

Susan wiped a tissue across her nose. 'Sure Dad? No one really likes cabbage. I think Mum just wanted you to feel good.'

Dad laughed. 'That's probably true.' His smile faded. 'A good woman. She wanted us to be happy, above all. You know, when she was carrying you, Susan, I nearly gave up work in the garage to be a Redcoat, Butlins. Sounds stupid now. I mean, I was already twenty-six, but it was a dream. I think I'd have been good and who knows where it might have led.'

'There're no Butlins round here.'

'That's why Mum was so special. She said, 'Do it,' and was prepared to follow me to Minehead or Bognor or Clacton. She'd have given up the house. She was braver than me.'

'And?'

'It was spring fifty-seven, we'd been married getting on a couple of years and she was pregnant. Still, she wanted me to take my shot when Butlins offered me a job for that summer, even when Lawrence gave me a pay rise to stay. April insisted we go, but she deserved better, and when you were born I knew I'd made the right decision. But every year, just after Christmas, she'd say it's never too late. She wanted me to try, she really did. And now I feel I let her down by not. Crazy, eh?'

That afternoon, rather than go into the shop, I worked hard on *Miracle Number Four* but didn't improve it.

Susan came home from work early and ushered me from the kitchen when I tried to help with dinner – unusual for me, I know. It was ready as Dad came home, and Susan insisted we sit while she dished up bubble and squeak. It was the best meal we'd had since Mum went.

There was no gig or rehearsal that evening. We watched tv together until Dad fell asleep, around eight. Susan whispered she was going to pop over to Bazzer's, she needed to talk to him. She said I should stay but I went with her.

Bazzer opened the door. He and Susan didn't kiss. They had been going out together forever, it seemed, but always they kissed, except tonight. I followed them inside where Steve and Sofia were curled up on the settee, Bruce at their feet. Vince was out, working at Zamara'z. Bazzer and Susan made tea for all of us then went up to his room.

Sofia was sleeping but Steve was watching *One Man And His Dog*. I laughed at sheep running the wrong way just as Steve asked me what I'd been doing that day. I managed, 'Graveyard, then we had bubble and squeak for tea,' before bursting into tears. Easing himself free of Sofia without waking her, he pulled a cigarette pack from a top pocket. He tapped out a joint, lit it and took a drag.

'I reckon your mum would understand,' he said as he exhaled and passed it to me.

Miracle Number Four

Chapter 31
Winter 1976/77
Algie's Challenge
'Gonna Make You A Star'

'Prog rock? Musos getting their dicks out hoping to impress the girls but mostly just showing them to their mates. Proper rock? That's using them to please the ladies,' Dimitri teased.

'Ignore him. He's a drummer and he's Greek.' I ushered Richard towards the stage.

'Just don't tempt him to get his dick out,' Susan offered advice. 'It doesn't take much,' she joked with Anika.

'It is a thing of beauty,' Dimitri said, more factually than boasting and with a hint of Greek accent that came and went according to his mood and the company.

Dimitri's 'prog rock' comment had been in response to Richard answering the question on what bands he followed.

Anika laughed easily. Her eyes were usually smiling with no guile and, though her nose and smile were slightly crooked it somehow made her beauty more real. Kay told Dimitri to put his tongue away. Anika chatted easily with Susan and Sofia, her Czech accent was charming, and she helped Vince and Kay make tea without being asked. When we rehearsed at Zamara'z, Algie trusted Vince with the keys. Even Steve was here this afternoon and I wondered if Richard or Anika might find it intimidating – the full Red Ice Rising 'family' in residence – but if so, they covered it well. Over the last couple of days, Richard had looked a little less pale but no stronger, and a couple of times I thought I'd heard him throwing up in the shop toilet off the stock room. He'd ditched the dodgy Fender baseball headgear for a new tweed flat cap. It suited him and didn't look to be hiding anything.

I enjoyed Sunday afternoons at Zamara'z. Algie encouraged us to use it and, even when empty, I loved the atmosphere and, oddly, the smell – Saturday night beer and fags, mixed with the washing up liquid used by the bar staff and the Flash detergent used to mop both the floor and tables; the dressing room/toilet smelt of weed.

Bazzer had got hold of an old Rhodes electric piano. He was teaching himself to play, coming up with some keyboard parts to enhance our sound. We hadn't tried it live – Bazzer might have an idea what the part should be but didn't have the skill to play it well, yet; I'd no doubt he'd pick it up quickly. When Richard had first started working in the shop, I'd hoped he'd be the answer to our search for a keyboard player, but after his revelation earlier in the week that was unlikely. Crazily, I had even resented that for a few minutes – I honestly felt he would have brought more than his playing to the band.

We spent half an hour going over and tidying up a few parts we'd cocked-up at the last gig, and a further half hour working on Bazzer's latest: *The Difference It Makes*. Richard and Anika occasionally applauded politely but it was nothing new to the others. Kay had brought a pad with her and spent the time sketching Dimitri wearing increasingly outrageous rock outfits. She even had a brand name ready for her imaginary fashion label: Rockware. When Algie came in, we took a break and knew something was up because he suggested Vince open the bar and the first round was on the house. Dimitri pointed out his generosity came from the cut he took out of getting us bookings and Algie laughed. I had a bottle of Coke, alcohol was still not a thing for me, but I did share a joint with Steve. Susan gave me a 'stupid boy' glare.

'Close to decision time.' Algie used his quiet, serious voice.

'Decision time?' Bazzer asked.

'On keyboards?' I asked, warily. I was still pushing for the extra band member and though the others agreed, we hadn't looked that hard, being so busy with gigging, rehearsing and writing. I glanced over to Richard. He and Anika were sitting apart from us. I didn't try to catch his eye.

'You guys need to sort the keys question, but I was talking about what happens this year. Things are going well, plenty of gigs, some music paper coverage, even a little record company interest. What next?' He waited and looked at us as if we should know what the hell he was on about. I was back in school, failing to understand the question never mind know the answer. Vince, standing next to Algie spoke for us, 'Give up the day job. Go full time or …'

'Go back to playing parties. Add some disco to the set and maybe play some weddings. Sofia and Kay as backing singers in spangly jumpsuits. Penscote's answer to ABBA,' Algie completed without humour.

'It feels like we're full time already, Algie.' Bazzer reacted first and cautiously. 'I'm knackered.'

'Because you still have a day job. I can't book you for anything too far from this side of London and I can't get you into festivals. You need to be up for work in the morning. I know, I get it. But …' Algie let the question hang.

'I need a rest Algie. I don't know about going full-time. I need a break.' Susan finally spoke, looking as tired as she sounded, then tearful. She pushed away the drink in front of her and went to the toilets.

We all looked to Bazzer.

'It's been a tough few weeks. We all need a break. And it's harder for Susie, always being watched, leered at. We don't know.' He looked to me and Dimitri. We both nodded but perhaps didn't understand.

'I get it,' said Algie, 'but you're booked up for a month, at least. Now is the time to go harder, faster, and if that means full-time then …'

'You're not our bloody manager.' Bazzer stood. He raised a hand, about to slam the table, but caught himself. 'We need a break,' he whispered.

I looked to Dimitri. We shrugged at each other. I didn't need a break. I reckoned I could play all night every night, full time or not. I guessed Dimitri would be the same.

Sofia went to see to Susan. Anika whispered something to Richard then also went.

Algie poured himself a scotch. 'Ok, I get it, a break. Tell you what. The first week of March is light. I'll cancel the two bookings already in the diary, they won't like it, and not book anything until the following week. You'll have it all to yourselves. Fair?'

Bazzer muttered, 'Not our manager.'

'But if you go full time you need one. I can do a lot more than book you into venues, but I need to know where I stand. I'm not the only one can do it, but ask yourselves who knows you best, who has already invested in you? Who's already getting the gigs? Who has a ready-made rehearsal stage, with bar? Who's gonna make sure you get that break you need?'

I did my David Essex impression of *Gonna Make You A Star*. Dimitri laughed, then Algie added, 'Look guys, I don't know how good Red Ice Rising can be, but I do know that unless you throw everything at it you'll never find out. And, if you ask me to manage, that's what I'll do, manage, not control. I promise.'

Algie told us to think and talk about it and left.

The girls came back in, Susan was quiet, and we chatted in circles for a while. Dimitri was relaxed about going full-time. He was already on his fifth job since leaving school and was happy to walk away from the latest – fitting tyres was not so glamorous and was risky to his hands. Steve had nothing to add, though not on stage he was still one of the band. He didn't have a job anyway and it occurred to me I didn't know where his money came from, though I could guess – it's not as though his share of band profits was enough for the bigger van he'd bought. As for me, leaving Patrick's Pianos would not be hard, though I briefly wondered what that might mean for Richard; vain, I know. I looked to Susan and Bazzer for a lead, but they said little. Our rambling indecision faltered, and I thought it might be awkward for the non-band members.

They were quiet until Anika said, 'I am not a part of this, so not for me to say, but don't you want to know what could happen? Is not taking the chance not the bigger risk?'

As I came to learn, Anika usually cut through the bollocks. I looked to Susan expecting some response, but she said nothing.

After a few more awkward minutes I went up to the stage, retuned my guitar and called to Richard, '*Blinded By The Light?* I think I've got the bass sorted.'

He shook his head as others looked at him, but we had done some work on it in the shop in the last couple of days.

'Shame to waste that practise,' I teased.

He pretended a smile but didn't move until Anika whispered into his ear. Hesitantly he came to the stage, but I wondered if I'd done the right thing as the few steps up were taken slowly and carefully.

'Ignore that lot,' I suggested as he stood at the Rhodes, pulled his cap down a little tighter and played a few chords and runs, feeling the keys, gradually easing into the song's opening sequence. I came in with vocals then bass and we muddled through a few bars until Bazzer came up, then Dimitri. Richard knew the song best and we took our lead from him. Within half an hour we had a rough version and I saw how Anika watched Richard with pride. I missed Petra more than I had in weeks. Our third full run through was going well until the keyboards dropped out. I looked to Richard who was staring at his hands. Even before the rest of us had stopped, Anika was up the side steps to the stage. The music faltered to silence as she moved to Richard's side. He was surprised she should be there and looked confused, though he nodded at whatever she whispered. She took his arm and led him off the stage. Susan asked if he was all right and Anika nodded while calling, 'Is there tea please? Much sugar but not milk?'

Sofia reacted first, making a chair available and going with Vince to the small kitchen behind the bar.

'Please, play,' Anika said to us as Richard sat with his hands in his lap and a vacant stare, but it seemed as good a time as any to take a rest. Anika helped him drink the tea, making sure he had a firm hold of the cup.

Richard didn't come into work until Wednesday and apologised for leaving Zamara'z early on the Sunday. I asked if he was feeling ok and he said he was fine. I didn't believe him.

We closed the shop for lunch and went out back. I'd made myself a peanut butter sandwich. Richard had a cheese and tomato doorstep made with fresh bread and a sprinkle of basil. He kept his cap on while eating. We swapped half rounds.

'Nice.' I mumbled with a mouthful.

'Anika made it.'

'Did she enjoy Sunday afternoon?'

'Yep. She thinks you guys should go full time, but maybe not yet. She thinks Susan might need a longer break. You're playing a lot of gigs.'

'Susan'll be fine. We'll have a week off in March.'

'Anika thinks that might not be long enough.' Richard spoke hesitantly, as if breaking a confidence.

'Why?'

'I don't know. Maybe she and Bazzer will get married and have a kid.'

'Nah, she's into the band too much. Why get married? And she wouldn't want a baby. Who would?'

'You wouldn't?'

'Maybe in a few years. When I'm too old to keep gigging. Maybe when I'm thirty or something.'

'You do know how old Jagger is?'

'Exactly.'

Richard looked confused.

I laughed. 'Anyway, kids gotta slow you down, right?'

'Slowing down might be a good thing. And they're a way of staying around.'

'What do you mean?'

'Just something Anika said.' Richard frowned. I needed to lighten this mood.

'So,' I took a sip of Vimto, 'let me get this straight. You're half Czech, half Vietnamese. Anika, who is …'

'Czech.'

'Is four years older than you …'

'Three years and ten months.'

'Makes you proper lunch, has beautiful eyes, charm to spare and a great figure. Can I say that?'

'I guess.'

'Just out of interest, while she's staying with you, where does she sleep.'

'None of your business.' Richard laughed.

'That's all the answer I need. Well, seeing how you're so fat, ugly and stupid I can only assume you have an enormous dick.'

Richard's pallid complexion showed a touch of embarrassment. I laughed until so did he, then he tried to deflect attention. 'What about you? Bass player in a band. You must have known loads of girls. Before Petra.'

I shrugged, pretending to be modest. I was about to make up a story or two about groupies, but I liked Richard. 'Not really.' I didn't mention that between Susan, Sofia and Kay it seemed I was never alone with a girl long enough. Not that I was sure how long would be needed. Besides, as I added, 'There's Petra. Shame she's in Ireland. We write a lot,' I lied casually. I hadn't heard from her in three or four weeks, not that I'd written. I also didn't add that I was still a virgin at the grand age of just over sixteen and a half – and that was because I suppose there had been enough in our letters to make me think Petra was still my girlfriend, just. She'd also written of plans to come back home in time to start college in September, but that was a long time to wait.

Miracle Number Four

Chapter 32
Winter 1976/77
Kay's Birthday
'Gonna Fly Now'

It was Kay's seventeenth birthday on the 3rd of February and Sofia was determined we should celebrate with her little sister. Between gigging and rehearsing no one was up for a mid-week party, and I felt bad for Kay, but Vince had an idea; it was easy enough to convince us because we didn't have to do anything. The idea came to him on the day Steve brought home a Sony Betamax player. Knowing how expensive it must have been, no one asked where it came from. Vince suggested we celebrate Kay's birthday with a film night. I didn't realise Kay was a film fan but Vince knew her better. And anyway, the idea appealed. I hadn't gone to the cinema since Petra had moved away and we all needed a night without playing, talking or thinking Red Ice Rising – every conversation kept coming back to Algie's question and Susan kept ducking an answer. I wasn't pressing her.

With Kay's permission I invited Richard and Anika, though I was surprised he was well enough to come. Sofia baked a cake, Bazzer and Susan supplied a couple of Party Seven tins and Vince brought a bottle of vodka from Zamara'z, donated by Algie. Richard and Anika turned up with a bottle of Mateus Rosé, and, thoughtfully, a present for Kay – a book on sixties' fashions. Steve got hold of a pirate copy of *The Omen* and Dimitri brought *Rocky* – he had been working out for a few months and now had the body of Atlas, or Stallone, to go with his luscious hair. Susan was desperate to trim it, but he wouldn't let anyone near with scissors.

Ten of us and the dog crammed into Bazzer's back room, squashed on sofa and armchairs, perched on kitchen chairs or, like me, cross-legged on the carpet. Sofia played hostess, continually to and fro the kitchen with fresh drinks.

The tv flickered images into the dark room. Bruce, the adopted dog, mooched from front to back room, unsettled at his usual havens being occupied.

Steve and Bazzer were smoking the more expensive weed and the sickly-sweet smell was settling on us. I felt a tinge of high even though I was getting used to smoking joints. Kay jokingly complained that she'd have to explain the smell on her clothes to her mother, to which Dimitri suggested she take off her dress. Sofia clipped the back of his head with a rolled-up *NME,* but Kay smiled at him.

The Omen was tense enough to keep our attention and I only looked away a couple of times. *Rocky* held far less interest. Whether it was because people were drinking or smoking joints, I don't know, but it wasn't long before Susan and Bazzer wandered off. Steve and Sofia went up to his room, taking the good weed with them. Dimitri went to the kitchen for a drink. When he was slow to return Kay went to look for him.

'You know they're shagging?' Vince said to me as Kay left the room.

'No, but I wouldn't be surprised. It's Dimitri.'

Vince looked downcast.

'Shagging?' Anika asked.

Vince explained.

'Ah, well anyone could see that,' said Anika, 'and I only just arrived.'

'After that cowbell attack we all knew he had a thing for her, but Sofia will kill him,' I said.

'Sofia knows.'

'And I thought me and Kay had a pact.' I half-joked.

'For what?'

'Doesn't matter.'

'Yes it does, what?' Vince pressed.

'We both agreed not to shag Dimitri, never mind how handsome he is,' I joked, then thought Vince might not find that funny.

'That is true. He is,' Anika agreed. 'We will go. Richard is tired. Hospital in the morning.'

Richard nodded and ran a hand over his head. His hair was returning but unevenly, so he kept it short.

'Coming to Zamara'z on Sunday?' I asked.

She looked at Richard who said, 'We'll see.'

They saw themselves out.

'Great film, eh?' I said to Vince.

'Not really.'

'So, Kay and Dimitri. You ok with that?' I asked.

'I guess.' Vince was unconvincing.

'You know, what with you and …' I hesitated, '… Algie being so pally these days?'

'It's not like that. He's not like that.'

'Really?'

'Really. You guys know fuck all.'

'Hey, I don't care.'

Vince went to a sideboard and came back with a tin of shredded leaf and some cigarette papers. 'Steve's back-up. It's not the good stuff but …'

He rolled two joints and passed one to me. I found myself humming the *Rocky* theme tune.

We heard a rhythmic knocking from above us.

'Steve and Sofia?' I suggested.

'Or Bazzer and your sister. Hang on, that's the room I sleep in. It's probably Dimitri and Kay. In my bed. Shit. And even your new pal, Richard, is paired up.'

I smoked the joint in the shallow way I'd developed; I was still a beginner. There was no taste as such but a mustiness that clogged the back of my throat. I coughed.

'He's married,' said Vince.

'Who is?'

'John. I mean Algie.'

I was a little dizzy and waited a few seconds before taking another drag while trying to make sense of Vince's words. 'Ah, Algie is John, right? I knew that.'

291

Vince nodded. His face was pale blue in the light from the tv. I was distracted by Rocky chasing chickens. That took a few seconds to work out. 'And Algie, John, is married,' I said.

'Not to each other.'

'No, I get that. Any kids?'

'He had a son, but he died, couple of years ago. He was only seven. Don't tell anyone. Algie will go apeshit. Likes to keep it separate.'

'Separate or secret? But really, what about you and him?'

'He's all right. He … helps. That's more than my old man ever did.'

'He helps?'

Vince drew deeply on his joint. 'No, I don't mean that. He's a nice guy. That's all. He listens then suggests things.'

'Like those rules?'

'Exactly. But he knows they're not right for me, yet. That's the thing about it.'

'I still don't get it, Vince.'

'Nor do I. But I don't want to go back home, and I didn't think I'd care about Kay and Dimitri, except I do.'

I touched him on the shoulder. 'If it helps any, so do I. Kay was my back-up plan if Petra doesn't come home.'

'She's too good for you, JB.'

'Kay or Petra?'

'Both, but especially Kay.'

'What about for Dimitri?'

'He's a Greek drummer.' He shrugged and I laughed.

The knocking sound upstairs grew louder.

'Yep, that must be Dimitri. He's speeding up,' I said and giggled at my own joke.

Vince and I watched the rest of the film. He lit another joint, I didn't. I was still dizzy and a little sick but didn't mind. Bruce wandered in and jumped up next to me on the settee, looking for a fuss. I wondered if he could get high and giggled at the thought.

Around eleven, Susan came down and needed less than one sniff before calling me all kinds of idiot, then slapping Vince and accusing Bazzer of being a total prick when he tried to calm her down. She dragged me into the garden and poured a glass of water down my throat. I've no idea why. I even swallowed some of it. By now I wasn't feeling any effects from the joint, but she was in no mood to listen or slow down.

'So, our pact, what happened?' I asked Kay. She was helping Sofia clear up.

'Well, to be honest, much as I like your hair, Dimitri's is longer, and I like his beard.'

'Is it too late for me to grow one?'

'More a case of too early.'

She was right.

'Anyway. You're still with Petra, right?'

'Sort of. She hasn't written in a while.'

'While you've been so regular with your letters.' She was being sarcastic.

'Have you?' I was defensive.

'Of course. She's doing all right and still plans to come back here for college in September. She might come and live with me for a while. We've a spare bedroom now that Sofia's moved in here with Steve. She also asked why you hardly write to her and if you've got a new girl.'

'What did you tell her?'

'That you'd write and answer that for yourself, this week. Don't make me a liar.'

'You could tell her I …'

'No.' She put a finger to my mouth. 'Don't tell me, tell her. I don't want to know before she does. Though I have told her you're obsessed with the band.' She made it sound a bad thing. 'She also mentioned a local lad asking her for a drink. So if you're still thinking of writing, better get a move on.'

'What do you mean?'

She didn't smile but her eyes sparkled with mischief. I could see why Dimitri would smack someone round the head with a cowbell for her.

'Did she go? For that drink?'

She didn't answer.

'Ok, I get it. I'll write. But if Petra doesn't want me, we still have that pact, right?'

'Too late for me, JB.'

I nodded.

'For what?' Susan asked as she came in.

'For Dimitri,' I said. 'He's fallen for Kay's charms. Can't see why though.'

Kay cuffed me round the head. I was destined to be the baby of the band.

Chapter 33
Winter 1976/77
999
'Maybe I'm Amazed'

That Saturday we played The Red Lion, Brentford. It was warm for February and there was a decent turnout. Even Algie and Vince came down, unusual for Algie on a Saturday. We played ok, but Susan wasn't her usual self.

'Well that was a bit shit,' Algie said in the car park afterwards. He'd stood and watched us pack away before gathering us together and offering his summary. We might not have been great but that was harsh. I thought Bazzer might stick up for Susan, at least, but before anyone answered Algie continued, 'Never mind deciding if you want to go full time. You need to decide if you want to bother at all. Thank God the guy from Swan Song didn't come down.'

He walked away, shoulders down, disappointed in us.

On the way home I asked Vince if Algie really had nearly got someone from Swan Song and he thought so. I didn't know whether to be further disappointed or relieved.

Richard came back to Zamara'z, with Anika, for the Sunday rehearsal, and we worked some more on *Blinded By The Light* but he didn't stay long.

I was surprised the next day when he came into the shop.

Mid-morning he was noodling at a Yamaha organ while I patched up a dodgy connection on a knackered Rickenbacker we'd taken in part exchange – soldering was another skill I'd learnt from Bazzer. We had the shop to ourselves. The boss was out, supposedly visiting another branch, but Richard reckoned he was giving piano lessons to bored housewives 'on the side'; he always came back happier than he left.

'Did you enjoy The Red Lion gig?' I asked Richard, while waiting for the soldering iron to heat.

'Nah, you were rubbish.'

With Algie's criticism still burning I may have looked upset.

'Only joking. You were good, as always. A bit … loud … on some songs but maybe it's just I sometimes don't like too much … loud.' He gestured vaguely to his head. 'You know, aches and stuff.'

And there was I feeling sorry for myself over a bad gig. What a prat. Though I was reluctant, this was a good time to ask Richard more about his 'Judas' but before I could come up with something subtle, Safety Pin Sally came in. Her hair was no longer violently sharp pink spikes – she had a bright red pixie cut. Her make-up was dark but there was less of it, and it was both more dramatic and less intimidating. She still wore black clothes, but it no longer looked second-hand or a big brother's and her Doc Martens had a sheen, if not an outright polish. Her smile was still cute and not in a cuddly toy way.

I put down the guitar.

'Oh. I forgot to tell you,' said Richard, 'Sally was there on Saturday. We got talking. I said she should pop in today as you could bring a couple of pairs of Dimitri's old sticks for her.'

'You didn't say.'

'I forget a lot,' Richard said with no humour.

'So what? No sticks then?' she said, sitting on the piano stool next to Richard. 'Oh, and my name's not Sally, cheeky fuckers.'

There was manufactured anger in her words and the swearing didn't suit her. I laughed. 'What is it then?'

'Mind your own.'

'Ok. Just tell me you're not here to steal something.'

'I need more sticks. And you guys were great Saturday by the way.'

'Liar,' I said.

She laughed.

'What happened to the safety pins?' I gestured to her ears where there were now studs.

'They kept going manky. No one needs pus in their ears.'

'No, I suppose not.'

'Still got one in my belly-button. You should get one.'

'What? A pin in my navel?'

'No, idiot. A stud, in your ear. And maybe a tatt.' She showed me her forearm and an inking of what might have been Marilyn Monroe. I nodded with what I hoped would be considered approval. 'Anyway, point is,' she rested a hand on Richard's thigh as they sat side by side on the piano stool, 'are you going to let me steal a pair of sticks or not?'

She flashed that smile. Richard shuffled uncomfortably.

'No. But you can share a joint with me.' I surprised myself with the suggestion.

'Funny boy.' She didn't believe me.

I took a battered roll-up from a top pocket and made a theatrical show of smelling it. Richard rolled his eyes.

'The boss won't be back until this afternoon.' I nodded towards the back of the shop. In the days following the graveyard visit, I'd made a habit of smoking half a joint in the stock room when the boss was out. I'd open the door to the delivery area and waft out the smell. Safety Pin Sally joined me there. We sat on the floor, there were no chairs, and I lit the joint, taking a couple of drags. We left the light off, but the low sun slipped in through the open back door and I had a memory of Lawrence's garage office. That seemed a lifetime ago; it nearly had been for Lawrence. I took another deep draw. I'd bought the joint from Vince, and it wasn't potent, but a welcome lack of concentration settled on me.

'I thought we were sharing.' Sally took it from me, and we smoked in silence for a couple of minutes before I asked.

'Is your name really Sally?'

'What makes you think that?'

'I dunno. Wait, I do. We gave you that name. Safety Pin Sally.' I laughed. 'Where did the pins go? Never mind. What is your name?'

'How am I gonna nick sticks if you know my name?'

'Good point. I'm JB.'

'I know.'

'So we'll stick with Sally. Which is a good name.'

We passed the joint back and forth and I learnt that Sally lived locally, had just passed seventeen and had parents with a few bob, much of which had been spent on her teeth, 'Explaining your cute smile,' I said.

She smiled, of course.

She was doing A levels at Cardinal Howard, Petra's old school, which I didn't mention, but spent most of her time bunking off,

'To nick drumsticks,' I added.

'A girl's gotta practise,' she said which made me laugh. I don't know why. But it was ok, she laughed too.

Perhaps the weed was stronger than I realised.

After ten or fifteen minutes I renamed her Chatty Sally as she told me why she liked Red Ice Rising but didn't like our music much and, though she loved that we played originals, hated that we didn't cover anything by The Damned, Clash, Sex Pistols or Ramones. She was annoyed that we didn't look punk, but glad we didn't wear poncy cabaret suits, though Susan was sooo good that it was a shame she dressed to please the men – I didn't think she did – and she was happy we played pubs but wanted to know when we'd be in the big venues. I told her – when I could get a word in – so did we. Oh, and could her band, Tatt Tramps, support us, just as soon as they got a few songs together, and I said I thought that was a great name for a band and then she stopped talking and just looked at me. For some reason I thought she was going to ask me why my smile was lopsided, but she didn't. She just looked, then edged a little closer and I realised she was going to kiss me. That seemed like a good idea, so much so that I giggled, thanks to the joint, but forced a serious face and leant towards her.

Sally hesitated. 'Do you mind that I'm bi?'

'By what?'

'You're an idiot,' she said, but, I thought, in a nice way, and I giggled again, like an idiot.

'Boss is back.' Richard knocked and called through the door.

We froze.

'Shit.' I stood up too quickly, blood rushed from my head, and I grabbed at the wall for support. Chatty Sally laughed.

'Shush.' I steadied myself, helped her to her feet and ushered her out the back door, wafting the smell behind her.

Next morning, Dad was up and out to work before either Susan or I were down. We both had cereal and tea, it was easy and, as usual, eaten mostly in silence. The radio was on, switched over to Radio Caroline; Dad listened to Radio 2 in the mornings.

'This DJ isn't half as funny as he thinks he is,' I said between mouthfuls.

'Bit like you then,' said Susan, without smiling.

'What's the matter?'

'Sorry. Nothing. Just, I dunno, knackered, still.'

'Anika told Richard you look tired.'

'Did she?' She left the table and scraped most of her soggy cereal into the bin. 'What do you think of her?' Susan stood with her back to the window over the sink. It was a grey, dreary morning but with the kitchen light off she was still almost a silhouette.

'She's cool. Looks out for Richard and he needs it. I don't think he'll be the answer to our keyboard question.'

'That's your concern?'

'No, I just meant … he's pretty sick. Good job he has Anika.'

'I like her. I think she's right about not taking the chance being a bigger risk. But ...'

'But?'

'Bazzer's finished his apprenticeship. We're both working, steady money and the band pays for itself, I never thought it would.'

'I always did.'

She smiled, close to patronising. 'Bazzer and me are thinking of getting a place together.' She made the suggestion sound ominous.

'Together.' I repeated. 'Dad won't like it if you're not married or engaged at least.'

'He won't care. But he thinks Mum would have, so he has to.'

'Last night, Dad asked me how the band is going.'

'And?'

'He reminded me of the Butlins story. How he was nearly a Redcoat, but you sort of stopped him.' I tried to say it in a jokey way but as I said the words realised they were never going to be heard like that.

'Oh yeah, my fault. Thanks for the reminder.'

'Sorry. I just keep thinking about Algie's idea. Why are you and Bazzer so worried about keeping jobs and living together? Unless ...?' I don't know the expression on my face, but I hoped it wasn't shock as I said, 'Oh shit. Bazzer's knocked you up.'

Maybe I'm Amazed was suddenly loud from the radio in the silence between us.

'You have such a way with words. Dick.' She didn't look at me.

'Well I guess that must have been a moment. When you found out I mean.'

'Ha bloody ha.'

'When's it due?'

'It? Shut up.'

'So are you?'

'Just ... leave it.' Finally, she turned to me and there were tears. She was right, I was a complete dick.

'Oh shit, I'm sorry, sis. I'm sorry. What you gonna do?'

'I don't know. I'm three weeks late. It might be nothing. But shit, Mikey, what am I gonna do?'

My first thought was to ask about Red Ice Rising but fortunately didn't. I muttered something about wishing Mum were here and what would she say?

'Get married quick.' Susan tried to joke but her tears turned to sobs.

'You keep playing that. What's it called?' Richard asked.

'*Miracle Number Four.* Remember?'

'Oh yeah.'

Wednesday afternoon. My favourite time in the shop. It was a couple of days after I'd almost been caught with Sally in the stock room. Actually, we hadn't almost been caught. It turned out the boss wasn't back for another half hour; Richard had been wrong. Still, I don't think the boss believed me when I denied all knowledge of the smell, but he had no proof and he still trusted us enough to leave us alone on half-day closing. Or maybe he was desperate to get to the next piano lesson he was giving.

I had some time to kill, and as worries over (a) Susan, (b) the band's answer to Algie's question, (c) Petra being asked out by a local lad and (d) Richard's Judas started to bother me, I did what I always did – ignored them, picked up a guitar and started playing.

'*Miracle Number Four.* Good title for a song. What's it about?' said Richard.

I hesitated, then, 'Peace.' It seemed he didn't remember we had talked about it before, even worked on it together a little.

'A protest song? Like *Give Peace A Chance*?'

'No. More like where is it?'

'Where?'

'And what. I suppose. Oh, and how.' I was vague, not wanting to talk about Mum – yet another worry (e) – if I was to think about it.

'Not sure I follow but that's ok. Need some piano on it?' Richard asked.

'Like you did before?'

'Did I?'

'Yep. It needs something. What do you …'

'Oi!' It was a muffled shout from outside followed by heavy tapping on the door. We'd dropped the blinds but peeking at an edge I saw Safety Pin Sally.

I let her in and found myself defending why I still hadn't got her some cast off sticks from Dimitri. She didn't bother defending the fact she still didn't have any money to pay for some. Richard laughed and I went out back to look for any old stock that we'd taken off sale for any reason. Sally followed me. The back door to the outside world was closed so I turned the light on.

'Time for a joint?' she suggested.

'Not today. I'm working on something.'

'Ten minutes?' She pulled a flattened roll-up from her purse.

'Shouldn't you be at school?'

'I'm older than you, cheeky git. But yes.' She sat on the floor, like a couple of days earlier, and lit the joint.

'You're just a rebel without a clue,' I teased. I don't think she got it.

'So, my band, Tatt Tramps? Gonna get us a support slot?' she asked, blowing smoke to the ceiling.

'Are you any good?'

'We're shit-hot. Honest.'

I closed the door to the shop and sat beside her. There was a silence which became less awkward as we shared the joint. Eventually I said, 'It's Algie you need to impress.'

'Algie?'

'Our mana … booking agent.'

'What about impressing you?' Chatty Sally giggled, then, as she passed the joint, leant over, ran a finger gently across the scar over my eye and kissed me.

I didn't protest. In truth, the kiss was as welcome as it was wet. Her tongue probed harshly, and I let her push deep into my mouth. Our teeth knocked and I worried for her cute smile. I stubbed out the joint on the floor as she sat astride me and was quickly hard as we kissed furiously, then she pulled away. I wondered if it was because she could feel my heart banging in my chest. Smoking weed did that sometimes but wasn't the cause this time.

'And you don't mind, you know, after what I told you last time?' she asked.

'Last time?'

'Some guys do.'

'Do what?'

'Mind.'

'About …' I let the question hang.

'Me being bi.'

'By what?'

'It wasn't funny first time you said that.' Her cute smile disappeared. My confusion must have been obvious as she added, 'So if me being bisexual bothers you, say so now.'

I didn't think I'd ever met anyone bisexual, though I wasn't entirely sure I knew what it meant. I remembered a headline in Susan's *Cosmopolitan* magazines and perhaps an article in a copy of *Mayfair* I'd nicked from Dimitri but, to be fair, I'd only been looking at the pictures. There had been an interview in one of the music mags with David Bowie where it had been mentioned and I'd got the gist of it but, like the situation with Vince, I understood that I didn't properly appreciate what it meant to Sally, though I could easily understand why a girl might fancy another girl – why wouldn't they?

Sally, still astride me, shuffled and, I'm sure, felt I was still hard. I think she took that to mean I had no problem with her being bisexual.

'Do you want to see my safety pin?' She lifted her t-shirt and arched her back so I could see her navel. Her stomach was not as flat as Petra's, but soft, smooth, rounded, feminine, perfect for gently stroking; so I did. The skin was pinched around the safety pin where it pierced, but not where it exited, and though it looked unnatural it was fascinating, sexy. I stared before pushing her t-shirt higher. She wore a bra, and her breasts, more full than Petra's, were, simply, beautiful, though she had no mole. The white cotton was stretched, showing them milky white and her nipples pink. I was even harder as I tried to slow my breathing and settle the desire to grab at her. She bent towards me, licking my ear with her tongue then whispering, 'Is it ok if I'm still learning? You can show me.'

I didn't know if I could, but with (a) my pulse racing, (b) her tongue back in my mouth, (c) breasts now pressing against me and (d) the biggest hard-on I'd had since I didn't know when, I was willing to try. She was breathing fast and smelt of weed, damp and grassy, but without the smoke, a smell of earth, of her sex. She struggled to undo my jeans just as a glimpse of Susan's pregnancy slipped into mind.

'Johnnies?' I mumbled as we kissed. 'I haven't got any.' The two Susan had given me, so long ago, were gone, taken by Petra. Petra. I wondered if she still had them; had used them? She was nine months older than me. Why should that matter? I had a sudden sensation of deep fear. Not of Sally's pregnancy but of telling Susan, Dad ... Petra ... Mum?'

'It'll be all right. I'm due on any day now.'

I had no idea why that might be helpful and, ridiculously, thought of Dimitri who always kept a few Durex in his stick bag.

'What's wrong?' she asked as my hands slipped from her arse, her sweet arse, and I tried to turn my face.

'Johnnies,' I repeated.

'It'll be all right.' Sally repeated.

And I was so hard, so desperate that I believed her and almost didn't hear the call, 'JB?'

I thought it was Sally until Richard half opened the door.

'Again?' Sally whispered.

'JB?' Richard repeated, quietly.

I couldn't see him and eased Sally away so I could stand, 'Coming, Richard.'

'Very nearly.' Sally laughed. 'You better wait a bit before going out there.' She indicated to my bulging jeans, and it would have been funny if it didn't sound like a moan of pain from the shop.

'Richard?' I pushed the door, but it only opened another couple of inches. Something was blocking it. I could put my head far enough round to see. Richard was half-sitting, half-lying, his feet preventing the door from fully opening. Vomit dribbled from his open mouth and pooled on his shirt. He held his spectacles in a hand laying limp at his side. I pushed a little harder, but slowly, until I could reach him. Sally was behind me. Together we propped him up against the wall. He dropped his head into his hands, pressing his palms hard against his temples. Moaning.

'No chance of any sticks then?' were Sally's last words as I let her out the front.

Richard's last word before I called the ambulance was, 'Judas.' I was crouched down in front of him, his face screwed with pain, sweat glistening on his forehead and upper lip, panting with agony, eyes red with fear.

I said the words, 'brain tumour,' to the call handler and sensed a new urgency in her voice. The ambulance was at the shop door in less than eight minutes – eight minutes that must have felt eight hours to Richard. He couldn't stop shaking to drink the water I tried to give.

West Middlesex Hospital A&E was busy but whatever I'd said in the 999 call made a difference. Richard was rushed past the waiting area to a bright curtained booth with shiny floor, a cream wall and metal framed bed that looked like a rack. The beige machines on trolleys looked to have come from a Sci-fi B movie, small dots of light blinked with a lack of rhythm that didn't inspire confidence. I was ushered outside as curtains were pulled. A nurse asked me questions before a doctor in a stiff white coat interrupted to interrogate me about the tumour. I was embarrassed, ashamed even, to know almost nothing about it, save it was called 'Judas', which sounded stupid as I said it, and the doctor's contempt was deserved. He told me to, 'Stay there,' as he pushed through the curtains. The nurse, with a white pinafore stiffer than the doctor's coat, resumed her questions and I tried to reconstruct Richard's surname – three vowels, two Ks, a J, S, R and a Z – but wasn't sure of the order other than it started with Z. I knew even less about Anika's surname, never mind a telephone number. The nurse stayed calm. I was close to panic. Behind me, through the curtain, I could hear the doctor questioning Richard, but only moans of pain in response. The nurse took me back to the waiting area while she rang round GP surgeries in Hounslow until she found one who had Richard Zakrajsek as a patient, known to have a brain tumour. Half an hour later a petite Vietnamese lady ran into A&E, her small steps clacking loudly on the polished floor, and was taken straight through.

The smell of chemical cleaner pretending to be lemon drifted through the waiting area, and I had a brief memory of sitting in a shiny corridor waiting for Mum and Dad to come out of the closed door at the end – a closed door with a small sign showing a long-forgotten doctor's name. When they came out they were both white, though Dad's eyes were red. They walked towards me down the hall, gradually forcing smiles, Dad uncurling from a hunch to his full height, bringing Mum up with him. I don't know why I'd been there. I didn't try to remember.

I wanted to leave A&E but waited, watching people come, a few go, but most sit and wait, like me. It was another hour before Anika came and I joined her at the reception desk.

I told her everything, except me and Sally in the stock room, and she screwed her eyes shut to stop herself from crying, took a couple of deep breaths and stood to her full height, matching mine.

'You know about Judas, yes?'

'Not a lot.'

'There's not much to know but what there is means much.' She looked directly at me, eyes tearful. 'Over six months, already. Did you know?'

I shook my head. No idea what she meant.

'Few make a year.'

Now I understood and was speechless. Of course I'd known it was serious. Now I understood. Now I felt something. Now I was terrified to think what Richard must feel.

'Do the others know?' asked Anika.

I guessed she meant the band. 'Susan.'

'Perhaps now they all should.' She said it as if some turning point had been reached and hugged me. 'And the band, they can finish learning Richard's song, yes?'

I assumed she meant *Blinded By The Light*. It was an odd request. I nodded.

'Thank you.'

I was left in A&E as she went to the ward where Richard had been taken. It was late afternoon, and we had a gig planned for that evening, so I caught the bus home, tired and useless.

Susan was in the kitchen. 'I need a change.' She sat at the table, a magazine of hair styles in front of her.

'Haircut? I wouldn't. Your fans wouldn't like it.'

'What? Both of them?'

'Haha.' I forced a smile.

'You look tired. Worried. About me?' she asked.

'I suppose, but also …'

She interrupted, 'Don't be. I came on, yesterday morning.'

'Came on? Oh, I see.' It explained her excited smile. 'So, a new haircut to celebrate?' I was disappointed not to have been told yesterday, though, of course, it wasn't really my business. Except I was pissed off at always being last to know.

'I think so. Also, Bazzer and I think Algie's right. We're giving up our jobs. It's all-in Red Ice Rising. We've got a week's break next month then we throw everything into the band. You in?' She spoke quickly.

'Wow, of course. And sounds like you two might have had something like a moment?'

'Sort of. Actually, the moment was probably a couple of days ago.' The smile disappeared from her eyes and froze on her lips. Then a solitary tear welled and settled on her cheek. 'I decided, if I was pregnant, I was gonna get rid of it.'

'Get rid?'

'Abortion.'

I held my breath, mind racing for words that might help, trying to guess what this meant to her. I bought some time. 'I see how that could have been a moment.' I tried not to make it sound flippant. 'But you didn't need to, so ...?'

'Just making the decision was moment enough. It means I'm not the person I thought I was, never mind being Catholic.'

'You never really were.'

'No, but Mum was. Think what it would have done to her. But I'd decided. That says something about me, doesn't it?'

'Mum would understand,' I said, but wasn't sure I believed it, and it struck me whatever peace she might have found might not be everlasting.

I took a can of Coke from the fridge and spoke without turning from the kitchen window. The garden was a promise of spring growth. 'Anyway, you might not have gone through with it.'

'Maybe. Doesn't matter now.' She stood and draped an arm round my shoulder, then took the can. 'So, what do you think? About Red Ice Rising. Happy to give up the shop?'

'Well, without me I suppose Patrick's will have to close but then again, without me who's gonna help Dimitri remember the songs? So, yep, I'm all in, but you already knew that.'

Susan laughed, 'I know. Bazzer has already checked with Dimitri so we can give Algie the news tonight.' As she removed her arm I said,

'Talking of moments. I nearly had what might have been one today. Now I think of it, there were almost two.'

'Really?'

'I was with Safety Pin Sally …'

'Safety Pin Sally?'

'A girl. Bisexual.'

'You don't say.'

'I don't think I've met a bisexual before. We shared a joint in the stock room and nearly got …' I hesitated.

'High?'

'Laid. But then Richard collapsed. Sort of ruined the atmosphere if I'm honest.' I tried to joke.

'Just as well. I don't mean about Richard, and I don't know who Safety Pin Sally is, but unless she has some impressive moves, the stock room doesn't sound like it was right for that sort of moment, bisexual or not. Though of course if it's the two right people then anywhere in the world can be the right sort of place. So, what about Petra?'

'Richard collapsed.' I repeated. 'I had to ring an ambulance. He's in hospital. Serious. Turns out he's dying.'

Susan took a breath and started to speak, but what was there to say? Except I said,

'That'll make for a moment, I'm guessing,' and wished I hadn't.

Miracle Number Four

Chapter 34
Winter 1976/77
One Night Only
'Blinded By The Light'

I was more nervous on stage than I'd been for months; all the more surprising for being here, at Zamara'z, home territory. These days, rather than play two sets we played just one, extended, and were near the end. We finished *Fire Charmer*, which always went down well, and I checked my scribbled set list before squinting through the spotlights, scanning the audience for Anika. She nodded, spoke to Richard and led him to the stage-side steps. Susan called to the crowd to welcome, 'Guest keyboard player, Richard Zak … Zark …Richard!'

Dimitri played a snare roll, and I led the applause. Anika helped Richard up the steps. My nerves were because I now feared Richard wasn't ready for this; wasn't well enough. I'd hoped this might be a moment for him but what if it went badly? Besides, why should playing one song with us be a moment? Especially when he was so ill?

It had seemed a good idea a couple of weeks earlier; not that it was my idea.

The shop had been quiet without Richard. Not that he was ever noisy or overly chatty – he mostly listened to my rambling gig stories and bad jokes – but it just wasn't the same when the shop was empty of customers and I played guitar alone.

A few days after he'd been taken to A&E, I'd sat behind the counter, nibbling at a ham and pickle sandwich. The boss was out. In between bites I was struggling to write a letter to Petra. I was trying to keep it light, matter of fact, humorous; impossible when you're thinking too much. The shop bell rang as the door opened. I felt the short burst of cold air and slipped the sandwich below the counter, hoping it would be someone wanting a guitar rather than piano. The woman wore a knee-length black skirt, plain white blouse and dark blue blazer. She shook the rain from the umbrella then lowered it and I was surprised to see Anika. My, 'Hi,' was genuinely as welcoming as I could make it, but my lopsided grin froze as it occurred to me she might have bad news about Richard.

'Hello, JB.' She held out a hand to be shaken formally and smiled.

'Hi,' I repeated.

'You are well? There's something on your chin.' She pointed.

I dragged my hand across my mouth. 'Pickle. Sorry.'

'Why sorry?'

Which was a fair question and I laughed, nervously. 'How's Richard?'

'I'm going to work but you will go and see him this afternoon. He needs ... company.' Her accent was as charming as ever and, as ever, at odds with the direct words.

'In hospital?'

'He is home.'

'I didn't know.'

'Why not?'

'Because no one ... doesn't matter. He wasn't in hospital long.' I thought that might be a good sign, but she said,

'No reason to be there when nothing is to be done. So he's home.'

'I'll go round after work.'

Anika wrote the address in a small notebook and ripped out the page.

'How is he?' I asked.

'I have to go to work. Enjoy your pickle.' She left me at the counter but stopped at the door. 'Oh, and Richard won't ask, but you should tell him. The band would like him to play that song again.'

'Which song?'

'Blinding light.'

Anika left and I spent a few minutes hunting through our small sheet music section to see if we had a score or tabs for *Blinded By The Light*. Though we knew the song well enough for a Sunday jam, we needed to tighten up and lock the structure. I found a copy and put it to one side, feeling sure the boss wouldn't miss it, then went back to the counter, took a bite from the sandwich but threw the rest away. I made a cup of tea and was daydreaming behind the counter when the doorbell clanged again.

'Did that make you jump?' Sally laughed.

'No, I was just in the middle of a stock count. Drumsticks. We're a few pairs short.'

'Haha. Funny.' She flashed that smile, looking a little older than before; make that more mature. Her red pixie cut was now auburn, her make-up far more subtle and she wore a simple blue dress under an expensive looking Crombie. I wasn't sure what 'look' she was going for. She still wore DMs, but it wasn't unattractive, and I wondered if she still had a navel piercing.

'No school today?'

'Nope. Nor yesterday, nor tomorrow. Suspended.'

'Really?'

'Why would I lie about that?'

'To impress me?' I tried a joke.

'I already know how to do that, remember?' She unleashed that smile again.

'Expelled for what?' I ignored the truth of her statement.

'Having a tattoo,' she tapped her forearm, 'and not turning up often enough.'

'That seems harsh.'

'That's what my dad said but it didn't make any difference. So I told school to stick it.'

'Which means?'

'My dad told me to get a job. So here I am.'

'Job?'

'Here. After all, you and the pretty dark-haired guy …'

'… Richard.'

'… work here so it can't be difficult.'

'Such a charmer,' I said defensively and came from behind the counter.

'I thought we'd make a good team, three of us.'

'I don't think the boss can afford three of us. Besides, we don't sell drums.'

'Ah, I get it, afraid of competition.'

'From a drummer?'

Sally laughed and took an acoustic guitar from the wall rack before I could stop her. It was an expensive Gibson, and I pulled a pained face. She strummed it. 'Got a tuner? A and D are out.'

'I don't think you should …'

But I was interrupted by her playing, and she was all right. It turned out several years of her dad paying for guitar lessons meant she played ok – better than ok, if classical and Spanish guitar is your thing.

'I thought you were a tub thumper.'

'I am, with Tatt Tramps, but this is my better instrument.'

I gave a crooked grin that I hoped she would recognise as a compliment, took the guitar from her and hung it on the wall, thinking about Richard not coming back to the shop anytime soon and me going full time with Red Ice Rising. So far I'd avoided telling the manager. 'Best pop back tomorrow. The boss will be in. I'll introduce you. Your real name is …?'

'Sally is close enough.

When she'd gone I saw another pair of sticks was missing.

The girl with jet black hair glided through the living room and into the kitchen. She was probably not even ten but carried herself with practised aloofness.

'That was Tina,' Richard said.

Following Anika's instructions, I'd visited after work.

'Kim!' a voice called back from the kitchen – the girl's voice.

'Oh yeah, forgot. She only uses her middle name these days.'

'And yours is?' I asked.

'Never mind.'

'Khuyen,' said Richard's mother. She was down the other end of the knocked through living rooms, gently dusting a shiny black upright piano. 'It has meaning. One who gives advice.'

'Thanks, Mum,' said Richard, 'but you didn't need to say.'

'See, giving advice.' The tiny Vietnamese lady laughed, and tousled Richard's dark hair then tucked the blanket tighter around him before going to the kitchen, saying, 'Tea. Green.'

'Khuyen?' I asked.

'Yes, and yes, it's tricky for me to spell.' He smiled weakly and loosened the blanket.

Richard had been home a couple of days. I'd only visited him in hospital once, but he'd been asleep. He looked better here, with no tubes attached and no oxygen mask, but still pale and had lost more weight. He was now bordering skinny. On the coffee table by his side were four tubs of tablets, a bottle of Lucozade and a half-eaten Mars bar. A dog lay on the sofa next to him, watching me suspiciously.

His mother brought a tray with tea and biscuits then excused herself – she was taking Kim to dance class. As the front door closed, Richard said, 'I heard you called the ambulance for me.'

'You don't remember?'

He shook his head. 'Last thing was you and Safety Pin Sally going into the stock room.'

'You did me a favour. Another minute and I'd have given in. On balance, probably not a good idea.'

'Given in?'

315

'She, we … nearly … never mind, another time.'

'I know she's fun, but she's not Petra.' Richard's eyes were dark, serious.

'True, and she's bisexual, not that that matters.'

'Probably to her,' Richard mused.

We were sitting in the back half of the through lounge, looking out to the well-tended garden. I took a biscuit from the plate and the dog's interest turned from suspicion to optimism. He didn't raise his head, but his eyes followed the biscuit as I dunked before asking, 'When you coming back to the shop? I've not sold a single piano or keyboard. The boss is losing patience.'

'I don't know, JB. I'm waiting for the docs to look at the last scan.'

'I remember my mum having those, and radiotherapy. She was in and out of hospital quite a lot for a while.'

'Cancer?'

'Breast.'

Richard nodded slowly and I thought I might know his thoughts, so quickly added, 'But that's not what, you know …'

He smiled, just.

'She got better, sort of. Dad called it a miracle.'

'Miracle?'

'Prayers to Saint Teresa's statue, Glaskild, near where Petra is, in Ireland …' I let the sentence drift, '… and hey, who's to say it wasn't. They stopped treating her and the cancer went, so …'

'Prayers to a statue? The sort of miracle I could do with. So how did she die?' He whispered the question and had to repeat it as I pretended not to hear.

'They don't know. Officially it was something like 'unexplained but not suspicious'. Seems to me it can't be both. Anyway, doesn't matter. She'd been ill in other ways. I think now, maybe she didn't know how to be with us. I don't mean us as in me, Dad and Susan, I mean as in just, well, here.' I rambled. 'Whatever, it wasn't a tumour or cancer.' I tried to sound upbeat. 'Meantime, I need you back at the shop. We have to get some practise in. We're playing *Blinded By The Light* at our next Zamara'z gig and need you on keys.' I passed him the sheet music as if to prove I was serious.

'I hope it's soon then,' he said, but it wasn't funny.

We lapsed into silence until Richard indicated to the music centre. 'That old cassette on the side? The song's on there, I guess we should listen to it properly.'

It was a compilation tape with a handwritten track listing, much like the one I'd given to Petra, and I wondered if she ever listened to it as I put on Richard's tape and fast wound to the song.

Richard had made it to the shop just a couple of times, with Anika's help. He didn't stay long, just enough to practise his part, and there was no chance to have a full band rehearsal. That was partly why now, as he carefully settled himself behind the electric piano on the stage at Zamara'z, I was nervous. But even more, I was scared this wasn't what he wanted anyway. I couldn't remember when he'd said this was a good idea or that he really wanted to play live. Too late now. Anika left the stage. The spotlights were harsh and Richard looked pale and small. I smiled across at him before looking to Dimitri who counted in the song – he and Richard were to come in together. Richard missed it. It didn't matter. Dimitri played on as if it was a planned drum intro then settled back into sixteenths on the hi-hat while he counted it in again. Richard was bang on. As we played so he sat taller and played harder; he could trust we had the song, and him, covered. A handful of camera flashes punched through the stage lights; Anika was taking pictures.

Blinded By The Light went down well and Susan encouraged the cheers for our, 'Special guest.' He was smiling broadly as he used the piano to push himself to standing and a tearful Anika helped him off-stage.

317

'Sounded great. Ok for next gig?' Susan asked Richard, lowered to her haunches and holding his hand as she spoke.

'Wembley or Earls Court?' He forced a smile then tapped the small denim pouch handbag at Anika's side. She pulled out some tablets.

'I'll get you a drink,' said Susan.

'Only Coke,' Anika called after her.

We were in the crowded toilet/dressing room – lots of new faces. I'd had to clear a path for Richard, he held Anika's arm, and Kay had stood from the sofa, pulling Dimitri with her, to make room.

Steve was at the back door, selling to those fans that knew the routine – speed leading up to the gig and joints afterwards. Kay and Dimitri were now crushed together on the battered armchair. Sofia was at the makeshift bar, crowded by six or seven others, some I knew by face but not name. It was darker than usual; someone had replaced the net curtain under the neon strip with a length of crimson linen. The red glow eased everything into slow motion. A radio was playing, probably loudly, but my post-gig hearing was dominated by the in-ear whistling which would take a couple of hours to subside. I started to ask Richard if he'd enjoyed playing but Algie pushed into the room, shouting 'Band only,' and ushering out others.

'Band includes Richard tonight,' I said to Anika.

'Oi Sunny. Not now eh?' Algie called to Steve who scowled, finished the sale and waved the last few customers away. They hung around the car park, waiting to be called back.

As the room cleared, cold night air came through the back door, lifting the smell of weed and alcohol. The breeze wafted the cloth under the strip light, throwing shadows out of time with Santana on the radio. Algie snatched the volume down, 'Meet Stewart,' and stepped aside to let the tall stranger come through. Stewart was skinny and hunched, with fast eyes, checking out the room, checking out us. They flicked from the makeshift bar to the sausage rolls to Steve counting the joints he had left. 'Hi, guys. Thought you were great tonight. Again.' He had an even smile, not as bright as Safety Pin Sally's and more plastic, tinged pink in the light. It was a smile that didn't reach his eyes.

Algie took centre stage again. 'Stewart is with Chrysalis.' He let the words hang. Dimitri looked up from the joint he was rolling. Bazzer slowly lowered the bottle from his lips. I looked to Susan. She was as surprised as me. 'Chrysalis,' Algie repeated slowly for effect. '… are running a showcase gig for new bands they want to sign, just for a couple of singles to see how they get on. It's a new idea and Stewart wants to offer Red Ice Rising the opportunity to take part.'

'Say that again?' Susan asked. She needed to. All I'd heard were the words 'Chrysalis' and 'sign.'

There was a dumb silence in the room then murmurs, open mouths, gradual smiles and ecstatic expletives. We didn't act cool. I think I even jumped in the air as Bazzer grabbed Susan and, as thrilled as I was for me, I was more for her. Sunny Steve slipped to Sofia's side and whispered something to make her smile. Kay hugged Dimitri. Richard smiled broadly, though it took effort, while Anika looked thoughtful then took some pictures, flashing the pink tainted light to short bursts of white. I turned to find Vince, but he wasn't there.

I lit a joint; a spare dick at a wedding. I took Anika's Instamatic and motioned she should snuggle up to Richard for a picture on the tatty sofa.

Algie exchanged glances with Stewart. They waited for us to calm then Stewart said, 'Congratulations guys, we've a good feeling about you,' and then to Algie, 'I'll be in touch.' He made to leave then turned, 'Oh, just to say, Chrysalis will deal with the band's management,' he nodded at Algie, 'and we need you to throw the kitchen sink at this thing. Don't want to see too much …' He mimicked drinking and smoking.

'Better piss off then,' Dimitri shouted and raised his bottle. Steve slipped away from Sofia to walk after Stewart.

Vince was standing in the car park, just outside the back door, drinking a Tennents with a picture of a bikini-clad girl on the can. I pretended to slap him, 'Made yer wince, Vince.'

He forced a smile. 'Don't be a baby, JB.'

'That's new.'

'Been waiting months to use it.'

'Why you out here?'

'Same as you I guess.'

We looked back through the door to the celebrations. 'It's a bit ... crowded in there,' I suggested.

'And yet empty,' Vince said.

'Deep,' I nodded and said, 'Pretty Penny,' to change the subject.

'What?'

I pointed to the can. 'Apparently she's called Penny. Pretty eh.'

'I guess.'

'I wonder if her name really is Penny. I hope so.'

'I doubt it.'

He offered me the can, but I shook my head, asking, 'Heard the Chrysalis news?'

'Algie told me.'

'Exciting eh?'

'I guess,' he said with no enthusiasm and my disappointment must have showed. 'Sorry, I'm just in a shit mood. I was thinking about my old man, after what happened today.'

'What happened?'

'His heart attack?'

'What?'

Vince looked at me, surprised, but surely not nearly as surprised, or shocked, as me. 'You didn't hear? It was this morning, at the garage. Your dad didn't tell you?'

'I haven't seen him. I worked at Patrick's all day then went to Bazzer's. You didn't say. Why not?' Vince hadn't been with us to help with the setup, but I hadn't given it much thought.

'I spent the afternoon with Mum, and you were already on stage when I got here. Afterwards,' he shrugged, 'I guess I thought it could wait. Anyway, it was bound to happen. He's not been well since … since what happened at the garage.'

'That was last summer.'

'Maybe, but Mum says me not being at home hasn't helped. I don't believe her but suppose I should go see him in hospital.'

'I suppose.' I think Vince was looking to me to tell him what to do but I didn't know. It had been a long time since I'd thought about Lawrence and Vi in the kitchen at the party or Lawrence being taken from the garage in an ambulance.

Vince looked away. 'It was my fault you know.'

'What was?'

'Dad's beating.'

If I'd any doubt it had been Will, that was now gone. 'Don't be daft,' I said vaguely, partly to avoid admitting I was pretty sure I knew what had happened, and partly to tell Vince it could not have been down to him.

'That morning, Will came round, and I told him about the office back door. He was angry. I shouldn't have said anything.'

'What if your dad had it coming?' I suggested as casually as I could.

'He probably did, if what Will told me happened at the party is right, with Vi.'

I was ashamed that my first thought was to find out if Vince knew that I'd seen, but done nothing. I wasn't about to ask outright but before I could come up with a leading question he said, 'So yeah, maybe Dad got was what coming, it's not like it was the first time,' and I thought he might cry.

321

'What do you mean?'

'It's what Will said. But you should ask your dad.'

'About what?'

Vince hesitated. 'Will said my dad needed a lesson and he didn't understand why your old man hadn't sorted him out.'

'What, because of the party?'

'No, I don't think that's what he meant.'

'What did he mean?' I pressed.

'I don't know.' He pulled his arm from my hand. I hadn't realised I was holding it.

'We're off, JB. Great news about Chrysalis.' Richard interrupted us. Vince span away, bumped past Anika and called to Sofia for a drink.

'By the way,' Richard indicated back into the toilet/dressing room. 'Sally has turned up. We saw her earlier, she said she'd enjoyed the gig. I think she has a thing for you.'

'Can't blame her.' I laughed.

'But she's not Petra, is she?' Anika said in that matter-of-fact manner that made it true – which of course it was.

'Petra's in Ireland,' I said by way of excuse for … something.

'Glaskild. I looked at the map. It's not that far,' she added. Which, of course, was also true.

I moved aside to let Richard and Anika out to the car park, shouting after them, 'Well played tonight Rick.'

'Rick?' he turned and smiled. 'Yeah, why not, tonight.'

Anika let him in to the big Citroen then came back, 'Thank you, JB. Asking Richard to play with you.'

'Hey, we've wanted to play that live for ages and couldn't have done it without him.'

'Of course,' said Anika in a way that was somehow both grateful and gently sceptical. She hesitated before saying, 'Richard told me about your mother. I'm sorry. The cancer that didn't kill her went away but the doctors don't know why?'

'Yes. I mean no.' I didn't know if she meant why it went away or what was the cause of death.

'That must matter, don't you think? Perhaps we pray too casually.' She looked at me, almost staring for a few seconds before pecking my cheek and leaving.

Later, unable to sleep, it occurred to me that Anika was asking what had happened to make Mum's cancer go away. The only answer I might have had, was the miracle Dad claimed.

Miracle Number Four

Chapter 35
Spring 1977
Need A Lift?
'My Sweet Lord'

'You made it then. Boss said you'd be late if there was a gig last night.' Sally was standing behind the counter. Both hands flat on the surface, claiming ownership.

I looked at the clock on the wall above her. The previous night had been the Zamara'z gig where Richard joined us but that was no excuse, yep, I was late again – not by much and, as it was my last Saturday, I didn't think it would matter. I'd already given in my notice. Now it was Red Ice Rising or bust.

'Boss isn't happy. Especially when I mentioned that I'd seen you at Zamara'z last night …' Sally was close to smug.

'… and yet you managed to be here on time.'

'That's exactly what he said. But then it is my first day.'

'Welcome to Patrick's Pianos.'

'Already done all that,' said the boss, bringing her a cup of coffee.

'On my first day I was the one making coffee.' I exaggerated a pout.

'I expect you were,' said Sally. Then she smiled and I was both sad and happy it was my last Saturday. I made myself a drink and when I went back into the shop Sally was demonstrating a guitar to a young woman. The boss caught my eye and nodded appreciatively.

Sally's first day went well. I introduced her to some of the regulars and she impressed them with her guitar playing and they took the mickey because she was a girl. She didn't seem to mind and I think it's because she understood she'd have the last laugh. The boss hung around all day as it was busy. He sold a piano and was so pleased, we were promised a couple of quid extra as a bonus. As five-thirty neared, we began tidying and Sally helped me re-order the sheet music that had been put back in the wrong place. We had a slight disagreement about where to put the sheets relating to songs starting with 'The', but I don't think she really believed they should all go under 'T'.

'So, c'mon then, what's your real name?' I asked as I passed her a copy of *My Sweet Lord* that had found its way to 'S'.

'Sally's close enough. I'm building an aura of mystery as part of my new image.' She took a step back as if to show me. Her DMs had been ditched in favour of plain black block heels, giving her an extra couple of inches, and she wore jeans and a plain blue blouse, probably from school. 'Are they ironed?' I teased, pointing to her jeans.

'Mum insisted. First day on job and all that. And thanks for helping get it. Dad's off my case, I get to play some sweet guitars and there's a chance to nick some gear for Tatt Tramps.'

My disapproval must have been obvious.

'Joking,' she was quick to add, 'I wouldn't. But did you, ever?'

'No, no way. The boss is all right.' Somehow the several packets of strings, plectrums and two, or was it three, mic leads didn't count.

She nodded, perhaps unconvinced. The shop bell clanged and one of our regular last minute roadie customers nipped in for a twelve-foot guitar cable. As usual he wanted to buy on credit, which I had to run past the boss. It was the last sale. The boss watched as I showed Sally how to cash up, then he paid us in cash and locked the door behind us as we left. It was cold and damp and Sally tipped up her Crombie's collar then touched my arm, 'Thanks again for helping me get the job. Today was all right.'

'My pleasure. And when the boss is out you can play all the guitars you like.'

She laughed. 'Speaking of which. Gig tonight?'

'Red Lion, Brentford. Coming?'

'Maybe.'

'Good.' I meant it and grinned lopsidedly.

'Hey, how's Richard? He didn't look well last night.'

'He's ... not well. Like really not well. Did great last night though.'

'Sorry.' She looked thoughtful, biting her bottom lip. 'By the way, I think maybe I should have mentioned. I went to school with Petra. She told me a lot about you and her before I ...' she hesitated,

'... started nicking sticks?'

'... let you get off with me.'

'Let me?'

'I know. I do feel a bit guilty. I always liked her. She was very cool and funny, though I don't know if she always meant to be, telling stories about her mum. Did you know when she was younger she had a donkey in her back garden?'

'Petra?'

'No, idiot, her mum. Another time, she said she saw a statue in a cave cry. Weird eh?'

'Who, her mum?'

'No, Petra.'

In the seconds it took me to think what that meant, Sally was gone, calling over her shoulder her dad was waiting. I watched her get into a dark Cortina.

Though just a little after half-five, the heavy cloud swamped the sunset. I felt it should be raining and regretted not wearing a jumper; my Harrington was not warm. I zipped it to the top and wandered to the bus stop, needing to be at Bazzer's to help prepare for that night's gig. But instead of ideas and plans for set lists, equipment checks and song suggestions, I was stuck with Sally's confession. That, and what Petra had told her, looped through my thoughts.

Richard's mother opened the door and offered a welcoming hug. Richard sat at the back of the through lounge and I thought he might be asleep, but as I neared I saw he was frowning out to the garden. The family dog was searching through shrubs as though for the first time. Richard seemed deep in concentration or lost in rambling reflection but, whichever, I didn't feel he was daydreaming lazily. I tried to remember how my mother had often looked out from our conservatory, but her face didn't come to mind and I was scared I'd forgotten it. Anika came from the kitchen and her loud welcome made Richard turn. His frown eased to a smile. Anika took my jacket and directed me to sit in the armchair while she sat beside Richard on the sofa.

'I just wanted to let you know how well everyone said it went, Friday night.' I nodded enthusiastically for emphasis.

'Thanks JB. It was good ...'

'It was great,' I interrupted.

Richard nodded. 'I guess. Sorry I was nervous. Got through it though.' He sounded tired and I hoped they didn't mind me coming. I'd waited ages for the buses – rubbish Sunday service.

'Of course. More than got through it. We couldn't do it without you. Made all the difference.' I meant it too.

'I'm still knackered today though.' His eyes were heavy, but he smiled.

'Yeah, gigs do that,' I agreed. 'We've a whole week off now. Susan needed a break.'

'She is ok about what didn't happen?' Anika asked me.

'Didn't happen?'

'No baby?' she said, and I assumed she and Susan had talked, so I nodded, not wanting to share more. I put on what I thought was a thoughtful expression and took a breath. 'Anyway, I had this idea, crazy I know. But,' I looked to Anika, 'something you said struck a chord and I wanted your opinion, Khuyen.' I turned to Richard, hoping he'd see I was both teasing and serious. 'The band have got a break for a few days, and I've been thinking about visiting Petra.'

'You should,' Richard agreed.

'Of course,' said Anika. 'And she's in Ireland, yes?'

I nodded.

Anika held Richard's hand in her lap. 'Where is also Saint Teresa.' It didn't sound like a question.

'Yep, in a cave at the beach.'

'How are you getting there?' Anika said, looking at Richard.

I hesitated.

'Need a lift?' she asked.

Miracle Number Four

Chapter 36
Spring 1977
Glaskild, Ireland
'Turn, Turn, Turn'

'Did someone famous once say it's better to travel than arrive?' Richard stood next to me at the rail. I was bent over it, holding tight.

'Fuck off,' was all I could manage. I squinted against the wind. The only difference between the rain and the spray was the taste of salt. I threw up again and something mushy and brown was blown back on to my jacket, adding to the yellowing stains. I'd have been disgusted with myself if not busy praying for the vicious nausea in my stomach to ease. I'd never felt worse. When you throw up at home, it stays in the bowl and you get a couple of minutes of blessed relief before feeling sick again. Not here, not on the deck of *The Avalon*. Here, the nausea didn't come in waves – no pun intended – it was just a constant, spiteful, deep, evil gnawing which didn't stop in my stomach; it crawled through my chest. We had been on board just over an hour; two and a half more to go.

The Avalon lurched as waves battered the bow and I was thrown against the rail. Through my slitted eyes I could see nothing but grey water with white foam topping. Then I was tipped backwards and there was nothing but grey sky. I groaned and threw up.

'They say it's better to stare at the horizon,' Richard offered meekly. He had moved a couple of yards away, probably to avoid sick and spit.

'What horizon?' I wiped at my mouth with a sleeve. The sea, sky, rain and spray merged; my vision blurred.

The ship rocked again, I rocked with it. Richard swayed gently with easy balance, as if this was a med cruise. I hated him. And the others. The deck was busy with tourists, none of them being ill. They strolled without fuss, shifting their weight effortlessly as the ship rolled and I heard someone suggest, '… a mild crossing for a change.' I hated them most.

Anika joined us, with two cups of tea, not spilling a drop, and apologising for not bringing me one, but she didn't think I'd keep it down. 'This is much bigger than the ferries my father worked on the Danube,' she said casually, passing Richard a drink. 'How are you feeling?'

I muttered something that was supposed to be a brave, 'I'm ok.'

'I was asking Richard. But yes, you do look better,' Anika acknowledged.

She stood at the rail, tall against the breeze, wearing a fitted mac and knee-high boots, seemingly enjoying the sense of movement and freedom. She pulled Richard to her side and linked arms. He wore a leather RAF style flying jacket that didn't look too big, despite his weight loss. His hair, though still short, had grown enough for a neat, deliberate side parting. They leant casually as one into the rocking of the boat. They looked cool. They looked happy.

So did everyone else on deck.

I loathed them all. I wouldn't be joining the navy any time soon. Anika passed me her Kodak Instamatic, insisting I take a picture of the two of them with the sea behind. Throwing the bloody thing overboard was a serious consideration.

It was three in the afternoon and we'd been travelling since early morning. Anika had driven us to Fishguard in the black Citroen DS – Richard's uncle's car. He'd lent it to her when she came up from Oakjack Ford to be with Richard. They both spoke often and with touching affection for Uncle Dudek, though to Anika he was an old family friend, not blood. I'd sat in the comfortable back as Anika drove us down the M4 and over the impressive Severn Bridge. Its towering supports were both brutal and elegant, and the suspension cables somehow satisfying in their simplicity and regularity. I enjoyed the rhythm of their passing, and it was the best part of the journey – the point at which I began to stop doubting the decision and looked forward to possibilities.

Those doubts had started a couple of days earlier, as I'd left Richard's house, and increased that evening when I'd written to Petra to tell her the plan. 'Plan' was rather a grand word for it. We couldn't leave until Tuesday as Anika had work on the Monday – she was a translator for some government department; a job that Uncle Dudek had found for her – and we expected to arrive in Glaskild sometime on Tuesday evening. My first attempt at writing started as an apology and slipped into excuses for the journey.

'That's really shit,' had been Susan's opinion when I showed her. 'What's all this?' She waved disdainfully at the page.

I started to speak. She interrupted. 'I know what it is. But where does it say you want to see her? Where does it say you want to hug and kiss her?' She screwed it into a ball and threw it at me. 'Whatever happens, be back for next Friday's gig.'

The letter that went in the post first thing Monday morning said simply that I was looking forward to seeing her and was bringing friends. I hoped it would arrive before I did.

I was still on deck when the ship's PA announced we'd be docking in twenty minutes. By now I was curled on a bench. I was no longer throwing up, but exhausted and already scared for the journey home – just the day after next – doubting this pain was worth it for such little time. I was also embarrassed that no one else seemed to have been affected. Anika told me to leave with the foot passengers and meet her and Richard dockside once the cars had disembarked. I found them and we sat impatiently kerbside for another fifteen minutes, she did not want to chance me throwing up in the car, we still had an hour's drive. I slept most of the way and it was dark by the time Richard reached behind to shake me awake, saying, 'Glaskild,' pointing to a sign that we passed before I saw. He neatly folded the map in his lap and tucked it in the glovebox. 'Got the address?'

I passed him the slip of paper I'd been holding since we left Rosslare.

We had little idea of Glaskild's layout or size, and the map didn't show street names. As far we could tell, it was a village with a crossroads at its centre and the plan had been to simply ask the first person we saw. I'd sort of imagined Petra had received my letter and would be waiting at those crossroads. She wasn't. There was no one around and we were through the village and out the other side before we realised. Anika turned the car around and stopped outside the first pub: *Hut Aoire* – its sign, a ewe and her lamb, was on the ground, leaning against the thick timber upright from which it should have hung. I waited in the car, and they were back in a couple of minutes with a rough map drawn on the slip of paper I'd given.

'They don't speak your English,' said Anika as we pulled away.

Richard gave directions and we pulled up outside number sixteen, a terraced cottage in a quiet street a couple of turns from the crossroads. The curtains were drawn and there were no cracks of light. I sat with nose pressed against the car window, steaming the glass, conscious of increased heart rate and tightness in my stomach – oddly welcome following the ship-nausea which had been draining. Bizarrely, I hadn't thought through what meeting Petra might mean – how I'd feel; how she'd feel. Instead I'd been thinking how exciting it would be. But now I didn't feel ready and what if Richard was right? It's better to travel than arrive. But here we were, and that we had arrived was success in itself. Wasn't it? I took a breath. I could still taste vomit.

'And?' Anika said.

'Have you any mints?'

Richard hunted through the glove box and tossed over half a pack of stale Polos. I sucked then crunched four in one go.

'And?' Anika repeated.

I swept straggly hair from my eyes and left the car, unzipping my Harrington so the pale blue Ben Sherman Oxford I'd borrowed from Richard was visible. It was too big for him now. I knocked on the door gently but not, I hoped, timidly. I shivered in the cold; my jacket and new trousers, from Harry Fenton, were still damp, though the rain had stopped and the sky was clear. The moon was close to full and, with no streetlamps, polished the still wet narrow pavement and road to a shine. The terraced cottages on both sides were grey and their doors, perhaps bright and welcoming in the day, were various shades of tired dark blues and mauves. I knocked again at Petra's. There was no answer.

Back in the car we sat in silence for a half a minute before Anika asked, 'Are you ok, Richard? It's time for tablets.'

And it suddenly occurred to me that despite my disappointment at no one being home, I still had the least to be worried about.

'Plan B then,' I said, with forced cheerfulness.

We'd known from the start that we might not be able to stay at Petra's. We needed to find a local B & B.

'And we come back in the morning, Richard is tired.'

She drove slowly as we scanned the cottages and houses for B & B signs, but this wasn't a tourist area. At the far end of the lane, away from the crossroads, was another pub: *Hogan's*. Above the door was a painting of a bodhran and a fiddle. The pub spread over a couple of cottages on a corner plot and there was a handwritten sign in the window: 'ROOMS'. We parked outside; the only car close.

The double doors opened into a small bar. I led the way. There was a counter only six or seven feet long with just a couple of beer taps and a short row of optics behind, suspended over a clutch of spirit bottles. It was dimly lit,

335

and the dark matt wood panelling soaked up any glare or reflections. There were three small tables, each with four chairs and at least five glass-bottom stains eating the varnish. Only one of the tables was occupied, by three men, each dressed in a heavy brown jacket and thick trousers. There was no fire, and I was disappointed not to feel immediately warmer. The men looked at us briefly then returned to their chatter, which was quick and melodious, and their laughter, which was sharp to rise and pass. They were loud enough to hear but I was only catching one word in a few. Anika guided Richard to a table then joined me at the bar. A young man in a grey suit came from a door.

'Welcome to Hogan's. Drink? Of course you will, why else be here?' The words were spoken so quickly they were as one and took me a couple of seconds to work through. His smile was welcoming though his eyes carried a question.

I was conscious, as ever when at a bar, that I didn't look eighteen – I wasn't yet seventeen, and probably looked younger; cold, pale and tired from the crossing. I didn't drink much at the best of times and was in no mood tonight.

'Two Cokes please and ...' I turned to Anika who finished,

'Vodka and lime.'

The bartender nodded and produced a couple of bottles of Coke and two smeared glasses, then poured vodka into a small tumbler, asking, 'When?' as he tipped in the lime.

I paid him and Anika asked about the rooms. He said he'd get the landlord. Back at our table, Anika took three small tubs from her handbag and a tablet from each. Richard swallowed them with his Coke. We sat in silence, deflated. In occasional lulls in conversation from the men at the other table I could hear singing and an acoustic guitar somewhere. Half-way through my Coke a big man in a black suit, black tie mostly undone, came through the door at the far end of the bar. I looked up, attention caught by the rise in volume of the music. Though the big guy almost filled the doorframe, behind him I saw through to another bar, much larger, crowded and with a young woman sitting on a stool playing guitar and singing softly, so softly that the drinkers were quiet to listen. That struck me.

'G'd evening. It's rooms you're after,' the big man boomed as the door closed behind him. Before we knew it, we had booked two – Richard and I would supposedly be sharing one – with breakfast thrown in for five Irish Pounds a night per room; we'd changed money on the ferry but as it was a pound for a pound less commission, that had seemed pointless, especially when the landlord said he preferred UK currency. He had asked a few polite questions about our trip, and we had been politely vague. I don't know why. He explained how to get to the rooms, left us the keys and went back to the other bar. The young woman was still singing and occasionally strumming. She was a much better singer than guitarist.

'Just gonna pop through to listen,' I told Anika and Richard.

'Of course,' they said in unison, which I thought sweet.

I went through to the other room. It had probably been the entire downstairs of the cottage next door, now with another bar stretching its width at the back. The wood panelling had been painted in cream, beige and light green and it was far better lit than the room I'd just left, though a pall of tobacco smoke hung under the stained ceiling. An open fireplace held a modest blaze, and it was a welcoming scene. There were nine or ten tables, most occupied, and though I was probably the youngest one there, I didn't feel out of place. No one turned to see as the door closed behind me. I stood to one side, near a corridor sign-posted to toilets, watching the brunette singing in the corner. Behind her was a blackboard advertising tonight's 'Open Mic' session. The girl sang *Turn, Turn, Turn* with a sweet, clear tone, and I couldn't help but cover the harmonies in my head. She was pretty and watchable, and the room listened. She finished with another chorus, this time encouraging the room to join in, which they did, then applauded her as she thanked them and left the small stage.

'Up next? You know you want to.' The soft Irish lilt was a whisper in my ear but still I started and span round. Petra's smile was as new as last summer. 'What the feck you doin' here?' She threw her arms around my neck, squeezed then pulled away to peck my cheek before I had time to squeeze back. It took another couple of seconds before my surprise was joy. I think I was holding my breath and she hugged me again before I could speak. As she released, I took half a step back.

She looked amazing, by which I mean I was amazed. Perhaps a little taller, not bigger but stronger, still slender but more full, pale but glowing. She wore flared jeans and a simple white shirt under a black bomber jacket that might have been leather. Round her slender neck was the delicate silver necklace I'd sent her for her birthday last September, the small 'P' nestling in the 'V' of her blouse. Her eyes were as green as I'd been imagining them and her hair as long. Instinctively I reached to brush a strand away from her cheek, muttering, 'Blonde.'

Petra laughed. 'Is it ok? I fancied a change but didn't want to cut it. Colleen helped me colour it.' She indicated to a table close to the stage. The girl there was looking at us; at me.

I just nodded. To me, her hair had always been that shade.

She asked a question. I was looking at her but didn't hear. 'So, what are you doin' here?' she repeated.

'You didn't get my letter?'

'Last one was weeks ago.'

'I posted it yesterday morning.'

'You could have rung. We finally had a phone put in last week.'

'Er, number?'

'Yeah, I was going to put it in my next letter.'

'Doesn't matter. The band's got a few days off,' I said, as if that was the reason I was there, realised what a cop out it was, took a breath and added, 'And I wanted to see you,' which didn't cover much but was a start Susan might have approved of.

'How long you here for?'

'Ferry is booked for Thursday morning,' I said quietly.

'That's a crazy long way to come for two days.' Petra's smile was frozen on her lips, gone from her eyes.

'I've got a gig Friday night.'

'Of course.' The tight smile faded but she hugged me again.

There was applause from the room and I tried to form a joke about them celebrating our reunion, but Petra said, 'So much to talk about,' and led me to a table as another singer took to the stool, this time with a separate guitarist. A young man announced them, then sat down at our table. There were five of us and Petra introduced me to, 'Colleen, her boyfriend Conor,' who was the announcer, 'and Liam.' Conor smiled broadly, the other two less so, but before they could speak the guitarist played the intro to *Landslide* and we sat in hushed reverence. I didn't mind, I liked the song, the girl was a good singer and Petra's thigh rested against mine. The only spoiler was Liam's occasional, but noticeable, glare. The song finished, the audience called for another, and Colleen said how good it was to finally meet me and asked about the trip over. Thankfully, before I felt the need to explain about the stains on my jacket, the guitarist began *Big Yellow Taxi*. The next half hour followed this pattern of snatches of conversation during which Petra's friends tried to question me but there was always a new singer and song to interrupt. I just wanted to talk to Petra alone, but she seemed comfortable with the situation. Then, as one of the acts finished, Conor, the announcer, asked if anyone else wanted to sing.

Liam gave me a nudge, saying, 'I hear you'd be up for a turn,' loud enough for Conor to hear.

I shook my head and my first reaction to Liam's smirk was to ignore him. 'Petra's told us about your band,' he added, in a way that suggested he didn't believe it.

I caught Petra's eye. 'You know you want to,' she said, and was right, but it was Liam's challenging sneer that made the decision for me.

The small audience applauded gently and there were a few encouraging calls to get up. I didn't need many and didn't mind feeling nervous as I took the acoustic guitar from its stand, fiddling with the tuning while thinking what to play. Conor asked my full name and made a joke that they had, 'Mike Open here for an open mic session.' The audience laughed and I nearly pointed out my surname was Oppen, not Open or even O'pen but knew better than to interrupt a happy audience.

The previous acts hadn't played traditional or folk songs, which was just as well – I didn't know any. Red Ice Rising didn't play many covers these days. But I didn't want to chance an unknown original. Something upbeat with some link to Ireland was called for but nothing cheesy like *Brown Eyed Girl,* which I didn't know anyway. I had been tinkering with a Thin Lizzy track and knew enough to busk the rest, so I played *The Boys Are Back In Town.* The crowd liked it and didn't mind when I had to repeat the second verse because I forgot the third. I added another chorus and had them singing along by the end. There were a couple of comments about 'the fecking English', but I paid no attention; I'd been heckled in Brixton and Mile End.

Liam scowled, but Petra's smile was reason enough to be there and, hey, she was wearing the necklace I'd sent. I wondered if she still had the leather bracelet from that day in the church yard. I did, it was in my holdall.

The announcer asked the crowd if they wanted another. Most said yes, or at least, enough did. I didn't have another up-tempo number up my sleeve, and anyway, variety is the spice of life, right, so I went back to my first and favourite acoustic song: *Seagull.* I knew it so well that the guitar took care of itself and I could concentrate on singing. I pretty much stared at Petra all the way through and hoped it didn't look creepy. The audience was silent throughout, but I think were listening. The applause at the end was a good place to leave things and I went back down to the table without milking it, much as I was tempted.

Conor pronounced my surname properly and encouraged the crowd to clap one last time.

I was the last act of the night – which suited me, I can't deny – and the drinkers gradually thinned out while I chatted with Petra's friends, though I was desperate to find time alone with her. As the barman called last orders, Richard and Anika came into the bar, and I was embarrassed I'd not thought to bring them through earlier. I made introductions, Petra already knew of them from my letters, but Anika was keen for Richard to get some sleep and we all agreed it had been a long day. Anika passed my bag and a key, and they went to their room. Colleen and Conor said goodnight and hoped to chat again. Liam offered to walk Petra home, to which she agreed but asked him to wait outside.

Eventually it was just me, Petra, and the barman. He turned off most of the lights and made a lot of noise clearing and wiping tables. The fire was dying and coldness seeped into the room. Petra and I were still sitting at the table, close, and I smelt her perfume; it was the scent of last summer, of our first kisses and our last. I hoped my jacket didn't smell of sick and wished I'd taken more mints from Anika.

'Is he ok?' I asked, nodding to the door through which Liam had just left.

'He's ok. Just a bit protective, like a brother, I guess. Likes to walk me home even though it's only two minutes. Anyway, how is everybody?' she asked.

'Ok, I guess.'

'Sofia ok?'

'What?'

'Just joking,' Petra laughed, just.

It didn't sound like a joke, but I didn't say anything.

She held my hand on the table. 'I'm so sorry about your mum.'

'Me too,' I said, and instantly regretted it.

'Still trying to be funny?'

'No, I'm sorry. It's been a while and people have stopped apologising and feeling sorry for me. Thank you.'

'And I'm sorry we didn't come to the funeral. We just … couldn't.'

'S'ok,' I pretended, though I remembered the hurt I'd felt at the time. Perhaps I looked sad as she said,

'But hey, I had no idea you were so good, like, really good …' she indicated to the low stage, 'I suppose I haven't heard you in …'

'Nearly nine months,' I said as she made a calculation.

'Yep, and then it was only in rehearsals. You're good, really.'

'Thanks. And the band is great. You gotta come and see us, honestly, Susan is another level. We play all our own stuff, and we might even have a shot with Chrysalis. We'll be recording a couple of …' I stopped. This wasn't why I'd come. 'You look great. Honest.'

Petra blushed.

The barman set down a glass on the bar heavily as Liam put his head through the door. 'Hey, Petra. Thought I was walking you home.'

I tightened my grip on her hand.

'I'd better go, it's late. I'm working at the farm tomorrow. I have to get the first bus at a stupidly early time but can get the afternoon off. Hey, I know, have breakfast at our house about ten, I'll tell Mum to expect you, then come on to the farm.' She looked back to Liam. 'There's a lot to catch up.' She withdrew her hand, pecked me on the cheek and left me there. I sat until the fire was out.

Chapter 37
Spring 1977
The Farm, Ireland
'Tie A Yellow Ribbon'

I slept well, eventually, after the mistake of smoking half a joint in my room. The gentle high had drifted away and I was left tired and cold but with my heart racing, keeping me awake. I'd resisted the temptation to smoke the other half, mostly because I didn't want the room to smell. Having said that, the room smelt. It smelt damp and, occasionally, of piss. There was a single bed, single wardrobe and small basin. The window looked out to Petra's street but I couldn't see her house, and the window was painted shut, though it still managed to allow a steady cold draught.

I hoped Richard and Anika's room was better.

Anika knocked for me at well past nine, saying Richard had needed a lie-in and wasn't hungry. She was going down to see if there was tea or coffee. The barman from the previous night welcomed us and explained, confidently, that we had missed breakfast; though he acknowledged we hadn't, 'missed much.' It wasn't funny. Anika asked if there was a kitchen where she could make coffee and he reluctantly led us through. There was barely enough instant coffee and milk for three cups. Anika resisted an argument and we took mugs upstairs in their double room. Richard sat on the bed and I took the chair to look out the window while Anika tried to sponge my jacket clean over the tiny basin. Richard was white and tired; a day's travelling had taken much out of him. He finished his coffee, downed his tablets, thought for a couple of seconds, took out another tub to down a couple more, and insisted he was ok to go to Petra's for breakfast.

343

Today's clouds were white and the pavements dry. The door to number sixteen was a deep red, and the brass number and knocker buffed to a worn satin finish. It gave a satisfyingly dense metallic sound and Vi was at the door in ten seconds and in tears at twelve. She hugged me for a long time, composing herself before she could say how sorry she was about Mum. Then she hugged Richard and Anika as if she knew them, or they'd known Mum.

Breakfast was bacon, eggs, beans, fried bread and black and white pudding, neither of which I liked but felt obliged to eat. Anika left hers and Richard had already settled for tea and toast. Vi didn't press him to eat more – my letters had said little of Richard's illness, but she seemed to sense his fragility. When Anika mentioned, in passing, that tomorrow would be Richard's birthday, Vi was straight to the larder, hunting ingredients for a cake and disappointed that she was low on eggs. Richard quietly insisted that Vi shouldn't go to any trouble, but we all knew that would make no difference.

I told Vi almost everything about the last nine months, including how much I'd been looking forward to catching up with Petra, but excluding how much I missed Mum. When I finished talking she took my hand across the table and said, 'Sorry we didn't get back for the funeral,' and cried again. I started to say it was ok and didn't matter, except it did, perhaps to Vi as much as anyone. I went round the table to hug her.

While drinking our third cups of tea the postman delivered my letter and we laughed more than was due.

Before we came away, Vi gave us directions to the farm where Petra worked and Anika asked her if it was, '… near that statue, Saint Teresa?'

It wasn't.

The farm was less than a couple of miles. The Citroen bounced up a track and, with condensation fogging the car's windows, I lowered the glass to see better. The country here was open and the overgrown hedges bordering the haphazard fields hemmed in sheep or cows, none of whom cared as we drove past. My chest tightened, with fear, I think, as it struck me both how far I was from home and what I'd risked by coming here.

'Remember the last farm we went to?' Anika asked Richard without looking over to him.

'Of course. I hope you haven't brought a gun this time.'

'Gun?' I asked to make sure I'd heard that right.

'Pistol,' Anika said.

'It wasn't loaded,' added Richard.

'Wasn't it?' Anika asked, deadpan.

Richard looked back to me. 'Long story.'

'Tell me later.' We were pulling into the farm's courtyard and I could see Petra walking towards a barn, wearing dirty jeans tucked into wellingtons, and a heavy, oversized brown woollen jumper. She carried a tangle of leather straps. Her hair was bunched under a blue cap. She turned on hearing the car and waited as Anika parked. I went straight to her, and we kissed cheeks as the first drops of rain fell.

Petra ushered us into the barn. It was damp, more damp perhaps than the rain, and there was a gentle, mechanical, rhythmic background noise I didn't recognise. There was also an unexpected awkwardness, and I was conscious of Richard and Anika watching.

'Hey, Petra, where's that feed?' was a shout from somewhere at the back of the warehouse sized building. The barns I'd seen on tv were old and rustic; this was industrial. Liam came from behind a huge, bright red, six wheeled, tentacled machine. He wore blue dungarees and black short sleeved t-shirt, and his muscled stance was at odds with his young face – smooth skin and clear blue eyes under a dark brown fringe.

I nodded at him. He nodded back, 'G'day,' and seemed more relaxed; home territory I supposed.

Petra led us through the barn and out to stables at the back. There looked to be five or six horses in their pens and a couple saddled outside.

'Morning exercise,' Petra said and looked to the dreary skies. 'They don't mind a drop of rain and it's not getting worse. Coming?'

It took a second to realise she meant me. I didn't particularly want to.

'Anika, Richard? We can saddle up two more,' Petra suggested.

Anika looked at Richard and, though nothing was said, their decision was shared, I'm sure. 'No thank you. I have fallen off a horse before but did get back on, so, I've done that.'

Richard smiled.

'You can wait in the house. Liam's mum will look after you. She's probably baking bread.' Petra pointed to yet another building; this site was more like an entire village than the farms I was used to – though to be fair, our nearest one to home was just so kids got to see a couple of goats, rabbits and a cow.

I didn't really want to be on the back of an enormous horse, but when Petra took my hand and started showing me how to climb into the saddle, the decision was made.

'Beautiful, isn't she? Her name is Ash,' Petra said as she slipped effortlessly up onto the other horse. 'And yours is Harley. She's older and very gentle.'

I wasn't convinced. Petra sat straight while I slumped. She pushed her heels down in the dangling metal things, my trainers kept slipping out. She held the reins softly; my knuckles were white. Harley followed Ash out of the courtyard and onto a track edging a field of sheep. We only walked, and though it wasn't comfortable, I didn't feel I'd fall off. Petra spoke about her newfound love of horses and the farm and how she wanted to come back to England to go to college and work as a veterinary nurse. I was happy to listen. Her voice was more softly Irish than ever and though the wind was cold it gave her usually pale cheeks some colour. I had a brief fantasy about this being a summer's day and riding – proper riding – to some leafy wood. While the horses fed, I'd lie with Petra, her eyes as green as the grass under her. But Petra was still talking – I wondered when she had become such a talker.

'JB? Can you? Stay longer?'

The summer day would have to wait. 'We're booked on tomorrow's ferry. It's a rush, I know. We've that gig, and Richard has a hospital appointment on Friday, getting ready to start more radiotherapy on Monday.'

Petra took a second. 'Oh, he's proper poorly?'

'Serious shit.' I sounded as sincere as I could. Perhaps when I'd mentioned him in my occasional letters I'd been understated. 'And he's a good guy, a really good guy. Funny, smart, plays piano, just seems to, I dunno, know stuff but never shows off. It's his birthday tomorrow.'

'How old?'

'Seventeen.'

'Looks older.'

'No, not older, just, I dunno, wiser or something. You'll like him.'

'Sounds like you already do. A lot.' She laughed. 'Not like Vince and Oskar, is it?'

'Not funny,' I said but laughed. 'Poor Vince. I don't think he knows what he wants. He and Kay are close. I don't get it.'

'She's a good friend to him. And what about the girl. Anika?'

'Czech. Even smarter. Funny too.'

'Pretty.'

'I guess. And what about Liam?'

Petra hesitated. 'He's ok. He got me this job. Not really a job. Just helping. Doesn't pay much but ...' she leant forward and rubbed Ash's neck.

'Are you and him ... you know.'

'No. Of course not.' She let go the rein to chew on a strand of blonde hair that had tumbled from under her cap.

'He fancies you though. And why wouldn't he?' I was feeling brave, despite gripping the reins ever more tightly. Heat rose from the horse, welcome as the clouds darkened again.

'This way.' She gave a little kick and Ash sprang into a trot as she turned from the fields and onto a track in the bordering woods.

Harley followed with no instruction from me, and I bobbled haphazardly in the saddle as we went into the woods. Ahead of me, Petra was gracefully rising and falling with the rhythm of the horse. I tried but as the horse came up, I went down. It hurt and winded me. A hundred yards into the woods Petra pulled Ash to a halt and waited for me. She had the good grace not to laugh.

'Some cover here,' she suggested.

But not much. The trees were still in winter, and though the bare branches caught some rain, they also gathered larger drips that fell more heavily, if less frequently.

The track was wide enough to ride side by side.

'By the way, you'll never guess who I met working at Patrick's,' I said, and waited, almost as if I was really expecting her to guess – idiot. 'Sally. Wait, that's not her real name.'

Petra raised an eyebrow. 'What is?'

'I don't know. She's from your school. Punk girl, safety pin earrings, good teeth.' I didn't add, 'Cute smile.'

'Might be Alison. Also has a safety pin in her belly button. Claimed to be bisexual but I don't know if she knew what that really means. I thought maybe it was because she liked the attention.'

'Er, maybe. Anyway, turns out she plays drums and is a decent guitar player.' I didn't mention kissed well too – I'm not that much of an idiot and not qualified to judge, either.

'I'm not surprised. She always talked about starting a band.'

'She did. Tatt Tramps. Good name. Considering the tattoo.'

'Tattoo?'

'Marilyn Monroe, on her forearm?'

'Ah, she finally did it then.'

'And got expelled.'

'Looks like I missed a lot.'

'You did. Kay and Dimitri are together now. Vince moved in to Bazzer's, the band are going full time.'

'I know all that from Kay's letters.'

'Yep, but still, you missed it all, and Mum's funeral.' I immediately regretted the way that came out, as a criticism. I was trying to say I was sorry we hadn't seen all those things together, but now, in my head, that sounded way too pretentious.

'I'm sorry, about the funeral.' She reached across for my hand. 'It's been hard. You must miss her, I'm sure. And she would be so proud of you and the band, I'm sure of that too. She once told me it's like you have a calling, like it was religious or something.'

'She said that?'

Petra nodded.

'You didn't say.'

'Didn't I? Sorry.'

We rode in silence for a while, holding hands awkwardly, me off balance and now scared of falling. The trail split in two and the horses stopped, waiting for direction. Petra let go of my hand and pointed left. 'That way loops back round to the farm. The other goes down to the beach but it's a half hour ride. Not much fun in this.' She indicated to the grey sky and the light drizzle. 'Maybe we can go down later, if the weather's better. It's a thing round here for the locals to spend Wednesday evenings drinking at the beach. We set up fires, take beer and blankets. If it doesn't rain it's a good night.'

'The beach?'

'Yep, and if it does rain then we can go to the caves.' She eased a rein and her horse walked to the left. Mine followed, of course. My bum was sore and my trousers damp. I was happy to be going back … except,

'Petra? Those caves. Is that where Saint Teresa is?'

She nodded.

'Sally said …'

'Sally?'

'I mean Alison said you'd told her Saint Teresa cried, last year when you prayed for Mum?' I turned it into a question.

'Did she? I don't remember telling her. Mind your head.' She pushed a branch out of the way, and I ducked as I followed her down the narrowing trail.

'But Alison wouldn't know unless you …' I stopped at the sound of heavy horse footfall and someone calling,

'Petra!' Liam came towards us, riding a bigger horse. 'Petra, the rain's getting worse. I thought you might need this.' He threw her a heavy green coat. 'And fer you Mikey.' He threw me similar.

Mikey. I wasn't keen on that but thanked him and, in truth, it was welcome. That he had brought a coat for Petra was nice on his part; that he had brought two was smart.

'Your friends are in the house, we've made soup.'

Petra and Liam took the horses away to unsaddle and dry them with, I supposed, enormous towels – which I tried to joke about but didn't raise a laugh. I found my way to the farmhouse where Anika and Richard were in the warm kitchen, holding steaming mugs, Anika chatting easily with a tall, wiry woman, Richard listening, watching. I caught his eye and mouthed, 'Ok?'

He nodded.

We had lunch there, Petra and Liam joined us, and it was pleasant enough, though I was frustrated not to be alone with Petra. At just gone one, the tall lady, I didn't get to grips with her name, said politely that she had, 'Work for two but less time than my own,' which I took as a hint we should go. As we said our goodbyes Petra pecked me on the cheek and suggested we go back to her house; she'd finish work early and meet us there. Anika said she'd like to see the caves she'd heard so much about and asked for directions. Petra looked out the kitchen door.

'It's clearing. We can go to the beach and caves tonight. It's on, right?' Petra's question was to Liam. He hesitated then,

'Fer sure, all you need is a blanket, firewood and some beer.'

We drove back to the B & B as a strong wind blew the clouds away, leaving a clear sky and bright sun. I changed clothes because they smelt of horse and sat in my room for an hour while Richard and Anika stayed in theirs; Richard napping, I think.

I wanted to go and talk to them about Petra and Liam, but they had enough to be worried about. An idea for a song popped up and I regretted not bringing a guitar, so I smoked the other half of that joint and vowed never to be without a guitar, or joint, again, which made me laugh.

Will came down from his room half-way through dinner at Vi's. He wasn't surprised to see us and was pleasant enough, asking after Susan and the band before telling us how well his current band was doing. I was desperate to mention the Chrysalis showcase gig and singles, but held back. If it went well he'd hear about it.

He made himself a sandwich, wrapped it to take out and said his goodbyes.

'Gig?' Petra asked him.

'Wexford, I need to get going. You guys going down The Orchard, again?' He raised a hand to his mouth and mimicked a yawn.

I pretended to laugh but left the table to follow him to the front door. 'Will?'

'What JB? Fancy jamming with us tonight? Wexford girls are top-rank.' He stooped to tie up his boots.

'Haha, no thanks,' I glanced at Petra, 'besides, no bassist ever pulled after playing *Tie A Yellow Ribbon*.' I pinched Dimitri's joke.

'Funny boy.'

'Anyway, did you hear about Lawrence's heart attack?'

He paused mid-tug of a lace. 'That was months ago, last year.'

'No, the latest one, last week,' I said, and was aware of movement behind me.

'Last week? No,' said Vi. She had followed me into the hall.

'Touch and go as to whether or not he made it.' I exaggerated what I'd heard but neither of them reacted for a couple of seconds, then Will said,

'Well, you know, maybe some people get what they …'

'Will …' Vi interrupted.

He looked from me to her and back to me. 'JB knows more than he's saying.'

'Everybody knows about last year at the garage, Will,' I tried to sound confident, 'and Vince's dad still isn't well.'

'So?' Will sneered.

Vi touched my arm. 'Come back to the table, Mikey, dinner's getting cold. Besides, you saw Lawrence in the kitchen at your mum and dad's party, while I was clearing up.'

So, Vi had seen me that night. Shame gripped my guts and throat and I struggled to whisper, 'Sorry.'

'Dick,' said Will and left.

Vi was still holding my arm. 'You couldn't have stopped him, the man's an arse, always has been. I've prayed for him since but it's a lie to say I feel sorry for him. May God forgive me.'

'Last year, Will said something to Vince about my dad and why hadn't he sorted out Lawrence. Why?' I asked.

Petra called from the back room that our dinners were getting cold.

'Coming,' Vi shouted back but took my hand and led me into the front parlour. The light was off. She didn't turn it on. 'It's an old story. April told me that a long time ago, before I knew her, Lawrence and Frank had a falling out. Ignore Will, I should never have mentioned it to him. Your dad handled it just fine.'

'What was the argument?' I asked.

'It doesn't matter now. It was before you were born.'

'Was it about Mum?'

'April always said nothing happened, but you've seen how Lawrence can be. He was an arse and ...' her voice tailed away.

'Mum?'

'April insisted it was something of nothing. You shouldn't worry, and your dad dealt with it.'

I had a fleeting memory of Lawrence's arrogant brutality towards Vi in the kitchen and felt suddenly sick that similar might have happened to Mum. And though Dad might have dealt with it, had Mum? Vi pulled me to her and held me as though I was a child until I eased away saying, 'I miss her so much.' Vi hugged me again, ever more tightly and I tried to catch my sobs. Petra called something but Vi held me tight and whispered, 'And you must never think April left us from choice. She was too good a Catholic and just wouldn't. She just didn't know how not to. Living was hard for her.' She let me go and went back to her dinner. I waited a further minute in the darkness, trying to work out what that meant while wiping my eyes. Back at the table no one asked, though I could feel they wanted to. I sat not eating while they finished dinner, chatting easily, Anika and Vi orchestrating conversation. It should have been a relaxing dinner, but I still hadn't talked much to Petra alone.

Afterwards, Vi brought through the cake she had made for Richard, and he was embarrassed but still blew out the candles and, prompted by Anika, made a wish. Vi presented him with a half-bottle of Jameson, playing it down by saying she'd, 'won it at bingo but didn't touch the stuff.'

We all helped clear the table and wash up then waited while Petra went to change for a night at the beach.

Chapter 38
Spring 1977
The Beach, Ireland
'Boogie Nights'

We left Vi's with armfuls of blankets, the half-bottle of Jameson, two flasks of sweet tea, half a birthday cake wrapped in aluminium foil and three torches. Petra wore two pairs of socks, wellingtons, heavy jeans, two or maybe three jumpers, one of Will's coats and a woollen hat that, just as we were about to walk out the door, had the bobble cut off. We stopped at the pub to gather as many warm clothes as we had, which was not many in my case. I tucked a couple of joints in my shirt's top pocket and slipped on the leather bracelet. Anika bought a few bottles of beer and we waited for the half hourly bus at the top of the road. Twice, Anika assured Richard she had his tablets, and three times pulled the sheepskin collar of his jacket more closely to his neck. With little breeze, it wasn't too cold and the sky was clear – the moon was just a night or two from being full. The bus driver welcomed us, not surprised by the expedition that clambered aboard. He let us off, not at a bus stop, but outside the track entrance to a farm. Next to the gate was a small doorless storage hut with baskets of chopped firewood. Petra dropped two Irish ten pence pieces into an open box marked '*Thank you*' and picked up a basket saying, 'We'll drop it back later.' She laid the blankets on top of the wood, motioning that I should take one handle while she took the other, then turned on the torch, 'just this one for now, save the others.' We crossed the road into a narrow pathway, created by footfall, through a patch of heath that turned into scrubland then grassy, sandy knolls. The breeze grew stronger and smelt of seaweed, so I supposed we were nearing the beach, as we wandered between growing dunes, decorated with clumps of rangy, waving tall grass, barely lit by the already dimming torch. The sand dragged our feet and we slowed, letting Anika and Richard stay close. Before we reached open beach, Petra took us through increasingly tall dunes. There was an orange haze and a smell of burning wood. The breeze brought snatches of music and fifty yards on we walked into a hollow, surrounded by dunes just high enough to shelter from the wind. At the centre was a careless pile of wood, burning fiercely. A silhouetted figure squirted a plastic bottle and the sudden burst of extra flame came with paraffin fumes.

Ten or more dark figures were standing around the clearing. Music from a portable cassette player came and passed on the breeze as the fire's flames flared and died.

'More wood is it? Good on yer.' Liam said, taking our basket.

Petra took a few seconds to choose a good spot – by what criteria I'd no idea – and laid down a couple of blankets, using bottles to weigh down the corners.

I'd never been to a beach at night and never to a beach party, full stop. I suppose I'd expected something more, I don't know, party-like? The people here were more *Teenage Depression* than *Boogie Nights*. They gathered in small groups, talking, drinking and smoking; silhouettes against the fire and shadows flashed to brief orange in the glare of a flame. As we sat on the blankets someone picked up a guitar and started playing.

'Don't,' said Petra.

'What?'

'Tell me whether he's any good or not. That's Finn. Nice guy.' She opened a can of lager.

I nodded then shook my head to refuse the offer of a drink, and we sat listening to the music and the conversation. Anika and Richard cuddled and occasionally whispered.

'You ok? Quiet since dinner,' Petra asked. We'd been sitting for a while, not saying much, which was stupid when I had so much to say.

'Just waiting.'

'What for?'

'You, I s'pose.' Which was true. I'd been waiting one way or the other since the funeral. 'Can I ask? What's with you and Liam?'

'Again?'

'You get on well and, what with the horses and all, have stuff to, I dunno, share.'

Petra smiled. 'He's like the big brother my real one isn't.'

'Does he know that?'

'Will?'

'No, Liam.'

'Well enough. And whatever, we're not as close as you and Sofia were.'

I couldn't tell if she joked or not, but it had been said, again, so still, things hadn't been put right. 'Is Sofia why you didn't come back for the funeral?' Or for me, I wanted to add.

'No.'

'Liam?'

'No. He just helped us when we moved here. Especially Will. He needed a job while trying to get another band up and running. Liam found him work at his family's farm. They were good friends for a while until Will fell out with him.' Petra looked at me. Side on to the fire she was mostly in her own shadow and I couldn't see her eyes. She sighed, as if preparing a thought. 'We didn't come back because of Will and what he did to Vince's dad. You mustn't tell anyone.'

'Anyone that might know, already does. We even had the police asking about him.'

'Police?'

'It's no secret. Some say Lawrence got what was coming,' I said hesitantly.

357

'Some might say my brother finished what your dad should have started,' said Petra. 'I'm sorry,' she touched my arm, 'I didn't mean that like it sounded. And you couldn't have done anything about Lawrence attacking my mum at the party that night. Could you?'

Of course she knew, and of course I could have; should have, done something, but instead of apologising asked, 'If Will hadn't attacked Lawrence, you wouldn't have left?'

'No, if you hadn't gone to bed with Sofia I'd have stayed at the party, and would have been helping Mum in the kitchen, and Lawrence wouldn't have dared.'

I started to protest but caught myself. Petra had spoken not with anger or accusation but with sadness. We went back to silence and were both grateful when Richard called,

'Hey, which way to the sea?'

'Through there.' Petra pointed to a gap in the dunes. 'You'll need a torch and don't go swimming,' she joked.

Richard led Anika away. I looked round the party again. 'I'd like to see it too.'

'Not much to see in the dark.'

'Moon's nearly full.' I took her hand and started after Richard.

Away from the dunes the breeze was stronger, and I heard the sea lapping on the beach though I couldn't yet see it. We walked towards the small, dirty white light from Richard's torch. He and Anika stood beach-side, just, of the landing waves, in an awkward cuddle that split as I called them. The moon was bright, flashing white ribbons on the water that rode the rolling blackness towards us, tumbling gently on to the dark, flat sand. The lights of the ferry out of Rosslare could be seen. They didn't move and yet were slipping out of sight.

'Here.' Anika passed me her camera; it now had a flash cube stuck on top. 'See if you can get the waves too.'

She and Richard held each other while Petra shined a torch at them, and I tried to guess what the camera was capturing. The explosion of the bulb made us laugh and momentarily blind.

'Did you get us and the water?' Anika asked.

'I think so.'

'It's a sweet-water night. That's rare,' said Petra.

'Sweet-water,' Anika repeated.

'It's what the locals say when it's calm. Mostly there's a mad wind and spiteful sea, scaring to drag you away.' Petra took a further step back from the water, as if remembering something.

'Czechoslovakia has no sea,' said Anika. 'We have lakes, but they can be still. Not without rest, like ...' she indicated to the blackness stretching out before us, then looked to Petra. 'And is Saint Teresa close?'

Petra started to ask a question, stopped, and looked down the beach, into the dark. The full moon could just pick out the change in light where the beach ended. 'There's a low rocky cliff with some caves. Well, not really a cliff, and not really caves, but holes and hollows, carved by the sea. Some you can stand in. She's in the biggest, out of reach of the water.'

'And you saw her cry for JB's mother?' asked Anika.

Petra looked to me and hesitated. 'Perhaps. But I couldn't see properly.'

'Really?'

'Honestly,' Petra repeated, 'I don't know.'

'A crying statue is something though, isn't it?' Anika smiled and spoke quietly, if not gently.

I remembered Susan saying something similar. 'Petra's not sure.' I defended her vagueness.

'Really?' said Anika. 'How can you not know?' Her smile was fixed.

Petra looked scared and I didn't want her to speak. Partly because I was also scared – I might not like the answer – but mostly because I could see it upset her.

'Did you see tears? Anika pressed. Not with anger or frustration but firmly, as if it would make Petra feel better to say.

'I don't know. I'm sorry.'

'Doesn't make any difference,' Anika turned to me, 'your mother didn't die of cancer. Whether Saint Teresa cried or not, something made a difference.' Anika pulled her mac tighter around her. 'Richard is cold, would you take him back to the fire please?'

Before either Richard or I could answer she was walking down the beach, the meagre light from a torch struggling to show the high-water line.

'Going with her?' I asked him.

'I thought it was a good idea when we came, but then we talked earlier and agreed not to ...but now she ...' Richard's answer tailed off and he gestured vaguely in Anika's direction. He took a step to follow her, but Petra put a hand on his shoulder.

'Here,' Petra handed him a torch. 'You guys go back, I'll make sure she doesn't get lost.'

It was already difficult to see Anika. Wisps of cloud now dimmed the moon which just occasionally picked out her light mac.

Richard and I stood close to the fire for warmth. The others acknowledged us with friendly enough nods and I could hear Liam and his friends' drunken rambling. They were boasting about their club's successful season. I had no idea what hurling was, but it involved tackling, cracking hurleys together, whatever they were, scoring goals and bleeding. It was like being back in school, sitting in the corner of the gym with the non-sports group, while the football squad alternately told each other how great or unlucky they were in the last match.

'We're ahead of the game all right,' Liam said to the youth next to him, who responded with a simple two-finger salute from his cap. Liam responded the same way. It was a small gesture but, clearly, it was theirs.

I thought of something witty to say and turned to catch Dimitri's or Bazzer's attention – except of course they weren't there. Liam had his team; I was suddenly missing mine.

'You ok, JB?' Richard asked. His shoulders were hunched, his head shrinking into the bulky collar of his flying jacket.

'Just wondering what the guys back home are doing. Do you think Red Ice Rising are ahead of the game? I mean, if the Chrysalis deal happens, that is. I thought it might take another year or two.'

'Maybe I'm not the person to ask.'

'What do you mean?' I asked then it dawned on me. 'Oh, sorry.'

'S'ok. For what it's worth I don't think anyone ever really gets ahead of the game. Whatever the game is. Sometimes we're on it, maybe like Red Ice Rising, and that's as good as it gets, to be at the right place at the right time. Though there was one guy I sort of knew who found a way to be ahead, in a way. Did I tell you about the saxophone player?'

I shook my head.

'Last year, remember when you played Oakjack Ford and I was outside the pub?'

'Sure.'

'I was staying with my uncle. Anika was there too. Next door was a woman who was dying, everybody knew, and every day the guy she lived with carried her to the garden, put her in a hammock and played the saxophone.'

'Saxophone?'

'I know, sounds odd, but it's true. Sometimes we'd sneak into the garden and watch and one day he, er, he killed her.'

'He what?' I couldn't possibly have heard that right. Richard was staring into the flames and repeated,

'Killed her. With a pillow.'

'Pillow?' I was close to making some stupid joke, but Richard's face was set, this was real.

'Suffocated her.'

'While you watched?'

'He didn't know.'

'Woah, that must have been a moment.'

Richard's gaze didn't move from the fire. 'A moment?'

'Never mind.'

'At first we were scared, then we wondered if we'd imagined it, but as the days passed, it all seemed quite natural. He loved her so much and she was dying and suffering, what else could he do? He was just getting ahead of the game. Afterwards he told my uncle that she deserved peace, and besides, hadn't left him. As long as he thought of her, told stories about her and tried to live as she'd have wanted, she was still there.' Richard stood away from the fire and looked at me. 'I think, pray, that's true. Don't you?'

I didn't answer. I was thinking about that word 'peace' again. 'Why didn't you go to the statue of Saint Teresa?'

'Because I know why Anika went. Of course I hope the statue cries, but I still have to be me if it doesn't. Why didn't you go?'

'I don't need to know.'

'You mean you'd rather not.'

Petra and Anika joined us at the fire and Anika hugged Richard, burying her face in his shoulder. Someone threw wood on the fire. I felt my face glow. I started to speak, but Petra stopped me and between the sharp cracks of burning firewood, I thought I heard Anika crying. She lifted her head, smiled and wiped her eyes. Without speaking, she led Richard to their space, pulled him to the ground and wrapped them both in the heaviest spare blanket.

Through the flickering flames I could see Finn on the other side of the fire. He took up his guitar to play and sing. I think it was an old folk song and didn't know it, but everyone else did, singing along with the chorus and clapping at the right times. A few more people had turned up and there were maybe twenty, huddling close to the fire or pulling blankets around themselves on the fringes.

'*The Wild Rover*,' Petra said, and I sang along with the next chorus and joined in the cheers when it ended, before asking,

'When are you coming home?'

Petra turned to me. 'I want to go to veterinary college and if I get in, that'll be September.'

'Why wait? Sofia's moved in with Sunny Steve. You could have her bedroom.' I tried to sound casual, as if this solution hadn't occurred to me weeks ago.

'I know, Kay told me, but what about Mum?'

'September then.' I stared into the fire and lit a joint.

'When did you start smoking?' Petra looked at me.

'Oh, it's ok, it's not a fag.'

'Oh, of course. You're a rock star, I forgot.'

I thought of mentioning the Chrysalis deal but that would not have helped. I took a couple of drags. Petra looked disappointed and I had a sudden image of what I might look like, hunched against the cold in a vomit-stained Harrington, staring into a make-shift fire, shuffling my feet to keep them from freezing, furtively smoking half a joint. Rock and roll? Hardly. I crushed the joint's end, put it back in an inside pocket, then drew myself to full height, shoulders back, and rubbed my hands towards the fire.

Finn began another song.

'Did Anika find Saint Teresa?' I asked.

'Yep.'

'And did the statue cry?'

'She said so.'

'You didn't see?'

'I didn't go in. What is it with you and that statue? Did you come here for me or your mum?' Petra asked, but not in an angry or offended manner, more sad, and added, 'It's ok I get it. I do. You think if St. Teresa cried, your mum's all right. Wherever she is.'

I took Petra's hand to lead her to our blanket. Away from the fire, my face and hands were quickly cold.

Next to us, Richard and Anika were buried under blankets, Anika's mac and Richard's flying jacket. We couldn't see their heads, and their bodies were one under the heap of covers. Occasionally we heard a moan but couldn't tell from whom.

I laughed but Petra looked serious. 'How old is Richard tomorrow?'

'Seventeen.'

'He seems so much older.'

'Hard to believe I missed your seventeenth birthday and you missed my sixteenth.'

'I'm sorry,' she whispered and leant into me, and I put my arm round her shoulder.

'S'ok. Tall enough at last.' Just. It wasn't comfortable sitting on the blanket like this, but I wasn't going to move away. I enjoyed Petra's weight against me, but she was so bundled in clothes that I could barely feel her.

'Eh?'

'Remember when we went to the pictures? I wasn't tall enough to put my arm around you easily.'

'I remember. I expect you've had a lot of practise since. Being a rock star and all.'

'Not really.'

'Not really?'

'Not at all.'

'What, so you've been waiting for me to … you know.'

This was my chance to say, 'Yes! Of course.' Instead I asked, 'Did you … wait?' and instinctively looked over to Liam.

'Of course, but if you didn't then I don't know why I bothered. You're an arse.'

Beside us the bundle of blankets and coats moved rhythmically, and the moans grew louder; definitely Anika.

'I waited. Honest.'

'You're a boy. Why should I believe you?' Petra asked, with mischief, I hoped.

'Or me, you?' I hoped my lopsided smile showed I was desperate to believe.

Petra wrestled a purse from one of her jacket pockets, showed me two small foil packs then slipped them back into the purse, laughing easily for the first time since I'd been back.

'Are they the same two?'

'Of course. Now, where's your proof? Mr Rock Star.'

I pulled my sleeve up just enough to show her the leather bracelet. 'But I only wear it on special occasions like ... like coming all this way to see you.'

She showed me her half of the bracelet. 'I believe you,' and pushed me to lie down on the blanket. She briefly kissed me on the lips, the first time since I'd been back, and leant across me to the spare blankets to cover us both. It was cold, the ground was uncomfortable, and there was no subtlety and little intimacy in our clumsy fumbling through layers of clothing. I was desperate to touch her bare skin, to see her mole, to cup her breast, to stroke her thigh, to kiss her flat belly. Our clumsiness was passionate but this was no sophisticated seduction. And that was ok. We kissed fast, then slowly, then hard; she let me undo her jacket and pressed against me; memories of our disco dance. Her breasts were heavier than I remembered though, to be honest it was hard to tell through three jumpers, a vest and a bra. With her hand outside my jeans she stroked my erection and I kissed her more furiously, wanting more urgency and she rubbed harder and more quickly and ...

'Whoa, whoa, no, not ... wait. We, I ...' I grabbed her hand.

'What's wrong? Isn't that right?'

I took a couple of breaths and gently pushed her hand away. 'Oh yes, too right. But I want to wait until we ...' I tried to find the right word. Most choices were too crude, like 'shag', others were too clinical, like 'have sex', and 'make love' just didn't sound like something I'd say – except I did.

Petra put both hands to my cold cheeks and kissed me firmly but simply on the lips. 'We will, I think we always were going to, don't you?'

Sometime during the night Finn stopped playing and the fire was left to die. Richard and Anika went still and silent. I didn't sleep much. In the dark early hours I heard Anika whisper, 'Happy birthday,' but Richard didn't answer. Perhaps he still slept.

Petra and I were huddled against each other with a couple of blankets over us, but as the night slowly lifted, the temperature dropped. I don't know if Petra slept much. I couldn't see her face, buried into her thick jacket's collar, but heard her steady breathing and could smell her hair. She occasionally nuzzled tighter against me, and I really didn't mind that we were waiting.

We took the late morning ferry back to Fishguard and though the sea didn't seem any calmer, and definitely wasn't 'sweet-water', I retched less. Anika came up on deck to find me, and we sat on a bench near to the rail, just in case. She brought me a black, sweet tea and a digestive.

'I'm sorry Petra didn't come back with us. I like her. She likes you. I think she will be back soon.' She sipped her coffee.

'I think so too.' I tried to sound sure.

'You could stay there.'

'Gig tomorrow.' I didn't add that besides, I needed to talk to Dad about Lawrence and my mum.

'Richard is below, sleeping. Last night was long. We are going to hospital for treatment on Monday and now we have Saint Teresa on our side, don't we?' She looked at me and I wondered what she thought Petra had told me.

'Maybe …'

She interrupted, 'Richard told me about your mother's fourth miracle.'

'I'd guessed.'

'I understand why you'd like to know but …' she sipped from her coffee, 'today, Richard doesn't need peace, he needs to be here. So it's important he understands Saint Teresa cried for him. Yes?'

'Yes.'

Miracle Number Four

Chapter 39
Spring 1977
Last To Know
'Don't Sleep In The Subway'

I sat up front. We stopped just once for petrol, keen to be home. Richard was stretched out in the back and, as far as I could tell, slept. I dozed and Anika was ok with that. We were too tired for small talk, as if that was her style anyway. She dropped me off at home and woke Richard. He was hard to rouse and took a few seconds to know who we were.

It was evening. Susan's Mini wasn't outside but Dad's Rover was on the drive so I went round the back. The house was dark, but music came from the lounge: *Don't Sleep In The Subway* – Mum had loved Petula Clark. Dad was in the conservatory and I called out as I went through, not wanting to surprise him. He sat in Mum's chair and looked up from his lap; a frown slipping into a warm smile.

'Safe and sound. It's a long trip. Is that Czech girl a good driver?'

'Of course.' I rested a hand on his shoulder.

'And how's the lad, Richard? Susan tells me he's very poorly.'

I nodded. 'Wotchya doing?'

'Resting. Busy day at work.' His hands were in his lap, holding Mum's apple blossom embroidery.

I wondered when he'd taken it from the wall and was a little ashamed that I didn't just hug him. 'Cold out here.'

'Little bit. There's half a chicken and mushroom pie in the oven. Susan's already gone round Bazzer's. It was her last day at the salon today. You lot are doing the right thing. How was Ireland?'

'Good. Could have done with longer.'

'I hear you've an important gig tomorrow night. I might come along.'

'You should.'

369

'Will I be allowed in?'

'Come with the band.'

'Maybe. Vi and Petra ok?

I nodded.

'Mum always liked Petra. Susan thought she might come back with you. She could stay here. In your room.'

'Really?'

'Really. Mum wouldn't have minded 'cos …,' he paused and I knew there was a punchline, '… you'd be on the camp bed in the front room.'

I laughed, embarrassed that he would have known my thoughts; of course he would.

'Oh, and Vince called earlier, wanting to know if you were back.'

'Is his dad still in hospital?'

'Yep.'

I wanted to ask Dad about what Vi and Will had said, about Mum and Lawrence, but instead, 'How ill is he?'

'He's due out tomorrow. I hope so, it's busy at the garage. Do you want that pie?' Dad asked.

'No thanks, not hungry. Better get some practise in. Big gig tomorrow.'

My thoughts spun and blurred: leaving Petra; Richard's illness; Lawrence and Mum?

I played my bass guitar, of course.

'Susan.' I called again, just a little louder, and tapped on her bedroom door. It was nearly ten on Friday morning and I'd slept for nigh on twelve hours. Susan didn't answer so I went in. She wasn't there and the bed was made. I looked out front. Her car wasn't there, nor was Dad's but then he'd have left for work a couple of hours ago. I supposed Susan had spent the night at Bazzer's.

Spring 1977 – Last To Know

I made tea and toast and took it through to the conservatory. It was a bright morning. The daffodil shoots promised a burst of yellow to catch up with the snow crocuses but the apple tree above them was still a skeleton. I left the crockery in the sink and took both my acoustic and bass to Bazzer's, nodding to the ladies in the bakery as I passed.

Susan led me through to the kitchen where Bazzer and Vince were close to arguing.

'Ok, I get it,' said Vince, 'you want to be managed by Peter Grant.'

'I'm not saying that,' Bazzer looked up and nodded 'hello' to me as I followed Susan in, 'I'm just saying we need to understand where the money's coming from.'

'And going,' added Susan.

'What's the matter?' I asked.

'Algie wants to increase his take of our gig fees,' said Susan.

'To help pay for the studio. Algie's out of pocket too.' Vince sounded hurt on his behalf.

'Studio?' I sat down next to Vince.

'For the two singles, which means cutting at least four tracks.' Susan was bordering on patronising. 'You got the bit about Chrysalis only paying for half the studio time, right?' That last bit was downright condescending,

'Yeah, 'course.' In truth, that might have passed me by.

'Which means someone else has to pay the other half.'

'Algie, right?' I guessed.

'But how do you think he pays for it?' Vince spoke quickly, to get in before Susan and Bazzer.

'Hadn't really thought about it.' I hadn't.

Susan sighed. 'He pays up front but recovers it from his cut of band earnings. And now he wants to increase his take.'

371

'Only until he's paid off Chrysalis, then it can go back to what it is now,' Vince explained.

'And Vince is the messenger we shouldn't shoot, yet.' said Susan.

I laughed. No one else did. Sunny Steve was now standing at the open back door, Bruce by his side.

Susan stood next to Bazzer, resting a hand on his shoulder. 'We've given up jobs for this. Money's tight.'

'It's just until he's paid off Chrysalis,' Vince explained again.

'Algie should be paying some of it out his own pocket.' Sunny Steve said, as he came into the kitchen. Bruce followed and I put my hand out for him to sniff. He was satisfied and went to his bed in the corner.

'I don't know. You guys signed a contract. I didn't.' There was strain in Vince's voice, a mix of fear and frustration.

Sofia joined us, kissing me on the cheek, 'Hi, JB. How was Ireland? You ok?'

I nodded.

There was a short silence which Vince was compelled to fill. 'I'll ask him about it later. I'll see him at Zamara'z. He's letting me move into the flat behind the office.'

'You're leaving here?' I asked.

Vince looked at Bazzer.

'Our dad is coming home earlier than we thought.' Bazzer was apologetic.

'Good behaviour. Supposedly,' said Steve. 'He'll want his room back and what with Sofia living here now as well …'

'Sorry Vince.' Sofia squeezed his shoulder.

'The flat at Zamara'z, with Algie?' I spoke without thinking.

'No, of course not with Algie. Just me. Rent free. I'm practically running the place already. It makes sense.'

'What about going back home?' Susan suggested.

'Mum wants that, but Dad said not over his dead body,' Vince looked down into his tea mug then forced a laugh, 'which was quite ironic really, considering he's still in hospital.'

There was a quiet few seconds before Sunny Steve took Vince upstairs, offering him a cutting from his 'best weed' to see if he could grow a little of his own in the flat at Zamara'z. Bruce seemed to sigh before reluctantly leaving his bed to pad after them.

Susan drove me home from the Friday gig. We'd played Brunel University, a good venue, and were keen to get on the university circuit. Bigger bands were listed and a lot of the up-and-coming London pub bands wanted to be. We'd still been playing the pubs but in the last few months, more of them were giving punk bands the gigs ahead of us. Susan was questioning me about the trip to Ireland; I was vague,

'We nearly … you know … but it wouldn't have been what it might, so …' I didn't finish.

'What? Like you couldn't get it up or something?' Susan seemed to find it both hilarious and shocking.

'What? No, it wasn't like that.'

My laugh was so obviously forced that Susan touched my arm and said, 'Sorry.'

'Maybe it'll turn out better this way, in the long run.' I remembered Susan's advice from the launderette.

'I get it, I think. When's Petra coming home?'

I shrugged, fed up with answering that question and turned the radio down, John Peel's show was finishing, and asked, 'Did Mum ever tell you anything about Vince's dad?'

'Lawrence?'

'Yep.'

'No.'

'Did Dad ever say anything?' My voice pitched higher.

Susan hesitated. We were close to home, passing the station. Susan pulled into the drop off cut-in. The streetlamps were a miserable shade of yellow and a couple of the neon strips in the station foyer blinked randomly. One of the telephone booths was occupied and I could hear the young woman swearing into the receiver. A late-night couple staggered from under the darkness of the station bridge into the flickering light, probably from a lock-in at The Railway. It was a long time ago we'd used that tatty upstairs room for practise.

'Did he deserve what Will did? Should Dad have done something before?' I pressed Susan. The windscreen fogged in the cold.

She spoke, finally. 'You know that thing with Dad not taking the Redcoat job?'

I nodded.

'I asked Dad if that was true, and he said yes, but there was more to it. Lawrence not only gave Dad a rise but also made him foreman after they had an argument.'

'About what?'

'Dad didn't say, but mentioned Mum didn't care about more money, she just wanted him to try the Redcoat job. There was more to it, but he wouldn't say. Sorry.'

This past of theirs; ours.

Susan, Vi, knew a little, even Petra and Will knew something. As usual, I was last. Susan's apology wasn't enough.

My silence was anger.

Chapter 40
Spring 1977
Side-Effects
'Angie'

Neither Susan nor I had to get up for work and were already used to having a lazy breakfast before wandering round to Bazzer's mid-morning. We, that is the band, had two decisions to make – the set list for the Hammersmith Palais showcase gig, just eight and a half weeks away, and the four tracks we wanted to record, four weeks away. It didn't take long to choose, we already knew which songs went down best live – though they would still have to be agreed with Stewart, our Chrysalis ... something or other, but still I was disappointed that I hadn't, couldn't, finish *Miracle Number Four* in time.

Afterwards I went to see Richard. Susan offered to drive me, but I needed time alone and buses were good for thinking.

'Guitar,' I said pointlessly, holding up the case.

'Oh, not a tuba then?' Richard raised a tired laugh. He had taken longer than usual to get to the door. I followed him into the back half of the through-lounge. It was quiet and full of plants. Not just a few pots dotted about, but tall, bushy, fleshy, dark green-leafed plants in corners, on tables and both mantelpieces. With the big brown and orange swirls of wallpaper behind them, it seemed the room was closing in. The dog lay in the middle of the carpet, ignoring us.

Richard guessed at my bemusement. 'Mum thinks all the extra oxygen they put out will be good for me.'

'Where is she?'

'Church. Kim is at school, Step-dad's at work, and Anika had to do something for Uncle Dudek, up town.'

'Your mum left you alone?' And, as I spoke I regretted it.

'It's nice sometimes.'

'I guess. Except, now I'm here.'

'Besides, she needs to keep her prayer count up or gets cranky.' Richard sat in an armchair and I took the settee.

'Aren't Vietnamese, Buddhists or something?'

'Some, and a few are Catholic. Hasn't been easy for them.'

'My mum was Catholic, for all the good it did her.'

'Did it?' Richard asked.

'I don't know. Doesn't matter. How did the radiotherapy go yesterday?'

He took a slip of paper from the table by his side, scrunched it into a ball, and tossed it over to me. It was a typed list on hospital notepaper:

Radiation to the brain can cause short-term side effects: Headaches; Hair loss; Nausea; Vomiting; Fatigue; Hearing loss; Skin and scalp changes; Trouble with memory and speech; Seizures.

I tried desperately to think of something funny to say, maybe about glowing in the dark, as I stared at the word: Radiation. Not radiotherapy. Radiotherapy carried hope. Radiation didn't. Radiotherapy implied treatment. Radiation threatened harm. I wondered which word Mum had seen.

'To be fair,' said Richard, 'it's too early for those. Give it a couple more sessions and maybe. But it wasn't too bad last time. Hey, do you think Susan would cut my hair short, really short? Then maybe when it falls out ...' the words faded.

'Worth it though. The radiotherapy worked last time,' I offered.

'Not really, else I wouldn't be having it again. They don't usually bother with two lots.'

I didn't know what to make of that.

'You'll want to tune up.' Richard indicated to the guitar case.

'Why?'

'Because you will. It's a comfort blanket. I don't know why they can't make one that stays in tune. It's nineteen seventy-seven for God's sake.' He smiled and stood unsteadily to go to the piano at the other end of the room. 'Imagine if I had to retune this every fifteen minutes.' He sat and fiddled with the stool, trying to get the right height, which made me laugh. The first thing I did with the guitar was tune it, twice.

'I've been listening to *Blinded By The Light*. I don't think I've been playing it right,' Richard said, as I pulled up a chair next to him.

We played it a few times but didn't improve it much and Richard eventually said, 'I miss working at Patrick's and playing … well, anything really.'

'I get it.' I played one of our favourites from the shop, *Angie*, and Richard added a few touches.

'We never did get past the intro on that,' he said, as the song petered out.

'What about *Miracle Number Four*? We played that a few times and it's still not finished.'

Richard was thoughtful, then, 'Do I know it?'

I began playing and sang the first verse and chorus, 'Remember?'

'Maybe.'

'It needs, you gave it, some piano.'

'Did I?'

I played it again and Richard tentatively tried a few enhancing parts.

I tried again but Richard didn't join in. His hands lay lightly on the keys, not moving. He stared at them. 'Sorry. Could you?' he pointed at a portable cassette player.

He put in a blank C60, pressed record, and I played the song through, though it was still missing at least one verse and maybe a bridge.

'Leave it here. I'll see what I can come up with,' he said, as the tape rewound.

We didn't play much after that and when his mother came home she insisted I have tea and biscuits – Richard had the second half of a Marathon bar and a Lucozade – while she chatted to me for perhaps twenty minutes without mentioning the 'R' word.

When it was time to leave, Richard came to the door and I remembered to say, 'By the way, thanks for taking me to Ireland.'

'It was a good trip,' he agreed, 'knackering, but good. I'm sorry Petra didn't come back with us. She's cool. Have you written to her yet?'

'I can phone her now.'

'Did you?'

'Not yet.'

'You should. Did you ask her to come back with us?'

'Sort of.'

'You know, you don't have to tell someone what you're thinking, but don't expect them to always guess right.'

'Petra knew, I'm sure.' I answered hesitantly, embarrassed.

'Of course,' Richard said, seriously, then laughed.

Early that evening, before going out to the gig, I rang Petra. I sat on the telephone chair in the hall. On my lap was a list of things to talk about. The last item on the list was (g) – Make sure Petra knows you want her to come home. She sounded pleased to hear from me and after item (a) – 'Sofia's still living round Bazzer's' and (b) – 'Kay says hi', I jumped straight to (g), saying, 'And she says you could have Sofia's old room.'

'I know,' said Petra, 'she already told me.'

'And I know you don't want to leave your mum but Will's there right? So you wouldn't be leaving her on her own.'

'I'd miss her. She'd miss me.'

'I know what that feels like …'

'Well, in that case …' She sounded sincere or was it teasing? I needed to see her smile to know.

'When?' I asked, in for a penny, etc.

There was a short silence, and I took heart from it being only brief before she said, 'Soon.'

Before I could press for a date, Dad was shouting from the lounge about the cost of international phone calls. We said quick goodbyes and it was ok she hadn't said when she'd be coming – I preferred 'soon'. It meant it could be, well, 'soon'.

Algie had been nagging Stewart at Chrysalis to pull a few strings and that night we played a support slot at The Nashville Rooms – a big deal. Afterwards, Stewart treated us to a round, then left, with Sunny Steve close behind. Steve was back in less than ten minutes.

Miracle Number Four

Chapter 41
Spring 1977
Mooching
'Rumours'

Susan came up with the name: mooch-time. She even wrote a song about it. It was rubbish. Few words rhyme with mooch, and who wants a song about an alcoholic dog. Mooch-time referred to those periods when we weren't (a) planning and rehearsing for the Chrysalis recording session and showcase concert or (b) grinding through the gigs Algie had lined up now we were 'full-time' and able to travel further afield.

Mooch-time was time lost in listless fatigue that was never long enough to fully recharge batteries. Mooch-time was half-written songs, half-hearted gear maintenance, half-listened recordings of other bands – even, or perhaps especially, *Rumours* – and half-met promises of exercise and proper eating.

I also used mooch-time to write to Petra. I occasionally telephoned, but Dad moaned about the cost. Our conversations finished with me asking when she was coming back and her answering, 'Soon.' I never pushed for a date but that, 'Soon,' was enough to make mooch-time bearable.

It was also during mooch-time that I introduced Vince to Safety Pin Sally. Algie had asked Vince to pick up new speaker cables for the house PA so I suggested he try Patrick's Pianos, and that if I came along he might get mate's rates.

We waited for the boss to go out, which meant hanging around in the nearby café. Two cups of tea and a shared Coke later I saw him leave. Vince followed me into the shop as I called, 'Hi, Sally. How're things?'

'All right. You?' She came from behind the counter.

'Good. I've been away. Ireland. Petra told me to say hi to Alison,' I teased.

There was a touch of surprise – or shock? – in her smile, but she quickly recovered. 'Ha. Tell her Alison wonders when she's coming back.'

'Soon.'

'Good. Maybe that'll stop you hanging round Alison.'

I laughed. 'This is Vince. Vince this is Sally, or Alison.'

'Sally, for now.'

Vince nodded his hello.

'We're after a couple of speaker cables. Got any twenty-four foot?' I asked.

Sally pointed to a rack. 'You know where they are.'

'Mate's rates?'

'They for Red Ice Rising?'

'No, Zamara'z, house PA,' said Vince.

'Oh yeah, I've seen you down there.'

'He's sort of our manager's right-hand man.' I held out a hand towards Vince, like an assistant introducing a magician's trick.

'Really? Can you get us a slot at the club?' Sally was straight in there.

'He can get you ten minutes with Algie,' I interrupted before Vince could speak.

'Give me your phone number.' She passed Vince a shop card and pen. He wrote the number down, asking,

'About those mate's rates?'

The argument about Algie increasing his cut of the band's gig take to help fund the recording deal didn't quite fester, but nor did it go away. To restore harmony, Algie hosted a dinner to celebrate the Chrysalis tie-in.

Dad had been spending more time down the Conservative Club, he was now both Assistant Treasurer and Entertainment Secretary, and offered us the use of the upstairs function room for free. They had a new chef who was keen to experiment – chicken or scampi in a basket was not so challenging – and there was a new menu for the night. Sofia and Kay were there early, decorating the room with Red Ice Rising posters and black, red and silver bunting – band colours. They placed some artificial flower decorations, in band colours, on the table and set up a cassette deck and speakers for background music – we weren't allowed guitars. Sofia and Kay were determined this was an evening for talking, listening, drinking and maybe dancing, not playing. They also insisted that we dress up – not fancy dress, but smart.

We met Richard and Anika at the club. He wore a dark blue suit and black hat. Susan took a few seconds to look him up and down, letting him know she thought he looked good and commenting on the fedora.

'Uncle Dudek's,' he said, pinching fingers to the brim and running them around the front.

It suited him, and though the dark clothes made his cheeks paler, his smile was bright.

Anika was overdressed in an evening gown of deep red, but could carry it off, and Susan looked great in a knee-length purple dress with a white cardigan draped over her shoulders, and a single string of pearls – Mum's outfit. It wasn't particularly glamourous but very classy, and, as I'd told her when she'd come down the stairs, 'Mum would be proud.'

I was scruffy in a pair of old grey school trousers that I'd found at the back of the wardrobe, but at least my black blazer looked the part – it was the first time I'd worn it since Mum's funeral. I wore my half of the leather bracelet so that Petra was there in spirit, or some such nonsense, as I later said to Vince even though he hadn't asked.

The doorman greeted us formally, almost certainly primed by Dad, complimented the ladies on their dresses, and pointed us upstairs.

Up in the function room, I sat next to Richard, opposite Vince and Sally. They were at ease together and he paid close attention to her conversation, which I couldn't hear because Kay turned up the music volume.

The room was a happy place; the conversation and music were loud. Wine and beer were topped up, and by the end of the main course I was beyond tipsy. I was still no drinker.

'Does it ever taste nice?' I leant in towards Richard to ask.

'What?'

'Lager.'

'I don't know.' He held up a glass of Coke. 'Doc says I shouldn't touch beer.' He smiled but it was a tired effort. 'But then I'm on so many tablets for headaches I don't need alcohol.' He took a small tub from his jacket pocket and gave them a shake. 'Doctor's specials. Not your everyday aspirin.'

'Do they work?' I asked, but he didn't answer. I tried to see his eyes, but they were in the shadow of the fedora he had not removed. He had asked Susan to give him a crew cut just a couple of days before.

'What's it like to have a joint?' Richard asked, indicating to Sunny Steve. He was drinking with his crew of two and their other halves, all smoking.

'They're smoking cigarettes.'

'I know, I'm not stupid. But I wondered what weed is like. Does Steve usually have some?'

'Or Vince.'

Richard was thoughtful. 'I've never tried. Perhaps I should.'

'What, for the headaches?'

'Not particularly. Just because, well we should all try stuff at least once, shouldn't we? While we can?'

I went round to the other side of the table, smiled apologetically at Sally then whispered to Vince.

He nodded, 'Not here, let's get some fresh air.'

I motioned to Richard to follow us.

The night air was cold, and we huddled together down the dimly lit far end of the car park. Richard pulled the fedora a little lower, trying to cover his ears. Bordering the car park were tall garden fences, providing some shelter from the wind. From here we could see the entrance to the club's foyer, brightly lit.

'Got them somewhere,' said Vince hunting through the pockets of his suit, which I told him,

'Looks sharp. Expensive?'

'Don't know. Algie paid. Said I needed to look the part if I was more or less running Zamara'z.' Vince found the cigarette ten-pack and took out three crumpled joints and a Zippo lighter. 'Thought you'd given up,' he said to me.

'All for one, one for all. As someone once said.' I took the joint as the door to the club was pushed open and light spilled into the car park. A woman was leaving – Vince's mum, alone. Instinctively, guiltily, we froze, though she didn't see us as she pulled her coat tight and left the car park, walking quickly.

Vince passed round the lighter.

'What do I do?' Richard asked, practising flicking the lighter flame on and off.

'Light it and suck,' I said.

He did and immediately coughed violently.

'But not too hard,' I added unhelpfully, looking at Vince. We sniggered. I took a draw and studied the joint as if it was a fine cigar. It wasn't. It was from Sunny Steve's cheap stash. 'So,' I tapped Vince's lapel, 'Algie bought you this cool suit and you're with Sally.'

'She sort of invited herself.'

'I can believe that. She's ok.'

Vince nodded.

'Cute smile?' I prompted.

'I guess.' Vince was suspicious.

'Is she bisexual?' I asked casually.

'Why do you ask?'

'Just wondered. That's good, right?'

'Why?'

'I don't know.'

'You know she is.' He looked serious.

'No.' I bluffed.

'She told me about the stock room.'

'Oh.'

'And you thought what, somehow we'd be kindred spirits?'

'No. Well, yeah, maybe.'

Vince drew deeply and held it for a couple of seconds before exhaling; the smoke disappeared into the semi-darkness. He laughed. 'You're an idiot, but it's ok. She's cool.'

'Good. Are you and she, you know?'

'What does that mean?'

'Getting together?'

'What, like you and she nearly did? No. She's a friend. Thinks I might be bi too.'

'What makes you think she'd know?' I asked.

'I don't know. She says everyone is, at least a little bit.'

'I don't know what that means.' I was confused.

'Bisexual. Likes guys and girls,' Richard explained to no one in particular.

'I know that.'

'You need to read more,' said Vince.

'I know what it means,' I protested.

'I read.' Richard drew more carefully on the joint and sniggered.

'Really? What with your dyselsis thing?' I asked.

'I read slowly.' He smiled patiently. 'Hey, Should I be feeling light-headed or something? I just feel sick, but that's nothing new.'

'Then why are you laughing?' Vince asked.

My own giggle was cut short as a man left the club. The silhouette approached our end of the car park.

'Your dad.' I tapped Vince's arm.

We moved closer to the fence, as if that gave more shadow. It didn't. As Lawrence reached his car, Vince carefully stubbed out his joint on the fence and put it back in the packet. Lawrence was parked a couple of cars away and didn't see us until close. He slurred, 'Is that you Vince? What are you doing?'

'Nothing.'

'Your mother said you were here tonight. You should have come to find her. Say hello.'

'I spoke to her today.'

'Oh, just me you avoid then.'

Vince hesitated. I laughed, with no humour, saying, 'Of course.'

'What?' He looked to me. 'That you Michael? What's going on?' His words were heavily slurred. He studied Vince for a few seconds. 'Oh, I get it. Dark car park, three boys. Pervs.'

'What are you on about?' Vince said coldly.

'I know about you. Your mother's told me everything. Disgusting.' Lawrence wasn't disgusted. He was drunk, stupid and angry. He was disgusting.

'Piss off,' said Vince, quietly.

Lawrence took a step towards Vince, 'You can still be given a lesson …'

'I don't think so,' I interrupted and stepped between them.

He stopped just short and spoke over my shoulder to Vince. 'Selfish little sod. Don't you think about your mother? And what about yours?' He turned to me.

'My mother?'

'What would she say? I knew her and …'

'No you didn't.'

'We were close.' He pressed his face close to mine. His breath was rank with alcohol.

'Bollocks you were. Prick.'

'You need to calm it son, else …' he raised his hand and I squared up, bracing myself for the slap, almost welcoming the confirmation it would bring, the question it would answer, the permission it would give me. No longer hearing him, deaf with sudden rage, I clenched a fist and took a step back to make room for a swing, but Vince pushed him away. He stumbled backwards, bumping against a car, falling, calling out as he hit the tarmac. There was silence. His face creased in pain and he drew his knees to his chest. The three of us watched him for a few seconds until he mumbled something to Vince, something about his heart, through gasping breaths, something about tablets, through clenched teeth and something about help, with grasping hands.

We looked at him.

'He needs help,' said Richard.

'Fuck him,' I said.

'He's a bad heart,' said Vince.

'So what.' I shrugged.

'He needs help,' Richard repeated.

'His heart is bad.' Vince repeated but not in a tone that suggested getting help.

'I don't give a shit.' I didn't, and bent over to spit, 'You didn't know my mother.'

In between quiet gasps he said, 'Better than you think.' There was such spite in his words I took a step back as Richard called,

'He needs help.' He was adamant, but didn't move.

'I suppose,' Vince said but didn't move either.

Seconds passed.

'JB,' Richard tapped my arm, 'Where's your dad?' He started for the club and had gone a few yards when I told Vince to stay and trotted after him.

'Lucky for Lawrence you guys were out in the car park,' said Dad. The celebration dinner had broken up shortly after the ambulance had left, and we were walking home. It was a leading statement that I side-stepped by asking him,

'Why do you hang round with him?'

'Him?'

'Vince's dad.'

'I don't, he's just my boss. What am I going to say when he offers me a drink?'

Dad didn't want to talk about Lawrence, but I wasn't going to let this opening pass. 'Vi said you had a falling out with him, years ago.'

'Did she?'

I looked to Susan, she nodded. I asked, 'Was it something to do with Mum?'

Dad didn't answer.

'I know what a prick Lawrence is.' I tried to prompt him.

'Dad?' said Susan, eventually, and stopped walking. So did I. We were between two sodium yellow streetlights, neither lit nor silhouetted by either.

'I told you,' he said.

Susan pulled her cardigan tighter around her, but it would not be warming. 'Not really.'

A couple of cars passed, noisy in the quiet night, before he said, 'When Mum was carrying you, Lawrence made a pass at her. She told me and said nothing happened, she wouldn't let it, but I … I threatened to beat crap out of him.' He lit a cigarette. 'It was when I was thinking of leaving the garage for Butlins, but Lawrence wanted me to stay, offered me foreman and a big rise. I thought that was because he felt guilty, though Mum insisted it was nothing. She was pregnant, Lawrence didn't know, and we needed the money. I thought leaving would make it look like I didn't trust her. So I stayed, even though taking Lawrence's offer made me feel like I was being bought off all these years, and that's a real shitty feeling Mikey. But I have to believe Mum. Nothing happened.' He rested a palm against my cheek for a second.

Susan took a step forward to hold him.

I was desperate to believe, but Lawrence's grotesque sneer was still fresh.

Miracle Number Four

Chapter 42
Spring 1977
At The Park
'The Last Waltz'

Richard's last radiotherapy session was on the penultimate Wednesday in March. That morning, the band met with Stewart from Chrysalis at Zamara'z to discuss the tracks we'd be recording in just three weeks. Problem: only one of his choices matched ours and there was no way we would record someone else's songs. Algie's diplomacy couldn't calm the chaos. We argued for an hour, and it was fortunate Sunny Steve wasn't there as Stewart's temper rose.

Eventually, Stewart dropped on the table a copy of the contract, highlighting the clauses about song choice. Perhaps he should have started with that. He might not have avoided our anger but could have saved his own, though I was to learn over the next few weeks that he enjoyed confrontation.

The meeting broke up with Algie taking Stewart to lunch. I took the bus to West Middlesex Hospital. It was nearly two by the time I got there and ten past by the time I found Radiotherapy. This was Richard's last day of treatment and, though I'd been to see him at home, I'd not been with him to hospital. Anika and his mum were sitting in the waiting room and welcomed me.

It was an age until a nurse came from a side room and called Richard's mum and Anika to join her. I was left in the waiting room and smiled at the middle-aged couple who came in but was then embarrassed as they didn't smile back – I should have noticed the man's grey pallor under his trilby.

Richard came out eventually, dressed in an over-sized heavy coat though it wasn't cold out, and wearing a new tweed flat cap. He didn't look too bad, but it took a couple of seconds for him to realise he was hunched and make a conscious effort to stand straight.

Reluctantly, Anika dropped us off a little before the house; Richard wanted to walk the rest of the way. We reached the entrance to the recreation ground at the top of his road and I followed him in. It was empty, save a couple of dog-walkers and youths kicking a ball around. One of them recognised Richard and waved as we sat on a bench, on the path that edged the park.

'That's Malcolm. Good friend. You met him at The Red Cow. With Julie. Did I ever tell you about her?'

'No.' I waited a few seconds, but he was silent until I asked, 'And?'

'At one time I thought we'd go out, but she suits Malcolm better. Still, I sort of miss her even though we were never together. Does that make sense?'

'Not really. Besides, you're with Anika.'

'Yep. She's the only girlfriend I've had. Does that matter?'

'God, no. I've only had one, Petra, and I'm not even sure about that. And I'm practically a rock star.'

Richard thought for a few seconds then hunched further into his coat and stuffed his hands into the pockets. 'You do miss Petra?'

I nodded.

'So if she turned up out of the blue that would be ok?'

'Of course.'

'That's a good sign.'

We sat quietly for a while, watching Malcolm and friends play football. I didn't mind sitting there, it was like my park, and I'd grown used to not having to talk when around Richard. After a while he said, 'Tell me to piss off if you like, but that thing with Vince's dad, couple of nights ago, what was that about?'

'Nothing.'

'Sounded like a serious nothing.'

I hesitated. 'It was nothing,' I repeated. 'Lawrence's just a prick. Everyone knows.'

'And?'

'It doesn't matter.'

'I don't believe you,' said Richard.

We sat in silence until I told him what Dad had said about Mum and Lawrence.

'Sounds like your dad's been living with it for years.'

I told him Lawrence's comment in the car park.

'Do you believe that?' Richard asked.

'I don't know.'

'And you can't leave it? I get that.'

'What if Lawrence did something that made Mum worse? She hadn't been well for a long time. I don't mean the cancer. Something else. They say life was hard for her, but I don't get why.'

'The easy thing is to pretend nothing happened. Harder to face him down and even then you might not like the answer.'

There was an unspoken challenge in Richard's words. 'You mean easy to let it go?'

'No, that's hard too. The easy way is to pretend nothing happened. See the difference?'

I wasn't sure I did. We lapsed into silence. A dog came and sniffed at us. Richard fussed him, then as it ran back to its walker said, 'Did I tell you about the saxophone player who killed his lover?'

'You did.'

'The song he played before killing her was *The Last Waltz*.'

There was a joke in there, surely, but even I wasn't that insensitive. 'It's hard to believe someone could do that.'

'Not really, I'm beginning to think it's harder to believe someone wouldn't, for someone they love.'

I thought about that for a while. 'Sounds like watching that might have been a proper moment.'

He gave me a quizzical look and I explained Susan's theory. He nodded, 'I get that,' and turned slightly to look at me, 'Ever had one?'

'I think so,' I answered, and though I avoided eye contact, the silence was compelling. 'When Mum died, or, rather, when I found her.' I finished quietly.

'Of course. Stupid of me. Sorry.'

I walked home with him. Anika was at the door, angry that we'd been so long. I stopped at the gate. As Richard went through he said, 'Hey, I forgot. I'm trying to write that extra verse *Miracle Number Four* needs.'

'We can share writing credits.'

'We are gonna record it one day, yes?'

'Of course.'

'Good. A way to capture time maybe.'

I waved and was five yards down the road when he called, 'JB, I could be wrong. Maybe sometimes that easy way is much harder in the long run.'

Anika led him into the house before I could ask what that meant.

Chapter 43
Spring 1977
That's The Way Of The World
'Landslide'

With just twelve days to the recording session we were struggling for rehearsal time. That wasn't a problem for the three songs of our own we'd be playing, but we needed time to work on another three – the songs that Stewart's 'people' had written. We complained to Algie that our gigging schedule was not easing. He agreed, but nothing changed.

Kay, meantime, was complaining that with just seven weeks until the showcase gig, Red Ice Rising needed to improve its stage appearance. Apart from Susan, we were getting by on jeans and t-shirts, except Dimitri who had taken to wearing white nylon shirts that stuck to his torso when he sweated, which he did profusely as the set cranked up through the gears. He claimed that, when wet, the shirts could pass for silk. I don't think that was the reason, and we took the piss out of him. He didn't care. Neither would I, if I worked out like him.

We played Reading university and had a decent crowd despite it being a Wednesday. After the gig, Kay insisted on silence as she passed round a few pictures she had taken. Her fancy new Polaroid meant she could print them immediately.

'So, what do you look like?' she asked after we'd passed the photographs round. Before anyone could reply – we understood we didn't know the 'right' answer – she said, 'I'll tell you. The band that was here last night, the night before and the night before that.'

'I don't think they have gigs on a Sunday,' said Dimitri.

'Shut up, Alan Freeman,' Kay said.

It took me a second to make the connection, 'Brentford Nylons,' and laugh.

'Point is,' Kay looked at Susan who nodded support – they had prepared this. 'You guys keep telling me you're better than those other bands. Yeah, you are. So why look like them?'

'And why do we advertise others?' Susan indicated to my 'Santana' t-shirt. She wasn't wrong, but we spent the next fifteen minutes arguing that our music didn't need an image, and no way were we dressing up like cabaret monkeys. Eventually, Susan put up her hand and suggested we look at one of the pictures again. We did. It wasn't even us and we hadn't noticed. Yes, it was taken from the back of some hall and was in black and white and out of focus, but even so, the point was made. It was agreed that we'd try some of Kay's ideas, starting with me, of course.

Late next morning, I went round to Kay's house. Her mum was welcoming, and we chatted more than was usual while waiting for Kay – Kay's mum did most of the chatting. She was a little taller than both her daughters and full and curvy of figure. She didn't look like a mum, wore a lot of make-up, for a mum, and had dark brown tumbling hair like her daughters. She was confident and laughed a lot, and I liked her, though she kept me a little on edge – somehow. Eventually, Kay came to explain her ideas for our 'distinctive but tasteful' stage gear. We wouldn't all wear the same but there was a theme. 'You'll pair smart with casual,' she said, as if that meant anything to me, and showed her sketch book of ideas. I pretended to be interested and, to be fair, they looked good, or at least better than my old jeans and t-shirts – her fashion course was clearly not just a way to pass a year before getting a job.

'And,' she said, 'I've already got some gear for you to try,' leading me into the lounge.

It was a comfortable room. There was a full bookshelf on one wall, a leather sofa facing a Sony thirty-two inch colour tv and a B&O hi-fi in the corner; Kay's dad had a few bob. She carefully placed the needle on the black vinyl to play *That's The Way Of The World*. She still loved Earth, Wind & Fire.

'How come a disco girl is going out with a rock drummer like Dimitri?' I asked, as she indicated to the clothes on the settee's arm.

'It's not disco, idiot. Don't worry, there's nothing tight or spangly.'

'Will Dimitri have one of these?' I held up the jacket.

'No. He can't play in that, but he'll look great in a plain white shirt. Real silk.'

'You two will have beautiful children.' I tried to sound sarcastic, but it didn't work.

'I know. Go on, try them on.'

I hesitated.

'C'mon, I've seen you get changed loads of times.'

'Yeah, in manky dressing rooms with everyone else. What if Dimitri turns up?'

'It's Tuesday, he'll be working out in his bedroom.'

'While thinking of you.'

'I expect so.' She laughed.

'What if your mum comes in?'

'You've nothing she hasn't seen before.'

'Funny. I'd love a cup of tea,' I said, and it was sort of true.

She exaggerated a sigh and left the room, leaving the door ajar while I tried on the clothes, shouting out, 'They fit well. And two sugars please.'

She returned and insisted I do a couple of twirls. 'See, straight jeans with proper shirt and light woollen sports jacket. I knew it would work. Just need to get you a dark tie, clean trainers and a belt.'

I looked at my tatty Adidas Sambas.

'Don't worry,' said Kay, 'You can get another pair of those and won't have to do up the tie.' She went to the hi-fi and changed the record while I checked my reflection in the mirror over the fireplace, wondering if I could play bass in this jacket. 'Not Fleetwood Mac,' I complained as *Landslide* began. She turned up the volume.

'It's one of Petra's favourites.' Kay stood behind me and tried standing up the jacket's collar. 'I don't know. There's something missing. What do you think Petra would suggest?' she asked, as another reflection came to the mirror. A slim young woman in a shirt dress, vertical pastel stripes, thin belt around a narrow waist, long, long blonde hair with brown roots, small face, mischievous smile and green eyes. The perfume was a memory of something close. The voice was both new and familiar.

'What about one of these?' The pretty girl held up her wrist to show the leather bracelet.

I didn't spin around, transfixed by the image in the mirror, scared that if I turned, she might not be there.

It was a mix of relief and excitement to see Petra and we spent the afternoon there, lightly making out when Kay left us alone and laughing with embarrassment when Kay's mum popped her head round the door, saying apologetically, 'No hanky panky under my roof. I promised Vi.'

Kay's head appeared immediately afterwards. 'Besides, remember what I told you,' she said to Petra, who I thought blushed, so I didn't ask.

Thanks to recent letters and phone calls we didn't need to catch up on much and were happy to sit in silence for much of the time, not even bothering to change the record.

That evening, Petra came to the gig and was welcomed by the Red Ice Rising family, not as some returning heroine or long-lost, desperately missed daughter, but as if her being there was simply natural and right – Susan gave her a brief hug, saying, 'About time,' and that spoke for everyone. She met Algie afterwards. He offered her a hand, took a step back to look at her and nodded, 'You're punching above your weight, JB,' then clipped me round the back of the head. 'Your job,' he told Petra, 'is to make him concentrate on the band. Today's prodigy can easily be tomorrow's one-hit wonder,' he explained, 'and don't tire him out,' he finished with a crude wink.

Petra and I laughed but didn't catch each other's eye.

She hadn't seen Red Ice Rising play before and The Half Moon was a top venue. We'd graduated to headline slots, albeit on less popular nights, and played there a couple of times a month. Petra was impressed. She stood with Kay at the back of the bar, chewing on a strand of blonde hair, watching intently – not just the band but the audience and drinkers. She'd brought a book to read – *Ulysses*, in case she got bored, she'd said – but as far as I could tell, it was never opened. Afterwards, she brought me a Coke and kissed me on the cheek to interrupt the couple of young women that were chatting to me as I packed away my gear.

On the way home, Susan dropped her back at Kay's. It was a disappointment but what else did I think was going to happen?

The next few days were spent gigging and rehearsing for the studio and the showcase. Petra came along in the evenings and job-hunted during the day, needing to find something to take her through until college in September.

That Saturday, we played The Red Lion, Brentford. Red Ice Rising was a slick machine these days. As well as the four of us on stage we had a crew of two or three, depending on venue, led by Sunny Steve. Kay took care of our new stage clothes while Sofia made sure everyone's food, drink and drugs needs were met – which wasn't difficult as we ate little, drank mostly beer, though I hardly touched it, and were hardly seasoned or heavy drug users. Joints and, occasionally, speed, was shared around but I'd not smoked much since returning from Ireland, and had no need for uppers to keep me going – playing live was all. Sofia and Steve weren't fussed about supplying the band – the audience were much better customers who actually paid. We also had our 'civilians' – a small and loyal group of fans that we were happy to have hanging around, and for whom we arranged free entry to those few venues where tickets were needed. So, while Petra seemed to enjoy the gigs she didn't feel useful or part of the band family, yet.

It didn't help there was no time for usual boyfriend/girlfriend stuff. We wanted to go to the cinema or maybe a meal at the new Greek restaurant that had opened near Ealing Broadway – Dimitri said to tell them he'd sent us – or maybe ice skating at Richmond or – Petra's suggestion – London Zoo, but there was never time. Physically, in snatched privacy, we had reached what I suppose the Yanks called third base. To begin with, the frantic, unplanned nature had added to the excitement but not even I wanted to reach fourth – or was it fifth? – base in the back of a Transit van at two in the morning travelling south on the A1 just outside Hatfield. We had a tacit agreement that it was worth waiting, but that didn't stop me thinking about her mole; a lot.

'Looks too permanent,' I muttered. We were standing at Mum's grave. It was blowy and cold but not yet raining. I hadn't been here for a couple of months but Dad was tending the plot. There were tulips and daffodils sprouting from the turned-over earth. The granite headstone had weathered a little but still looked clean, if not new. It also looked too permanent.

'What do you mean?' Petra looped a hand through the gap between my arm and body; my hand was stuffed into a pocket. It had been her idea to come here, a week after her return.

'Like it's always been here and always will.'

'I suppose it will.'

'That doesn't feel right. I'm not sure Mum's there at all. And she wasn't there before and that's what's most important.'

I could feel Petra looking at me but didn't mind the silence. Then she let go of my arm to take a small camera from her handbag. 'Lovely inscription, Susan's a poet,' she said, taking a picture. 'Mum wants to see it. We're sorry we didn't come back for the funeral. Honest.'

We watched the grave for a little longer but when I felt raindrops and Petra shivered, I led her over to the yew tree. 'I get it. I blame Vince's dad.'

'Not Sofia?' She asked as we cuddled under the canopy. I was maybe three inches taller than her now, and kissed her lightly on the forehead.

'Still?'

'Joking. Sofia spoke to me. She cares a lot about you, but not in that way. She was drunk, or high, or both.'

'Oh.' I pretended to sound disappointed.

Petra laughed and hit me on the arm. 'She did give me some advice though.'

'Hmmm.' I was suspicious. 'About?'

'You and me.'

'What?'

'That's for me to know and you to find out.'

She leant back against me, head on my shoulder so I couldn't see her.

'And?' I pressed.

'When the time comes,' she said, and I could feel her smile.

We stood that way for a couple of minutes as the rain became heavier, but I didn't mind. 'Thanks for coming today.'

In the afternoon we went to see Richard. I had a routine of popping in every couple of days and had left a guitar there. When he had the energy, we played a little music; *Miracle*

Number Four was completed apart from missing a verse. Other times we just chatted about stuff, and other times he was sleeping. Today, Anika let us in saying, 'He sleeps JB. His head hurts.'

'Headache?'

'Not really. You and me have headaches, maybe. Richard's head hurts. Deep.' She looked tired. I followed her to the lounge. The curtains were closed, and the room was in darkness. Richard sat in an armchair, blanket over his legs, sunglasses over his eyes. The dog was sprawled on the sofa and had to be nudged aside for me and Petra. The air was stale, despite the plants.

'Has he taken any pain killers?' I asked.

'Oh no, we forgot.' Anika looked at me with a hint of contempt.

'Sorry.' What an idiot.

Anika sat opposite Richard. His mother came in and offered us tea. I shook my head. Today she didn't press me. Richard stirred and perhaps mumbled something. Anika's eyes reddened.

We didn't stay long. I explained, 'We're in the studio soon and I need to practise.'

Chapter 44
Spring 1977
From The Heart
'When Diamonds Cry'

Wessex Sound Studios was in Highbury but Algie had arranged for us to meet at Zamara'z. He led the way in a black roadster I hadn't seen before, MG I think. The convoy followed: Band Transit; Susan's Mini; Sofia's Vauxhall Viva; Vince bringing up the rear in the Escort estate that Algie had bought him, in case anyone broke down – Algie had also paid for Vince's lessons as the estate was, 'Handy for Zamara'z business.' There wasn't much talk in the Mini, though I did compliment Petra on her smart trousers with pleated front and a light woollen v-neck jumper.

'Smart?' she repeated.

'Er, stylish, cool?' I tried. Susan laughed.

'It was Kay's idea. You never know who might be there,' said Petra.

The studio was in a converted church hall and our convoy filled the small car park. We followed Algie, our quick chatter fading as we entered the studio space. There were no windows, the lighting was barely adequate, and it smelt of stale air freshener. I took a few seconds to look around. There wasn't much to see. The floor was mostly clear with a jumble of instruments, mic stands and heavy sound partitions, pushed to the walls. Someone, I assumed the studio engineer, welcomed us nonchalantly and quickly pointed round the space, 'Drums go there, guitar, bass, vocals. No keyboards or piano, right?'

'Right,' I said.

'Shame. I like a touch of piano. You must be the boy wonder Stewart talked about. I'm Pete, but you can call me Fader.' He laughed at his own joke – no one else got it –

and checked his watch. 'Are you paying by the day or hour? Is someone bringing in the gear for you?'

Steve and Vince were waiting outside. We took the hint to go and help. Algie went to the office to find Chrysalis Stewart, while Fader offered Petra, Kay and Sofia tea in the control room on an upper level, overlooking the studio. He left them there, with instructions not to touch anything, while he came back down to supervise setting up. It took an hour and a half to place the gear, partition the drums and vocal areas, and set up mics. The girls were soon bored and came down to tell us. We had a quick lunch in a local café and, when we returned, Chrysalis Stewart was up in the control room. He indicated we should each put on the nearest set of headphones and gave a motivational speech. Algie nodded along enthusiastically, which made Dimitri laugh.

Fader then assured us he had a fool proof method for solid results, and told us to stay calm and enjoy. I was concerned that we weren't here for 'solid' results; we wanted 'great' and started a question but was closed down.

'I know you've all read of Floyd or Genesis or Queen spending five weeks to record one song. But, let's be honest, you ain't Floyd, Genesis or Queen, and we're not remaking Sergeant Pepper. So, let's crack on and work through these tracks. Oh, and trust me,' said Fader.

'Trust him,' said Stewart.

'Trust them,' said Algie.

'Ok,' said Bazzer into his mic to be heard in the control room, 'but we record our own songs first.'

'Makes no difference to me,' said Fader and I really think it didn't, which seemed a shame.

It took an hour and a quarter to record four false starts, three unfinished and five completed versions of *When Diamonds Cry*. Between takes, Stewart and Fader tinkered with mic placements and issued criticisms, instructions and some praise, with Fader predicting the third take would be the best. Eventually he congratulated us, almost sincerely, said we could listen back to it later and maybe add some guitar and vocals, if Stewart agreed, but now was a good time for a ten minute break.

Out in the fresh air of the car park I blinked against the brighter light and nearly took the joint that Vince offered but saw Petra's disapproval.

'What's happening up in the control room?' Bazzer asked.

'We don't really know.' Sofia answered. 'We've been moved through to an office. There are speakers there so we can hear what's being recorded but we can't hear what's going on in the control room.'

'This isn't what I expected,' I said. 'How do we know if it's any good.'

'And I've made a ton of mistakes.' Susan was down.

Bazzer gave her a hug. 'We all have, but it'll be fine and anyway, we won't know until later, when we hear it back. It will be fine.' He wasn't convincing.

Disappointment settled on top of silence. A cloud slipped across the sun and the shadow was chilly. It seemed we all huddled closer. Petra shivered and I gave her my jacket.

'Control,' she said quietly.

'Eh?' I muttered.

'Control,' she spoke louder. There was a short silence then Susan asked,

'What do you mean?'

'You don't have it. This must be killing you and Bazzer.' Petra spoke hesitantly.

'Because …?' Susan prompted.

'It wasn't until I came home I realised how good Red Ice Rising are.'

'Really?' I tried to sound offended.

'Really.'

'If you'd known, you'd have come back sooner?'

Petra laughed, 'Yeah, maybe. Point is, I know you're all good at what you do, even JB …'

'Even me?'

'Ok, especially you,' she patted my cheek, 'but seems to me Susan and Bazzer know what's needed, have, like, a vision of what you're going to sound like …'

'A vision of sound?' I teased.

'You know what I mean. They,' she indicated to Susan and Bazzer, 'call the shots. Make decisions. They have control and that gives you confidence to let go your inhibitions. There's always a path to get back to. It's why you're so good live. But here, it's the Chrysalis guy and that jerk Fader. Algie's just along for the ride. You guys know what's best for Red Ice Rising. Not them. You're rushing to get all the songs recorded. Isn't it better to record just the right ones the right way?'

I nodded appreciatively. Petra was smart.

Vince was thoughtful. 'Something's definitely missing. I've heard you loads of time and even on off-nights you're playing your nuts off, from the heart. But today sounds like a rehearsal when you'd rather just be down the pub, drinking, not playing.'

'He's not wrong,' Kay's arm was draped around Dimitri, 'and it's much better when you play your nuts off.' She kissed him lightly.

'Right guys, time!' Algie called from the door. 'And time is money. Really, in this place.'

We looked at each other and began an unenthusiastic trudge back to the studio; except Susan who called on us to wait, adding, 'Petra and Vince are right.'

Algie shouted something, but Susan was waving us back.

'What's the matter? Stewart and Fader are waiting in the studio.' Algie reluctantly joined us in the car park.

'This isn't us,' Susan said cryptically. Algie's confusion was obvious.

'We can do much better.' Bazzer added.

Algie lit a cigarette, trying to be patient. 'Clock's ticking, which means money's burning. A lot of it's mine and I have no idea what the fuck you're on about.'

'I'll tell you what the fuck we're on about,' said Susan, and she did.

They argued. Later it struck me that for all Susan and Bazzer's passion, neither made the case as well as Petra and Vince had. Eventually Algie said he, '… understood, really, I do. But so what. No one's walking away from the deal. It's record their way, or go home. As if.'

'Or,' Petra said quietly, 'the band could try just two songs, their choice, that are recorded well and they …' she looked to Vince,

'… play their nuts off from the heart,' he finished.

'It's my nuts on the line if this goes tits up,' Algie said and though it was funny, I daren't laugh. 'We carry on as planned. Come on. Stewart and Fader are waiting.'

'Fader doesn't care much. He just wants to get through the session,' said Vince.

'As do I,' Algie all but shouted. 'This is your … our, chance.'

'What if it's the only one we get?' I asked. 'If it's not the chance to be Red Ice Rising then it's no chance at all. One good single's better than two shit ones.'

'Bollocks.' Algie checked his watch. 'I'm not arguing this. We have a contract. You've five minutes to get your arses in there and play.' He walked away, slightly hunched against the increasing breeze. I thought he was going to turn and wait. He didn't, not even at the door. Vince ran after him.

The rest of us shuffled around for a couple of minutes, muttering things to convince each other we were right. No one mentioned that we might have made a mistake – we were as one, for good or ill.

Bazzer lit a cigarette. Dimitri lit a joint. Kay picked it from his mouth, took a drag then carefully put it out. Sofia and Steve went to sit in the Transit, comfortable with waiting. Susan whispered something to Bazzer. I stretched an arm around Petra that I hoped showed I was both relaxed about events – I wasn't – and proud of her – I was.

Vince came back into the car park, striding confidently, calling, 'Problem solved, maybe. Algie gets it. He's speaking to Stewart. Come back in.'

'What did you say to him?' Bazzer asked.

'I reminded him of his promise, to manage not control. Remember that?'

I didn't but others did.

'It took some persuasion but he's a good guy. He'll try to keep a promise,' Vince said when the muttering had died away.

We followed him back to the studio. Algie was at the foot of the stairs to the control room, looking up at Stewart, a couple of steps above. Stewart was red in the face, brandishing a sheaf of papers and shouting at Algie, '... and right now I don't give a shit either way.'

'And that's the problem.' Algie was calm and spoke quietly. 'Remember we're fifty-fifty on costs for today. That buys the band a say. We say it's better to lay down two great recordings for one single. Band's choice of song.'

'Bollocks. We're doing it my way. Though from what I've heard so far we could be here all day and not get half a decent track.' He waved the papers closer to Algie's face.

There was a snigger from the top of the stairs: Fader.

'In fact,' Stewart continued, 'you lot can piss off home. We're done. And you can forget the showcase gig.'

Algie lit a cigarette and looked round to us then back to the sneering Stewart. 'You're an arsehole. But I'm fair. Tell you what. I'll pay the studio costs for today and you fuck off.'

'I don't need you.' Stewart took a step down closer to Algie.

I hadn't noticed Sunny Steve come back in with us, but from nowhere, he was between Algie and Stewart, who flinched as his upper arm was grabbed. Steve leant up to whisper something. When Steve let go Stewart muttered, 'Until nine tonight, but you're paying for all of it. And still no showcase gig. And if the recording's shit, no single.'

Stewart brushed past Algie and left. There were a few seconds silence then Susan went to the top of the stairs, calling to Fader,

'Hey, you can do better right? 'cos I know we can.' He looked confused. Susan continued, 'I mean, you can help us do better, and I bet you know how to get the best on tape too.'

'I guess.'

'Looks like you've just been promoted to producer. We've got six hours to get down two tracks, and your foolproof method for solid? Well solid isn't good enough anymore. What's the best recording you ever worked on?'

Fader smiled. 'I was in on some of the sessions for *A Day At The Races.*'

'That's the bar set then. We'll be playing our nuts off, from the heart.' She looked down to Vince and smiled, then back to Fader, 'You just need to capture it. Come and tell us how we can help you.' Susan took his hand and led him down the stairs.

I asked Sunny Steve, 'Did you threaten Stewart? Not that I mind.'

'Nah, it was just a friendly reminder that he owes me.'

'Owes you?'

'Nothing big, just a few joints, a couple of lines and an introduction to some guys I know that invited him to their special parties.'

'Special parties?'

'You don't want to know. I don't want you to know.'

'Good,' I offered, because it seemed appropriate, though I really did want to know.

'Oh,' Steve said more loudly to catch everyone's attention, 'and don't worry about the showcase gig. Stewart's not cleared what he owes yet.'

Petra and Vince went to Algie, standing by the open door to the car park, drawing heavily on a cigarette. I couldn't hear what they said, but his frown turned to a smile.

It took a couple of hours to finish *When Diamonds Cry*. As a guide track we used the best version we'd already laid down, which turned out to be the third as predicted by Fader, and re-recorded the various parts. We played and sang our nuts off. By the time we heard Fader's voice through the headphones, inviting us up to the control room, I was mentally knackered. I entered last, as Fader told us to, 'Give this a listen. It's not the final mix but not bad. What do you think? Better than solid?' and his pride was obvious. He pressed PLAY and gently pushed up the main slider volume control.

I heard parts to the song I'd never noticed before and the clarity, energy and detail was absorbing. I was spellbound by Red Ice Rising and a little astounded that I was part of it. I looked to Petra, the pastel colours of her outfit showing against the black walls of the control room. Her small smile and subtle nod were high praise, and I hoped she was proud of me. I looked to Susan and Bazzer; they weren't smiling. The track finished and they asked to hear it again. This time they managed to smile even though Susan said, 'Sounds great Fader but we can do better. The solo needs more volume and another voice on the harmonies wouldn't go amiss.'

'And I'd like to add another guitar to the second bridge,' Bazzer interrupted, 'and can we shorten that last crashing chord? And can Dimitri add some tambourine on the last chorus?'

Fader looked disheartened but Susan and Bazzer were right. It needed to be better. We needed Red Ice Rising to be better.

'Not down to you, Fader,' Susan placed a hand on his shoulder. 'You captured it great. Especially love the drum sound. It's an eight out of ten. We just need to get it to nine.'

'Oh, so not a ten?' Algie stepped from a dark corner.

'Because then there's no way to make it better, and there'll always be a way,' I guessed.

'Not to mention, I didn't bring a tambourine.' Dimitri added.

'Well as I'm paying, you better get on with it. Another half hour, that's all. Then on to the next track.' Algie tried to take back control.

We finished forty-five minutes later but instead of being called to the control room to listen, Algie told us to get a cup of tea and ten minutes of fresh air then straight back for the next track: *Dreams That Kill.*

Back in the studio, we made quicker progress; we were getting used to the process which prompted Fader to tell us, in clipped headphones' tone, 'Don't get complacent just 'cos you know what it feels like now. Gotta make each attempt sound like the first. Gotta attack each take.'

'Good advice, Fader, thanks,' Susan spoke sincerely into her mic so we could all hear, and I could see Fader up in the control room, smiling.

'Nuts off from the heart.' We heard Petra speak into Fader's mic.

And we did. But by gone eight we were flagging and Bazzer called for another tea and fag/joint break. There was a solitary streetlamp trying to light the car park and it was cold, but we found a corner and stood mostly in silence, Algie occasionally muttering a quiet word of encouragement or giving a pat on the back; we were like a football team waiting to start extra time. Kay took a few pictures and Sofia handed out Mars bars and crisps. I shared a Lucozade with Petra and wished I could have a joint instead, but wouldn't.

I jumped at the half-hearted 'toot' of a car horn. The black Citroen DS lumbered into the car park and bounced to a stop next to Susan's Mini. Anika was out first and helped Richard. He held on to the brim of the fedora; the wind was picking up. 'I really hope you haven't finished. I've just necked a day's worth of tablets to get here.'

'Sorry we're late. Richard's been sleeping most of the day, then we had to stop on the way,' Anika said in explanation more than apology.

'Yep, threw up outside Islington Town Hall, next to the mayor's limo I think. The chauffeur was not impressed,' Richard added, quite cheerfully. He was chewing as he walked over but stopped by the hedge to spit something out. 'What have we missed?' he asked.

'Something. I think,' Anika said, taking in the scene.

Petra told of the day's events as she led them to the now crowded control room, Anika helping Richard up the stairs. As we settled in the studio to re-record some vocals, I heard Richard through the headphones, 'Don't forget, play your hearts off, out your nuts,' and laugh.

It was good to have Richard here; I attacked the vocals with new energy.

It was half-ten by the time Fader finally called us up. The control room was packed and Sofia handed round tea and digestives – very rock and roll. We listened back four times, discussing ideas for improvement, but even Susan conceded it would be better to come back another day,

'Or not at all,' suggested Algie, thinking of his bank balance.

Steve and Vince went down to the studio to start packing away, while Dimitri produced a bottle of brandy and sneaked into the office, taking Kay, on the premise they were looking for glasses.

'What's wrong with the usual,' I called to their backs as they left the control room, 'straight from the bottle?'

Dimitri gave me a two-finger salute.

Susan and Bazzer asked Fader if they could listen back again, through headphones.

Richard asked if he could see the studio and Petra and I led him and Anika back down.

The studio had a forlorn air; instruments were scattered, the drum kit was partly dismantled, an untidy pile of cables was jumbled in the centre.

'What did you think of the sound?' I asked Richard. He thought for a second before taking something from an inside pocket and putting it in his mouth. He started chewing and I caught the smell of something like flowers that had been in a vase too long.

'Khat,' he said in answer to my unspoken question.

'Cat?'

'Yep. For chewing. Uncle Dudek knows a guy who has a contact in Kenya. It's hard to get fresh over here.'

'Of course. But, er, what is it?'

'It helps,' he said vaguely.

'With the pain,' Anika added. 'Tablets don't do enough and slow things down.'

'Khat speeds them back up,' Richard said cryptically. 'Want some?'

'Nah, smells.'

'You get used to it. Or, rather, I don't notice it. Actually, I don't taste or smell anything anymore,' he tapped his hat, 'Something else Judas has taken. Makes dinner boring. The band sounded good. The track we heard? Very good. I'd buy it.'

'You can have a signed copy for free.'

'Signed? I didn't like it that much.' He laughed. He was still wearing the fedora and I couldn't see his eyes. 'Hey, an old Bechstein.' He sat at the piano, pushed over to the wall.

Anika sat next to him on the piano bench, and he played a few chords and runs. I pulled over a couple of taller stools for me and Petra. It looked like we were just about to sing while they duetted on the piano.

'Glad you made it today,' I told him.

'Me too. Glad to have made it anywhere.' It wasn't as funny as he hoped, especially when he added, 'It's been a rough few days.' His shoulders slumped, as if suddenly deflated, and his head dropped, the brim of his hat almost touching the piano's music stand. Quietly, he asked, 'So, when will the single be out?'

'I don't know. After today's arguments with the Chrysalis guy, maybe never.'

'Don't say that.' Petra slapped my arm.

'Doesn't matter,' said Richard, 'it's on tape now, forever. A little piece of you will live on. Cool eh?' He was still chewing.

'I suppose.'

'Of course it is. It's like part of what you leave, part of you, don't you think?'

'Richard, don't.' Anika spoke gently and rubbed his arm.

'I've been giving it some, a lot, of thought about what we … I, might leave.'

'Please, Richard,' Anika tried again.

'And I was chatting to Uncle Dudek, just yesterday,' he stopped to put some more of the khat leaf into his mouth, 'and we agreed what's important.'

'Not tonight,' said Anika but Richard continued,

'People think it's important to leave shit in wills. Money and jewellery and houses and stuff. It isn't. We agreed, Uncle Dudek and me, it's the other stuff that counts. It's the stories of what a person was like, what they did, how they laughed, when they cried, why they loved, what they did wrong, when they did right, how they fucked up. And it's what they cared about. What they felt was right or wrong, and why, and how that made them act. What mattered to them. Stories,' he looked at me, 'of when they took the difficult choices, didn't let go too easy.'

His stare was uncomfortable, and I nodded, looking for a chance to slow him down but he was rambling.

'That can all be told. Then there's the stuff you can touch and feel. Not money or gold or that shit. Important stuff. Like, I dunno, like the comp tape I bet you made Petra, or a photo album, or a scrapbook or a diary or a ...'

'Homemade leather bracelet?' Petra interrupted and showed her wrist. I showed mine.

'Exactly,' said Richard, 'or your single, JB. Only you, only Red Ice Rising could have made that. It might sell thousands, it might sell a dozen, you might have to give it away, but that doesn't stop it being your stuff, left to others. All part of your ... what did Dudek say?' he asked Anika.

'Doesn't matter. He's a stupid old man who talks too much. Like you when you chew that rubbish.'

'Legacy, that was it,' said Richard. 'I think it would be good to leave one, but then I'm only seventeen.'

'You'll be eighteen, you'll be nineteen,' Anika said.

Richard looked from her to me. 'Thank you.'

'What for?' I asked.

'Not agreeing with her.'

I hadn't seen Richard like this before and was ashamed to have been so naive.

'Richard, it's late. You're tired,' said Anika.

'It's ok, I can take more tablets and chew more khat.' He coughed hard and Anika took a tissue from her bag so he could spit out the leaf. He did so, but complained, 'I'm not a child.'

She left the stool to find a bin.

Richard watched her. 'Hey, maybe I can record something on the piano. Part of my legacy.' He played *Chopsticks* then started *Happy Birthday*, shouting up to the control room, 'You getting this?'

I put my hand on his to stop him playing. He didn't resist.

'What about *Miracle Number Four?*' I asked quietly.

He looked puzzled, then, 'No, dumb idea. I'll cock it up.'

'You won't. And it doesn't matter if you do.'

Ignoring the protests I went up to the control room and asked Fader for a favour. He was reluctant until Susan said gently, 'It's ok, we're paying for the studio, right?'

It took only five minutes for Fader to mic up the piano. I recorded acoustic guitar and vocals for *Miracle Number Four,* just well enough for a guide track. Richard could play the piano part along to it while Fader recorded. I told Richard it didn't matter the song wasn't finished, it just mattered that we had the piano part to work with, and it needn't be perfect.

'Perfection? I can't even remember it.' His sarcastic bravado of just minutes before was gone.

'It'll come to you. Don't suppose you brought that cassette?' I forced enthusiasm and la-la'd what I could remember of the part. After a minute or two he played along, and it was close enough. I handed him the headphones. 'You'll get the guide track in these. You just go with it.'

'I can't.'

'You just did.'

'No, I mean I don't want to … wear headphones.'

'Why not?'

'They won't fit over hat.' Anika answered for him.

'Take it off.' I said.

Richard shook his head.

'Ok, we'll, drape them round the back of your neck and hope the cans stay on your ears. They do stick out a lot.'

Richard pretended to be amused.

I shouted at Steve and Vince to stop packing away. Twenty minutes later we had four takes. Richard was nervous and there were mistakes, but I was confident there was enough for Fader to cut together what was needed. Anika slipped the headphones from his ears.

'Nicely done,' said Petra, 'Can't wait to hear that with the guitar.'

'We'll put it on the album,' I said.

'Then I hope it's coming out soon.' Richard looked down to the piano keys. Anika sat back alongside him and took his hand.

'*Miracle Number Four*. Good name for a song,' said Petra.

Richard took his hand from Anika's. 'Is it? Do you know what it's about?'

'Sort of.'

'What about miracle number three?' He looked from Petra to me and back. 'Remember Ireland. Do you think Anika saw Saint Teresa cry?' he asked Petra.

'Do you?' Petra glanced at Anika and tried to bat the question away.

'Well, I kind of have to, don't I? Cos I'm in big trouble if not. Haha.' Richard's sarcasm returned. He looked at Anika. She was frowning. 'Don't say anything,' said Richard.

Anika walked away.

'It's hard for her,' I said, to fill the silence.

'Yeah. Hard. For you too I expect.' Richard's voice was suddenly raised. 'For all of you. So hard. So fucking hard. All that recording and gigging and planning a future? God that must be difficult. You're so brave. And maybe scared and angry too? Of course you are, your Mum died. Are you angry?' he asked bitterly, 'I am. I'm fucking angry but you know what, at least it will be over and you can all get on with your lives and it'll be ok because you can tell each other it doesn't hurt anymore and I'm at fucking peace.' He was shouting. 'And what a miracle that'll be, right? Fucking peace all round. Oh, and my, what's it called, legacy? Yeah, you'll all have my legacy 'cos you can say I played piano on *Miracle Number Four*. So it better be a hit fucking single. Don't you think? Don't you!'

His face was flushed red and his eyes dark with tears that didn't fall, and none of us had the right to tell him he should be calm; none of us had the right to offer sympathy; none of us had the right to claim we understood.

He was suddenly old and drained. He took off his hat to wipe away sweat. We saw the scars on his head where he'd

417

used a razor to saw at the clumps of hair the radiotherapy hadn't stolen.

A couple of days later, we went back to the studio. Stewart was there. I expected there to be a ruck but he was suspiciously calm and friendly. He'd heard the tapes and liked them, not a lot, but enough to warrant spending money to add some guitar, vocals and percussion. He emphasised the 'spending money' bit, adding, 'If it's good enough after the final mix we'll put it out. *When Diamonds Cry* can be the A side.'

We were quick to record the additions, and in a break, Susan brought coffee and cake from the cafe for Fader and Stewart. Later, taking him to one side, I asked Fader if he could make sure the tape with the rough recording of *Miracle Number Four* was kept somewhere safe. He pointed to a rack. 'Third along. It's labelled but if I were you, I'd sneak it out before someone records over it. Don't tell Stewart. Tape is expensive.'

'Fader, when we're big I'll insist on you as our studio engineer.'

'JB, get me a date with Susan and I'm in.' He laughed. I think he knew about Susan and Bazzer, but I smiled back.

I waited until Stewart and Algie were in the office and took the tape out to Susan's mini. We finished recording early afternoon and Dimitri, who had proved he could play a tambourine, wanted to celebrate down the pub, any pub, but I wanted to go home. I didn't enjoy our second studio day as much as the first; Richard's anger was somehow still there and I hadn't seen him since.

Chapter 45
Spring 1977
Challenge
'Lonely Boy'

Dad put down yesterday's newspaper as I came into the kitchen. Surprised, he looked from me to the clock on the oven and back. Point made: It was early, for me. He took a sip of tea from his favourite mug and turned the radio down as *Lonely Boy* finished. 'Did I wake you?'

'No. Got stuff to do.'

'Ok.' He didn't follow up. Fortunately.

Truth was, I hadn't slept well, or hardly at all. After finishing in the studio the previous day I'd come straight home. Susan had spent the evening round Bazzer's and Dad went down the Conservative Club to finish preparations for a Queen Elizabeth II jubilee party in a few days. Petra had gone to bingo with Kay and Sofia. I'd tried to watch some telly but Richard's outpourings, a few nights previously at the studio, were a distraction not even my guitars could combat. I'd tried reading a book – first one since scraping through English at school – but Dad's copy of *The Godfather* hadn't held my attention, and I'd not dropped off until the early hours then woken with Dad's alarm.

I put some bread in the toaster and we sat in silence until it popped. As I spread butter, Dad said, 'I'm thinking I need a change.'

I followed his line of sight. 'Painting the walls a different colour?'

'Haha, funny.'

I wasn't trying to be, but didn't say so.

'No,' he continued, 'Bigger.' He took a slice of toast. 'What would you say if I gave up working at the garage?'

From his tone I knew he expected me to feel this was important, so waited a few seconds to appear as if giving it serious thought, then answered, 'It's up to you.'

He looked at me, disappointed, so I asked, 'What would you do instead?'

'There's a job going down the Conservative Club. General Manager. It doesn't pay as much and I'd be there almost every evening. Would you and Susan mind?'

As he was down there almost every evening anyway, or we were out gigging, I could honestly say I didn't and that it sounded a great idea. I told him, asking, 'Does Vince's dad know?'

'Not yet. He's out of hospital after what happened in the car park but not back to the garage. He's still poorly, though I hear he's finally taking it serious and walking round the park three times a day to get fitter. I'll tell him soon as he's back at work.' He reached for the cigarette pack next to his cup then changed his mind.

'You don't care what he says though, do you?' I asked.

'No.'

'Good.'

It was cold, sitting here in the park, mid-morning. I was on the bench nearest the spot we'd found Mum having her 'picnic', so many months ago. There had been a couple of dog-walkers and a few mums taking toddlers to the playground area, but, mostly, it was just me sitting there, waiting, and the longer the wait, the more doubt grew. This wasn't a great idea and, in many ways, wasn't even mine. It was a seed planted by Richard that I couldn't weed out. Even so, I was close to giving up when Lawrence jogged into the park wearing a dark blue tracksuit which neither fit nor suited him. He'd pass me in a few minutes. I sat still, breathing fast.

'Hi, Mike, how're things?' Lawrence panted on reaching me.

I didn't answer. The words I'd been working through for the last half hour were not there.

'You ok? Thanks for helping the other night, in the car park. I don't remember what happened but heard you helped.' He smiled; as if I gave a monkey's.

I still didn't answer. Had he been so drunk that he'd forgotten the confrontation?

'I need to keep moving. Doctor's orders. See you on the next lap,' he said and started to walk away.

'I saw you and Vi at our party,' I blurted out.

He took another step, stopped, and waited a few seconds before half-turning. 'So what.' He was calm, but it was a challenge.

'In the kitchen. You grabbed her.'

'No.'

'She pushed you away.'

'You're talking bollocks. I never touched her.'

I stood from the bench. 'I was there. And what about my mum? Did you grab at her? Back in the day?' The question was rushed.

'What have you been told?'

'Did you force her to, to do anything?' I stood as tall as him now, but far smaller. My heart beat an irregular, heavy tattoo and I wanted to back off, maybe run away, but this was my park. I wished I was angry instead of scared. He considered his answer before saying,

'Your mum didn't mind.'

'Mind what?'

He hesitated. 'A cuddle.'

'She told Dad nothing happened.'

'She would.'

'You're a fucking liar.' I spoke with as much venom as I could.

He puffed out his chest and came towards me.

'Everything all right, JB?' I heard Sunny Steve call, as Bruce trotted over to smell me. Lawrence took half a step back and shrank an inch. I didn't answer. Sunny Steve was still a good thirty yards away, walking towards us.

Lawrence gave a smirk and walked on. Steve repeated his question as he reached me, though he watched Lawrence.

I remembered what Susan had once said to me about Steve not being for hire. 'All good Steve. Just having a chat with Vince's dad.'

'He's a wanker,' Steve said and sat down. Bruce explored around us. 'We like it here this time of day. Time to think, but the good part is, I don't bother.' He offered me a joint. 'We just take it in, don't we Bruce?'

Bruce looked up on hearing his name.

The sun tried to warm us, raising a mist from the lawn. I watched Lawrence leave the park at the next gate even though it wasn't nearest for his house. I shook my head at the joint. We didn't talk, but it was good to have Steve here. I felt better at confronting Lawrence – would Richard be a little proud? – but angry that I was no wiser. His words, 'She would,' swirled with different meanings.

That afternoon, I went round to Richard's.

Chapter 46
Spring 1977
The Festival
'Yesterday'

It was the week after Easter, one of the first festivals of the year, and our first festival ever. Though only small – four or five fields somewhere outside Brighton – we jumped at the chance to play. Algie negotiated a Sunday evening slot and we arrived early that morning. It wasn't Glastonbury and it wasn't summer but still, it was a festival and we weren't stupid, we packed jumpers and wellies. We were directed to the field immediately behind the stage and put up an old eight man scout patrol tent for the band that Sunny Steve had brought. I think it was called an eight man tent because it took that many to put it up. There was black mould speckled across the khaki canvas but the smell wasn't too bad. Besides the band, we had three crew and nine or ten 'civilians' with us, the usuals plus a few I didn't know, organised by Sofia and Kay. They'd brought their own tents. By ten, Sofia had supervised setting up our little village in a corner of the field, including a private two man tent for Richard and Anika – we hoped they'd turn up though it was a long journey for him. By eleven, breakfast was frying over an open fire. By half-past, the beers had been opened, and a few minutes later joints were being lit. Cows in the next field watched as if they were interested and it was calming just to watch them back. Musicians and fans from the other bands wandered over to chat. A few had heard of us, or at least said they had, and bummed joints, and though the weather wasn't summer, the atmosphere was. We did a sound check around one, then wandered through to the next field, packed with tents and larger marquees: St. John Ambulance; food and drink provisions; hemp products; tattoo parlour; real ale; vintage vinyl; Friends of the Earth.

Steve and Sofia made for the hemp tent, impressed that they sold hemp milk and juice, while Susan and Bazzer checked out the old vinyl next door. Petra and I were in the tattoo parlour, flicking through a book of designs, Petra trying to talk herself into a shamrock, inked somewhere hidden. I suggested high on her thigh but then didn't like the idea of the tattooist 'working' there. Sally was encouraging her, and I hoped the conversation didn't wander to include piercings, it might be tricky if Sally asked what I'd thought of her belly button safety pin in front of Petra. I joined Vince, and pretended to be interested in the small bird design he was checking out, a swift I think, or a swallow.

'How's your dad?' I asked when we ran out of conversation, but didn't think it safe to go back to Petra and Sally – the tattooist was showing them piercing bars. 'Has he said anything about that night in the car park?'

'I haven't seen him.' Vince didn't look at me, more interested in the tattoo designs. 'But he's out of hospital.'

'I heard. My dad went to see him. He gave in his notice.' I wanted to tell Vince of my conversation with his dad in the park but had no good reason.

'Leaving the garage?' Vince was surprised.

'Yep, after, I dunno, twenty odd years.'

'Finally had enough?'

'I guess. He's already got a new job. Manager of the Conservative Club. It's right up his street. Just don't tell the committee he's voted Labour all his life.'

Next to us were a couple of guys, just a little older, discussing the best shoulders on which to have matching Celtic cross inks. They left the tattoo tent holding hands. I nudged Vince. We watched them go. One of them said something funny and the other laughed and pecked him on the cheek. I'd never seen such openness in public – nor in private come to think of it. It was, to me, a fascinating curiosity, but to Vince I could see it was something more.

'Bold eh?' I tried to sound admiring.

'Bold?' Sally was by my side, from nowhere. 'You're a caveman.'

I remembered Petra saying similar.

Sally and Vince left the tent. Petra and I followed. The two men wandered, hand in hand, to the tea stall at the back of the hemp tent where they were warmly welcomed and offered drinks and a biscuit.

'Fancy tea?' Sally said to no one in particular and went after them.

We followed. Tea and cake were a cool way to spend half an hour and the guy serving from behind the trestle table made us laugh by asking which of us was with who. Petra and I stayed at the table while Sally and Vince went over to the rack of Gay Pride leaflets at the back of the tent. We left them there, with a shout not to miss our set.

The field was only half full when we went on stage but that was ok, there was room for people to spread out and enjoy the sun. A few came close to the stage while others lay on the grass drinking and smoking a different grass. It was a lazy atmosphere and though we played full-on we didn't work the crowd. Susan was dressed 'Joplin hippy' – perfect for the sunny afternoon – and I'd borrowed one of Kay's old tie-dye t-shirts. Richard and Anika finally arrived and found a place in shade from which to watch. Vince and Sally stood at the back of the field, next to the guys we'd followed to the hemp tent. After our set, we grabbed beer, wine and joints from our tents, found the burger van and went back to watch the final band. They were a folk-rock group with an enthusiastic following. Clapping along with choruses was infectious and many of the crowd knew the set well enough to sing along. The stage had been positioned so the sun wasn't in our eyes as it dropped. Instead, the sunset's vivid blend of orange, yellow and red was behind us, lengthening shadows and gradually inviting darkness to close in, drawing focus onto the band as the stage lights brightened in contrast.

'Next festival, Red Ice Rising gets sunset slot,' I shouted to Petra above the cheers as the band started a song the audience knew.

Afterwards, we sat outside the band tent, most of us on blankets, Richard and Anika on rickety campchairs. The fire was smaller than on the beach in Ireland, but it was warmer here. Someone a few tents away was playing an acoustic and singing *Yesterday*. They finished to polite applause and started another song but someone else took the guitar, tuned it and began *Pinball Wizard*.

A verse in, I had to admit, 'He's good.' Petra rolled her eyes. I watched the guy for a while. Even though his small audience was, I assumed, band mates and friends, he wasn't playing for fun, he was performing. I recognised him as the singer from the band on before us that afternoon. 'Bit too keen though?' I said to Petra.

'Desperate,' she said.

'To be a star,' added Richard, 'and maybe you have to be.'

'What?' I took two beers from the hamper and offered him one, despite knowing he probably shouldn't. He shook his head.

'Desperate. Maybe if you want to be a rock superstar you need more than love for music, performing, being good at it. Maybe you need to be desperate to be the centre of attention, to be adored, ruthless, surrounded by people telling you how good you are until you believe it and shit on those who don't.' Richard's words were slurred and slow, but his tone was matter of fact.

'I could do that,' I said.

'No JB, you couldn't.'

I lay back on the blanket, next to Petra. 'My mum did say don't try to be liked, just play what we feel, not what others want. Or something like that.'

Susan shifted on her blanket to rest on one elbow. 'She said similar to me.'

'She never wanted you two to be dickhead superstars,' Bazzer said, flat on his back, smoking a joint.

'Did she tell you that?' Susan asked.

'Didn't have to. No one wants their kids to be arseholes.' He passed the joint to Susan, who rarely smoked.

'But what if I want to be superstar?' She took a drag and coughed hard. We laughed.

'I won't let you,' said Bazzer, 'in honour of your mum.'

'What if the single is a hit? It'll be released in a couple of weeks.' Susan passed me the joint.

I took a light drag. 'S'ok, we don't need it to be. We're gonna be more of an album band, that'll be our ... what's the word?' I looked to Richard.

'Legacy,' he almost whispered.

'Legacy,' I repeated and passed the joint to Petra. She feigned taking a drag, watching us watching her, laughed and passed it to Sofia.

'Sorry,' Richard said, barely audible.

'Richard?' Anika looked to him.

'Sorry, JB. I'm sorry for being a dick in the studio, when you recorded the single. I was stupid angry. I don't chew that crap now, just take more tablets.' Our fire cast more shadow than light and he still wore the fedora so I couldn't see his face. 'But I'm sure the single will sound good, and it doesn't have to be a hit to last. It'll always be yours and who knows who might come across it in years to come and think of Red Ice Rising. That's cool.'

'And we will put *Miracle Number Four* on the album.' I said.

'If you ever finish writing it,' Richard teased.

'Your piano part makes it.' I stretched over to tap his foot. I don't know why.

In a flicker of yellow flame I thought I caught him smiling. 'And that, JB, is why you'll never be a dickhead superstar. But it's nice to think my name might be on the album, for posterity.' There was an awkward silence.

I preferred him angry to sad. I preferred his old self to both. He was staring into weakening flames as Anika sat forward in her chair and said, 'Guess what?'

No one did.

'You have to try.' She insisted.

No one did.

'You lot are rubbish. I ... we ...'

Richard put up a hand to interrupt. Anika looked to him, reached to hold his hand, and continued, '... are having a baby.'

It was a couple of seconds before Sofia and Susan shrieked, almost in unison, 'Oh my God!' and, in unison, were quickly on to their knees to hug her awkwardly in the campchair. Anika pulled them to her, and they collapsed to the ground with the chair. Richard smiled, embarrassed.

I caught his eye and nodded, 'Congratulations. Great news,' I said as sincerely as I could and meant it.

'Thanks.'

'When?' Susan asked as the girls rolled free of each other. Sunny Steve put the chair back together and placed it so Anika could sit even closer to Richard.

'I'm only a few weeks. We think it was in Ireland, on the beach. Richard's birthday,' said Anika, 'but don't tell anyone yet. We weren't careful and Richard was so ...'

'Er, they don't need details,' Richard interrupted and though I couldn't be sure in the poor light, I thought he was blushing.

'Of course we do,' said Petra, 'everyone will want to know everything. Especially my mum. She'll love that it happened in Ireland, on our beach.'

'Well ...' Anika looked at Richard, 'it did feel special.'

Richard struggled to raise himself from the chair to kiss her. She met him half-way. He pointed to the Czech Airlines flight bag at Anika's feet. She counted out, and passed him, four tablets. He swallowed them without a drink; practised.

'What did your mum say?' Petra asked Richard.

'She doesn't know. Please, no telling. It's too early.' He looked down to his lap, his face back in darkness under the fedora, 'But she'll be very excited, something to remember me by.' It was a real shitty joke, and no one laughed. 'It's ok. It's true. Uncle Dudek can talk about stories and keepsakes and what we care about, but what we leave doesn't get any more real than a baby. To be honest, I can't quite believe it.' He looked to Anika.

'C'mon, names!' Susan called to fill the silence. 'What you got?'

Before Anika could answer there was a confusion of suggestions – I threw in Ziggy – then a discussion about the baby's sex and likely hair colour and the contrast of Richard's handsome part Vietnamese features with Anika's Czech beauty, then debate over what instrument the baby should learn first and whether Red Ice Rising would still be going by the time he or she was old enough to join us and we all agreed, of course she, Richard now insisted, would. Beer and a joint were passed round, and the conversation slowly settled and faded.

The night grew cold.

Sofia and Steve took their blankets to the patrol tent. Susan and Bazzer followed. Kay and Dimitri were already there; I could hear his snores. Vince and Sally – she still used that name around the band – had gone to the tattoo tent an hour or more ago and weren't back. Across the field, most had slipped into their tents. The would-be superstar was still strumming and singing, but almost in a whisper, and there was little light from adjoining fields. Occasionally I'd see someone pick a path through the tents, lighting the way with a torch. I heard a low from the cows next door and wondered what they did at night.Anika checked her watch and pulled a different box of tablets from her bag. Richard indicated I should pass him one of the half full bottles of light ale left by the fire.

'More pain killers?' I asked.

'Different. They help me sleep too. Anika won't let me take too many. But sometimes I like to be asleep.'

'Know what you mean. I quite like sleeping.'

'It's not the same thing. I like being asleep.' He emphasised the '*a*'. 'It's when fear goes away.' He looked at me and I hoped I'd read him right when I asked,

'Are you? Scared?'

He nearly smiled. 'Of course. I'm sick, not thick.'

'Of …?' I prompted hesitantly but Richard answered quickly,

'Not of what's coming. I hope there's something, in fact, God, I hope so, God or not, which is funny, right?' he waited for me to laugh, just, 'But if not, then either way I figure at least it won't hurt anymore and I don't have to watch Mum, Anika and the others be eaten away. That's the worst kind of mirror. And I don't believe any bollocks about Saint Teresa's tears, never mind what Anika might say.' He touched her cheek.

She pressed his hand into her face then kissed the palm. 'Ha, what do you know. God might be out of fashion but we're not giving up on miracles. I also prayed for a baby.' She patted her belly, but the humour was forced. She stood. 'Come, no more talk. Take me to bed.'

'In a minute.'

Anika bent and kissed him then said to me, 'Don't keep him talking,' and then to Petra, 'Don't let him.'

Richard watched her go, waiting until she was in their tent before whispering, 'But I throw up, terrified, when it hits me, of not being here, of what I'm going to miss. All those moments, proper, big, small, whatever, I'll miss them. I won't feel them. I won't make anyone feel anything new and maybe there'll be a hole where I was, but that'll shrink and you'll stop wondering what it might have been like and I'll be just half a memory, less, because of what I've missed, and the more I miss, the more the memory shrinks.'

I pulled the campchair as close as I could and sat to put my arm around him. He was thin and light, easy to pull in. He cried into my shoulder.

After a minute he eased away. He took a deep breath, but it didn't calm him, and he asked, 'Was your mum scared?'

This mattered. I thought before answering. 'Maybe for a long time. And I was too stupid to know. But on that last day? I don't think so. Maybe by then she was no longer scared of missing her future. She didn't always make sense.'

'Perhaps that's what she meant about the fourth miracle. Maybe it's that simple. It's when you aren't scared of what you might miss. Maybe that's the peace she meant, and I think you should believe she found. It's not the same as wanting to go, but when it's also just too hard to stay … and people talk about peace when they really mean not suffering anymore. Shouldn't there be more to it? Fuck, JB, I'm shit scared. And it's great that a bit of me will be here with the baby but it's crushing that I'll miss all that too.'

We sat quietly for a minute or two before Richard said, almost in a whisper, 'I still wonder if the sax player's lover was scared. I know you find it hard to believe he murdered his love, but it's true.'

'I believe it.'

'I just wish I was as brave. Anika is but …'

Petra started to ask a question, I told her I'd explain later.

We lapsed into silence. Finally he asked, 'How do I stop being scared, JB?'

The time for false hope had gone. All I had was, 'It doesn't stop you being the bravest person I ever met. Come, Anika's waiting, it's late.' I helped him to the tent. He leant heavily against me, having to concentrate to walk, almost dragging his right foot. When had that started? Richard sensed that I'd noticed.

'Just wait 'til I start pissing myself.'

It was hard to laugh but we tried.

I stared at the near-dead fire. Though not comfortable it was warm with a blanket around me, and the fresh air kept my head clear for thoughts of Richard's sadness and fear.

'What was that about the sax player earlier?' Petra asked. We were sitting back to back, leaning against each other.

I told her what I knew of the story.

'What, the sax player couldn't watch her suffer, so he suffocated her? Wow. True?'

'I think so. And when she was at her most scared, the sax player was there.'

'True love or not, that's heavy.' She shuffled round to rest her head on my shoulder. I would have been happy to sleep there, cuddling like that night on the beach in Ireland, instead of the crowded tent. And to wake with the rising sun might have changed something, though I've no idea how. But Petra nudged me, 'Bedtime?'

I was reluctant; I could still hear Dimitri's snores, but Petra stood and held out a hand to pull me up. I took a step towards the patrol tent, but she indicated to the second two-man tent that had been put up earlier and which no one was using, 'That's ours. It's got a blow-up mattress.'

'No, the mattress was for Richard and Anika,' I said, not connecting the dots.

'They have one too. That's our tent.'

'No one said.'

'Susan did. I'm pretty sure you were there.' Petra led me and unzipped the flap. As we crawled in I gave a backward glance to Richard and Anika's tent. There was no light, and I hoped he was sleeping well – was sleep a respite from his Judas or so temporary it was just a fitful taunt?

Our tent was not big enough to stand, and the blow-up mattress took all the floor space. Petra suggested we take off our trainers so as not to get the double sleeping bag dirty. I turned on the torch hanging from a hook by the entrance, the swaying light threw shadows.

'JB, you're singing.'

'Am I?'

'*Blinded By The Light,* slowly.'

'I don't think so.'

'You most definitely are. You ok?'

'I was thinking about Richard. It's …' I faltered.

'Really shit. I know.'

We sat quietly for a few seconds then Petra asked, 'And?'

'I'm thinking that it didn't have to be Richard. It could have been Dimitri or Bazzer or Vince or you. Just like it didn't have to be my mum. Could have been Susan or me. Might still be, one day.'

'Would your mum or Richard want you to think about that too hard?'

'Probably not.'

Petra took my hand. 'You know I came back earlier than I was going to?'

'I guess.'

'Because Richard wrote to me. He didn't say why exactly, but he just made coming home seem the best thing to do, a good idea.'

'I think so.'

'So do I. We should thank him.' Petra leaned over to kiss me, and I was suddenly nervous. We had spent a lot of time together since her return and had even slept together, which I'd enjoyed, but it had, literally, been sleeping, in a van or a dressing room. We were still waiting for this. The longer we waited, the more important it became, though it was almost crippling me as our petting had become increasingly intense. I suppose I'd thought the wait would be over in a scene of rich romance, with time, privacy and a sophisticated mutual seduction. Well at least the tent was private, and we had all night – two out of four – hopefully, the romance and seduction would come naturally.

'Should we get in?' Petra unzipped the sleeping bag.

It was a struggle to open and slip into the bag while sitting on it. I was close to wishing I'd brought a joint to calm my nerves then glad not to have – this feeling was anticipation, not fear; to be encouraged, not dampened. I

433

smiled at the realisation and hugged her tight. I hesitated to say, 'At last,' not wanting to speak in clichés, but it was true, so I said it.

'I know. Even if it is a set up.' Petra half-smiled. 'That's really something about Anika being pregnant. Which reminds me, have you got, you know?'

I kissed her gently, taking a few seconds to smell sweet almond. 'Of course. I bought a pack the morning after you came home,' then I pulled away, 'but they're in my guitar case, in the other tent. Idiot.'

'S'ok.' Petra struggled to reach into a pocket before pulling out two crumpled foil packs.

'They're not ...'

'They are.'

I laughed and kissed her harder.

'But they're old so,' from the other pocket she produced a new pack of three Durex.

'So we've just the five then?' I joked.

'I'm on the pill too. Susan's idea. She came with me to family planning a couple of weeks ago but until my next period we need to be double-safe.'

'Susan's idea? Of course.' I pretended it was not embarrassing to have my sister organise my sex life.

'Susan also gave some advice.'

'Not sure I want to hear it.'

'Ok.'

We kissed more passionately.

'I suppose we should get undressed?' Petra made it a question. 'That doesn't make me sound, I don't know, easy, does it?'

'Of course not.'

'Good. Anika said it's about time we got on with it.'

'Anika? Ever practical. So that's Susan and Anika. Anyone else been giving advice?'

'Sofia had some, but I can't tell you what, yet.'

'I expect I'll be the last to know, as usual.'

'But the first to find out,' she said cryptically.

We tried to undress in the bag. There was no room and I elbowed her in the head while she kneed me in the stomach. We both apologised and I said it could have been worse; a few inches lower. I didn't want to be the one to say it would be better getting undressed outside of the bag, but it was her idea, and we reversed the struggle to get back out. Undressing kneeling wasn't much easier. Petra turned away from me and I was quickly down to my underpants, any embarrassment overridden by growing excitement. Petra slipped her t-shirt over her head then lay on her back to shimmy tight jeans over her hips. She smiled without catching my eye. I looked at her, trying hard to appear as casual as ever I had, desperate to fix the image without staring. The sun had given her usually pale cheeks a pink tinge and her hair, longer than ever, was a tangle down and onto her white chest, leaving glimpses of her bra but hiding that mole.

Petra rested up on one elbow, saying, 'Kay also had some advice.'

'Of course she did.'

'Nice undies.'

'Undies?'

'Bra and panties. Not tarty, but sexy.'

'That sounds like Kay.'

'Sorry, mine are … grey. I tried some of hers. Red and lacy but didn't fill them. Does that matter?'

'God no,' I said, and meant it and nearly added a 'thank you' for letting me see her this way. Instead I asked, 'Are you nervous?'

'I was until Mum said I didn't need to be. She said to remember you're the lucky one.' She gave the laugh that was such an enticement to kiss her.

'You spoke to your mum as well?'

'Of course.'

'Wow, still sharing everything. Are you sure she's Catholic?'

'Both practising and practical. Don't tell Father Andrew.'

'He's the last person.'

'Though I might, at confession.'

I couldn't tell if she joked. Her poise was unexpected – it shouldn't have been – and I may have looked unsure as she said, 'Are you ok? Still thinking about Richard? Do you want to wait?'

Had she asked me that outside, ten minutes earlier, there's a very, very outside chance I'd have said yes, but now, seeing her so close to naked, no way. Dimitri's Playboy and Mayfair mags had nothing on the elegant lady lying so effortlessly seductive, skin both soft and taut, complex, shallow curves organic and shadowy, an intoxicating sculpture, precious and primal.

'You ok?' she asked quietly.

'Just admiring your necklace.' She wore the silver letter 'P' I'd bought.

'Mum said that as it was a present, you'd appreciate the thought.'

I tried to match her confidence, 'She's right. And did your mum give any other advice, you know, seeing how we've waited this long?'

'She said not to worry if the first time isn't great. As long as it's the same for both of us, good or bad, that's ok, and afterwards, not straight away but a little afterwards, we should make sure to laugh.' She shifted slightly and the long hair slipped away showing more skin.

'You have no idea how much I think about your mole.'

'That's weird. But good. I think. And oddly I think a lot about your lopsided grin.' She ran a finger across my mouth.

We went back into the sleeping bag. We cuddled and kissed, and, despite my anxious excitement, I unclipped her bra first time. Feeling her bare skin against mine dispelled any lasting nerves.

'Feels like you better put one of these on.' She passed me a condom.

'Only one?'

'JB, no jokes unless they're really funny. That wasn't,' she said, as she removed her panties and waited for me to tear open the foil and fumble the condom into place.

Our touching and caressing were awkward but that didn't matter, our kisses were natural, and our passion was honest. I tried to remember the *Cosmopolitan* articles I'd read on foreplay, but our desire was running fast – or Petra had read different articles. She pushed me on my back and sat astride, shifting her weight a little at a time, feeling for the right position. I felt a slight give in resistance but then she gave a small gasp, of pain I think, and stopped pushing down. I froze.

She tried again but I could see it hurt. I eased her aside and lay over her, moving deliberately slowly. Resting up on my arms I hoped my crooked smile was a sign of calm rather than an idiot grin and kissed her. She used a hand to guide me. I felt the same resistance but this time her eyes shut tight, and she pulled me in.

A couple of days later, when Susan asked me how it went, I said, 'That's between me and Petra.' But if pressed to answer I'd have added something like, 'All that romantic bollocks about symphonies and fireworks and ecstasy and being as one and intense pleasure to the point of pain and feeling both lost and found? Turns out it's true.'

I don't know if the sudden release of tension I felt through Petra's body was her final loss of control or if she felt mine. I shuddered and she pulled me down until I took the weight off my arms and rested on her heavily. We stayed that way for maybe a minute, then I rolled away and we lay on our backs breathing deep. I desperately wanted to ask if it had been ok but didn't – maybe later, maybe in the morning; it was important to know. Instead I just watched her and relaxed when she turned to face me and gave that special, open smile; no pretence. I remembered Vi's tip and said, 'Everyone gives advice but no one tells you what to do with a used condom if you're in a tent.'

Petra shook her head. 'Shhh. I think my mum was wrong about the laughing afterwards.' She kissed me lightly and reached for her bag to take out, and hand me, tissues.

'Don't tell me. More of Anika's practical advice. And what was Sofia's?'

'I'm not saying, though as far as I can tell it worked.'

I laughed.

'I can tell you Susan's advice though, if you want.' She settled back, looking up at the tent's ceiling.

'I've heard everyone else's, so why not. In case she asks me.'

'She said it wasn't essential, but it would be better if ...' she hesitated.

'If what?'

'If ... I mean it's not like it has to be Romeo and Juliet or anything and probably not like the sax player and his dying girlfriend, thank God. And it doesn't have to mean forever, or maybe even much longer, though one summer at least would be cool, but she thinks it'd be better, for both of us, if, right now ...' She was flustered; I'd never seen that before, '... you know, when we finally stop waiting, at least, just at that time, we, you know, are ... in love.'

'Aren't we?'

'You don't know?'

'I guess I just always assumed so. Feels like it, especially now. Doesn't it?' I didn't add that I had no idea what this type of love was meant to feel like, except I was sure this mix of desire, desperation to spend time with her, enjoying a sense of wanting to look after her and hoping to be looked after in return, anxious to please her and desiring her – I know, I said that twice – had to be the real deal. So what if I was still two months away from seventeen. I had no reason to think being older would make these feelings any stronger or deeper.

'Good. Susan told me it might turn out to be a moment. Not sure what she meant but …'

We cuddled into each other, pulling the sleeping bag to our necks and I told her Susan's theory about moments.

'Is that why Richard was talking about them earlier?' she asked.

'I guess.'

'Poor Richard. And what about you? Have any?'

I hesitated, then, 'Definitely one.'

'When?'

'Story for another time.' I brushed hair from her face and stroked her cheek.

Miracle Number Four

Chapter 47
Spring 1977
The Missing Verse
'Miracle Number Four'

The corridor split the hospital wing in two. On each side were single bed rooms, and at the end it opened into a ward behind the nurses' station. It was mid-morning but there were no windows to the corridor and the unnatural neon lighting bounced around the polished floor and walls. I supposed time was passing but it could just as easily have been circling, along with the nurses's repeating routines.

I sat outside Richard's room, feeling conspicuous at first, but less so as I realised the nurses and doctors were far too busy to take notice of a skinny kid with shaggy hair – as long as that kid kept out of the way. And I felt like a kid. I shouldn't – I was just two months from turning seventeen, a soon to be rock star, feted by fans and critics, the envy of my peers, haha, and Petra's boyfriend – but here I was just a kid.

Uncle Dudek brought me a cup of tepid tea with too much sugar. He found a smile as he patted me on the shoulder and went into Richard's room. I'd met him a couple of days earlier and he was everything they'd said; a caring man as generous and loving as he was big, and I watched him fight to help his family as they watched Richard die and I watched as he shrank under the weight of the tragedy.

I considered asking if I could go back into the room – I'd been in when first arriving, just for a couple of minutes, though Richard was unconscious. It had been awkward with Anika, his mum and stepdad watching me – not that they were, of course – and I wondered where Kim, his sister was, but didn't ask. In truth, when the nurse had said, 'Close family only from now,' and ushered me out, I had been relieved. The silence in the room was a blanket that

441

suffocated, not cosseted. My mum had died almost in front of me on a peerless summer's day and I had been of no help, had offered no comfort. Here, on a miserable, damp, airless Friday in May, I was less than useless and then ashamed to think that what I felt was of any consequence.

Anika came from the room, asked if I was all right, sat for a few minutes then went back. I guess even her control was stretched to breaking point. I'd seen that earlier.

When I'd arrived, Anika was at the nurses' station. She was much younger than the white-coated doctor in front of her. They stood face to face and the older man was frustrated that the young woman in front of him was not persuaded by his platitudes nor cowed by his authority. Anika's fists clenched and unclenched, fighting to hold back tears, and her voice was increasingly loud as she repeated, 'I will not let him be in pain. You will not let him be in pain.'

'He isn't.' The doctor tried to sound convincing.

'How do you know?'

'He's unconscious.'

'How do you know he is not suffering? You have given up treatment.'

'There's nothing more ...'

'You have given up,' she almost shouted, then took a breath and was quieter, 'You have given up. And he is in pain.'

'He isn't. He's unconscious.'

'I watch him. He looks in pain.'

'We're giving him morphine.'

'I, we, will not see him in pain. What if he needs more?'

'He doesn't.'

'How do you know? All you know is enough to give up.'

'We can't give him more. It would be dangerous.'

'Ha. Now we see. Coward. You can't save, but you won't do anything to help him pass.'

'We're doing all we can.'

'Coward. It's not enough.'

'You know what you're asking. It can't be done.'

'Coward!' she screamed. Doctors, nurses, patients, visitors turned to see. 'Coward,' she whispered and started to sink to her knees. I ran to her, taking her arms, holding her. 'Let me do it.' She looked up to the doctor. 'He trusts me, he is brave enough. I can be too …'

The doctor looked away.

I'd taken her back into Richard's room. She muttered something about the saxophone player while his mother held her, and they sobbed quietly in the corner. I sat by Richard, watching his chest barely rise and fall and his eyelids occasionally flicker. The steady drip of fluids from the bag metronomically and relentlessly marked the passage of his life.

Sometime in the afternoon, I've no idea when, Uncle Dudek called a doctor to the room – they didn't delay, Dudek had a way about him. The doctor called for a nurse. The nurse called for matron.

Anika eventually came out to see me, red eyed, pale, aged. We hugged and I thought maybe I should be crying too. I supposed I would later. She gave me a piece of paper, saying, 'From Richard but he wanted me to wait. He hoped to give it to you himself, if … well, you know, if he didn't …'

At the top of the page was written *Miracle Number Four – missing verse*. Followed by eight lines of lyrics in his neat style.

One of the nurses let me ring Dad and he left work, picking up Petra on the way, to come and get me. They both held me, and Petra cried. I expected to but didn't. It was Friday the 29th of April just twelve days since the festival; twelve days since sitting by that fire. How could it have been so quick?

Except, for Richard, perhaps it had also been so slow and that was terrifying.

Miracle Number Four

Chapter 48
Spring 1977
Blossoms In The Park
'Blinded By The Light'

Five days after Richard died, I woke up late, having slept on the sofa at Kay's. We'd played a gig at Slough College the previous night. I didn't think it went well and the van broke down on the A4 in the early hours. It was a week before the showcase gig at Hammersmith Palais and I wasn't feeling ready. Dimitri brought me coffee. I sat up with the blanket around my shoulder, cradling the mug.

'Not a great night,' Dimitri said, looking down.

'What, the van breaking down? I'm knackered.'

'Not the van, the gig. We weren't as tight as usual,' Dimitri almost whispered.

'Oh. No, guess not.' I'd made a lot of mistakes. Dimitri was being kind to say 'we'. 'Sorry.'

'We get it, we do. It's ok.' He gave me a hug and kissed me on the cheek. 'My mother says it hurts because it matters and if it matters it's worth the hurt.' The slight accent should have made it way too cheesy, but instead made it more sincere.

'Is that an old Greek saying?' I called as he went back to the kitchen.

'No. Of course not. She comes from Stoke Newington.'

Petra brought toast and jam. Kay's mum let Dimitri and Kay sleep together, but not me and Petra. I guess she was determined to honour her promise to Vi.

Kay took Dimitri shopping for a new shirt for the showcase gig. Petra and I hung around for a while, getting in Kay's mum's way while she tried to vacuum, so we went out.

I rang the bell and we waited. I heard the dog bark so rang again, beginning to think it wasn't a good idea to come round unplanned. Eventually the big man opened the door, except the big man, Uncle Dudek, wasn't so big anymore. He was hunched over, one hand clasping Richard's dog's collar, and looked up to us, rheumy eyes in a sallow face with a slack jaw. The dog barked again, but even that was half-hearted, and Dudek needn't have held him.

'Yes?' the once big man said. He didn't recognise me until I removed the flat cap, then invited us in. He explained that Anika and Richard's mother were at the funeral directors, making arrangements, taking care of things. He apologised to us that it wasn't him 'taking care of things'; it wasn't him making arrangements; not him looking out for the family; not him finding the way to celebrate a life; it wasn't his shoulders anyone was crying on. He was broken.

We left when he composed himself. I think he was glad to be alone.

'Let's go home the other way,' I said, taking Petra's hand and leading her to Richard's park. We slowly walked the path running just inside its perimeter. The park was all but empty and the playground unused on this chilly afternoon. The sky was uneven with patchy clouds that slipped slowly across the hazy sun and let fall a scattering of rain; hardly enough to dampen. I liked it here. It was similar to our own park.

Some way round was a couple sitting on a bench. I recognised them and whispered to Petra, 'Malcolm and Julie. Richard's friends. We've met, sort of.'

Malcolm looked up as we neared.

'Hi,' I said. 'Malcolm, right?'

He nodded but took a couple of seconds to recognise me. 'JB. Hi.'

He looked tired. Julie, at his side, raised a hand in welcome.

Malcolm went to stand then changed his mind while I took off, and fiddled with, the flat cap. Julie and Petra exchanged sympathetic smiles. Malcolm and I had a lot to say to each other, probably, but no real inclination to say it.

'You ok?' I asked.

'Not really. You?'

'Not really,' I agreed.

'It's all a bit shit, isn't it?'

'Yep.'

He nodded. 'See you around.'

'See you around,' I copied, put my cap back on and walked, but only a yard when he said,

'Richard loved playing *Blinded By The Light* at Zamara'z.'

I turned back. 'You saw?'

'It's one of his favourites. He also said there's a chance his piano playing might turn up on a recording one day. Is that right? He was excited about it.'

'I hope so. And maybe some of his lyrics.' I felt the back pocket of my jeans. The sheet with Richard's words was still there, increasingly crumpled but unread since the day Anika had passed them.

'Richard would have loved to see the band next week, down the Palais. We'll go. Big gig. It's still on right?'

'Maybe.' I gave a half-wave and continued walking. Ten yards on Petra asked,

'What do you mean, maybe?'

'Nothing.'

Petra stopped. 'Really?'

'I don't know. The last couple of gigs haven't gone great. I'm wondering if we … I'm, ready.'

'What do the others say?'

'I haven't talked to them. But they've noticed. Dimitri said it's ok but …'

'Bollocks. Why wouldn't you play the showcase?'

I shrugged. 'I don't know. I'm not sure it matters so much now.' Petra looked at me with another question, unasked. She took my hand and we continued walking.

'Pretty, isn't it?' she said.

'What?'

'The blossom.' This top end of the path was bordered with cherry blossom trees. Tiny white and pink blooms smothered the branches and the colours were more vibrant for glittering with raindrops.

'Not really.'

'No?'

I looked up at the darkening sky. The drizzle was still light but becoming constant. We sheltered under one of the taller trees. 'I'm sorry. You're right. It is pretty, very pretty. Mum liked it. She was embroidering blossom when she died. It took months. She finished it the day she died. I didn't find it until ... why did I go to the park that day? I just ...' I didn't finish.

She put her arms around my waist. 'I know you feel guilty but ...' her words fell away.

'But what? I should have been there.'

'You were.'

'Not when it might have made a difference.'

She squeezed me tighter and we stood for a minute.

'Was it just too hard for her to keep living? And what if I was just too stupid to know?' I whispered.

'I don't know, JB. Richard said he thought she was ready and, of any of us, he should know, don't you think?'

'Richard thought peace was something you should feel, not just freedom from pain.'

She stroked my cheek. 'Maybe you just gotta let it go. It's ok not to know.'

I took out Richard's lyrics and passed them to her. 'I haven't looked at them yet.'

She read through a couple of times and handed it back. *Miracle Number Four?*'

'The missing verse.' I read it.

'When it's too late to be scared
You will find a way to trust
Your special moments still are shared
By the ones that love you most

Spring 1977 – Blossoms In The Park

When your stories still are told
And your pain and burden cease
Know your loved ones still can hold
And trust the miracle of peace'

At the bottom Richard had written:

Yea, all a bit cliché, I know. But I'm beginning to think there's a lot of truth in cliché. Don't forget to put my name on the credits. P.S. Mum helped with the spelling.

'Maybe you just gotta let your mum go,' Petra repeated.

I nodded and squeezed her hard.

'And remember that other stuff Richard said about the stories we leave?' she asked.

'Of course.'

'No one writes them for you.' She kissed me lightly. 'You have to play the Palais.'

Miracle Number Four

Chapter 49
Spring 1977
Hammersmith Palais
'Miracle Number Four'

The sound-check was in the early evening. We were excited by how loud the house PA was, and how far we could push the guitars and vocals. Dimitri was beside himself with joy at the punch from his kick drum through huge bass bins, and the sound guy had to tell him to play more quietly – as if.

'Hey, Dimitri!' I shouted as he reluctantly stepped away from the kit, 'How many drummers does it take to change a lightbulb?'

'Don't answer!' Kay shouted from the wings.

I finished, 'Five. One to screw the bulb in, and four to talk about how much better Bonham would've done it.'

There were four bands, each playing a thirty minute set and we were on last. Naturally, all the bands wanted to headline, but it turned out Sunny Steve knew someone who knew the guy that supplied the floor manager at the Palais – so we took the prized last spot.

We hung around the dressing room, Sofia limiting us to one joint each and Kay allowing just one beer; I gave mine to Dimitri. There was a minor argument when going through the short set list, again, and Susan and I insisted we play *April Blooms Again.*

A guy dressed entirely in black denim, including fake cowboy hat, stood at the door saying there were people wanting to come in, claiming to be with the band. Steve went with him and came back with a couple of our, make that Dimitri's, regular fans, and Anika. The room was dark and she took a second to look around, as always, controlled. No, not always. I had seen that time, with the doctor. Now

451

she stood tall, wearing the light mac I'd first seen on the Irish trip, but with a dark fedora: Richard's. She could carry the look and her eyes were in shadow. Susan went to her. They hugged – no words – and separated as Black Denim Guy called us to the stage. I walked towards the door, holding Petra's hand, not knowing what I would say when I reached Anika, but she just smiled and stroked my face. The band, crew and civilians followed Black Denim Guy to the stage where we waited in silence while the group before us finished. They were good but I wasn't afraid to follow them. This was the biggest stage we had played on, but I had no doubt we would fill it. This was the largest crowd we'd played for, and I was sure we would move them. Besides, I understood what Richard and Mum had told me. I looked out to the packed hall and whispered to Susan, 'Hammersmith Palais. We play to them but for ourselves.'

'And Mum and Dad.'

'And Richard,' I said and led the band out. With stage lights off I could see out to the packed crowd. There were muted cheers from some of our regular fans who had come along, and sarcastic shouts and abuse from others. We plugged in and tuned up.

Susan nodded to the sound and lighting guys, ignoring the wolf-whistles as she shone in the sudden spotlight. 'Once upon a time,' she spoke into the mic quietly but loud enough to catch attention, and waited for the crowd to settle. 'Once upon a time, someone we knew danced here and fell in love. It was a moment.' She looked to me and started to speak but choked, swallowed, said, 'Fuck it, we're Red Ice Rising, let's play,' and ripped into the opening chord.

The needles danced in the red zones.

Petra and I sat on the stage at Zamara'z. We'd gone straight there from the Palais. The club's lights were dimmed, except for the bar area where the others drank and chatted.

'And that's really where your mum and dad had their first dance?' Petra asked.

'So he says. *Unchained Melody*.' I smiled at a memory.

'That's nice. A moment for them?'

'I hope so.'

'Was tonight a moment for you, playing the Palais?'

'Probably not. But now you mention it, I do remember having another one.' I paused.

'Should I guess? If so, something to do with our night at the festival?'

'No.'

'Oh.' Petra looked disappointed.

I kissed her cheek. 'It was ages ago.'

'And …?'

'The lockups. Live band, pretty girl with long blonde hair, green eyes, bobbing on a tea chest with perfect timing, style and a smile that was just for me. Rock found me and I found the girl.'

'It wasn't blonde.' She laughed.

'Of course it was. What about you? Any moments?'

'Funny you should ask. I was in a pub in Ireland, listening to friends at an open mic, when some skinny kid with a lopsided grin and a Frampton haircut walks in. He came all the way from the suburbs. Turns out he's gonna be a rock star.'

We kissed slowly and rested against each other. I didn't mention that I'd probably had a third moment too. I was starting to feel Richard's death would count, and that was a good thing.

All the others were down the bar area. Petra slipped off the stage, 'Anika's on her own.'

'I'll be there in a minute,' I said, but before I went, Susan brought me a beer.

'Tonight was a triumph,' I said theatrically. 'You were sensational.'

'You too.'

'*April Blooms Again* went well.'

She chinked her bottle against mine. 'I think so too,' and gently ran a finger across the mark above my eye. 'You've grown into that scar nicely. Mum would think it dashing. Did you know Dad was coming?' He was resting against the bar, chatting to Dimitri's fan club. They laughed.

'I think he's just told one of his better jokes,' I said.

'I'd better go and rescue him.' One of the girls was holding on to Dad for support. Susan went over.

Vince was behind the bar, Safety Pin Sally next to him. They talked across it to Algie, who was like a proud father, both for the band and Vince, who was showing off his new tattoo – a small swift, or swallow. Algie shook his head, but kindly. Sally had all but moved in with Vince. He assured me it wasn't a romantic thing, but they were close and, in some way, needed each other while they found out what they wanted, which I guess is a sort of romance in itself. He was right about the rules and their paths; he was looking for a different way, or bravely writing them as he went.

Steve and Sofia shared both a joint and red wine, drinking from the bottle. She said something and laughed. He didn't, until she brushed his cheek with a light kiss, then he smiled: Sunny Steve.

Kay sat on Dimitri's lap, kissing and necking, but gently these days, with affection rather than lust. Kay was simply too cool and confident to be threatened by Dimitri's fan club, and he knew how lucky he was. On the way to Dad, Susan collected Bazzer and they chatted arm in arm, sharing glances and smiles, something unspoken but tangible. Petra was at the bar, talking to Anika. They looked serious, but then, of course, Anika must still have been lost. I wanted to go and hug her but what difference could that make? Petra smiled sympathetically. Anika took a deep breath, touched her belly, and let Petra place her hand there.

I watched them all. I saw each of them.

That I'd not told Dad and Susan what Lawrence had said in the park was a shadow, but they deserved to believe the best. Besides, Lawrence was a bully and a prick and who's to say he wasn't a liar? That afternoon I'd gone round to Richard's and told him what had happened. We talked about it until I chose not to believe Lawrence; the risk of hurting Dad and Susan was too great. Richard said I'd done well to confront Lawrence; learning to let go is not the same as pretending it didn't happen.

God, I regret going to the park the day Mum died.

Was Mum's cancer cure a miracle? I don't think so. Did she find peace before she died, as Richard said? I think yes, and who's to say that isn't a miracle? She deserved one – anyone that loves that much does. As for peace after she died? I don't know what that means.

And Richard? I don't think peace was found before he died, which is beyond sad. And after? Again, I don't know.

They wouldn't want me to go crazy thinking about it.

Standing, I reached into my back pocket for the paper Anika had given me in the hospital. I took an acoustic from the back of the stage, tuned it and started strumming. No one paid attention. I watched them all as I played and sung quietly – *Miracle Number Four* – and Richard's new verse fit perfectly just before the solo. It felt like the song might finally be finished and I had no doubt he and Mum were with me on that stage. When we have their stories, when we know and live by what made them laugh and cry, when we believe in their love, they're still here.

Petra caught my eye and smiled, and I figured this was a moment as good as any.

END

Author's Thanks

I started thinking about what has become *Miracle Number Four* back in 2014, whilst writing *Three Weeks In The Summer*. I'd introduced the character of Michael 'JB' Oppen into that novel and felt there was a lot more to come from him and the people around him. I was also encouraged by readers' positive reaction to two key characters in that book – Richard and Anika – and wanted to find a way of both continuing and bringing their stories together. This book is the result.

The process from conception to production of any creative endeavour is dependent on the help, knowledge, enthusiasm, encouragement, talent, skills and support of many people. My thanks go to:

Paul Swallow (editor), Kath Kyle, Howard Fletcher, Chris Downs, Sue Murphy, Neil Rendall, Peter Olive, Angie Sherritt, Peter Thomson, Tony Thornton, Chris Troughton, Nicola Canon, Peter Thomson, Linda Laurie, Debbie Marriner, Alexander Marriner, Eve Marriner, Chris Troughton, Ray Munro, Colleen MacMahon, Nicole Russell.

Thanks are also due to my fellow Faber Academy alumni friends: Jacqueline Sutherland, Darragh O'Reilly, Scott Taylor, Stephen Kenefick, Sinead Nolan, Blanka Hay, Osman Haneef, Shayna Wilson, Charles Adey, Ruth Nares, Yinka Ayeni, Katharine Lewis, and our tutor Sabrina Broadbent – all talented writers who inspire me to keep trying.

There is, I believe, a fifth miracle not mentioned in this book but one which I hope the story celebrates: Music. May it transform, calm, excite, inspire and guide you as much as

Author's Thanks

it has me since hearing my mother's transistor radio in our kitchen, 1964, play Petula Clark's *Downtown*.

Making music is a 'team sport' and I am fortunate to have played alongside, and learnt much from: Tony Thornton, Howard Fletcher, Jim Murphy, Dave Murphy, Liz Sims, Tara Keatley, Adi Heesom, Andy Riches, Luke Riches, Paul Sherritt, Mark Evans, Nicole Russell, Paul Drewett, Paul Herbert, Jordan Overton, Noel Warn, George Younger, Maureen Hardman, Teresa Jennings, Mark Wright, Chris Vicary, Craig Malcolm, Mark Horswell and Clare Jerome. Thank you all for your skill and enthusiasm over the years – it's been joyful.

Lastly, special thanks to three people without whom music would not have been the force in my life it is. June Marriner for always playing that kitchen radio and singing along, Raymond Marriner for buying me my first pair of sticks and building an entire shed just so I could play drums, and Joseph 'Tibby' Hall for driving me around, telling me stories and giving me the belief that anything is possible.

... by Paul Marriner and available through www.bluescalepublishing.co.uk .

Three Weeks In The Summer

Innocence Lost, Grief Found

1976. Richard (16) has finished his exams and a long, hot summer beckons, but his crush on the new girl in town is unrequited. He leaves the stifling suburb to spend time in The New Forest with Dudek, his Czech uncle. Dudek is being cared for by Anika, a vivacious young Czech woman. Anika introduces him to village life and when he meets Jennifer, a girl his age, he finds his attentions torn between them. Teenage emotions and needs are laid bare as relationships with the two girls develop.

The summer's experiences intensify as forest fires threaten the village and Richard learns more of the events that led to his father's death. As the summer break ends, Richard has been touched by love and death and understands more of his father's history.

The story concludes the following New Year when Richard returns to The New Forest, needing to pick up where the summer ended.

… by Paul Marriner and available through www.bluescalepublishing.co.uk .

The Blue Bench

A beautifully written story of yearning and love in 1920 as a nation grieves - one soul, one person at a time. The body of the Unknown Warrior is coming home, can Britain find peace?

'..an important novel..'

Margate 1920. The Great War is over but Britain mourns and its spirit is not yet mended.

Edward and William have returned from the front as changed men. Together they have survived grotesque horrors and remain haunted by memories of comrades who did not come home. The summer season in Margate is a chance for them to rebuild their lives and reconcile the past.

Evelyn and Catherine are young women ready to live life to the full. Their independence has been hard won and, with little knowledge of the cost of their freedom, they are ready to face new challenges side by side.

Can they define their own future and open their hearts to the prospect of finding love? Will the summer of 1920 be a turning point for these new friends? As the body of the Unknown Warrior is returned, can the nation find a way forward?

'..a brilliant story told brilliantly..'

… by Paul Marriner and available through www.bluescalepublishing.co.uk .

Sunrises

… moving and thought provoking …

A story of a family learning how to love, lose, mourn and, ultimately, find peace.

When Anthony and Christine's daughter dies the void is unimaginable and unbearable. Grief is driving their family apart and they struggle to find peace. Mark, their son, is growing to manhood not sure of his place and seeking his own way forward.

Big questions have no answers and important truths hide hard lessons.

Love, grief, hope, sorrow and joy – bringing truth to a life.

Printed in Great Britain
by Amazon

10089268R00264